T he moon scythed between the filmy curtains and across the bed. But at the man's face it paused, deferential, and melted into molten silver. His features luminesced.

She shivered again, this time not from cold but from the look in his eyes. Her body flushed with excited heat as his hand clenched on hers where they held the washcloth. With her other hand she covered his, barely touching. The cloth tumbled away onto her lap, and suddenly his fingers traced the lace-edge of her shirt, leaving a hot trail on her moist flesh.

"Jordan." Why did her voice sound so husky? Still scraped by the river water, of course. Jordan's brows had drawn together in the tiniest of frowns, and she smoothed it away with a light touch of her index finger. Rachael licked lips suddenly gone dry, but it wasn't water she craved.

It was her feverdream, she reasoned. She'd do what she wanted. She moved her hand around to the back of Jordan's head. Curled her fingers in the thicket of hair. Tugged him gently toward her. Met him in the kiss....

ALSO BY DAYLE IVY

Novels

Blackwood House (forthcoming)
Waking the Witch

Short Stories

The Best Catch
Flowers for Marjory

What Beck'ning Ghost
a gothic romance

Dayle Ivy

*For Marcelle,
My OWN & booksigning buddy!

With affection,
Dayle Ivy*

WHAT BECK'NING GHOST
by
Dayle Ivy

Print edition published 2013 by Soul's Road Press

Copyright © by Dayle Ivy. All rights reserved, including the right of reproduction, in whole or in part in any form, without written permission of the publisher, except in the case of brief quotations embedded in critical articles and reviews.

This is a work of fiction. Names, characters, places, and events are either the product of the author's imagination or are used fictitiously, and any resemblance to actual persons, living or dead, business establishments, events, or locales is entirely coincidental.

First Edition

ISBN-13: 978-0615829890 (trade paperback)
ISBN-10: 0615829899 (trade paperback)

Inquiries should be addressed to
Soul's Road Press
http://www.soulsroadpress.com

Cover art © davidhills/iStockPhoto and Dani Simmonds/BigstockPhoto
Cover and Soul's Road Press logo designed by Designs by Trapdoor

For my father, Walter George Dermatis,
who shared his love of the mountains with me.
I miss you.

Acknowledgements

I grew up in the Adirondacks, and although Heather Mountain doesn't exist, parts of it are inspired by Keene and Keene Valley, New York, as well as the farm my grandparents owned, where my father built a cabin when I was in junior high school. I wandered the woods, spending many an hour in an old cemetery at the edge of our property, where I sat on tree branch and dreamt up stories. Thanks to Tolkien, I was sure Elves lurked just out of sight. The forest was magical to me, and still is.

Although writing a book is a solitary endeavor, many people are involved with making it fit for public consumption, and that includes keeping the writer sane. Sarah Husch, Teresa Roberts, Joan Dermatis, Lynn Nauman, and Lev Kosegi gently pointed out weird phrasings, impossible plottings, and the usual other errors. Lohr McKinstry's readily available and cheerfully shared arcane knowledge of newspapers, police procedure, and other such things was invaluable. Lisa Feeney cheerfully gave me insights into the mysterious mind of a ten-year-old. My thanks go to Colleen Kuehne for her eagle-eyed copyediting skills (any mistakes are entirely mine). And Kristine Kathryn Rusch and Dean Wesley Smith continue to offer their wisdom, advice, and friendship, which I humbly and gratefully accept.

Of course, none of this would be possible without the love and support of my beloved, Ken. Thank you for letting me show you the magic of the forest and the brook and the waterfall.

What Beck'ning Ghost

a gothic romance

WHAT BECK'NING GHOST, ALONG THE MOONLIGHT SHADE
INVITES MY STEP, AND POINTS TO YONDER GLADE?

— Alexander Pope
"Elegy to the Memory of an Unfortunate Lady"

Prologue

Despite her precautionary sweater, Rachael found the cellared chill taking its toll; even as she felt the sneeze building she was scrabbling in the pocket of her worn jeans for a tissue. Tucking her clipboard under her arm, she blew, dislodging an errant spiral of black hair from the ribbon at the nape of her neck. She'd tied her long mane back for convenience, but it never fully responded to her taming attempts. She poised her pen over the clipboard again.

Monsieur LaFayette was gone.

Rachael muttered a minor curse under her breath, not really angry. She was used to the curator's self-absorption when it came to "his treasures."

Part of the Musée des Arts charm was that it was housed in an historic château buried deep in France's wine country. The catacombing wine cellars that ranged beneath served as storage for most of the artifacts not presently on display, walls and floors now carefully sealed to lock out damaging moisture. Fluorescent track lighting provided an unearthly glow. Crates and boxes of assorted sizes, although stacked neatly and efficiently, made each underground room a maze in itself.

"I still should've left a trail of breadcrumbs," she said aloud, propping one ink-stained hand on her hip and leaning against a towering crate marked *Full Suit of Armour, circa 14th Century; left gauntlet dented.*

As if in response, something seemed to rattle within the crate. Rachael gasped and jumped away, imagining the side of the crate swinging open and a metal-covered arm silently dragging her in next to the missing man. Still, she moved closer and peered around it, and spied the half-hidden doorway through which Monsieur LaFayette must have gone. Resisting the urge to make a notation on the wall to help her find her way back, she ducked through the low stone opening. At five-nine, she had swiftly and painfully learned to duck when she went through old doorways.

She found the rotund curator standing before a cabinet, his head barely peeking over the open door, bald skin glinting between the carefully arranged strands of sparse hair. In the cabinet were individual drawers, each labeled in the man's precise handwriting.

"Mademoiselle is not coming down with a cold, one hopes?" he asked, not looking up. His voice reflected the concern he couldn't display while he was intent on his work.

Rachael smiled, ever amused by his formal speech. If it was the last thing she did at the Musée, she was going to get him to address her by her first name.

"I'm fine," she replied honestly. The chill really didn't bother her. Her year-long study in France—and her Master's in French History—completed, she had been ecstatic to get the plum opportunity to be apprenticed to a museum curator. She'd grown to love the small Musée. What it lacked in size, it made up for with some extraordinarily rare and unique pieces of art and artifact.

In the two months she'd been there, with another month and a half to go, she'd learned nearly every facet of directing and running a museum. She felt as if she unearthed buried treasure with every artifact they systematically categorized as they moved through the storage rooms.

Monsieur LaFayette began examining each piece of jewelry in the cabinet to ensure it was undamaged. Rachael dutifully marked them down, adding notations as to what would be done with each object: remain in storage or be put on display, and in the latter case, where it might go.

"This one would go perfectly with the green velvet evening dress," Rachael said, marveling at the intricacy of a delicate silver chain studded with glinting emeralds.

"Oui, mademoiselle—that is a lovely idea," Monsieur LaFayette said, carefully replacing the necklace in its slot. "Please write that down. We will finish here today, and tomorrow we shall begin on the top floor."

The top floor was where the more perishable objects—clothing and documents—were housed. Rachael made the note on her clipboard and returned her attention to the case of jewelry.

"Gold brooch, cross-shaped, set with 4-carat, 36-point topaz," Monsieur LaFayette knelt and read off the next label, the first on the lowest row of drawers.

"That sounds like a royal jewel," Rachael commented, as he jingled his heavy set of small keys until he found the right one.

"We believe, well…" He shrugged. "It was possibly owned by Marie Antoinette," he finished softly, and sighed.

"Possib—*really*?!" Rachael couldn't contain the excitement that leapt in her belly like a frightened hare. "What's wrong?" she asked quickly, as she saw the look on the man's ruddy face.

"We believe it was given to her by a friend just after the Cardinal of Rohan was acquitted of wrongdoing in the Diamond Necklace Affair in Versailles in 1786…but we have no documented proof," he finished sadly.

"This could be the pièce de résistance of the Musée's collection, but we will never know."

"May I see it?" Rachael asked softly.

Monsieur LaFayette sat back on his haunches and smiled up at her. "Of course, mademoiselle," he said. "The brooch is quite beautiful. It is still a treasure—no matter who owned it." He slid the drawer open and, almost devoutly, brought out the carefully wrapped pouch. Rachael took it from him with solicitous hands.

As she did, she felt a chill prickle and twitch its way up her spine, a chill not caused by her current underground location. She had seen and touched many a historic object in her studies, but this one affected her differently. Could it have belonged to Marie Antoinette?

Holding her breath, she let the brooch slip from the velvet bag and cradled it in her palm. The curator was right: It *was* beautiful.

It was shaped like a cross, one long piece bisected by a shorter piece, each end flaring out into three scallops. Smaller pieces overlapped, ended in points halfway up the longer pieces. An oval band looped under all four ends, connecting them. Delicate carvings covered each piece's gold surface. The gold and topaz glimmered in the fitful fluorescent light. Rachael reverently traced a fingertip over the design. Around her, the room began to shimmer, fade at the edges.

The woman sat awkwardly in the ornate chair, her swollen belly preventing her from pulling herself close to the small writing table. The room was hot and cloying, the heat from the fireplace making Rachael's face flush. The scent of flowery potpourri was thick, almost overwhelming.

Years of study made Rachael automatically identify the woman's garments as eighteenth-century French court garb. Awed, she realized she recognized the woman from numerous portraits. Even without that, the flowery signature—"Marie Antonia"—gave no question as to the woman's identity.

"*June 1, 1786,*" *she had written.* "*Yolande: Come and weep with me, come and console your friend. The judgment that has just been pronounced is an atrocious insult. I am bathed in tears of grief and despair.*" *On the envelope, she carefully printed* "*Comtesse de Polignac.*" *She stretched uncomfortably across the desk for the sealing wax.*

Rachael fought off dizziness.

The scene changed. The woman, her figure now slim, sat very still, holding a small baby on her lap. The brooch clung to the fabric at her throat.

"*T'was a gift to cheer me,*" *she said to the painter, who had commented on the pin's beauty. Her lips thinned at the memory of why she had needed to be cheered. She forced a smile.* "*And to welcome Sophie Hélène Beatrice,*" *she added, juggling the baby, who gurgled appreciatively.*

Rachael shuddered, and instinctively closed her hand over the ornate pin. The images intensified.

Now the woman was gaunt, dressed in plain black, no jewels. She tried to remain regal, but her pale blue eyes revealed her fear as she was led to the guillotine. Blood red hazed the view.

Rachael pressed her hand against her mouth, muffling her own screams....

"Mademoiselle? Are you unwell? Mademoiselle de Young? *Rachael!*"

Shaking her head, Rachael pulled herself away from the images, half-reluctant to detach herself from the seductive vision. She clutched the gold-and-topaz brooch in her fist, feeling a desperate need to protect it, hide it. Monsieur LaFayette gently pried her fingers apart and replaced the jeweled pin in its case.

"Mademoiselle?"

"I—I'm fine, Monsieur," she said, staring at her hand. A pinpoint of blood initialed the spot where the pin's clasp had pricked her skin. She curled her hand into a fist again, hiding the crimson dot that reminded her of the wash of blood that had darkened her vision. A vision that had seemed—felt, smelled, sounded—entirely real.

"Monsieur LaFayette, doesn't the Musée have Marie Antoinette's diaries and letters on file?" she asked, remembering what she had seen.

"We have them on microfiche, oui."

"May I look at them?"

"By all means, Mademoiselle."

*

Rachael rubbed the spot at the small of her back that ached interminably. She'd been studying the microfiche of Marie's writings all evening, but had only found the letter Marie had written to Yolande. At first she'd been startled, almost frightened to find something that confirmed her vision. But then she rationalized: Surely in her studies she'd come across the letter before, and simply forgotten until her subconscious regurgitated it.

In all the 'fiches, she'd found no mention of the brooch. She'd hallucinated everything, of course. She hadn't eaten much that day; hell, she hadn't eaten much since becoming a starving student in France. Bread and cheese had become her usual sustenance. There was no way she could have seen Marie Antoinette and those events. The thrill of seeing and holding the brooch had sparked an already overactive imagination.

She arched her back, purring with pleasure as her vertebrae untwisted. Her mind, however, remained twisted around what happened, and yet couldn't have happened. The images had seemed so *real*, though; and not just images—all her senses had been violently, acutely involved. She glared at the microfiche reader, wishing she could lay the blame on it for not divulging the information she needed.

She'd started reading the diaries on the day the Cardinal was acquitted of wrongdoing in the Diamond Necklace Affair—a twist of fate that had stunned and angered Marie, Rachael knew—and worked her way forward, day by day. The going was slow; though she knew French well enough to get by during her stay here, the unfamiliar spelling and grammar of the language in the eighteenth century hampered her progress.

There must be some other way.... Rachael snapped off the machine and turned on the small reading lamp that squeezed a place for itself on the desk next to the machine. She flipped open the spiral notebook on her lap. She'd scribbled down everything she could remember about the brooch and her hallucination after she and Monsieur LaFayette had finished the inventory. Almost without thinking, she began to sketch the pin on the opposite page. Her hand seemed to work independently of her brain—a line here, a curve here, delicate shading there to give the illusion of facets in the jewel. The tiny flowers and curves of the etched design blossomed and swirled beneath the tip of her pen....

Rachael stared at the sketch, awed and a little frightened. She'd never been able to draw much more than stick figures, but the brooch seemed to glimmer from its place on the page. Perhaps it was the dim light? She leaned forward, somehow realizing that if she'd kept going, Marie would have come to life beneath her pen as well, soul flowing out with the ink to stain the paper with sorrow.

Maybe she'd been going about this the wrong way. A slow, tingling realization infused her. Shutting the book, she crossed the hall and stuck her head into the curator's office.

"Monsieur, was there a portrait done of Marie Antoinette to commemorate the birth of her daughter Sophie?"

The small man looked up from his paperwork and frowned thoughtfully, squinting as if to visualize the picture about which she asked.

"There was a small one commissioned when Sophie was three months old, Mademoiselle," he said. "The birth of a daughter was not a momentous occasion, of course, and the portrait is relatively insignificant. I have never seen it, and I am unsure of its exact date. If you think that is the one you mean, try the catalogues from the Musée de France—that is where the portrait of which I am thinking is hung."

Rachael gathered up the heavy catalogues from the bookcase and carried them, pressed possessively to her breast, back to the other room. She set the stack on the floor and settled the first one on her lap, tucking one leg beneath her as she sank into the chair. She leaned forward, trying to make the most of the light from the straining lamp.

Three catalogues to find it. Then, there it was: Marie, skin pale, dress blood-red as if to symbolize the blood that would someday spill. And at her throat, what had to be, despite the size of the reproduction, the brooch. She sat, one hand half-lifted to the jewel, a small smile on her lips, but a haunted, distant look in her eyes that had once been described as "imperial blue."

Rachael gripped the catalogue in suddenly sweat-slick hands, the chill down her back belying the moisture on her palms.

The picture proved nothing. It was too small to conclusively say the brooch was the one tucked away in the cabinet in the wine cellar, a masterpiece of topaz and gold languishing away in anonymity for simple lack of proof. The portrait itself would clinch it, but that was away in Paris, and she had to know now. *Now*.

Then she read the description next to the picture.

Of course. Portraits took more than a few days. She had to look in the diaries four months after Sophie's birth....

"I wore the lovely brooch from Yolande for the portrait sitting today. The painter commented on its beauty. Yolande was a dear to give it to me, but it will always remind me of the Cardinal and his forever unpunished treachery."

Searching back, Rachael found the entry where Marie spoke of receiving a brooch—a topaz-and-gold cross, described exactly like the one in the cellars—from her friend.

So it had really happened. She dropped the catalogue on the floor and drew her legs up into the chair, hugging her knees and rocking, ever so slightly, back and forth. Somehow, when she'd held the brooch, she'd been able to see the past, see directly into moments in its history.

One thought rose above the growing belief, the faint shock-fear and the swirling implications:

Would it happen again?

Chapter One

October, seven years later

"Have a nice vacation, eh," the cab driver said, and heaved the suitcase over the lip of the trunk.

"Thanks," Rachael said absently, handing him the money, her eyes and thoughts on the grey-and-tan stone house before her. The faintest hint of apprehension trickled down her back, like a single bead of perspiration; then it was gone, swiped away by excitement and curiosity. She wasn't here for pleasure, but for work.

Behind her, the cab kicked into gear and motored off down the driveway that ribboned its way through a row of stately evergreens. And she heard, over the silence of the Adirondack Mountains, only the faint, distant purr of a lawn mower.

Manor MacPherson spread out before her, the late afternoon sun glinting off its many windows. The massive front door, located up a wide flight of low steps, was flanked by two bulging towers. On either side of the towers unfurled the wings of the house; except for the towers, the building was shaped like a capital I, because each wing ended in a front-to-back-facing hall.

Above the front door, in a semi-circle sweep of stained glass, Rachael saw the MacPherson family crest, a cat sejant, proper, and the words "Touch Not The Cat Bot A Glove." She wondered what had prompted the ancient MacPherson clan, far away and long ago in Scotland, to adopt such a warning for their motto: "Don't touch the cat without a glove."

The ominous motto somehow disturbed her, and she reminded herself that this was a job just like any other she'd had in the past few years. Simple genealogical research, back through the MacPherson family tree. She was eager to get started.

Hauling her laptop case and overstuffed suitcase up the steps, she opened the door and maneuvered inside. She stopped. Slowly setting the suitcase back down, she looked around, enchanted.

The front room was as fabulous as the outside of the house promised it would be. On either side, a massive staircase began its ascent; halfway up, each split into two sets of stairs, heading forward and back to connect with walkways along the second floor. Above each staircase was a high skylight allowing a view of the wispy cirrus clouds outside. Hallways led left and right along the front of the house, as well as back beneath the staircases. Straight ahead were two pairs of paneled double doors, one door slightly ajar. A gilt chandelier hanging from the two-story ceiling provided crystalline flashes of light. The room smelled of fresh pine and a light, sweet scent Rachael couldn't identify.

There was no front desk, but a small sign beside a half-open door on the wall to her right said "Manager." Leaving her suitcase and computer inside the front door, Rachael crossed the parquet floor and peered in. A short woman, wearing a pinstriped blue-and-white blouse, khaki skirt, and Docksiders, was sliding a manila folder into a filing cabinet drawer. Rachael knocked lightly, and she looked up.

"Hi! Welcome to Manor MacPherson," the woman said, closing the drawer. Some of the freckles on her face vanished into the grooves of laugh lines around her eyes as she smiled. Rachael guessed her to be in her early thirties. "What can I do for you?"

"I'm Rachael de Young," Rachael said, extending her business card. Embossed in purple on the marbled lavender card were the words "Rachael S. deYoung, Genealogical Researcher & Historian," and her contact information.

"You made it," the woman said, sounding pleased. "We've been looking forward to your arrival. Let me go tell Celeste you're here. I'm Karyn Cappricci, hotel manager, by the way." With barely a glance, she plucked a key from a pegboard and swung around the desk, her hip skimming the corner with practiced ease. "I'll be back in a sec—have a seat."

"Thanks," Rachael said, sinking into the indicated chair outside Karyn's office. But she'd been sitting all day—cab to plane to train to cab—and moments after Karyn had hurried off, she was up again, restlessly prowling the front room.

A host of MacPhersons had trod the floor where she walked, and she felt a heavy wave of history undulate beneath her feet. For a fleeting second she had the sensation of standing in the middle of all of them, as they surged and wandered and lived and died around her. Suddenly she felt as though she were no longer alone, and whirled. For the briefest of moments she thought she saw a pair of haunting green eyes, but she was still alone in the hall.

The MacPhersons, she knew, were known for the rich green of their eyes, and yet she couldn't shake the sensation that someone had been with her—not watching her, but being with her.

She was standing before a sweeping oil painting of what could only be the original Manor MacPherson in Scotland when Karyn returned to the front hall and returned Rachael to the present.

"I'm sorry, but Celeste is on an overseas business call," she said. "She'll be half an hour at most. Why don't I take you up to your room?" At Rachael's nod, she swept up the heavy suitcase. "Not only am I the manager, but I'm also the bellhop," she said with a grin as she marched across the polished floor toward the right-hand set of stairs. Though her hips were roundly curved, she wasn't overweight or, obviously, out of shape. Rachael's long-legged stride allowed her to keep up with the energetic woman, and she was only one step behind as they mounted the staircase.

"I was really excited to hear you were coming," Karyn said, her blunt-cut pageboy swinging at her shoulders. "I studied history for a few semesters in college, and I wish I could have taken more classes in it."

"What kind of history did you study?" Rachael asked, now curious.

"Just your basic survey courses. I didn't have many free credits to blow, and history didn't have much to do with my major, Hotel Management. It was a real treat to get the job here—this place is fabulous."

"It is," Rachael agreed admiringly. She wished she could stop and look at every object, picture, and architectural feature that they passed, but she restrained herself, knowing she'd have ample time in the ensuing days.

"This wing, the east wing, is all guest rooms," Karyn explained, leading her down a long, narrow hall. "There are a few in the upper west wing, but most of that is the MacPhersons' private living quarters. We're putting you in one of the business suites, since we figured you'd need some room to spread out your research stuff."

She had stopped about halfway down the hall, and, putting Rachael's suitcase down, inserted the large brass key into the lock. It turned easily, but Karyn had to use a shoulder to help encourage the heavy door to swing in. "Here you go," she said, standing back so Rachael could enter first.

The two-room suite enthralled Rachael, right down to the bowl of fresh flowers on the highboy and the crystal decanter of brandy and two glasses on the night table. She pulled her laptop out and set it on the desk, then slung the case back over her shoulder while Karyn laid her suitcase on the steamer trunk at the foot of the four-poster bed.

"Do you want to freshen up before you meet with Celeste?" the manager asked solicitously. "I know how tiring your trip must have been."

"No, I'm fine," Rachael said quickly. Her curiosity—what had led her to this field of study in the first place—demanded some immediate appeasement. "This is a huge house—how many rooms do you rent to guests?" she asked as she re-locked her door and pocketed the key in the comfortable jeans she'd worn for traveling.

"Twenty. We have eight regular rooms, four honeymoon suites, and six executive suites. We also have two rooms that each have an extra bedroom attached, in case a couple is traveling with a third person. We discourage small children, though—too many delicate antiques lying around."

As Karyn led her back downstairs, she pointed out the frescoes on the stairwell ceiling and the detailed carvings of the wall panels, which she said were exact copies of the originals in Scotland.

"I'm also the tour guide," she joked. "I know as much about this house as Celeste and Ian do."

"What about the family history?" Rachael asked. "Are you an expert on that as well?"

Karyn paused on the landing. "If you're talking about the tragedy, then no. It's not discussed. Since you'll be researching the MacPherson history, I'm sure Celeste will speak to you about it." Her voice wasn't unfriendly, but held a firmness that Rachael knew better than to push. She wondered if Karyn fielded this question often, because of the guide book or simply local gossip. At any rate, Celeste had hired her, so she was the one to question.

"You can wait here, in the parlor," Karyn said, pushing the double doors open further so they could walk through into the room across the front hall. "Celeste will be with you in a jiff. If you need anything, I'll be in my office. Make yourself at home." She smiled and left.

Rachael dropped her attaché case on a settee and walked to the wide bay window. She knelt on the built-in, cushioned bench and looked out at the wide expanse of lawn, smooth as a putting green and dotted with small copses of trees and, Rachael saw with delight, a stone fountain. The lawn sloped away to a thicket of trees. With the afternoon sun upon them, the tops of the trees looked afire, the leaves crackling vermilion, pumpkin, and citron flames. And beyond the trees loomed the mountains that made up the Adirondacks. The majestic peaks ringed her vision, some tree-lined and colorful, others grey with shale and slate; the highest already snow-capped, fading into blue and purple in the distance. Rachael, a Midwestern-born-and-bred flatlander, never ceased to be awed by the presence of mountains, and her attention was only drawn away when she leaned farther into the oriel and saw the edge of a garden peeking out from the right side of the house. She couldn't wait to explore the grounds. But her first priority would be the massive house.

No, she realized ruefully as she slid off the bench, her very first priority would be to find a bathroom. Finding her makeup kit, which was buried in the bottom of her attaché case, which doubled as her purse, she crossed the parlor to the door, and saw that Karyn's office door was shut. Well, she could certainly find a bathroom by herself.

"Pick a direction—any direction," she muttered cheerfully. Well, she'd been in the east wing already; perhaps it was time to explore the West. Karyn had said the family quarters were upstairs, but had given no indications that the lower level was private. She headed down the back corridor, carefully opening doors on both sides. She found two closets, a TV room, a staircase and two generic sitting rooms, and was beginning to give up hope when she discovered a short hall leading right, toward the back of the house. A whining noise caught her attention. That would mean a person, she deduced; she could ask on the whereabouts of the bathroom. She knocked, but no one answered; the whining clatter continued. She opened the door, and, surprised by what she found, she took an involuntary step inside.

Although the paneled walls, stained-glass window edging, hand-woven carpet and heavy dark furnishings definitely belonged to the manor, the rest of the office was thoroughly modernized; so much so that Rachael felt physically jolted. Two computers, each with a large, flat-panel LCD monitor, two printers (one a combo scanner/fax machine), and two telephones completed the high-tech array. The noise was from one of the printers, which was choking helplessly on a piece of paper. Rachael moved to succor the afflicted printer, tucking her makeup case under her arm. She opened the side of the printer, tugged at the paper, and it uncrinkled, revealing several more sheets that had built up in the mechanism.

And then someone grabbed her from behind.

Rachael cried out in surprise, a bright ribbon of fear twisting and knotting itself about her midsection. Her makeup case tumbled to the floor. Heart pulsing frantically, she reached deep for strength and twisted in the powerful grasp, trying to free herself from the vise-like hands that gripped her upper arms.

"Don't turn around," a voice rasped close to her ear. Rachael smelled expensive, subtle aftershave and a hint of smoke—not cigarette, but more carbon-like, as if a match had suddenly flared. She stopped trying to crane her neck around, knowing if she continued, she would only anger her assailant.

"What are you doing in here? Don't you know this is a private office?"

From his words, Rachael realized this was no baseless attacker, but rather, a servant or security guard. She tried to determine why his voice contained the unnatural raspiness, wondering if he were trying to disguise it. His strong fingers bruised her biceps. She gritted her teeth and said, "I was looking for the bathroom. I heard a noise and saw that the printer was jammed."

"The bathroom is down the hall, second door on your left," he said shortly. He released one arm to swipe her makeup case off the floor. He handed it to her, then turned her and propelled her to the door. "Stay out of my office."

As he pushed her out of the room, she caught a glimpse of the hand that held her left arm. It was smothered in a supple black leather glove.

The door shut firmly, with finality; not a slam, but neither a soft click. Trembling, Rachael didn't stop walking until she was in the bathroom. Then she sat down.

By the time she'd finished washing her hands, they'd stopped shaking and she felt calmer. She'd intruded on the man's office, and of course he'd been angry. Yes, he'd been more forceful than the occasion warranted—he'd deliberately tried to frighten her, it seemed—but on the other hand, he'd walked in and seen a stranger messing with his printer. Still, she couldn't fathom why he'd not allowed her to see who he was.

A critical look in the mirror showed her that, as she'd expected, the hours of travel had done little to damage her makeup. Rachael found the stubby end of an eyeliner and brightened the line around her eyes in a cerulean that mirrored and accentuated her eyes. A few quick dabs of powder around her nose and on the slant of her high cheekbones completed her work, and she headed back to the parlor, hoping she hadn't missed Celeste.

Celeste was nowhere in sight, and Karyn's office door was still closed. Too shaken from her encounter with the strange man to sit and stare out the window, Rachael plopped down on the loveseat next to her attaché case and pulled out the heavy, banded folder that held her notes. She wrapped the wide rubber band around her wrist.

HEATHER MOUNTAIN, N.Y. — Tragedy struck last night at Manor MacPherson when fire ravaged an outbuilding, killing three family members and seriously injuring another.

Killed in the blaze were Jordan MacPherson; his brother, Shane MacPherson; and Shane's wife, Emilie Shaw MacPherson.

Mr. and Mrs. MacPherson's son, Ian, aged 6, is in critical condition at Mercy Hospital with burns on at least 50% of his body, hospital officials said.

Heather Mountain Fire Chief Wayne LeFevre said it is unknown at this time how the fire started in the unused cottage located approximately one-half mile from the manor.

The blaze was first noticed at about midnight by friends leaving the manor after the MacPhersons' annual All Hallows Eve Costume Ball.

By the time firemen put out the fire, the cottage was gutted.

Funeral arrangements for Misters MacPherson and Mrs. MacPherson are incomplete at this time.

No further details were available at press time.

Rachael practically had the words memorized, but the clippings still fascinated her, drawing her back again and again to read the blurred words. She fished in the folder for the next article.

HEATHER MOUNTAIN, N.Y. — The New York State Police have been called in to investigate the Manor MacPherson tragedy because they have learned two of the deceased were killed not by fire, but by gun shot.

Police have determined that Jordan MacPherson and his sister-in-law, Emilie Shaw MacPherson, were both shot sometime before the fire was started. Shane MacPherson, Mrs. MacPherson's husband and Jordan's brother, was not shot, police said. He was killed by the ensuing fire.

Fire officials continued their investigation today of the Manor MacPherson fire that destroyed an outbuilding on the manor property following the family's annual All Hallows Eve Ball.

"When we learned there had been a shooting as well, we started to look for signs of arson," said Fire Chief Wayne LeFevre. Someone had spilled lamp oil around the building, a cottage located about one-half mile from the manor, he said.

Ian MacPherson, aged 6, remains in critical condition at Mercy Hospital. Dr. Joe Billings said he is unsure whether the boy will survive.

Due back at the manor today from New York City are Celeste MacPherson Jenner and her husband, Arden Jenner. The rest of the immediate family are currently in residence; letters have been dispatched to relatives in Scotland.

A wake will be held at Manor MacPherson on Friday and Saturday. Burial will be held at 3 p.m. Sunday at the family plot in Heather Mountain.

Rachel spoke into her digital recorder.

"Reminder: See if the State Police will release the investigation records. Also, see if the Heather Mountain Fire Department has records concerning the fire investigation. And see if the chief or any firefighters who fought the fire are still around."

The mysterious fire. In the past few years, Rachael had made a career of solving mysteries—of the genealogical type. She wasn't sure what intrigued her about unraveling family relationships and charting the place of people in history, but she did know she'd chosen a rather limited specialty in the field of history. While most of her colleagues found teaching jobs and worked to get grants for projects, or settled into jobs at museums or universities, Rachael had chosen to create her own niche.

The rest of the *Northwoods Press* articles she'd found contained little information, finally summarizing that police were baffled by the violent crime. The charred remains of a gun had been found in the shell of the cottage; it was believed to have been Shane's, but there was no way to tell who had fired it: whether someone had shot Jordan and Emilie with it or whether Shane tried to defend them. There were no clues pointing towards who might have set the fire. Young Ian, though badly scarred, had survived.

A sheet of heavy, cream-colored paper slipped from the folder as Rachael shuffled through the papers. The letterhead displayed the MacPherson family crest, and along the bottom was a strip of the MacPherson modern dress plaid, black, yellow, maroon and cream. Rachael fingered the fine stationery, looking at the bold strokes making up the signature of Celeste MacPherson Jenner, the person who had commissioned her for this project.

The matriarchal woman sat behind a wide desk topped with black slate, a Mont Blanc fountain pen poised in the act of signing the paper before her, a sheet of ivory stationery. An expensive perfume rose discreetly in the air.

"I've made up my mind," she said. "It needs to be done." Her voice held conviction, but her eyes were troubled. The person to whom she spoke stood before her; Rachael could only see his broad-shouldered back, and his hands where they rested on the edge of the desk—

—his left hand shrouded in a black leather glove.

The man began to turn....

Rachael gasped, the letter fluttering from her fingers. She pressed a trembling hand to her lips.

She hadn't meant for that to happen. She must be more tired than she realized—or more shaken by her confrontation. In the seven years since she'd discovered her psychic ability, she'd learned to control it. Images no longer came unbidden, unwanted, unexpected, when she held an object. But her control had just slipped, and the loss of restraint frightened her.

If she concentrated, Rachael knew she could learn a great deal about Celeste from this simple letter, including things that Celeste probably had no intention of sharing with her. She had already seen Celeste in her office in the act of signing the letter. She'd heard Celeste speak to the mystery man, smelt her perfume. That much, in a few meager seconds, from a single, simple piece of paper—and so much more was possible.

That, Rachael refused to do.

She was glad her talent for psychometry hadn't revealed itself until she was in her early twenties—when she was mature enough to deal with the implications of the power. If she decided to misuse her ability to see images by holding an object, she could delve into the most intimate and private matters a person had. Oh, occasionally the temptation was strong, as it had been when she returned from France to learn of her boyfriend's betrayal. But she'd swiftly decided that, when it came to that situation, what she didn't know wouldn't hurt her. And, she decided soon after, what she *could* know *could* hurt other people.

On the other hand, psychometry could be an extremely valuable tool for an historian. So Rachael had laid down a simple law for herself: Never use her psychometric powers on something that belonged to a living person. Sometimes that wasn't easy, for an object could be passed down through the generations, but, with practice, Rachael had learned how to focus her ability on the time period she was aiming for.

If the object had a particularly powerful event attached to it, however, images of that event might come unbidden, and she would struggle to retain her own identity and control the visions that swept her in. She had worked hard at that control, still knowing it would always be a frightening experience—consciousness snatched away, dropped into a pit where senses sharpened, experiences were unwanted and difficult to escape from. The recent shudder to her nerves had damaged her control as well.

The MacPherson project, she guessed, would be particularly difficult because the potent event had happened a mere forty years ago. The traces of memory of it would be fresh, unblurred by the passage of time, of hundreds of years of later memories pressed on top. Most of the recent history of the families she studied was relatively bland; usually the older events were more exciting. By the time Rachael handled them, the emotional aura on the objects had faded to a manageable level. But there was something about this project that had intrigued her from the moment she received Celeste's first letter.

Intrigued her—and frightened her. Frightened her in the same way that her slip when holding the letter frightened her. That was, Rachael realized, exactly why she had been apprehensive in the first place. The history of the fire hadn't been laid to rest yet, and she would no doubt continue fighting to keep herself from getting tangled in the strands of time.

She squared her shoulders. She was overreacting. She was here to study the entire MacPherson genealogy—the Halloween massacre was only a tiny part of their history, and not what she going to be spending her time on.

Despite everything, she *was* excited about this undertaking, and looked forward to spending some time in the beautiful Adirondack Mountains of upstate New York. Celeste MacPherson had said in the letter that autumn was the best time to visit the Adirondack Park. Rachael knew that the word "park" was a misnomer, bringing to mind tidy, open lands prepared for maximum visitation for city-dwelling vacationers; in reality, much of the alpine land was either privately owned or still in a state of untamed, often dangerous wilderness.

Although she'd never seen the North Country in the other seasons, Rachael had to admit she couldn't imagine a more beautiful setting than the one outside the bay window. Right now, a family of deer placidly munched their way across the lawn near the border of trees.

She shuffled through the papers on her lap, choosing not to reread the relatively unhelpful obituaries of Jordan, Shane, and Emilie, and selected a page she'd photocopied from a guidebook called *Where to Stay in Northern New York*. Pulling the rubber band from her wrist, she twisted it absentmindedly around her fingers as she read.

Manor MacPherson Built in 1850, this majestic hotel is one of the oldest buildings in the North Country. Copied almost to the stone from the historic MacPherson manor in Scotland, the hotel is still home to the MacPherson family. They opened to the public in 1956. Currently, Celeste MacPherson Jenner and her cousin, reclusive businessman Ian MacPherson, jointly run the operation. The MacPhersons also own MacPherson Syrup, Inc., one of the leading providers of maple syrup in the country.

There are few tales of ghosts or spirits at Manor MacPherson, despite a tragedy that the family steadfastly refuses to discuss. In 19--, three members of the family—Ian MacPherson's mother, father, and half-uncle—were killed one night: two by gunshot and the third in a mysterious fire, all in the same cottage on the property. Intense rumor at the time speculated that an illicit affair had been going on between two of the deceased, though no concrete evidence supports this. Some visitors to the manor say the faint notes of a piano are sometimes heard wafting from the music room when no one is inside—but it is doubtful that this romantic notion can be linked to the fire.

As if to divorce itself from that tragic night, the family still holds a gala, full-costume-required Halloween Ball every year, carrying on the family's hundreds-year-old tradition despite the fact that one took place on the night of the 19-- fire.

October is certainly a wonderful month to visit Manor MacPherson, not only for the sumptuous ball but also for the famous spectacle of fall leaves in the Adirondacks as well. Also to be noted is the foliage on Heather Mountain—the area was so named for the Scottish Highlands heather that the MacPhersons transplanted on their land when the manor was built. The hardy plants, blooming with sweet-scented flowers of purple, grey-blue and white, are another special touch that makes a stay at Manor MacPherson unique.

Manor MacPherson has managed to perfectly combine the brilliant architecture of the 1500s with the modern conveniences of the twenty-first century. Open an antique cupboard in your room and you'll find a hotpot, mugs, and a variety of imported teas atop a tiny fridge. Light switches are cleverly disguised to blend almost seamlessly with the surrounding woodwork….

"Rachael de Young?"

An older woman with impeccably coifed short white hair stood in the parlor doorway, smiling.

"Mrs. Jenner?" Rachael moved the overflowing file from her lap to the brocaded loveseat cushion so she could stand.

"Celeste, please," the woman said, coming forward and taking Rachael's hand between hers. "We can't have such formalities when we'll be working so closely together."

Rachael smiled back, feeling the last of her anxieties melt away before the gracious woman. She stuffed the photocopy back in the folder and shoved the whole thing into her attaché case.

"I'm sorry I kept you waiting," Celeste continued as they left the parlor together. "It was a phone call that simply couldn't wait."

"No problem," Rachael said. The woman was several inches shorter than Rachael, and if it weren't for her snowy hair, her erect carriage and slim figure would easily cause her to be mistaken for a woman twenty years younger. Her navy suit and simple, high-necked red silk blouse spoke of both elegance and comfort. Rachael felt grubby in comparison in her jeans and soft grey knit shirt, but Celeste seemed not to notice—or if she did, she didn't mind. "It gave me a chance to look around a bit."

"And what did you think?" Celeste held open a door and allowed Rachael to enter first.

"Everything is beautiful—gorgeous," Rachael said lamely.

"Thank you, dear," Celeste said, and moved around to sit behind her desk.

Her black slate-topped desk.

At Celeste's gesture, Rachael sank into the comfortable burgundy-leather armchair across from her. So. Even unbidden, her visions continued to be accurate to the last detail.

A cluster of framed photos held court at one corner. Rachael tilted her head around to see them. Most were older, sepia-tinted. One, of a dark-haired man, struck her soul; even though the color couldn't be in the picture, she saw him with familiar eyes of green.

"Now, I do want to go over a few things before you get started on your research," Celeste said. "Let me give you a brief overview of the family. Of course, I will always be available to you—I'll give you whatever information I can. The rest of the family is to do the same, not that there are many of us left."

"You said that's the reason you wanted the family history charted," Rachael said. Celeste's office also contained modern computer equipment, but Rachael noted that it was recessed in the back wall and doors could be closed to hide it, better retaining the manor's antique charm.

"That's definitely one of the reasons," Celeste agreed. "Really, Ian and I are the only ones of this line, and we don't seem to be leaving any heirs. I've lost track of all the different groups in Scotland—you'll track most of them down, I'm sure—but I gather they're diminishing as well. Smaller families, fewer marriages, that sort of thing. My main interest, where I'd like you to concentrate, is on our line of the family since we came to America." She leaned forward. "Another reason, Rachael, is that, besides the manor itself, the one thing everyone knows about the MacPhersons is a tragedy we had here a number of years ago. I don't want that to be the only thing everyone remembers."

"The shootings and fire," Rachael supplied.

Celeste's green eyes narrowed. "You know about that?"

"Only because I did some research before I came here," Rachael said quickly, seeing the woman's discomfort. "I'd be a poor historian if I didn't do some preliminary study before I dove into a project."

"That's true," Celeste said, sounding relieved. "So, you know of our tragedy." She breathed in deeply, the sides of her aquiline nose hollowing. "Yes, I'll admit I'm sensitive about the subject—although not nearly as much as Ian is, poor boy." She paused, considering the neat arrangements of objects on her desk: leather blotter, pen holder, closed date book. "I don't want the only thing people remember about us to be that night, and especially not the rumors about it," she said slowly. "But I admit there's a concurrent reason why I hired you."

Rachael waited.

"In the course of your research, if you can, I wonder if you could find out who murdered three members of my family forty years ago."

Chapter Two

"Excuse me?" Rachael gasped. The warning flicker about this assignment that had been lurking in the back of her mind flared to life, Celeste's words like a piece of paper tossed on glowing embers. What, was she getting precognition to go along with the psychometry? What next? Spoon-bending? Reading auras? Astral projection?

"I'm sorry, Rachael, did I startle you?"

"A little," Rachael admitted. "I just don't understand—why do you think I could find anything more than the police did?"

Celeste rose and went to gaze out the window, which overlooked the back lawn that Rachael had been contemplating not long ago. The sun had nearly set, the blue of twilight overtaking the scene. A light in the base of the fountain turned the bubbling water to liquid crystal. The deer had gone.

"Let me tell you a little bit about my family," Celeste said finally. "My mother, Letitia, was twenty years older than her brothers, Jordan and Shane. As a result, I was seven years younger than Jordan and only five years younger than Shane; they were more like brothers to me...."

"We had already left Manor MacPherson that night."

Rachael knew she meant the night of the shooting and fire.

"My husband and I were living in New York City, where he had a business. We had come up for the Halloween Ball, but left on the last train out that night because Arden had an important meeting the next morning. Of course, we came back as soon as we heard the news."

Rachael remembered reading that Celeste's husband had died about a year ago. She wondered if that had sparked Celeste's interest in the family geneology.

Celeste turned and walked back to her desk, sitting and folding her hands before her. Her short, carefully manicured nails shone with a clear polish.

"As the youngest member of the family, and a woman to boot, I wasn't privy to much of what went on in the higher echelons of the household." She laughed shortly, derisively. "I was, however, a good listener. I still am. I heard the rumors, and I heard the whisperings of my family, and I put two and two together." Her eyes, hued the legendary MacPherson green, ensured Rachael's attention. "You've done your homework, so you know what some of the rumors were. I believe my family preferred there not be an intense investigation into the murders. I don't know if they were protecting anyone—perhaps it was simply the family honor."

Celeste smiled, a bit sheepishly, and Rachael nodded for her to continue.

"I thought that since you're already here doing research on the family, you might be able to find some answers," the older woman said. "Oh, I may be being foolish; sentimental and suspicious in my old age. But I truly would like to know what happened that night. Lay the ghosts to rest."

"Do you believe there are ghosts?" Rachael asked, remembering the tour book's offhand comment.

Celeste laughed. "Oh no, my dear, that was a figure of speech. I don't believe in spooks and spirits. I'd like to know more about my ancestors, but I don't expect them to come back themselves to tell me." She sobered. "Rachael, I would appreciate it if you didn't recount our discussion to Ian," she said. "As you must know from your research, he was seriously injured in the fire." At Rachael's nod, she went on. "Apparently he saw someone—his father or mother, probably—head to the cottage, and he snuck away from his nanny to follow. He was caught in the fire, and seriously burned on half of his body. The scars, both physical and mental, can never be erased.

"Because of his disfigurement, Ian has been tutored at home all his life. He even graduated from college with the highest honors through studying at home. Modern technology has allowed him to run his business activities and transactions from his office here in the manor. If a situation demands his presence, he sends a stand-in. He is well-known and well-respected in the business community, but never seen."

Celeste toyed with the black Mont Blanc pen in its holder. "Ian is very self-conscious about the way he looks, of course. But you're a mature woman, Rachael; I don't think you'll have any problem seeing beyond Ian's scars."

"I'm very impressed by what he's accomplished," Rachael said honestly. "It is a true testament to his spirit and drive that he has achieved what he has. I respect hard work and intelligence in anyone."

"Good for you." Celeste rose again. "I don't know how much help Ian will be to you with regard to the fire," she said as she moved around the desk. "He never speaks of it; says he can't remember, which is common in trauma cases like that, I understand. I can't imagine a child going through such an event without experiencing great shock. No matter how long ago it was, it must still bring him great pain."

"Perhaps it would be best if I let him bring up the subject," Rachael said, gathering up her bag. "He knows why I'm here—he may volunteer some information eventually."

"He might," Celeste said as they walked to the door. "We can speak about this some more at a later time. I hope that you'll have dinner with us tonight, Rachael. Guests dine separately, but as you'll be working here, I'd like you to get to know us. Karyn will be dining with us as well—we consider her part of our little family."

"I'd like that," Rachael said.

"Dinner will be at seven o'clock. We don't dress too formally, but you'll want to wear a skirt. We put out a buffet of hors d'œuvres in the parlor at six thirty; you'll be able to meet some of the other guests then."

"That sounds lovely," Rachael said, and they parted ways.

She hadn't realized how travel-grimy she felt until she'd stripped off her clothes. She found her toiletry kit and hair dryer, and carried both into the adjoining bathroom. That room was dominated by a huge, claw-foot, white porcelain bathtub. Rachael noted with delight the basket of bath beads, soaps, and powders on a stool near the tub.

The plumbing at the manor was definitely modern. Water cascaded over her, the pounding spray attaining the high temperature she preferred. Lathering up a loofah, she mentally replayed her meeting with Celeste MacPherson Jenner. She found that now, upon reflection, she felt less surprised by the woman's request. She was, after all, a historian, trained in research. If the family had suppressed an investigation into the fire, then she wouldn't have much to go on; then again, with the family pressure turned off, someone might be willing to divulge some long-secret information.

There was another possibility for Celeste's entreaty, however. Biting her lip, Rachael wondered if somehow, impossibly, Celeste knew about her power. If she did, she would certainly believe Rachael was capable of solving the forty-year-old, hushed mystery.

But there was no way Celeste could know, because Rachael had never told anyone of her gift. Whenever she came close, whenever she was tempted to ease the burden by revealing its existence to another, she closed her eyes and visualized the tabloid headlines. She would not, absolutely would *not* allow herself to be known as one of those sleazy psychics who solved murders, tracked down missing children, pointed police in the direction of criminals.

After the surprise of discovering her psychometry had worn off, after she'd returned home from France, Rachael had been woken night after night by dreams of people chasing her, clawing at her, begging her to find their children, their wedding rings, the treasure they were sure their ancestors had hidden: "Touch the handkerchief—oh please, this watch—can you see if you hold these strands of hair—?" They wept, they pleaded, they cajoled, they threatened. They wouldn't stop until she appeased them, and then others would take their places, crying out for the same help; the stories differed, but the desired end was the same. They beat upon her until she acquiesced, and more came and demanded until Rachael dropped of exhaustion. She would wake shivering in her bed, more tired than she had been when she lay down, feeling physically pummeled and sore.

Those nightmares had been interspersed with dreams of cowering as others taunted her as a freak, a crazy, a psycho. Even the gentle faces of her parents would surface, swimming to the forefront, their eyes questioning and fearful.

So Rachael had rented a cabin on Nag's Head for a weekend, and sometime Saturday night, in the dream-suppressing haze of vodka, she had sworn to herself that she would tell no one. She accepted the power, agreed with herself to use it discreetly in her work and never for personal gain.

The dreams never returned.

Rachael wondered if Ian had had such nightmares, or worse, had experienced the taunting, the pity or the fear. He hadn't been born with his scars, they had been thrust upon him as her power had been thrust upon her. But unlike her, he had no way to hide them.

A trail of conditioner tickled down her cheek, breaking Rachael from her reverie. No, there was no way Celeste could know of her psychometry; there was no reason for her to panic. She was tired, and feeling vulnerable; that was all.

After her shower, she put on her favorite dress, a comfortable turtleneck that hugged her upper figure and flared out at the waist. She knew the teal blue brought out her eyes and the form-fitting cotton knit accentuated her slim waist. She worked hard at her figure, having inherited her mother's bountiful bosom and thus the tendency to gain weight, despite slim hips gained from her father's side of the family. Rachael was unable to resist a twirl before the mirror, flaring the calf-length skirt nearly to her stocking-tops…but in mid-twirl her ankle twisted and she nearly fell, catching the wall just in time.

"Damn heels," she muttered as she eased into the chair in front of the floral-skirted dressing table. She crossed one leg over the other and glared at the black, spike-heeled pump. She grasped the heel, and it wiggled obligingly. "Damn," she repeated. She made mental note to take it in to a shoe repair shop in town, and leaned forward to apply her makeup. A silver Victorian-inspired necklace and matching heart-shaped earrings, a jingling cluster of bangle bracelets at her left wrist, and her grandmother's silver-and-diamond ring on her right hand, and she was ready.

She didn't hurry downstairs; instead, she lingered, admiring the manor and all its intricacies: the ornate carvings, the surprises of tiny portraits and landscapes tucked in unusual nooks, the occasional well-placed antique chair or table. An object propped on a built-in shelf caught her eye, and she paused to examine it. It was an old cloak pin: a crest badge, and a MacPherson one at that; Rachael could just make out the faint letters of the motto on the curve of the gold circle. After a brief hesitation, she picked it up. She needed to find out whether she was back in control of her power.

Cupping the cloak pin in her palms, Rachael stared at it until she had its curves and clasp memorized. Closing her eyes, she pictured the pin, and hefted its weight in her hands, the metal heavy and cool. Then, carefully, she blanked her mind of all thoughts and opened herself to whatever might come.

The room smelled of tallow and peat, of unwashed bodies—and of death. By the fire it was warm, but the rest of the room felt cold and damp. The fire provided the only illumination, for it was twilight outside the small, unshaded window.

A man lay on a pallet, eyes shut, unmoving. A woman gently unfastened the cloak pin from his woolen wrap and straightened, turning to face a young boy of no more than fifteen, his face pale beneath his shock of red hair. He stood, back straight, as his mother pinned the badge to his cloak with trembling fingers.

"You're the eldest, now, Ewen," she said, her eyes bright with unshed tears. Rachael had to struggle to understand her words, garbled by her thick brogue. *"You're the laird of our house. We'll send word to th' MacPherson in the morn."*

Rachael let out a whoosh of air and opened her eyes, blinking to reorient herself in the brighter-lit hallway, and the present. She gently replaced the pin on the shelf. She longed to retreat to her room, find the art pad and colored pencils as yet unpacked, and dust the fine freckles on the boy's cheeks. Though she had no real talent for art most times, after she used her power she found she could render the scene in exquisite precision, often revealing details she hadn't noticed.

Realizing she was now late, Rachael hurried the rest of the way down the hall to the staircase. Halfway down the stairs, she paused on the landing, listening. Subtle music drifted out of the parlor between the open double doors; she identified the faint droning wail of bagpipes. From this angle she couldn't see inside, but she heard the murmur of voices as well. She quickly started down the last flight of stairs.

And then the heel of her shoe snapped. Rachael felt herself pitching forward and grabbed frantically for the banister, her stomach lurching. Her fingers skidded along the finely polished wood, unable to gain purchase. She cried out.

A firm hand grasped her elbow, stopping her fall, hauling her upright. She clutched at the banister again, and this time, steadied, she managed to grab hold of it. Gasping, she gripped the sturdy wood with both hands, and turned to thank her savior.

No one was there. She could see both flights of stairs after they split, and there was no way someone could have gotten down one of the hallways before she turned. She slowly sat down.

"Rachael, are you all right?"

The voice was Celeste's. The woman had emerged from the parlor. Several other faces peered from the room in consternation.

"I'm fine—my heel broke, and I stumbled," Rachael said, willing her heart to slow its incessant drumming. She held up the offending shoe; the heel dangled. She took a deep breath. "I'm fine."

The other faces receded politely. As she approached the doors, Celeste asked, "You're sure you're fine?"

Rachael nodded. "I need to go get another pair of shoes."

"No, you rest for a moment. Maria?"

The black-and-white clad servant paused in the doorway to the parlor, looking up at them.

"Could you run an errand for me, please?" Celeste asked. Maria passed her tray of shrimp cocktail to another maid in the parlor and came up the stairs to where they were. Rachael described the shoes she wanted, and gave Maria her room key and the pumps.

"You're still pale," Celeste said. "Would you care for a drink?"

Rachael requested a whisky sour, and when Maria returned, Celeste passed the order on to her. The servant, her reddish-brown hair caught in a neat hairnet, smiled and hurried off.

"How many people do you have working here?" Rachael asked, slipping on the lower-heeled burgundy pumps.

"Nancy Rabideau is in charge of the staff, as well as being our full-time cook," Celeste answered as they walked down the stairs and across the front hall. "Her husband, George, is the groundskeeper. You've already met Karyn, of course. We hire out for daily maids and other servants."

As they entered the parlor, Maria arrived with her drink. Rachael smiled and thanked her.

"Now, let me introduce you to the other guests," Celeste said.

Rachael made brief small talk with all the people currently staying at Manor MacPherson. Doug and Ally, the honeymooners, giggled and said hello and went back to their contented murmuring at one another. Businessmen Brian, David, and Kevin each shook her hand gravely and then delved back into their quiet, earnest discussion; and William and Janet, a couple from nearby Plattsburgh who were celebrating their twenty-fifth anniversary, welcomed her to upstate New York.

"A couple from Alabama will be arriving Sunday," Celeste added after they had made the rounds. "Then there'll be a brief lull before the All Hallows Eve Ball crowd."

Rachael sipped her drink, feeling the alcohol warm and relax her. "You keep busy," she commented.

"We try," the older woman said, surveying the group. "Guests are the lifeblood of a hotelier, of course."

They chatted for a few minutes, and then dinner was announced. The guests filed into the formal dining room, and Celeste led Rachael to where the family would be having their supper.

If this was the small dining room... Rachael gazed around the expansive room. The white vaulted ceiling was crossed with dark beams, and a dark, carved wooden screen half-hid a door on the side wall that probably led to the kitchen area. A tapestry on the back wall depicted, appropriately, a medieval feast scene. A long heavy table dominated the room, a drape of milky lace upon it. The table was set with Bird of Paradise china and a delicate crystal that glittered in the light provided by an overhead chandelier, carefully dimmed, and candles on the sideboards and dining table.

Rachael was several steps into the room before she realized there was someone already seated at the rectangular table; at the long end, away from the door. His profile was to the women as they entered, the candles causing his silhouette to flicker. He was studying something on his lap, pausing only to type some figures into the calculator that sat on the table next to him; his plate had been pushed aside to accommodate the small machine.

"Ian," Celeste said affectionately as they walked toward him, "Can't you set aside your work long enough for dinner?"

"I was just going over a few figures before everyone else showed up," he said, his fingers swiftly tapping. He examined the calculator's display out of the corner of his eye, made a notation on the paper on his lap, then flicked off the machine. He slid something, which seemed to be a book of matches, off the table and into his jacket pocket.

"Ian, this is Rachael deYoung, the historian I hired."

"Ms. deYoung." Ian stood, and, smiling, extended his right hand.

Rachael was glad Celeste had prepared her for Ian's looks. She could imagine how it must hurt him when people unwittingly flinched at the sight of the shiny, puckered skin on the left side of his face. He had grown his hair longer and combed it down to cover the burned area on the side of his scalp where no hair now grew. No left eyebrow remained, and the scars tugged up at the left corner of his mouth. The burn scars continued down his neck until they disappeared into the starched collar of his shirt. His left hand was shrouded in a black leather glove.

"Good evening, Mr. MacPherson," Rachael said calmly, returning his firm grip, remembering how his hands had painfully gripped her arms and shoved her from his study.

"I'd like to apologize for my actions earlier this evening," he went on. "I didn't realize who you were."

"That's quite all right," Rachael replied. "I can imagine how it must have looked to you, finding me fiddling with your printer."

"I hadn't realized you two had met," Celeste said, looking from one to the other.

"We ran into each other earlier, briefly, when I was waiting for you," Rachael said quickly, not wanting to embarrass Ian by relating the whole story. Before she could continue, however, another voice called out,

"Oh, dearie me, I'm not late, am I?"

Rachael turned to see a petite, elderly woman enter the dining room. She walked with a cane, but seemed to be using the instrument not as crutch, but as a way to propel herself faster toward them.

"No, Felicity, you're not late," Celeste said warmly. "Come and meet Rachael."

"Rachael!" The woman took one of Rachael's hands between hers. Rachael expected frail hands, but instead felt wiry strength beneath the papery, cool skin. The woman's green eyes were bright and seemed to regard her—and the rest of the world—with bemused contentment. Paint, bright orange, smudged her cheek. "How good of you to come! I'm Felicity MacPherson. You must call me Felicity—don't be stuffy just because I'm old; I won't stand for it."

"Thank you, Felicity."

"Felicity is my aunt—she and my mother were twins—and Ian's half-aunt," Celeste explained. "She's an artist."

"So I gathered," Rachael said.

"Whoops!" Felicity looked down at the paint-spattered smock she still wore. Leaning her cane against a chair, she reached behind and untied the apron. She looked around thoughtfully, then opened the credenza along the side wall, wadded up the smock and tossed it inside. Shutting the door, she leaned against the credenza with an innocent smile that was negated by the wicked twinkle in her eyes.

Celeste cleared her throat. "Felicity is quite well known in the Adirondack area, as well as central New York and Vermont. She had several shows in New York City that were rather successful."

"You might want to include some of Felicity's work in the volume of family history," Rachael suggested, delighted by the whole interchange.

"That's a lovely idea," Celeste agreed. "I had been considering a gorgeous oil she did of the manor."

Maria slipped into the room through a back door and informed Celeste that the guests had been served.

"Please tell Nancy we'll wait a few more minutes," Celeste told her. "Karyn hasn't arrived yet."

"Rachael, may I refresh your drink?" Ian asked. At her nod, he took her empty glass to the row of crystal decanters on the far sideboard. She noticed that he walked with a slight limp, as if the left side of his body were stiff. When he returned, she sipped the cold, sour drink and asked him about the business of running a hotel. He was describing their different forms of advertising when Karyn hurried into the room.

"I'm sorry I'm late," she said breathlessly. "Brett's sitter cancelled at the last moment, and I had to drive him to a friend's house in town. Brett's my son," she added for Rachael's benefit. "I'm also a mother," she said with a grin, continuing her earlier listing of her duties.

"You don't live in town?" Rachael asked.

"Karyn and Brett, as well as Nancy and George, live in cottages on the grounds," Celeste supplied. Seeing Maria peering into the room, she nodded at the servant's unspoken question. "Why don't we sit down?"

They clustered at one end of the long table, Ian at the head, Celeste on his left and Felicity to his right. Ian poured everyone wine as Maria and a plump, middle-aged woman, who was introduced to Rachael as

Nancy Rabideau, brought in the first course, a crisp green salad with bright cherry tomatoes and Roquefort dressing.

The conversation flowed with the wine, enhancing each course of the meal. Karyn asked Rachael about her work, and so Rachael found herself at the center of attention during most of supper. Everyone seemed honestly interested in her career, although she noticed that Ian grew quiet when she discussed the family studies she had done.

"It seems to me," he said finally, "that the past is the past. What do we really gain by spending so much time and energy studying it? Isn't it better to look to the future, work toward it?"

He didn't speak antagonistically, and Rachael wasn't offended by his questions. He brought up a debate in which even historians took sides.

"Some say we can learn about the future from studying history," she said, dabbing cream sauce from the corner of her mouth with her napkin. "You know the old idea: that we must learn from our mistakes or forever repeat them."

He set his fork gently onto the china dinner plate. "But isn't it better to learn from our own mistakes, instead of trying to interpret someone else's?"

"You've got a point," Rachael said, warming to the debate. "The farther we go back in history, the harder it is to learn exactly what happened. The outcomes are easy to see, but it's harder to determine what caused them."

"Let the past be the past—let it rest," he said.

"Ian," Celeste said.

"'The circumstances are in a great measure new. We have hardly any landmarks from the wisdom of our ancestors to guide us'," Felicity quoted. "Edmund Burke," she added as they all looked at her, and popped an asparagus tip into her mouth.

"Felicity," Celeste said in the same tone of voice she had directed at Ian.

"Oh no, that's okay," Rachael said quickly. "I've had this sort of discussion many times before. Many people feel the way Ian does. Unfortunately, sometimes those are the people holding the grant money."

Karyn and Felicity chuckled, and even Celeste had to smile.

"Well, what Rachael does is different," she said. "Researching a family's genealogy is a way to make the past relevant."

"I don't agree," Ian said. "In fact, I see less of a point in finding out that, oh, one's ancestor owned twenty head of cattle or fought in the Battle of Hastings."

Rachael chewed a piece of chicken, savoring the creamy wine sauce. "Some people simply find it interesting," she said. "For others, it's a matter of pride to be able to say their great-great-great-whoever came over on the *Mayflower*."

"I've always felt our ancestors helped shape who we are today," Karyn spoke up.

"What a lovely way of phrasing it!" Celeste said. "That's exactly what I was thinking—I've just never been able to put it into words."

"I like to believe I've shaped myself." Ian looked up. He rolled his knife between his fingers; candlelight glinted off the blade. The scars on the left side of his face seemed to pulse a deeper red. "I am who I am because I've worked, and struggled, and learned—and yes, failed, and learned from my own mistakes. My great-great-great-whoever had very little to do with it."

"'People will not look forward to posterity, who never look backward to their ancestors'," Felicity said complacently. "Also Burke."

"Then you're not in accordance with Celeste on this project?" Rachael asked Ian.

He set down the knife carefully, the end of the blade resting on his plate. "Celeste and I discussed the matter at length before you were hired," he said finally. "While I may not be in total agreement on the necessity or value of this research, I will give you my full cooperation." He smiled slightly. "I was overruled, but that doesn't mean I'm not a graceful loser. Please don't hesitate to come to me with questions, Rachael. I do want to help you."

"Thank you," she said. The strained atmosphere escaped out the door as Nancy and Marie brought in the dessert, a fresh fruit sorbet and slices of spongy, light pound cake.

*

After supper they retired to one of the sitting rooms Rachael had found on her quest for the bathroom. Large mirrors on the walls, gilt-framed, made the room seem larger without reducing its intimacy. The fireplace held a careful placement of birch logs, a fire unnecessary this early in the season.

Finally feeling the effects of her day of traveling, Rachael declined an after-dinner crème de menthe and chose another cup of coffee instead. The French vanilla aroma was rich and comforting.

Celeste asked Rachael where she would be starting her research.

"I'd like to interview each one of you," she answered. "You'll all have different memories, have heard different stories about the past. I'd also like to go through whatever family papers are available. After that, I'll see about getting whatever certificates—birth, marriage, death—and other official documents. My first goal is to put together as complete a family tree as I can, and then work on details from there."

"I know there's a family Bible in the library," Celeste mused. "I'll see what else I can find."

"Why don't I give you the full tour of the manor on Sunday?" Karyn suggested. "I should have the afternoon free after the Alabama couple check in. They're due at one, I think."

"Didn't Grandfather have a file of papers in his office that were related to the family?" Ian spoke up.

"I think you're right," Celeste said. "Can you find that?"

"I'll try. You know how Grandfather's study is."

Celeste turned to Rachael. "The man had a truly unique filing system," she said.

"If you don't mind, I'd love to look through his files myself," Rachael said. "There's no telling what may crop up. No offence, but you might not know if something was important or not," she said to Ian. "I've learned the hard way that anything can be useful: a receipt, a scribbled note, a ticket stub...."

"No offence taken," Ian said. "I'll look for that particular file, and you can go through the study later, at your leisure."

Rachael felt a yawn coming on, and her coffee cup clinked in the saucer as she hastily set it down and covered her mouth. "Well," she said with a laugh, "if I'm going to get any work done tomorrow, I'd best get myself to bed."

"I'll walk you to your room," Ian offered, and she accepted. She said goodnight to the others, and they left.

"I want to apologize for my actions this afternoon," he said. "I had no idea who you were."

"It was my fault as well," Rachael said. "I shouldn't have gone into your office uninvited."

"I overreacted," he said. "We should just agree to forget it happened."

"Good plan."

They lapsed into silence, Ian so silent that Rachael thought he was brooding. She noticed that he made a point of walking at her left, so his unscarred side was presented to her.

"I hope I didn't offend you with my remarks at dinner," he said suddenly. "I was in no way trying to demean your work."

"I wasn't offended," she assured him. "You presented some valid points. I'd rather debate with you than to argue with some pig-headed fool who doesn't even listen to what I'm saying."

He smiled. "I meant what I said—I'll help you in any way I can. Though I don't think I'll be much of a source for you."

"You might be surprised," Rachael said. "If you spent any time with your grandparents, you might remember some of the stories they told you."

They began the ascent of the stairs, Rachael discreetly slowing down so Ian wouldn't overextend himself.

"I won't be much help to you with regard to the night of the fire," he said suddenly. "I remember nothing."

"Celeste told me," Rachael admitted.

"I know that you will have to include that night in your research, because it is a part of our history," he said. She could hear the tension in his voice, saw the way his shoulders tightened beneath his suit jacket. "But I ask you not to dwell upon it." They were nearly to her room, and Rachael was already reaching into her small handbag for her key when he swung to face her, placing his hands lightly on her arms. "That part of the past is very painful for me—for the whole family. There is no need for you to do more than mention it in the book. That night did not shape me: I shaped myself from what remained of me after the incident. And there is nothing to be learned from the past."

"I understand," Rachael said. It was best not to argue with him, nor to agree and have him challenge her work later. "My job here is research. While I intend to produce as complete a history of your family as I can, I don't want to hurt anyone."

His shoulders dropped slightly, and he let her go. "Thank you. Good night, Rachael."

She put her shoulder to the door and bumped it open. "Good night, Ian."

*

The room was dark; but then, neither man needed light to know the other was there. One could sense the other's presence, and the other needed no light to see.

"She has power," one said. "Strong power."

"I know," the other said. He stared out the window. Soft fingers of clouds lovingly caressed the cold half-circle of the moon.

"You will not harm her," the first man said evenly. His words nonetheless conveyed a subtle threat.

"I will not let her learn the truth," the second man said. There was the barest hint of desperation in his voice. His fist clenched. "I *cannot*."

"But you will not harm her," the first man repeated, his words a cold presence. "I will not allow that."

Chapter Three

Rachael slowed to a light jog and wiped her brow where the sweat had trickled below the twisted bandanna. Ahead, the driveway curved, snaking between the rows of evergreens. Trees blocked most of the early-morning sunlight, but here and there golden light trickled through, rippling on the pavement as the breeze gently shook the branches, as if to shake the trees awake to greet the day.

She'd chosen to send her early-morning run down the mile-long drive and back so she could see how Manor MacPherson revealed itself to outsiders; yesterday, confined in the taxi, she'd been unable to catch the first glimpses, had seen nothing of the house until the cab left the trees and entered the gravel drive that circled through the front lawn.

No such disappointment now. As she resumed her steady pace and followed the bend of the road, she spied the stone merlons of a tower battlement thrusting above the tall trees. A little farther, and she was able to see more through the latticework of branches: a window, more stone, the second tower. Like a faerie castle, it seemed to tease her, taunting by revealing bits of itself and then vanishing again into the realm of magic and shadow. Then she came to the end of the trees, and stopped as the full view of the house struck her again as it had yesterday afternoon, sprawled across the lawn like a pair of arms flung wide in invitation.

From this angle, she could see an enclosure of tall, golden oak boards to the left of the house, and a figure closing the gate. The person, wrapped in an ankle-length, dark beach robe, turned and headed toward the house. Even from this distance, Rachael could detect his slight limp. That explained one of the house rules: that the pool was closed to guests between 6 and 8 a.m., and guests were requested to avoid the pool area during that time. She imagined that swimming was good therapy for Ian, a way for him to get exercise and remain limber without causing undue strain to his ravaged body.

That thought made her aware of her own body, and the fact that her calves were beginning to tighten from the sudden cease of movement. She resumed jogging, heading down the right side of the circular drive in front of the house and then striking off across the lawn toward the east wing.

She'd awoken early to the sound of two birds playing tag against her window, dark forms darting and swooping behind the delicate white curtains that lifted gently in the morning breeze. Knowing the day would be busy, she'd decided to head out on her daily run, and use the time to go over what she had to do.

The family tree was a top priority, she decided as she jogged over the smooth lawn. The hardest part would be when she had to delve back into the ancestors in Scotland. It would be easy to trace the movements of those in America, but when she started digging into information overseas, the work's difficulty would increase tenfold.

She discovered the gardens around the side of the house. To her delight, she found that they were an extension of a greenhouse that thrust out from the back of the east wing. Beyond the gardens was an arboretum, white latticework urging vines to seek the sky. Rachael jogged past, making a mental note to visit the area later. She loved greenery, although most of her experience had been with the house plants scattered through her apartment.

Although she hadn't consciously planned it, Rachael wasn't surprised when her feet took her to the edge of the grass, where carefully planned lawn met less-tamed forest. She slowed to a brisk walk and followed the path that led into the woods. Slipping her iPod earbuds out and draping them across her neck, she listened instead to the gentle whispers of the forest.

The path led to a wooden bridge over a swiftly-running stream. Rachael walked to the bank and squatted down to splash water on her warm face. The water was deep here, the rocks on the bank suddenly plunging down to shadowy depths from which an occasional fish streaked silver to the surface and then back down. Beneath the bridge, Rachael could just make out the dark, gnarled fingers of a tree branch that had gotten trapped between the rocks below the surface.

Straightening, she decided she could explore the land beyond the stream later, but then the red flash of a chattering squirrel caught her attention. From the other side of the stream, it watched her with alert, bright black eyes, nibbling occasionally on something between its paws. What made Rachael curious was what it was sitting on. It didn't seem to be a tree stump....

She stepped onto the bridge, and her movement caused the squirrel to flee, leaving an annoyed chatter in its wake. Halfway across, she saw what it had perched upon: a foundation stone. She could see the others, nearly covered with weeds: a rectangular arrangement marking where a building had once stood.

But she had no time to investigate now; and as she followed the path back out of the woods, she realized she had little reason to investigate. Old properties often bore the remains of ancient buildings. When she was young, she'd been friends with a girl who lived on a farm, and there had been a number of places where old buildings and stone walls had once stood.

Rachael walked briskly across the lawn toward the house, having agreed with herself to cut her usual three-mile run short today. Ahead, a large dog gamboled with a young boy clad in jeans and a red-and-white striped shirt. As she drew near, the boy noticed her approach and perched on the edge of the fountain, watching her.

"Hello," Rachael said, smiling, when she reached him. "You must be Brett Cappricci." His blond hair and smattering of freckles had given him away. He nodded gravely, and she said, "I'm Rachael de Young. I'm staying here, and researching the MacPherson's family history. I met your mother yesterday, and she told me about you."

"This is Chewie," he announced, ruffling the dog's fur. He watched her expectantly, as if daring her to guess the origin of the dog's name.

"Short for Chewbacca, obviously."

Admiration flickered in Brett's eyes. Rachael smiled. She'd passed his test. She was a "cool" adult. She mentally thanked her nieces and nephews, who were obsessed with *Star Wars*. She had to admit even she enjoyed it (the original series, at least).

Chewie the dog was of no determined breed, but seemed to have some German shepherd in him. He panted at her, still staying protectively close to Brett. She held out her hand, palm up, and he sniffed it cautiously. She apparently passed his test, too, for he licked her hand.

"I'm a Han Solo fan myself," she said.

Brett pursed his lips. "Greedo shot first," he said accusingly. "Han wouldn't do that."

Whoops. Trust a kid to care about something like that. "You have a good point," Rachael said hastily, and searched for a way to change the subject. "So, how do you like living here?" she asked.

"It's nice," Brett said with a shrug of his slim shoulders. "There's lots of room to play." He looked up at the house, and Rachael followed his gaze. "Mom's happy here," he added. "It's cool. Hey, did you see it?"

"See what?"

"The ghost." He pointed at the west wing.

Rachael briefly saw an indiscriminate figure standing in a window just before the curtain dropped.

"A ghost, Brett?" she asked gently, keeping her voice nonjudgmental. "That was probably just a guest."

"Nope, it was the ghost," Brett said positively, dropping to his knees to hug Chewie's neck. "Couldn't've been a guest, 'cause that's where the MacPhersons are. I've seen him—the ghost—before. He doesn't hurt anyone."

"Well, what does he do?"

But Brett was no longer interested in the alleged specter. "He just hangs around, I guess," he said. "You wanta go exploring with me and Chewie?"

"Maybe later, okay?" Rachael suggested. "I have to go in and shower before breakfast. Will I see you there?"

He shook his head. "I ate at home. See you later. Come on, Chewie." He took off down the lawn, and with a gleeful bark, the dog followed.

*

After showering and dressing in a pair of comfortable jeans and a purple shaker-knit sweater, Rachael discovered the breakfast buffet set up in the formal dining room. Doug and Ally were sharing a cozy table for two in one corner and feeding each other bits of buttery croissants; the businessmen were at a larger table and waved for her to join them after she filled her plate.

Unlike the family's dining room with its one long table, this room was arranged with more intimate tables in varying sizes, each covered with a different lace tablecloth. The scent of fresh flowers came from crystal vases on each table; silver candelabra clutching half-burnt candles in carefully polished arms accompanied the vases. Ceiling-high windows urged the daylight to flood the room. The hunter-green velvet drapes framing the windows were held back with loose ties that could be easily released when evening fell.

"We're in advertising—this working vacation was supposed to stimulate our creativity," Brian answered her question after they had exchanged comments about the manor. He bit into a slice of toast, his teeth white against his dark skin.

"What are you working on?" Rachael asked, arranging lox on her cream cheesed bagel half.

"Some new soap that's supposed to make your skin glow," David answered with a crooked grin. "Real exciting."

"What made you pick the manor?"

"That was my idea," Kevin said, pointing at himself with a forkful of sausage and tomato. His eyes, though light, were very intense, burning beneath his close-cropped hair. "We don't make nearly as much as we're worth, y'see. I really pushed for this vacation, even if it's a working one. I used to work up here, and Manor MacPherson was one of my clients, so the company got a decent rate. They're so cheap, we wouldn't have been able to do this without the discount." He snorted.

"And what about you?" David hastily asked Rachael. "Last night you said you were here to research the MacPherson genealogy—how did that come about?"

Rachael explained about Celeste hiring her.

"Going to do any ghost hunting while you're here?" Kevin asked.

Rachael stopped in the act of raising the bagel to her mouth. This was the second time in an hour someone had mentioned ghosts. "Ghost hunting?" she repeated.

Kevin set down his coffee, and some sloshed onto the saucer. "The MacPherson Fire is local legend, and there's always been a rumor of ghosts."

"I've never been much for hunting," Rachael said lightly. "And my focus will be all of the MacPherson history—as far back as I can trace in Scotland—so I won't spend much time on the fire."

"Well, if you ask me, it's not a ghost that haunts this place," Brian said. "This Ian guy—he seems to be a pretty weird dude from what you've told me, Kev."

"He's a gracious man," Rachael answered before Kevin could. "He's a brilliant businessman as well, from what I'm told."

"Doesn't he do all his work from right here in the hotel?" David asked.

Rachael nodded. "Apparently he has quite an impressive computer set-up," she said, unwilling to mention that she'd seen it. "Kevin, since you're from the area, maybe you can give me the names of some locals who might be able to help me with my research—local historians and so on."

Kevin squinted his hazel eyes. "I'll have to think about it," he said. "Let me make a few calls and get back to you."

"Great."

"Speaking of getting back..." David said, glancing meaningfully at his watch.

"Right," Brian and Kevin said simultaneously. "Back to the salt mines," Kevin added, not quite smiling, as the three scraped their chairs back.

Rachael finished her bagel, her thoughts not on her breakfast. Ghosts. In her work in Europe, she'd explored legendary haunted places without finding a trace of specters. Now, in a grand hotel in upstate New York, of all places, rumors abounded. She couldn't discount the idea of ghosts—her own experience with parapsychology had swiftly taught her not to summarily dismiss a theory, no matter how amazing it sounded—but neither did she outright believe in every conjecture, hypothesis, or tale she heard.

She flashed on the unrelated memory of her near-tumble down the stairs the night before. Even now she could feel the impression of the firm grip on her arm, steadying her for just a second until she could grab the banister. But when she'd turned, no one was there. Or *was* the recollection unrelated? Had a ghost, a guardian angel, saved her from a nasty fall? She rubbed her elbow, trying to banish the memory sensation of the hand.

Maria's arrival at her table with an offer to refresh her coffee brought her back to the present.

"You were here last night, you're back this morning—don't you ever take time off?" Rachael asked as the young woman refilled her cup. The steam from the silver coffeepot coaxed loose a wisp of hair from her neat bun.

"I work weekends and nights, mostly—I go to Adirondack Community College during the day," Maria explained, straightening. "After I get my Associate's, I should have enough money saved to go on and get my Bachelor's in Microbiology."

Rachael nodded, impressed. "Good luck," she said. "By the way," she added as the dark-haired servant began to turn away, "whose room is the third from the end in the west wing on the back of the house?"

Maria thought; one finger moved in counting each room and its occupant. "That would have been Jordan's room," she said finally.

Rachael wasn't surprised. Maybe she'd guessed that already. "Does anyone else use that room?"

"No." Maria shook her head. "Well, Ian goes in there once in a while, but not often. We keep it clean, but other than that, it's pretty much left untouched."

Rachael nodded her thanks and sipped the pungent vanilla coffee, half-watching Maria refill the newlywed's cups and leave the room. She and Brett could easily have seen Ian or a servant in the room earlier that morning. But Ian had just returned from his swim, and it was doubtful he would have gone to Jordan's room before drying off and changing.

And would the servants be cleaning an unoccupied room this early in the morning?

Maria came back by, this time with a folded slip of paper.

Rachael: The papers you requested are in the library. I'll check to see if there are any others hidden about. Ian.

Rachael smiled, and borrowing a pen from Maria, scrawled "Thank you!" across the bottom of the page. She handed the paper and pen back to Maria, who gave her directions to the library before leaving the dining room.

With a last gulp of coffee, Rachael rose and headed back to her room.

*

"Hi, Mom, it's Rachael."

"Rachael! Hi, honey, how are you?" Elizabeth de Young's voice was warm as she greeted her second-to-last child and only daughter. "Have you started that new job yet?"

"Yep. I'm here at Manor MacPherson in Heather Mountain. The cell service in the Adirondacks is really sketchy, so let me give you the phone number here." Rachael relayed the information and set the scrap of paper on the floor next to the cushioned window seat in her room. Then she asked, "Where's Dad this morning?"

"Out golfing as usual." The fond tone overwrote any suggestion of ruefulness in Elizabeth's voice when she spoke about her husband's favorite pastime. "He's trying to get all the games in that he can before winter. You'll have to send us glowing reports of the courses where you are, so I can convince him to take me on a long-overdue vacation."

"What about your trip to Spain?" Rachael asked. She scrunched farther into the seat, absentmindedly regarding a thread pull in the toe of one of her purple socks.

"That was two years ago, and your father hasn't forgiven me yet for the archaeological tour of Barcelona that I dragged him on. This time, he says he wants to relax."

Rachael laughed. Vacations were a traditional family joke. Her parents comprised a deadly combination—her mother taught grade school; her father, high-school economics—so vacations always had to be a "learning experience," much to the chagrin of Rachael and her three brothers. No matter how often they had pleaded for Disney World, they had gotten whale-watching excursions, science conventions, and art tours. Rachael had finally learned to appreciate the unique holidays, and credited a trip to Bodie, a ghost town in California, with sparking her interest in history. Now, with the children grown, her father wanted to spend more time golfing, but Mom saw no reason to change tradition.

"Relaxing vacation?" she said. "I think not! Dad will hit the golf courses—and learn the history of each one in the process—and you won't rest until you find the Lake Champlain Monster."

"Ooh, a monster? Has it been documented? How often has it been sighted? Tell me," Elizabeth commanded.

Rachael laughed again. "Champy, as it's called, was first sighted by Samuel de Champlain, who discovered the lake in 1609," she said. "I'll pick up a guide book for you."

Elizabeth laughed, too. "Now I really want to visit. Father's doomed. So, tell me about this job you're working on."

"Another genealogy. It's pretty neat, Mom: The family came over from Scotland in 1839 and built a replica of their manor house here in the mountains. They got involved in the maple syrup business, and in 1956 turned the manor into a hotel. It's beautiful—you'd get a kick out of the antiques, and how they've tried to keep things as authentic as possible while still offering modern conveniences."

"You sound like a guide book yourself," her mother said. "Well, it sounds wonderful; I know you'll have fun. Just don't find any ghosts."

"Ghosts?" Rachael gasped. Her palms suddenly got slick, even as she felt a chill ripple down her back. The phone nearly slipped from her moist hand, and she gripped it firmly, half-using the contact to stabilize herself.

"Don't dig up any skeletons in the closet, I mean," her mother said. Rachael forced herself to relax. If one more person mentioned ghosts....

"You know what I mean," Elizabeth continued. "Like that lovely book you put together on our family history, the one you gave to everyone for Christmas last year. I swear to you, Aunt Gertie is still in shock over that delightful piece of information about Great-Uncle Norman being a rumrunner."

"Oh, she's in shock, all right," Rachael said dryly. "That's why she sent me a bottle of rum with the deYoung label for my birthday!"

There was silence on the other end of the phone, then her mother burst into peals of laughter.

"Did she really?" Elizabeth asked, gasping. "Oh dear. She never said a word."

"I think Aunt Gertie knows a whole lot more about the situation than we ever gave her credit for," Rachael said. "And so help me, I'm going to get her to tell me everything if it's the last thing I do."

"Good luck," her mother said. "Well, darling, I don't want to run up your phone bill, and besides, you know how your father gets when he finds out he's missed a call from you. We'll try to give you a call next weekend."

"Great," Rachael said. "Give my love to Dad, and Reed and Robert and Rich."

"I will, and I'm sure your brothers would send their love if they ever bothered to call. 'Bye, sweetie."

"'Bye." Rachael settled the phone into the cradle and stood, bending swiftly to touch her toes and pop the kinks from her back. With her attaché case slung over one shoulder, she went in search of the library and the paperwork Ian had dug up.

*

The library occupied the north of the west wing's side hall. The main part was a cavernous, two-story room with a high, sparkling chandelier that couldn't quite dissipate the shadows in the corners and niches. Two spiral staircases led up to an open-railed catwalk that ringed the room, providing access to the second level of bookcases. The fireplaces at either end of the long room contained leafy plants in brass planters, although sets of fireplace tools and spark screens testified to their usual use during the winter months. Couches, comfortable chairs, and small tables were scattered throughout the room, and paintings hung on walls not covered with shelves. Rachael noted that the Adirondack landscapes were by Felicity.

Rachael wandered the circumference of the room, trailing a finger along a shelf as she went, pausing once or twice to examine a book more closely. The wide variety of books didn't surprise her, nor did most of the topics: Scottish history and authors, antiques, business manuals, an entire set of *Hotel* magazine, modern novels. An anteroom contained older books, probably passed down through the family. Rachael noted on her digital recorder that she should examine the books further to see if they contained any information she could use.

Back in the main room, Rachael found several piles of papers on a table. Atop them was a piece of paper with her name in large red letters, and the initials *IM*. Feeling the adrenaline rush she always got when starting an investigation, Rachael pulled out her laptop, flicked on the lamp, and settled down to work.

The rush sustained her well into the afternoon, for when she looked up again, tired, hungry, and extremely frustrated, she discovered shadows slinking silently toward her like half-seen enigmatic cats.

"Damn," she murmured in surprise. She didn't have to glance at her watch to ascertain how late it really was; on the back lawn, the deer had arrived for their evening graze, and the tight grumble in her middle reminded her that her last meal had been breakfast.

The shadows curled and languidly stretched, and she shivered, tugging her sleeves down to her wrists from where she'd shoved them up and out of the way. With a sigh, she began straightening the stacks of papers on the desk, unhappy with the way her research had gone thus far. The paperwork had definite gaps in it, and, in turn, so did her grasp of the history. However, she'd managed to put together a respectable family tree, tracing the lineage directly back through the eldest male to Birney MacPherson, who in 1839 had brought his wife Elisa and their daughter Glynis to the New World and built the replica of his family home in what could be called the Highlands of New York.

But beyond that, she found much information about some relatives, and next to nothing about others. Jordan, Shane, and Felicity's father was Malcolm John MacPherson, who remarried after his first wife's death. This second marriage, to Anne McKenzie, had produced Shane. Rachael had found Malcolm and Anne's wedding certificate, but very little to show that Marion Roark, the first wife, had existed. She was also surprised to find little about Shane's wife and Ian's mother, Emilie Shaw, but she surmised that Ian may not have thought such recent paperwork necessary yet. She made a voice note to ask him for information dating from the 1920s to the present.

Still, the afternoon had been far from wasted. In one folder, she'd found a copy of the charter that gave the MacPhersons their family crest, along with a modern translation. Rachael knew that period of history would take up a fascinating chapter of the book.

She finished tidying the desk, having already divided the papers into several stacks by fifty-year blocks of time. Another stack represented the papers she still had to review. From that stack, she pulled an old, slightly musty-smelling photo album, the edges of its black pages crumbling with age.

This was too enticing to put off. Food could wait a little longer. Tucking one foot beneath her other leg, Rachael set the book on her lap and carefully opened it.

She quickly placed the time period from the meticulously hand-lettered captions beneath the sepia-toned photos at the early 1900s. Young Felicity, in a paint-spattered smock, clutching a paintbrush; her twin, Letitia, posing next a piano. Celeste, a babe in the arms of her mother, a now-older Letitia.

Malcolm, straight-backed and stern-looking, but with approachable-looking eyes. A lone picture of his first wife, Marion Roark MacPherson, a friendly, open smile on her face. A photo of Malcolm's second wedding to Anne McKenzie, who wore a dropped-waist, pearl-buttoned dress.

Rachael muttered to herself, annoyed, as she turned the pages and found blank spots where photos had once been, lighter-toned spaces framed by black sticky tabs that once held the corners of pictures. Someone had probably removed them to have negatives made, or to give away, or to include in a school project. Whatever the reason, the precious photos had never been returned, and now they were either tumbled in with other belongings, or, worse, lost forever.

Her mutterings became spotted with more violent curses when she discovered someone had torn whole pages from the album. Rachael ran a finger along the ragged edge where a page had been ripped out. The heavy, construction-paper-like page had left a soft frayed border where it had succumbed to a greater strength.

Rachael closed the book and looked around the vast room again. The shadows twined about her feet, sinuous and intangible. She heard a creak, and quickly glanced in its direction, feeling the hair stand up on her arms. "Paranoid," she chided herself, trying to shake off the feeling of not being alone. Definitely time to pack up for the night.

Twisting to crack her spine, she stretched her arms up and hung her head back. And saw someone on the catwalk, nearly hidden by shadows.

She jerked, and the photo album slipped from her lap. Her historian's instincts took over and she lunged, catching it before it hit the floor.

When she looked back up at the catwalk, the figure was gone.

"Lovely—all this talk of ghosts has me hallucinating now," she said aloud, her voice sounding flat because of the walls' padding of books. But despite her words, her heart pulsed painfully in her chest, and her stomach roiled with the aftershock of fear.

She still clenched the scrapbook in her hands, and now she set it on the desk. Only then did she notice the corner of a picture thrusting out, as if trying to escape. She slid her fingers beneath the corner in an attempt to open the book to that page. Instead it flipped one page farther, and she saw that two pages had stuck together; the photo had wormed its way out through a space not glued by moisture and time. With gentle motions, she coaxed the pages apart, wincing every time she imagined a tearing sound.

Finally the pages parted, revealing pictures inserted in tabs on both sides. A glance at the captions showed they were all of Jordan MacPherson.

The only pictures of him in the entire album.

Rachael stared at the slightly blurred, uncolored photos in fascination, glad for the chance to study him, which she'd wanted to do ever since she'd seen the picture on Celeste's desk. The man's eyes—which she somehow knew were the MacPherson green—caught hers so intently that she felt she was looking at a real person, not a picture. His dark hair curled to his shoulders. A strong nose and a smile she could only describe as wicked quirking his full lips kept his features from being unassuming. Looking at the one full-length shot, she saw that his broad chest narrowed to slim hips and well-muscled thighs; at the picture of him seated at a piano, she found herself quite aware of his artistic, slim-fingered hands resting possessively on the black-and-white keys.

Suddenly her vision blurred, shifted.

But yesterday's incidents had her on alert, and Rachael kept her mind firmly in the present, refusing to allow her power to give her any unwanted images. This album had been handled by many people, including several who were alive today. She couldn't risk using her second sight and hitting the wrong time period.

The pictures of Jordan fascinated her, and she wished they were in better focus. Were there family portraits? She'd have to ask. Reluctantly, she closed the album.

She gratefully snapped off the chandelier's switch, pulling the doors shut and preventing the room's shadows from escaping out into the bright light of the hallway. Her unintended discovery cheered her; the day's work seemed less frustrating now that she had found some parts she'd thought were missing. Her hunger surely had contributed to her earlier defeatist attitude.

She snagged a banana from the fruit bowl in the parlor, and as she headed through the front hall, she saw that Karyn's office door was open, so she stuck her head inside.

"Working on a Saturday evening?" she asked.

Karyn looked up, and smiled tiredly.

"A manager's work is never done," she said. "That's one of the advantages of living on the premises—I can come in at odd hours. To make up for it, I can leave at odd hours as well, which is handy when one has a small and very active child."

Rachael slid into the chair in front of Karyn's desk. "I met Brett today. He seems like a great kid."

Karyn glanced at a framed photo on her desk. "He is," she agreed fondly. "He can be a nuisance at times, but I love him. Did he talk your ear off when you met him?"

"We had a discussion about *Star Wars*," Rachael said. "I got points for recognizing Chewie's name, but lost points because I didn't immediately agree—"

"—that Greedo shot first," Karyn finished. "Brett got you with that one, did he? I have the most moral child on earth, I tell you. Sometimes I don't know how he could have come out of my body."

"Oh, you two are a lot alike." Rachael remembered Brett's talkativeness and friendly openness. "He's got quite an imagination, too. While we were outside talking this morning, Brett said he saw a ghost standing in one of the windows."

Karyn nodded, her lips briefly tightening into a concerned frown. "He's still talking about that, is he? He's told me several times that there's a ghost here, and I brought it up with his school psychologist. She said kids his age often make up stories like that, since that's the age when they get into slumber party stories and such." She shook her head. "It just isn't like Brett to do that, though. Oh, he likes to make up stories, but he insists the ghost is real. He's never been one to lie, so I wasn't quite sure what to make of it. He hadn't mentioned it in a while, and I thought maybe he'd outgrown the idea."

"We both did see someone in the window," Rachael assured the older woman. "He may have just automatically said it, or he might have been trying to see what my reaction would be."

"Well, he doesn't seem concerned about it, so I suppose I'll just let it slide," Karyn said. She looked at her watch. "Is it that late already? I have to collect the little tyke and shovel some dinner into him." She surveyed the files on her desk, many dotted with scrawled Post-It Notes. "Oof, what a mess. I'll be back here tomorrow morning, that's for sure. I've got tons to do before that couple from Alabama arrives."

"Why don't you finish up here, and I'll go find Brett for you," Rachael suggested.

"Oh no, I couldn't impose on you like that," Karyn said quickly, but Rachael heard the layer of hopefulness beneath her polite words.

"It's no problem," Rachael said, standing. "I need to work the kinks out before dinner, anyway. Where is he?"

"Last I saw, out on the back lawn. He and Chewie were defeating the bad guys and making Manor MacPherson safe for humanity once again."

Karyn directed her to a sunroom at the back of the house, and leaving her bag in the office, Rachael found her way there.

Closing the glass-paned door behind her, Rachael stepped onto the porch and surveyed the green carpeting. The scene was the same as when she'd looked out the library window, and she realized that she hadn't seen Brett then, only a deer. The deer in question had meandered to the edge of the wood, and as she stepped off the porch, it vanished with one graceful, sudden bound.

Rachael cupped her hands around her mouth to holler Brett's name, then let her arms drop, unwilling to shatter the peaceful silence of the mountains, now blue in the twilight as they settled down for slumber. To her left, the final arc of the sun left a farewell present of long bright beams that caressed the lawn.

Then, she heard Chewie begin to bark, a desperate, angry warning that brooked no avoidance or ignorance.

Rachael took off down the lawn, shoes slapping against the ground as she sprinted, her muscles loosening and lengthening. Her breathing rasped her ears, punctuated by the hoarse frantic sound from Chewie. Her foot caught in a shallow cavity; her ankle twisted painfully, and she stumbled, catching her balance just before she would have pitched onto the ground. She resumed her stride, a twinge of pain snapping up her leg each time her left foot met the ground.

Into the trees, and she slowed, the path here too uneven to run over at full tilt.

"Brett?" she called out. No answer, but Chewie's barking continued, unabating. "Brett!"

Seeing the dog perched on the edge of the riverbank made her heart constrict in her chest. Her feet skidded into the moist earth and wet ferns at the bank as she came to his side. "Oh God."

In the middle of the swift-running stream was Brett, half-draped over a rock near the bridge she had admired earlier that day. Both arms gripped the boulder as he struggled to pull himself up, but his bare feet kept slipping on the wet moss. In one hand he clutched a fluorescent green Frisbee.

"Hold on, Brett, I'm coming!" Rachael called, but she didn't know if he heard her in his exertions. She left her shoes on, hoping they would help her not slip, and waded in.

The icy water made her gasp, and she felt the cold claw viciously into her shins before her lower legs went numb. She stepped forward, feeling for a foothold, and then stepped again…and the streambed dropped out from under her.

Rachael plunged into the frigid brook, and came up gasping for air. Her feet scrabbled for the bottom, and found purchase on the pebbles below. She stood, discovering that the water was chest-high. Grimly, she moved forward, fighting against the current that threatened to knock her off her feet again. A few more steps, and she was at the rock, and Brett.

"Hold on, buddy," she said in greeting.

"I-I th-threw the Frisbee too hard, and it went in the river," Brett said, his teeth clicking together with cold. "I knew Mom would be mad if I lost it, s-so I waded in, but—"

"That's okay—your mom will just want you safe," Rachael said as soothingly as she could without letting her own teeth clatter. Her fingernails were turning blue in the bone-chilling water, and she didn't know how long it would be before she couldn't feel anything at all.

"Now listen to me carefully: I'm going to take a hold of the back of your collar and pull you back in. I want you to lie on your back and kick your feet, okay?" At his jerky nod, she continued. "You have to remember not to struggle, or I won't be able to hold on. It's not far to the bank—you can do it. Ready?"

His head bobbed again, and she reached up and got a firm hold on the back of his T-shirt with nearly numb fingers. "Okay, slide off the rock—slowly. Just slide into the water. There you go."

He relaxed, and floated on his back as she had told him, still holding on to the Frisbee. The cold stream, fed from springs high in the mountains, gently began tugging him along with the flow, and his body slowly turned parallel to the bank, his feet floating in the direction of the bridge. Rachael took a cautious step toward the bank, then another, barely able to feel the pebble-strewn bottom shift beneath her feet. She wondered if she should swim for it, but realized the swift-flowing river would push her too far along. As it was, with most of her body under water, she drifted downstream with each step. The added pull of Brett's body only made the movement worse.

Rachael considered, then pulled Brett's head closer to her, tugging with her other hand to bring him around perpendicular to the bank, his feet facing forward. If she pushed him ahead of her, then he could climb out and she could make the rest of her way on her own. She nudged him forward, and stubbed her right toes on the rock that made up the ledge she had tripped from earlier. She put her right foot on the rock and stepped up, only to overbalance and tumble backwards. Her unfeeling fingers slipped from the collar of Brett's shirt, and she barely had time to take a deep breath as she went under.

Rachael kicked her legs, her arms turning slow pinwheels against the water, her heavy clothes weighing her down. She felt herself dragged downstream with the current, and scrabbled frantically for a foothold. The river was even deeper here, and she only smacked her left ankle against a rock. Pain bit through the numbness.

Desperately, she kicked upward, but something jolted her to halt before her head broke the surface. She squinted in the murky depths, and saw that her sweater had gotten caught on the submerged tree branch she had seen earlier.

The branch clawed at her face as she fought to free the right arm of her sweater from the grasping clutching fingers. Her lungs burned, and she desperately needed to take a breath. Her left hand worked awkwardly, her fingers lifeless. She jerked her arm away, but the branches stubbornly kept hold. The water pushed her farther into the limb, and her hair floated forward, obscuring her vision.

Her vision filled with exploding stars, then nothing more than darkness.

Chapter Four

The afternoon shadows had blended into evening's twilight gloom, but neither man moved to turn on the room's lights. One man stood motionless by the window, arms folded across his chest, his face impassive and turned away; a dark profile silhouetted against the darkness settling outside.

"Why are you keeping things from her?" he asked suddenly, his voice like the surprising, painful glare of high-beamed headlights on a nighttime road. "Why do you hide things?"

"The history she compiles will be the best for everyone," the other man said shortly, from his seat behind the desk. "It will be as complete as it needs to be."

"The story will either be complete or not. There is no in between. And who are you to decide what is best for everyone?"

"The past is the past. Let the dead rest."

The first man chuckled, humor-lacking. "That's an ironic thing for you to say, considering—"

"Considering nothing." The second man jerked his hand as if to physically cut off the other's words. "History is dead, the past is dead, and so is most of our family. Even—"

Now it was the standing man's turn to interrupt, suspend the thought before it could be spoken and thus recorded, unerasable, on the very air that hung between them.

"She'll keep searching," he said. "She won't stop because something's not there. She'll just dig deeper and deeper, try harder, and then who knows what she'll find? You can't hide every photograph, every incriminating scrap of paper; sooner or later she'll find something that will lead her closer to the truth."

"You're a fine one to talk about truth."

The words were meant to wound, but the first man was beyond feeling the pain from such stinging darts. "I have nothing to hide," he said simply, honestly. "My existence can be laid bare."

The second man made no response.

Finally, voice soft, the first said, "She'll learn. You can't stop her, and I won't let you push too hard."

There was no response from the seated man; no acknowledgment that he had heard or cared. But the first man knew he had, and did. That knowledge only added urgency to his concern.

Outside, Rachael began her frantic sprint down the lawn. One of the men saw. Without sound, almost without perceptible movement, he left.

*

Rachael coughed, and winced as ice-fire pain seared her lungs. But breathing felt delicious, despite the pain, and she drew in another ragged breath. Her head ached, her sinuses throbbing. She was very cold, but a comforting, numbing cold, and all she wanted to do was close her eyes and sleep…

No. Something was wrong; there was something she urgently had to do, though she couldn't remember exactly what. Reluctantly, she opened her eyes. Trees bent solicitously over her, red-and-gold-leafed branches rustling fussily over her prone form. Beyond the trees, the sky was the specific indigo hue that signaled the coming of night, one more shade to go before the stars pricked through the black fabric of heavens.

Funny. She could hear the wind in the trees, but the leaves weren't moving.

Then she realized that the sound was of rushing water, and she remembered what had happened.

Rachael struggled to sit up, managed to prop up on her elbows. The sight of Brett's unmoving form on the river's bank gave her another burst of energy, and she rolled over onto her hands and knees. The sudden action sent her head spinning, and darkness groped at the edges of her sight. She ducked her head down, willing herself to stay conscious.

Without warning, she heard a crackling noise that developed almost immediately into a frightful roar. Fits of light flickered over the grass, nipping at her hands, filling the woods.

"What—?" She hauled her head up and stared, horrified, at the fire consuming a cottage across the river. Even on this bank she could feel the heat emanating from the conflagration, warming her wet, chilled body. A scream tore from within the inferno, a shriek of agony and fear that spiraled higher and higher until Rachael buried her head in her arms and covered her ears.

Then, again, just the sound of the rushing brook, punctuated by a fearsome growl that sent the hair barbing down her neck. Cautiously, she looked up again. Chewie was standing over Brett, hackles raised as the low rumble emanated from his throat. What was he protecting the boy from? Rachael looked in the direction of the dog's gaze, saw nothing. But when she looked back, she thought she saw something gleaming pale out of the corner of her sight.

She looked again. Nothing. Like trying to look at a dim star: If she looked directly, she couldn't see it; but if she looked away, it would become clear and bright in her peripheral vision. Concentrating, she directed her eyes on Chewie and Brett.

There. A slender-built, dark-haired man, clad in a white shirt and dark pants, standing a few feet away from the boy and dog. He held out one hand, but Chewie would have nothing of him. He turned, and looked at Rachael, his eyes startlingly intense. Even in the darkness, Rachael got the impression that they were green. He nodded and smiled briefly, as if glad to see she was conscious.

That did it. She instinctively moved her eyes to look at him fully, and he was gone. She shook her head, angry and frustrated. But he had been trying to help Brett, and despite the curiosity that wailed for her to investigate further, she turned her attention to the boy. Unwilling to risk standing just yet, she instead crawled toward him.

Chewie's threatening snarl stopped her.

"Chewie, it's me. Hey, puppy, take it easy," she cooed. She held out her hand, palm up, hoping the loyal dog wouldn't somehow equate her with the man and snap off her fingers. "I want to help Brett, Chewie. I can't do that unless you let me."

The dog whined uneasily, glancing from her to where she had seen the man. She didn't dare look over there herself. "Come on, Chewie."

The big dog stretched toward her hand, and she forced herself not to jerk away. His black, wet nose hesitantly snuffled her palm. He yipped in frustration, then stepped away from Brett, putting himself between the boy and the man.

Rachael scrambled the last few feet and pressed her fingertips against Brett's neck. His skin felt clammy and cold, but she could feel a faint, slow throb beneath her probing touch. However, he wasn't breathing, and even in the dimness she could see his lips were unnaturally shaded and dark.

She took a deep breath, centering and calming herself, forcing herself to think clearly even though her stomach jittered with fear. Carefully, she slid her left hand beneath Brett's neck and firmly tilted his head back.

With her other hand she pinched his nose shut. She took another breath, then bent over and covered his chilled mouth with hers, and pumped air into his unworking, unwilling lungs.

The next few minutes blurred into a rhythm of breathing and pausing, cocking her head between breaths to put her ear close to his face and listen desperately for a whisper.

Breath, pause. Breath, pause, all the while some part of her brain mentally begging, bargaining with whoever might listen and grant favors. How long had he lain there unbreathing? she wondered. How long had she been unconscious?

Breath, listen. Breath, listen.

Please.

Then, without warning, Brett's narrow chest heaved. Rachael rolled him on his side away from her and felt a clog of relief break free as he spewed up brackish water, coughing and spitting and sobbing weakly as he gulped air.

Chewie padded over and dropped the neon Frisbee on the ground beside the boy, then licked his face, shoving him into Rachael and nearly knocking them both over.

"Hey, you're doing fine," Rachael said, hugging his wracking shoulders.

"I don't feel good." His voice was weak and sad.

"I know you don't. I don't feel too great myself." Rachael laughed shakily. "Let's go back to the house. Think you can walk that far?" She didn't think she'd be able to carry him, though he was small for his age.

A hesitant nod. "Think so."

They helped each other up, and Rachael, squinting in the darkness, guided the boy over the rough patches in the path to the lawn. They walked slowly, unsteadily toward the house, Brett leaning with one hand on Chewie's broad back, supported also by Rachael's arm. By the time they reached the sunroom he was shuddering uncontrollably from both cold and delayed shock. Rachael was little better. Her sodden sweater weighted her shoulders, and her still-numb feet squished in ruined shoes.

Karyn, in the act of locking her office door, turned at the sound of their grim approach across the front hall.

"Oh God!" One hand flew to her mouth, then she dropped Rachael's attaché case and reached out to enfold Brett as he stumbled the last few steps to her maternal grasp. "What happened?" she asked, her blue eyes darkened with concern as she cradled her son.

Brett's voice, muffled in her embrace, provided a disjointed, rambling explanation. Karyn looked to Rachael for translation.

"Apparently he waded into the brook to retrieve his Frisbee—" The toy in question was trapped in Chewie's jaws, and the dog's tail beat on the floor at her words. "I found him clinging to a rock and went in to get him."

"Rachael saved me," Brett said, pushing away slightly so he could look up at his mother, earnest. "She got me out and gave me mouth-to-mouth res—reski—rescitution."

"I *guess* I got him out," Rachael said, flushing at the wordless gratitude that flared in Karyn's eyes. "It's all sort of hazy." Which was a lie: the memory of the fire, the screams, and even the half-seen (and yet so star-clear) man stained bright in her memory like the bold swathes of paint on a canvas.

Karyn didn't seem to notice her comment, just as she seemed unaware that Brett's wet clothes soaked her. They all stood for a time-trapped moment, giving silent blessings to someone for life.

Then the moment was broken as curious faces peered from the parlor, and Celeste appeared from within. Rachael was reminded of the night before, when she'd nearly pitched down the stairs. Celeste paused long enough to politely but firmly shut the parlor doors, then she crossed the hall, begging an explanation.

Karyn and Brett seemed to have answering well under control, and for that Rachael was glad. She didn't seem to have the energy to go through the story again. In fact, she didn't seem to have the energy to keep standing, and while the others talked, she found herself drifting to the nearest wall. Once there, she leaned against it, and moments later discovered that she'd unaccountably slid to the floor, where she found herself huddled, limbs tight, for warmth.

"Oh dear," Celeste said, finally noticing. "You're chilled to the bone, aren't you?"

Rachael nodded mutely up at her, feeling vaguely like a wide-eyed puppy. The vision of herself, tongue hanging out, made her giggle. My, but she was feeling giddy.

Karyn excused herself to get Brett dry clothes and drive him to the emergency room, just in case. She offered to take Rachael, but Rachael refused.

"I wasn't in the water as long as he was," she said, pulling herself to her feet. "I just need a hot bath, and some food. Sorry about your floor," she added to Celeste, looking at the water puddled on the polished wood.

"The floor will dry," Celeste said briskly. "The important thing is that you and Brett are all right. I'll explain your absence at dinner. Now, go and dry off and warm up. Shall I have food sent up to your room?"

"Some soup would be great. I'll call down to the kitchen when I'm ready; is that okay?"

"Of course. We always offer room service, although most people prefer the dining room—it adds to the atmosphere. Now, off with you." Celeste shooed her toward the stairs, then went back into the parlor.

Rachael slipped off her shoes and socks, and made her ascent barefoot rather than risk slipping in her sodden footwear. She was on the landing when she heard a voice call, "Rachael!"

She turned to see Kevin shutting the parlor door. He took the stairs two at a time until he was next to her.

"Celeste told us what happened," he said, not the least bit breathless from his dash. "I wanted to see if you needed help. Can I carry your bag?" he asked, reaching for it, but Rachael moved it from him.

"All I did was go for a swim," she said easily, shaking her head. "I'm fine. But I accept your company for the long, arduous journey to my room."

She wasn't sure whether to be appreciative or annoyed by his offer, and something she couldn't quite identify nudged her into the latter category. Growing up amidst three brothers had taught her independence early, and she hated being assumed the "weak female." And it wasn't as if she were ill. Except for the brief dizziness, she felt fine. But Kevin's solicitousness seemed sincere, and she couldn't fault him that.

They turned the corner at the top of the stairs. Rachael cast a sidelong glance at Kevin. He was wearing a white shirt with grey pinstripes, and a pair of charcoal-grey pants. For a flashing moment, with his dark hair and light eyes, he reminded her of the man she'd seen—thought she'd seen?—by the brook.

She shook her head. Perhaps she *was* still light-headed. Kevin's hair was cropped in a businesslike style, though it ringed untamable around his ears, and the other man's hair had curled to his collar. Kevin was huskily built—she suspected he put in several hours at the gym every day—and the man had been slender-hipped, though strong-shouldered. And Kevin's eyes were not the striking green that the man's had been.

But she couldn't have seen the man's eyes...and, yet, she had.

Kevin asked her about her day and she briefly told him of her research, which she seemed to have conducted eons ago. Though she didn't mention them, she was again reminded of the oddly few pictures of Jordan and some of the other family members.

"How about you?" she asked. "Are you three getting ready to head out tomorrow?"

"We're begging for a reprieve," he answered. "We've gotten a lot done, but we think with one more week we can wrap the whole package up and have it ready to go. Our boss is impressed with the work we've done so far, but he has to clear things with the Big Boss. We should hear tomorrow morning." He shook his head, his tone again becoming bitter. "Lord knows we deserve it, doing all the grunt work and getting none of the glory, much less any of the real proceeds."

"I hope it's good news," Rachael said politely, still unsure of her feelings toward him. Maybe it was his profession that made him seem too slick, layered over with false solicitousness. Then again, he'd seemed honestly willing enough to look up some names and information for her.

She fished the key from her briefcase, but it promptly fell from her numbed fingers and skittered across the hall. Kevin retrieved it and would have opened the door for her but for her insistence that she was capable. He handed her the key, exclaiming at how cold her hands were.

"Nothing a hot bath won't cure," she said firmly, putting her shoulder to the door and discovering it sore and bruised as she nudged the protesting door inward.

"You're sure you don't need anything?" he asked again, trying to lean around the door.

"I'm positive. You're sweet to ask, though," she said. Annoyance returned. "Really, go on."

He did, and soon she was immersed in frothing, apricot-scented bubbles. The antique tub was long and narrow and deep, and she slid down so the water nuzzled her chin, feeling the heat penetrate, layer by layer to her core. A shiver claimed her body, and water splashed onto the tiled floor. She filled the tub twice with steaming water, as hot as she could stand it, and by the time she reluctantly set the water to swirling down the drain a second time, she felt downright toasty. She slipped into a pair of pajamas—an oversized T-shirt with lace-trimmed stretch cotton shorts in a matching dark floral print—and disdained socks as she padded across the suite to call the kitchen.

Maria commented on her lack of warm footwear when she brought up the light supper.

"You're awfully flushed," the servant added, raising a hesitant hand as if to feel Rachael's face; then, instead, she simply set the tray on the side table.

"Hot bath," Rachael explained. She realized she'd used that phrase in her last three conversations, and giggled. Maybe she should've majored in Roman history, so "hot bath" would've fit better in every other sentence. *The Romans had a system of aqueducts, so they had hot baths.*

Maria looked worried, but Rachael shooed her out with promises to eat and get right into bed. The missed lunch and near drowning had left her famished, and she barely paused to savor the hot, thick oxtail soup, which Maria had ladled into a deep earthenware crock, and the accompanying crusty French bread and marinated cucumber salad. When she finished, she set the tray outside her door and climbed into bed, flopping on her stomach and tugging the quilts up to nearly cover her head.

Her last, guilty thought was that she really ought to get up and put the batteries from her digital recorder into the battery recharger.

*

Rachael walked up a spiral staircase, the steps like wedges of stone pie, narrowing to points at the center of the staircase. She guessed she was in one of the towers at the front of the house. She wore a long, filmy white gown, and carried a candelabrum. The candles flickered fitfully, though she could feel no breeze.

"Oh, this is ridiculous," she said in disgust. "I look like the bimbo from *Dark Shadows*. 'My name is Victoria Winters,'" she mimicked, high-pitched, plucking at the skirt. "'I am a simpering idiot.'"

So then she was wearing her pajamas. Well, that was interesting. She'd read about controlling your dreams, but had never had one respond, much less so obediently. She still had the candelabrum, though, not a handy flashlight.

Her feet drew the stone's chill into her body, and she wished she'd put on socks before she'd gone to bed. But she'd been so hot then, and now she was getting so cold. In fact, now she could feel the whispers of the winter-laden draft that toyed with the candleflames.

She reached the top of the stairs to find a heavy wooden door with iron crossbeams and an old-fashioned latch. She lifted the latch and pushed. The door swung easily inward, and the ensuing wail of wind snuffed the candles and shivered her skin.

Waking, she felt the breeze puffing at the curtains, blowing into the room. She tugged the covers tighter to her, curling her feet up and slipping her hands between her thighs to warm them. Sleep reclaimed her, and gave her back the dream.

The door hadn't swung in, but outward, depositing Rachael on the bridge over the brook. The darkened candles were unneeded here. Bright roaring flames shot upward from the cottage and out its windows, straining toward the night sky, and she feared for the trees huddled around the building. Acrid smoke curled and coiled like a rattler about to strike; then did strike, biting at her eyes and her lungs still pained from the water. She coughed, blinking furiously and wiping away at hot tears. The blistering heat rolled over her in waves. Her pajamas clung wetly to her skin, soaked with her sweat.

Rachael pushed the bedcovers to her waist and tried to kick them off the bed, but they tangled in her legs and she fell back, exhausted, defeated.

Someone drew the covers back over her.

"No," she protested. Her voice sounded thin, whiny and petulant. "Too hot."

"You're fevered," a low, smooth voice said. "You'll catch a chill."

"I said I'm *hot*. If I were chilled—" Wait. Who was she talking to? She must be still dreaming.

"Well, I was only trying to help." The man's voice offered gentle, patient amusement.

She opened her eyes. No bright firelight. Instead, the moon scythed between the filmy curtains and across the bed. But at the man's face it paused, deferential, and melted into molten silver. His features luminesced.

"Oh yeah," she murmured, delighted, "my hallucinations are getting better and better all the time."

Her curiosity about Jordan MacPherson had caused her subconscious to deposit him on the edge of her bed, details exact right down to the scar on his chin, just below his jaw line. One heavy dark eyebrow quirked upward; beneath, eyes glittered with unvoiced laughter. His sensual lips also quirked in a smile as he regarded her.

"You're feverish," he repeated.

"I am most definitely feverish," she agreed. "I am flushed with barely contained rapture." She coughed again, and moaned—even in her dreams she couldn't escape from the reality of her tortured throat and lungs. She touched the corner of her lips with the tip of her tongue, found cracked dryness.

"Boy, do I need a drink of water," she announced to her hallucination. She tried again to untangle her legs from the bed coverings.

"No, you rest. I'll get it." Jordan rose and crossed the room to the bathroom, nearly vanishing into the forest of dark as he left the path of moonlight. Rachael began to drift into sleep again, the sound of the running water growing distant, obscured, otherworldly.

Somewhere, far and away, she heard his voice. Dreamily she opened her eyes, and found him sitting on the bed. How odd. She didn't feel the bed move when he sat down. She must've really fallen asleep.

He set the glass down and fluff-plumped the pillow against the headboard when she sat up, and she drooped against it as a wave of lightheadedness made her vision shimmer. When her head cleared, she accepted the glass from him. His slim fingers stayed under the glass until she had it firmly in her grasp. Before he could completely pull away, she reached out and traced a fingertip along the tickling of hair on the back of his hand. At her touch, he stilled, watching her with eyes turned suddenly smoke-green.

"Such nice hands," she murmured. "Graceful. Artist's hands."

"In a manner of speaking," he said, slowly, pulling his hand away. But he didn't pull his gaze from her face.

Holding the glass in both hands, Rachael drank greedily, the coolness of the liquid a balm to her raw throat.

"Easy," Jordan said, reaching out to take the emptied glass even as she came up gasping for air. She nestled back into the pillow again, still feeling float-headed, fever-light.

"I brought a cloth for your head," he added. His voice seemed faded, waned, to her.

"That's nice," she said, listening not to his words, but to the sonorous voice. A singer's voice.

A lover's voice. *Now, what made her think that?*

Through nearly closed eyes she watched as he laid the cloth on her forehead, and she reached up to help him press it to her temples. Her brow cooled, she gently grasped his wrist and moved his hand, and the cloth, to her throat. She squeezed the cloth, and water trickled down her chest, vanishing into the lace-edged V of her pajama top. She arched her back, her eyelids fluttering shut, reveling in the feeling of the cool water.

The room was silent. Languidly, she opened her eyes. Jordan was staring at the point where the water droplets vanished beneath her shirt. She glanced down. The cotton clung to her breasts like a lover's kiss. She shivered, suddenly cold again, and her body's reaction to the goose-chill caused him to sharply suck in his breath.

She shivered again, this time not from cold but from the look in his eyes. Her body flushed with excited heat as his hand clenched on hers where they held the washcloth. With her other hand she covered his, barely touching. The cloth tumbled away onto her lap, and suddenly his fingers traced the lace-edge of her shirt, leaving a hot trail on her moist flesh.

"Jordan." Why did her voice sound so husky? Still scraped by the river water, of course. Jordan's brows had drawn together in the tiniest of frowns, and she smoothed it away with a light touch of her index finger. Rachael licked lips suddenly gone dry, but it wasn't water she craved.

It was *her* feverdream, she reasoned. She'd do what she wanted. She moved her hand around to the back of Jordan's head. Curled her fingers in the thicket of hair. Tugged him gently toward her. Met him in the kiss.

This was, Rachael thought, the most lucid dream she'd ever had. Not like a dream, really; no fuzzy edges, no strange inconsistencies save for the fact that the man she kissed had been dead for forty years. This wasn't like her visions, either, for in those, even though she could feel and smell and hear the scene, she still stood apart, an unseen onlooker.

She was definitely involved in this dreamscene. The kiss surrounded her, caught her, drew her in. She could tell Jordan was startled by her actions, and then he responded. His mouth grazed hers, his tongue sensuously stroking the sensitive skin inside her upper lip. But she wanted more. Her fingers flexed in soft strands of hair at the base of his neck, and she pulled him deeper, harder into the kiss. Their lips fought in mock battle, until she, victorious, caught his lower lip between her teeth. A benevolent captor, she tortured him by nibbling gently, chuckling softly as she heard his quick indrawn breath of pleasure.

No model prisoner he—he slipped beneath her guard and snared her lip in a tender trap. Her turn to gasp with delight, to indulge in momentary, delicious surrender. Then the game began anew, their tongues combating teasingly. Feinting and darting, they proved evenly matched contenders, the contest made all the more challenging because each sought not to win, but to give enjoyment to the other as well as receive it.

His hand, trapped between them, fluttered, and his fingers moved to cup her breast, touching, teasing. His lips kissed a trail along her cheek, her jaw, down to her throat, following the path of his fingers along the neckline of her shirt. His tongue dipped down, ever so briefly, beneath the vee-edge of lace, as if trying to capture the water droplets that had slid below. Licking his way back up, he kissed her throat again, biting with passion tempered by tenderness at the suddenly sensitive skin.

Rachael arched her neck, the gentle pain and the feel of his hand at her nipple enflaming her body. She moaned somewhere back in her throat, again floating, but this time on a cloud of swirling passion that spun her around and around, a mad twirling dance.

Spinning, twirling, whirling dervish... Blackness nudged at the edges of her sight. Spinning, falling...

"Rachael? Rachael!"

"Hmmm?" Though he had pulled back, her hand still wound through his hair, and she toyed aimlessly with the curls.

He sighed with relief. "I thought I'd lost you, there."

"Hmmm." She smiled languidly. "Be honored. I've never almost passed out before."

Even in his concern, he smiled. "As much as I'd like to think so, I'm afraid it wasn't because of the kiss." A frown chased off the smile. "You're burning up with fever. I'll wet the cloth again for you."

He did, and cooled her head and neck, his touch no longer that of a lover, but of a caregiver. He set the cloth in a delicate glass bowl that had been artfully arranged next to her bed table lamp, drew the covers around her again, and rose.

"No, don't go." She caught at his hand.

"Rachael." She could tell he struggled for control. He drew in a ragged breath. "You're in no condition for this."

"No," she agreed. Already she could feel her body drifting again, more gently and yet more insistent than before. Sleep stung at her eyes. "Sing for me," she said, unsure whether her voice was audible.

"Sing for you?" In a half-lidded glance, she saw the surprise flare, green-flash, in his eyes.

She nodded, her hair tangling on the pillow at the motion. "Sing me to sleep."

She somehow knew that he sat back down, though the bed didn't move.

"Alas, my love, you do me wrong to cast me off discourteously, when I have loved you so long, delighting in your company. Greensleeves was my delight, Greensleeves was my only joy...."

*

Rachael awoke with "Greensleeves" still echoing in her head. The hallucination's memory settled around her like a shower of fall leaves, and she smiled, pressing a hand against her mouth in mild embarrassment at her own dream-actions. She had no problem being forward with a man, but she certainly never grabbed one *before* the first date.

She stretched languidly. A lovely dream, still. How fitting that she should have him sing "Greensleeves," one of her favorite songs.

Her limbs felt weak, but her head clear, and she knew the fever had broken. The bed sheets were a crumpled mess, making her glad for room service. As she padded barefoot to the bathroom, she ran a hand through her hair. Her fingers caught, and she looked in the mirror to see the tangled witchnest. She sighed, fluffing the hair back from around her face.

And froze. Her reflection looked shocked, stunned, just as she felt.

On her throat, a red mark. Passionmark.

Rachael traced the spot with her forefinger. Tender. But it couldn't be. Dreams left no physical evidence.

She flung open the bathroom door, and stared. No. But yes. On the bedside table, an empty glass, and a still-damp washcloth sitting in a low bowl next to the lamp.

What kind of hallucination left traces?

Chapter Five

The tiny MacPherson chapel solidly claimed a plot of land beyond a small pond. The view opened up as Rachael stepped from the trees. Her journey here had meandered through MacPherson grounds, past a delightful collection of outbuildings, including a now-unused ice house, pump house, and dog kennel. Regarded seriously by a splattering of geese turning lazy circles in the water, she made her way around the pond to the white-trimmed, grey-stone chapel.

"Good morning, Rachael!" Celeste said, turning in the small pew as Rachael entered the chapel. "How are you feeling this morning?"

"Good as new," Rachael replied softly. Though she wasn't particularly religious, she always felt the need to pitch her voice low when she was in a holy place, out of deference to the builders and believers.

This chapel proved no different. Small from the outside, it was even smaller within due to the thick stone that comprised its walls. Six narrow white pews, three to a side, provided seating for no more than twenty people. At the front, a simple, polished wooden cross hung on the wall behind a podium. Multicolored sunshards of light littered the floor.

Rachael slipped into the pew next to Celeste, glad she had thrown a black blazer over her black sleeveless turtleneck shirt and dark sage green pants, for the stone walls made the building cool. She had taken breakfast—simple toast and tea, unwilling to chance anything sturdier—in her room. The maid who'd brought it up carried with her a message from Celeste inviting Rachael to meet her in the chapel if she felt up to the walk.

"You had no problems finding the chapel?" Celeste asked.

"The map is wonderful," Rachael enthused. Felicity had sketched the official map of manor grounds, which had been printed up to be given to all guests who wished to explore the outbuildings. The whimsical map included sketches of the buildings, as well as native flora and fauna and surrounding mountains, all meticulously labeled.

"We get many comments on it," Celeste said with a smile. "One person wrote and told us she'd framed it as a souvenir of her trip."

Rachael pulled the map from her back pocket. "There's so much to see," she said. "I can tell how the manor grounds were laid out similarly to how the Scottish landholdings must have been."

Celeste nodded. "Apparently Birney MacPherson, for all his enthusiasm about settling here, was homesick, and so made everything as similar to his home as possible. Most of the outbuildings are no longer in use, of course." She pointed to the map. "The cowshed, for instance, and the stove ash house."

"The dog run looked vacant, too," Rachael said. "I take it Chewie doesn't think much of it?"

"That he doesn't. But the kennel saw its share of use in past times, I can tell you." Celeste smiled fondly at the memories that filtered back to her. "We boarded sled dogs here in the summer for a few years. And we all had our pets. I saw my Springer spaniel through several litters; what a darling she was. Jordan had a beautiful Irish setter—raised it from a pup, and he was only ten or so when he got him, I think. Finn, his name was, after Fionn mac Cumaill of Celtic legend. Jordan was quite a romantic, even at an early age."

She paused long enough for Rachael to prompt, "And Shane? What sort of dog did he have?"

Celeste's brow slid into a frown. "Shane never had much luck with animals," she said finally. "He went through a whole succession of dogs, as I recall. They just...they never seemed to live long. Ian's never been one much for pets, either, come to think of it."

They fell silent again for a while. Finally, Rachael said, "What can you tell me about the night of the fire? I realize you weren't here, but if you can give me the basic timeline of events, I can fill in the missing pieces from there."

"Certainly," Celeste said. She glanced down as Rachael eased the small black recorder from her jacket pocket, but didn't protest. "Let me give you some background first. The All Hallows Eve Ball is a tradition dating back in the MacPherson family for as long as anyone can remember. Certainly the family has been hosting it here since this Manor MacPherson was built. It was always a gala event, and in its heyday—from the mid-1800s when trains were introduced into the Adirondacks, and up to the 1950s—guests came from all over. Those who traveled the furthest often stayed for several weeks. Much of the local population have traditionally been invited as well. That year, we had an average crowd of a hundred and fifty or so.

"Arden—my husband—and I had left earlier that evening to take a sleeping-car train back to New York City. I believe we had, oh, twenty-five people still staying at the manor that night. The family was in the front hall saying goodbye to some of the locals, servants were cleaning up, and so forth. Everyone was so busy that the fire wasn't noticed until it was out of control."

"Who noticed it first?" Rachael asked.

Celeste thought. "I believe Felicity and the groundskeeper, who was closing up the greenhouse, noticed it at nearly the same time. The fire company was called immediately, of course, and everyone ran down to the cottage...."

"The one just across the brook, right?" Rachael asked.

Celeste nodded, startled.

"I saw the foundation stones, and guessed," Rachael explained, remembering her vision but unable to mention it. She still wasn't sure what had caused her to see the fire, for she hadn't really been touching anything that would have carried the memory. "There aren't too many other places where cottages may have stood that would have been visible from the house."

"A number of them lined the brook at one time, but most fell into disuse as the servant staff was reduced and the number of long-term family guests went down," Celeste said. "The cottage that burned was almost directly across from the bridge. Even in winter it was invisible from the house because of the evergreens around it. Only the light of the fire could be seen."

"Jordan, Shane, and Emilie were all in the cottage?" Rachael wished she had thought to bring pen and notebook, and hoped her recorder's batteries would hold out.

"Yes, although no one knew what they were doing there, or who'd gone to the cottage first."

"Didn't anyone wonder why they weren't saying goodbye to the guests?"

Celeste shrugged. "I don't know. Perhaps they had already said their goodbyes." She slid a slim gold cigarette case from the pocket of her tailored wool plaid skirt and said, "Do you mind if we talk outside for a while? I don't like to smoke in here."

Rachael followed her out and sat on the single stone step leading to the chapel door. Celeste cupped her hand against a sudden puff of wind and lit her cigarette with a monogrammed lighter that matched the cigarette case.

"There's not much else to tell, really," she said finally. "The fire and ambulance companies came. Poor Ian had stumbled around from the back of the cottage, his clothes on fire. He was in the hospital for months. Arden and I returned for the others' funeral."

"Are they buried here? Is there a family cemetery to accompany the chapel?" Rachael asked.

"No. There's a family mausoleum at the Heather Mountain Unity Cemetery—I'm sure they'd provide you with the records if you asked. There's another, tiny cemetery just past our property line that the county is supposed to keep care of—not that they do, mind you, so I try to send the groundskeeper out there once a summer to clean the place up. It's just a tiny plot, but the names on some of the tombstones are familiar. For example, there are Bartletts buried there, and the road up to our land is the Bartlett Road. For all I know, the Bartletts were family friends sometime in the past."

Rachael made a mental note to visit the mausoleum—she knew she'd be reminded to when she transcribed this tape. She rubbed her left ankle, wincing at the pressure from her fingers. While she hadn't done more than twist it when she was running, she was sporting an impressive bruise from where she'd smacked her foot on an underwater rock.

"At the time of the shooting, did your family have any enemies?" she asked. "Do you know of anyone who might have wanted anyone killed?"

A thin, blue-white stream of smoke drifted from Celeste's nostrils. "None that I know. I gather Shane had racked up some minor gambling debts, but that doesn't explain why Jordan would have been killed, unless someone botched up. Emilie was from Scotland—Shane met her on a trip over there—and she barely knew anyone outside the family. My grandfather was still running the family business, and he was well-loved in the community and by his employees."

Rachael sifted the information, squinting out over the sun-dappled pond. A duck dived, and several others followed suit in a flurry of splashes. Finally she broached the question they both knew she had to ask. "What about the rumor that Jordan and Emilie were having an affair?"

Celeste's eyes were directed at the ducks as well, but her gaze peered into the filmy past. "I really don't know, Rachael," she said. "I wasn't around long enough to know. I barely knew Emilie—she was such a quiet thing that I never got to talk with her. As for Jordan, well, he was so attractive and charming that women flocked around him. But he never took advantage of that; he was always a gentleman. I can't believe he would ever take another man's wife. Shane…Shane had a temper, and was quick to judge, but I honestly cannot believe that Jordan would be involved in such a thing."

"And none of that explains who set the fire," Rachael murmured thoughtfully.

*

When they got back to the manor, Karyn was still helping the couple from Alabama settle in. Rachael took the opportunity to seek out Felicity. She found the sprightly woman in her studio in the east tower. An elevator had been installed for convenience. Although Rachael normally preferred to take stairs, she chose the elevator out of deference to her ankle.

Felicity's studio was a jumbled amalgam, much like Felicity herself. Mess contrasted with order like absentmindedness contrasted with sharp wit. A dusty heap of pastel crayons half-tumbled from the drafting table, but all the artwork was neatly covered and stacked around the octagonal room.

"I remember the night of the fire well," Felicity said in answer to Rachael's question. "That's one of the curses of getting old, my dear: You might not remember what you had for supper yesterday or if you cleaned your brushes, but you remember the far-flung past with clarity. Too much clarity, sometimes."

"Where were you when the fire broke out?" Rachael asked.

"Up here, painting." Felicity glanced out the back window. Past the roof of the house, the far edge of the lawn could be seen, and beyond that, the woods that concealed the cottage's foundation. "I'd already said my good-byes to the guests, and I came up to work on the paintings I was doing of the All Hallows Eve Ball. I'd done sketches at the party, and was working on the paintings rather zealously."

She looked back down at her current work, and daubed the brush once, twice. Pursing her lips, she considered the new marks. "I saw little Ian head off down the lawn—it was dark, but he had a lantern. I was going to tell the nanny, but I thought since Shane was down there, he'd be safe. I get rather obsessed with my work, you see, Rachael," she said, a bit apologetically. "I really didn't want to be bothered to go all the way downstairs to find the nanny. I thought Ian would be fine."

"You said Shane was already at the cottage?" That fact intrigued Rachael; as yet, no one had been able to confirm when Shane arrived at the cottage. "Did you see him go down?"

"Oh yes, a few minutes before Ian did." Felicity swirled her brush in a cup of water. "I suspected Ian was following him. He absolutely worshipped his father."

"Did you see Jordan and Emilie go down as well?"

Felicity halted the swirling, thinking. "Can't say as I did," she admitted. "I was engrossed in my work—I only happened to glance up when Shane and Ian went out because the lamplight caught my eye."

That could mean that Jordan and Emilie were at the cottage before it got dark...or that they deliberately went without light so no one would know where they'd gone. Rachael considered how to phrase her next question.

"Did you tell anyone that you'd seen Shane go to the cottage?" she asked.

Felicity had been dipping her brush in the paint, and now she paused in the act of applying it to the canvas. "No one ever asked," she said. She painted, considered, painted again. "Besides, Jordan asked me not to," she added. Her words were low and off-handed, as if she were commenting to herself.

Rachael's brow creased. "But if Jordan was already at the cottage when Shane went...then afterward...he was dead."

The brush stilled. "Why, so he was," Felicity murmured thoughtfully, and continued painting, her strokes sure and firm. Rachael realized she was intent on her work, Muse perched on her shoulder.

Instead of bothering her again, Rachael stole out, her mind filled with Felicity's words and their implications.

*

"Hey, how's the 'Bama couple doing?" Rachael asked, sticking her head around Karyn's door.

"They're insane. You're going to love them," Karyn laughed, the skin around her eyes crinkling. "Mildred just kept going on and on about how 'ya'll just must go nuuuuts tryin' to dust awl those chan*de*liers'—accent on the second syllable."

Rachael giggled. "Well, don't ya'll? Ah know Ah get so dizzy jes' lookin' up at 'em!" She craned her neck back and wobbled a few steps.

"Stop, stop." Karyn waved one hand helplessly while groping for a tissue with the other. "No, really, they're wonderful people. Every year they take a trip somewhere else in the country, and apparently their enthusiasm never dims."

"That's what's important," Rachael agreed. "So, can you tear yourself away long enough to give me a tour? I'll understand if we have to postpone again."

Karyn glanced at the clock on the wall, a simple octagon framed in white birch. "Tell you what: How about half the house today, half tomorrow?"

"Lay on, MacDuff," Rachael said gallantly.

Karyn kept up a running commentary of information as they moved through the west wing. She avoided any private rooms, simply stating what they were, but Rachael was delighted at the number of rooms to which she was allowed access.

"You're going to die for this room," Karyn said, stopping before a set of doors identical to those that provided entry to the library. In fact, if Rachael had her bearings straight, the room should front the library and occupy the south side of the west wing. "Voila: the ballroom," Karyn said, and flung the doors wide.

The manager's comment proved correct. Rachael found herself immediately enchanted by the exquisite room. She entered almost reverently, trailing her fingers a hairsbreadth from the pale blue wallpaper hand-painted with tiny gold fleur-de-lis. Midnight-blue, gold-fringed velvet draperies smothered narrow windows along the west wall. Beneath her feet, each tile of the floor presented a fleur-de-lis in its center.

"Wow," Rachael said. Then again, "wow," drawing the word out in many syllables, singing the Kate Bush song of the same name. The word reverberated off the walls, acoustically perfect.

Karyn wandered to the end of the long room and sat on the broad set of steps leading up to a low, wooden-railed orchestra balcony, wrapping her arms around her knees. "Knew you'd like it. Just wait until the All Hallows Eve Ball, when it's full of crazily costumed people, champagne and music flowing. It's a hotel manager's nightmare. I *love* it."

Rachael, in the middle of the room, grinned at her. The room's spell bewitched her, and she began to twirl about, dancing with an imaginary partner. She tossed her head back. Heavy gold chandeliers tugged in vain to bring down the ceiling, which was covered with a sweeping mural of a masked ball. Spinning faster and faster, until the scarlets and evergreens and blacks of the tartans above blurred round and round.

She felt as if she *did* dance with someone, someone who rested one hand intimately on her back and controlled her wild jig, kept her from spinning away. Without thinking, without looking, she guessed it was Jordan; somehow, her mark-making hallucination followed her into today.

She slowed her twirl, and heard the hum of "Greensleeves." But she was the one who hummed, and she heard a low chuckle before he was gone, as sudden as he'd come.

She stumbled back, dizzy and breathless.

"Oh! Oh, do I have something to show you," Karyn said, leaping up and gesturing.

"Did you—?"

"What?" Karyn asked, turning back.

"Nothing," Rachael said, glancing back over her shoulder at the center of the room. She shook her head and followed Karyn around the left side of the balcony to a curtained window along the same wall that backed the balcony. No, not a window, Rachael realized; that wall didn't face outside—just as Karyn pulled back the cumbersome folds of thick, heavy velvet to reveal a narrow door.

"A secret passage!" Rachael delighted.

"Not particularly secret, actually," Karyn said dryly, jostling through her key ring. "Usually we don't tell all the guests about it, but we do leave the door open during the ball, as a fire exit, and we make sure everyone knows there's another way out. Here we go." The door swung inward on silent, well-oiled hinges, and Karyn fumbled for a light switch. Pale bulbs disguised in simple wall sconces flickered to life, and the door swung shut behind them. Karyn relocked it, and led her a short ways down the narrow, shadow-cornered corridor. She stopped in front of a door in the long wall, and pointed the rest of the way down the hall.

"That's the way out. Now *this* is what most guests don't see," she said, searching for another key. In the dim light, the keys looked muted, unsilvered, dark. Rachael refastened her hair in its tortoise-shell clip while she waited. "Unless they specifically mention they have an interest in it. I nearly forgot about it, and here it's perfect for you."

The door opened, a little less smoothly, a faint grumble of protesting movement. Air whiffed out, heavy and stale. The lights came on, sconces the same as those in the hall, and then Karyn turned on the other lights. The ones illuminating each portrait.

"I'd thought there might be a portrait hall," Rachael murmured, drifting to stand in front of the first painting. *Birney MacPherson*, proclaimed the gold-inscribed plaque. "I hadn't seen any portraits hanging anywhere else, so… Oh, Karyn, this is wonderful." She moved to the companion picture, of Elisa and Glynis, and continued wandering around the small, boxy room until one of the final portraits brought her up short.

The smoke-green-eyed, slender-fingered man of her hallucination. Jordan MacPherson.

The photos had been small, grainy and dim; the moonlight had warred with shadows on his face. Here, now, she could see how he truly looked. He was just as he should be, just as she would have guessed from the photos and her dreams.

While the first portraits had been simple, seated representations of each person, the later ones provided more setting. Unsurprisingly, Jordan's reflected his love of music. He stood by a black grand piano, one hand resting on its gleaming top, leaning almost insolently. One dark eyebrow cocked ever so slightly as he stared out, daring the painter to bring his soul to life, daring the portrait viewer to see him fully. His dark hair curled over the collar of his front-ruffled white shirt. On the piano behind him, the candles in the bronze candelabra seemed to flicker with light of their own.

Entranced, Rachael took another step closer. Visually she traced the hair that curled under his ear, along his firm jaw where she could imagine the faint shadow of stubble, to the pale scar just visible under the curve of his chin....

Scar. Rachael remembered running her finger along the pucker of skin in her dream last night. The small blemish certainly hadn't been visible in the photographs she'd seen, so how had she known to add that detail in her imagination?

Rachael shivered. The harder she tried to convince herself she'd had a very lucid hallucination the night before, the harder Fate threw at her facts to the contrary.

"Rachael?" Karyn jittered the keys in her hand. "I need to be getting back. I can give you the key anytime you want to come here, though."

"Oh...okay." Rachael felt as if she were swimming up from a hypnotic trance. "Let's go."

*

Rachael stood before one of the windows in the library. A low ray of sun hit the glass just right, so that instead of the lawn outside, she had a clear reflection of herself. She tugged at the collar of her turtleneck, pulled it down so she could see the mark, purpled against pale skin.

Troubled, she rubbed at it lightly with one finger. The faint pain reaffirmed the reality, the existence of the mark, and of the fact that something had happened last night. Could her dream have been so vivid that her subconscious had projected the mark on her neck? She shook her head, dislodging a curl from the haphazard pile on the back of her head she made to keep her hair out of her way while she worked. No, that theory smacked of stigmata, and that condition only appeared in cases of intense religious fervor. Her growing interest in Jordan wasn't to the point of fervor or obsession.

Then what would explain it? Explain any of it? She let her collar slip back into place as she returned to the table where she'd been working. How had she known about Jordan's scar? She leaned on the solid back of the chair and stared at the piles of papers and books, trying to remember. She'd inadvertently seen Celeste and Ian when she held Celeste's letter, but she hadn't seen Jordan, then or in any vision.

Was she suddenly showing some talent in telepathy? she wondered. Was she picking up Jordan's image from someone who'd known him? Celeste, Felicity and Ian were the only ones in the house who would remember exactly what Jordan looked like, and Ian probably only faintly, since he'd been so young when Jordan died. She drummed her fingers on the chair back. Doubtful, for wouldn't she be aware of the telepathic vision?

Well, that left only one other explanation she could think of: that—

A noise—a book slapping to the floor. She whirled, eyes searching the library. The afternoon was beginning to wane, and she hadn't turned on the lights yet, so much of the room was dim, corners murky and gloom-filled.

A squeak—a door opening? Then silence. Someone was definitely in the library with her. She put her back to the chair, one hand gripping tightly.

A shuffle—someone moving slowly—purposely lurking? Rachael tensed, wondered if she should make a dive for the fireplace and a heavy brass poker. Then again, it might just be a maid... Or her hallucination...

No, don't think about that. She cleared her throat.

"Come out, come out, wherever you are," she said, keeping her voice light. She glanced at the fireplace again. The last sound had been kitty-corner to that end of the room, she might still have the element of surprise.

"Hi!" A head poked out from one of the small anterooms.

Rachael yelped.

"Sorry, did I startle you?" Kevin walked across the room to her, one of his sneakers making a loud squeaking sound on the wood.

"A little," Rachael said, and smiled, somehow not wanting him to realize how frightened she'd been. "I didn't hear you come in."

"Oh." He didn't explain when he'd entered; instead, he thrust a piece of paper at her. "I put together a list of names for you—people you might want to contact locally for your research," he said.

"Thank you," Rachael said, accepting the page. She'd completely forgotten about their discussion—had it only been yesterday morning? An age ago.

"Research going well?" Kevin asked, glancing around her at the table.

"Just fine," she said, not offering to let him look at the papers. She hated discussing her work when she was in the middle of it, and she doubted he was really interested; he was just being polite.

"I'm surprised you don't use a computer," Kevin said. "It would really help you get organized."

"I do, but I prefer to do my initial research this way; it keeps me closer to my subject matter." It annoyed her that she felt defensive.

"Let me know if you need any help setting up spreadsheets," Kevin said, further annoying her. "I'm great with data crunching."

"Mm," Rachael said noncommittally, wondering—idly, absurdly—why she'd ever thought him attractive: He simply wasn't her type, too slick.

"Well, you're busy, I'd better be going," Kevin said, finally starting to make movements away.

"Thanks again," she said, lifting the paper in explanation.

"You bet." And he walked out, his sneaker squawking rhythmically until the door shut behind him, blocking the sound.

Rachael dropped the paper on the table as she sat down, and picked up the pages she'd transcribed from that morning's conversations. After her tour with Karyn, she'd taken lunch up to her room—somehow unwilling to face the guest's questions about her soggy entrance the night before—and listened to the tapes of Celeste and Felicity.

Not surprisingly, the information so far was raising more questions than it answered. That's how it usually worked in research like this, and she wasn't concerned. She had to perform a delicate balancing act between what people told her and what facts she could find. Much of Celeste's story was hearsay, and would be hard to prove, because few of the people who had been around that night were available to back up her words.

Felicity's words had only given her more to mull over. What had she meant, "Jordan asked me not to"? The wanderings of an elderly woman? Or something more, something very much more?

Rachael leaned forward and pulled the photo album toward her, and opened it to the pages of Jordan. She fingered the loose picture, the one that had initially alerted her to the stuck pages. Jordan stared back at her, watchful and knowing, his secrets unrevealed. What was his part in all of this? Was he, like many suspected, the loose philanderer, dallying with his brother's wife? Or was he an innocent bystander in some greater story?

Rachael propped the picture up against the wall that backed the table, and continued sorting through the documents before her. Deeds, letters, certificates of marriage, birth, and death. Business records of the MacPherson's maple syrup business, later a corporation and the source of their current and continuing wealth.

She was scrawling notes on a piece of paper to set atop a stack when she heard another noise—a scuffle this time, up above her on the catwalk. *Not again*, she thought wearily, barely able to get nervous.

"Kevin?" No answer. "Kevin, is that you again?" No answer. Her neck muscles went taut, and she felt the first stirrings of a headache as it insinuated itself between her temples. She was in no mood to play games.

She turned quickly, looking up to where she thought the noise had originated. A flash of movement? She frowned, the headache smacking against the backs of her eyes. No, no one was there, but she was annoyed enough to go up and check.

As she ascended the closest spiral staircase, she kept her eyes on the area where she'd heard the noise. Nothing seemed out of place, but the impression that someone had been there seemed stronger. She paused halfway up, and looked slightly away from the spot, to see if it were the same situation as the man by the bridge. No one. She climbed the rest of the way anyway, stubborn and intent.

As she walked around the library, she ran her hand along the thick polished railing that separated the narrow catwalk from empty space. Heights weren't a problem for her; in fact, she admired this view of the cavernous, book-lined room. Admired everything except for the fact that there were too many nooks for people to hide in.

She reached the place where she'd seen the moving shadows, and looked down. She had a perfect view of where she'd been sitting. A well-aimed book from this angle would have smacked her right on the head.

Rachael turned and surveyed the rows of books. As she'd somehow suspected, there was a glaring gap in the shelf directly before her. She rubbed her finger along the fissure in the otherwise smooth line of books, feeling a sort of psychic heat that told her the book had been taken within the last half hour. She kept her power in check, though, unable to allow herself to give it free rein and show her who had taken the book.

She glanced down again. She couldn't see the other spiral staircase from here, so the person could have snuck down while she was climbing. She could see the doors to the hall, but there was no reason why the person couldn't still be here. Or maybe the person had taken the book earlier, and she'd somehow seen a memory-trace of him or her on the catwalk.

Chewing her bottom lip, Rachael turned back to the books. From the surrounding titles, she really couldn't tell what type of book had been taken; up here, the books were less ordered than below, the titles and subjects mixed and mingled. With a sigh, she leaned back against the railing. It hadn't been a very wide book, from the looks of the space it had occupied, but that was all she could tell.

Then she heard a sickening crack, and with a thudding bolt of nausea, she felt the railing begin to give way, begin to open the way for her to plunge to the floor far below.

Chapter Six

Rachael felt the railing lurch beneath her, and without knowing what she did, she pushed away, flinging herself forward toward the shelves. For an eon-second she seemed to hang, suspended, with nothing below to hold her...then she plunged away from the edge.

The catwalk was narrow, and she slammed full-body into the shelves. She almost rebounded back, but clutched frantically at the books, desperately trying to regain her equilibrium and not fall backward.

For a moment she clung there, gasping and dizzy, pressing herself against the shelves as if to a lover's form—desperate and appreciative. Then, reluctantly, she turned, keeping her back against the books, and looked at the railing.

An angry crack split the wood, though no chunk had actually fallen down. She held no illusions that it wouldn't have completely given way had she left her weight upon it. Almost hesitantly, she touched the wounded rail, and jerked her hand back when a splinter bit into her forefinger. Sucking the pained finger, she cursed herself for being so stupid. Old house, old wood; what had she been thinking? Everything was so well-tended here that she'd been lulled into forgetting the possible hazards.

She made her way back to the stairs, still shaken, superstitiously keeping away from the railing. Knowing she would be unable to concentrate on work any longer, she packed the more valuable papers in her attaché case and left the library.

Karyn was horrified when Rachael told her of the incident, even though Rachael toned down the story and insisted she was fine.

"I don't understand it," the hotel manager said, pulling her oversized appointment book toward her as she spoke. "The MacPhersons have people go over this place with a fine-tooth comb to ensure its safety. How awful if you or another guest had been seriously hurt!"

"Old houses are unpredictable," Rachael tried to soothe her.

"But the liability...! Ian will be furious; we'll all just have to stay out of his way for a while." Karyn rolled her blue eyes. "I'll call the carpenter first thing in the morning," she said, marking the note in her book.

She got up and went to the closet, emerging with a battered, gun-metal grey toolbox. She heaved it up on the desk with a clunking thud, and reached over to snag her key ring from the pegboard. "I am also the interim handyman-person," she said, a trace of her easy-going attitude surfacing. She picked up the heavy toolbox and followed Rachael out of the office, pulling the door shut with her foot. "I'm going to do a quick patch-up job until tomorrow, and lock the library. Is there anything in there you need before tomorrow?"

Rachael shook her head. "I'm set for the night."

"Good. By the way, the family traditionally eats with the guests on Sunday, so cocktail hour will start half an hour early—so if you want to get to the good food before the other guests do...."

"Thanks for the tip," Rachael said, heading in the other direction, up to her room.

*

"I warned you not to hurt her." The first man's posture was tense, tight.

"She wasn't hurt," the second man argued calmly. "She was warned."

"She could have been hurt, or killed," the first man said, frustration evident. "I won't let you continue this."

*

Deciding she didn't need to shower again before dinner, Rachael chose the easiest route and paired her sleeveless turtleneck with a long skirt. Although the garment boasted a great deal of flowing material, it somehow clung to her in silky waves. Atop the black skirt, on which swirled muted blue and purple flowers, she cinched a purple belt; below, she drew on black hose and her flat black shoes. She made a second mental note to take her wounded black pump to a local cobbler.

In the bathroom, she tied her hair back in order to scrub her face before redoing her makeup. Even that small gesture made her feel refreshed, and helped her put today's near-accident behind her. With a pleased sigh, she buried her face in the thick, fluffy towel, then lowered it to look in the mirror.

And in the reflection, she saw Jordan MacPherson standing behind her.

She froze in shock—almost fear—the sight startled her so. Over her shoulder, past her wide, disbelieving eyes, she saw his lips move, his own eyes conveying anxiety and concern.

"Be careful, Rachael. That was no accident in the library."

She whirled, the towel falling from nerveless fingers, and lunged at him, arms outstretched. Her hands didn't quite connect with anything, and yet they did. Her momentum was slowed by something, but not something solid. Like a pool of water—no, thicker, more like porridge, only not moist or grainy. Something that you could feel and move through, but that didn't leave a trace.

Then the feeling was gone, and she stumbled forward a step as the resistance vanished.

Strangely, Rachael didn't find herself terrified by the apparition in the mirror, though any number of late-night horror flicks would have told her to. Jordan hadn't seemed threatening; in fact, his message had been of concern for her safety.

And what she'd felt when she'd turned, as he melted away somehow, proved this wasn't some sort of elaborate hoax: no hidden projectors, no—she had to grin at the thought—trick with mirrors.

But that didn't really bring her any closer to an explanation of what she *was* seeing and feeling. Rachael turned back to the mirror and, with one eye cast over her shoulder, began smoothing foundation on her face.

So far as she knew, no one else had ever reported seeing the ghost of Jordan MacPherson at the manor. The only exception to that was Felicity, and for all Rachael knew, she could have been rambling or confused about time. Brett had also said he'd seen a ghost, although he didn't name who, and goodness knew kids had wild imaginations....

The fact remained that there had been no widely reported sightings of Jordan's ghost by a guest or servant. The only mention of ghosts at all had been in the guide to Northern New York hotels—and all that had mentioned was the occasional sound of sourceless music—and Kevin's offhand mention of local rumor that seemed little more than an offhand quip.

Only an idiot would fail to make the connection between ghostly music and Jordan, the accomplished musician, Rachael thought sourly as she brushed dark purple eye shadow in the crease of her lid. Maybe that was why she was seeing him, or at least thinking she was? Had she made a subconscious connection...?

But no. That didn't explain any of a number of things. Pursing her lips, she pulled her hair out of its tortoiseshell clip and shook it out. The curls tumbled down, and she made a face. Being shoved haphazardly up all day meant that now it just looked goofy, sticking out on one side and squashed in on the other. She flicked through her hair with a pick, trying to decide how to salvage the situation.

As she did, another part of her brain considered the mystery of Jordan. She was an historian, but in many ways her work resembled that of a scientist, gathering facts, testing hypotheses. If one answer didn't fit, or if there wasn't enough information to form a logical answer, then she had to get more information, perhaps test other theories and ideas.

Rachael went to her suitcase at the foot of the bed, and rummaged through until she found a long purple scarf shot through with metallic gold streaks. Back in front of the mirror, she pulled her hair into a low ponytail and wrapped the scarf around, tying it in a big floppy bow at the nape of her neck.

She fluffed a few spiral tendrils around her face, smiled at the effect. That problem was solved, and she had a very good idea what to do to gain more information about Jordan's ghost.

*

Rachael barely made it to the parlor before she was descended upon by Mildred Shay from Alabama. She finally gleaned from the woman's heavily accented, roundabout explanation that Mildred had had a genealogical survey done of her family's participation in the Civil War. Mildred had been just *thri-illed* with the results, and had been so excited to learn there was another genealogist staying at the manor.

Rachael smiled, finding the woman's enthusiasm pleasant, albeit a little overwhelming. She was beginning to feel as though she raced with a speeding train when a short, balding man joined them. Mildred interrupted herself to introduce her husband, Earl, who smiled and nodded to Rachael. Mildred pushed up her thick, large-rimmed glasses and continued on. Earl wandered back to the buffet.

Dinner was a relatively quiet affair. Karyn and Celeste didn't appear until nearly the end of the cocktail hour; both looked grim, and Rachael knew why. Mildred was seated next to Doug and Ally, the newlyweds, and strove to keep their attention for most of the meal. Ally smiled gamely; by the end of supper, she looked bravely wilted.

Afterwards, Karyn excused herself to go home; Rachael and Celeste joined Ian and Felicity for brandied coffee.

"Rachael, I cannot apologize enough for what happened," Celeste said as soon as they were out of earshot of the other guests.

"I'm fine." Rachael brushed away her reparation. "I shouldn't have leaned on the railing anyway. I found the weak spot, so now you can repair it."

If it had been a weak spot at all, she amended silently. Jordan's words had hovered about her ears all evening. Would the carpenter be able to determine if it had been an accident or deliberate?

In the sitting room, Celeste poured the coffee into the delicate china cups, and Ian added a shot of brandy to each. Celeste had told him what had happened, and he, too, expressed his dismay. Rachael repeated what she had said to his cousin, adding good-naturedly, "Everyone's making far too much out of this. I grew up with three brothers: I'm used to being bruised and battered." In an effort to change the subject, she turned to Celeste and asked, "Do you have any idea how Jordan got that scar on his chin?"

A rattle-clatter of china against china. Ian set down his teacup carefully, his saucer liquid-laden, and dabbed ineffectively at the coffee stain on his tan trousers.

"How clumsy of me," he said, a half-smile fluttering across his lips. "It just slipped out of my hand."

But Rachael had seen his expression in one of the gilt mirrors. He had been genuinely startled by her question. Why? She remembered Karyn commenting that Ian would be furious and he'd best be avoided for a few days. Was he very upset about the broken railing?

Celeste rang for the kitchen staff, and Maria swept in to remove the cup and offer Ian a damp towel. After she left, Celeste said, "Now, you asked about Jordan's scar? To be honest, Rachael, I really don't remember."

"How did you know about that?" Ian asked curiously. He held his new cup very tightly, his hand shaking every so slightly from the grip, and Rachael knew he forced the question to be casual.

"Karyn showed me the portraits in the gallery," she answered. "I've always thought family portraits were such a wonderful way to preserve memories. With photography being so simple now...."

"Oh, of course; I'd nearly forgotten about them," Ian said. "I've never found them to be very practical—but then, you know my position about obsessing on the past."

"Be careful," Celeste warned lightly. "Now you're venturing into the realm of art, and you might just raise Felicity's goat."

Felicity paused in the act of pouring more brandy into her cup. "'That's my last Duchess painted on the wall'—"

"'Looking as if she were alive,'" Rachael continued.

Felicity got an evil glint in her eye as together they finished the line, "'I call that piece a wonder now.' Browning," she added.

"'My Last Duchess'," Rachael supplied, grinning.

"Oh dear, now they're both at it," Celeste said with mock dismay.

Felicity made a face at her, turned back to Rachael. "I should like to paint your portrait, I think," she said. "Such bone structure you have. And it would look lovely hung next to Jordan's."

"Well, I'm not exactly a member of the family...." Rachael felt flustered.

Felicity sipped from her cup. The stain of blue paint under her fingernails contrasted with the delicate gesture. "That's true," she said, and sipped again. She smiled brilliantly. "But at least it would fill up that empty space next to his portrait."

As they bantered lightly, Rachael glanced in one of the mirrors. Ian was watching her, but she couldn't read his hooded expression. His gloved fist clenched rhythmically in his lap. Why had he been so startled by her question? What did he know about Jordan?

*

Rachael curled on the window seat, swathed in the peach terrycloth robe. She'd poured a finger of brandy from the decanter into a glass, and she swirled it absentmindedly as she read the slim volume propped on her knees.

The book, a brief history of Clan MacPherson, was the type anyone could pick up in a gift shop in Scotland, but it could provide her with some basic information. Even though Celeste had privately asked her to concentrate some of her research on the night of the fire, she had been hired to chronicle the entire MacPherson history relating to this branch of the family, and she knew she needed to get to work on that.

She'd already skimmed the book before she arrived. MacPherson County, she'd learned, was just about smack in the middle of Scotland, south of Murray Firth. The family probably descended from Gilliecattan Mhor through a priest named Muirich—hence the name MacPherson, or Son of the Parson. And since the name Gilliecattan Mhor meant "the big servant of St. Kattan," the clan motto, "Touch not the cat bot a glove," probably descended the same way. The MacPherson clan first began making its mark in history in the late 1300s during a quarrel with the Mackintosh clan over the leadership of the Clan Chattan Confederation, she read.

Propping the book open upside down, she took a sip of brandy and glanced outside. Pale moonlight filtered across the front lawn, turning the flaming autumn trees to stark shades of grey.

"I know you're around here somewhere," she said aloud, firmly. "So you might as well show yourself." Her lips quirked. "I'm not supposing I can outwait you, but I warn you, I can be quite stubborn."

She sensed him, saw him suddenly reflected in the window a breath before he spoke.

"Very well," Jordan said, and she heard the amusement in his voice. "You win."

She turned. He stood in the middle of the sitting room, hands in his pockets, one eyebrow cocked. The single light from the table lamp next to her gently brushed his dark hair.

"Thank you," Rachael said, uncurling from the window seat and standing. "Would you like a drink?"

His smile deepened. "Please."

She went to the crystal decanter and poured a shot of brandy into a glass. The liquid swirled, molten, fiery. She handed him the glass, and he dropped gracefully into the armchair. She resumed her perch on the window seat and toasted him silently. He returned the gesture and drank, closing his eyes as he swallowed, obviously enjoying the feel of the brandy sliding down.

"How do you do that?" Rachael asked.

His eyes opened. "Do what?"

"Drink. Hold the glass. Sit in the chair." *Touch me*, her mind added, and she fought back a rush of desire. "It may have been a product of my delirium last night, but I'd swear you didn't move the bed when you sat on it. And you must've just come into the room through a wall, unless you've been here since I came back from dinner."

"Ah, that." He regarded the glass, looked back up at her. "What do you suppose I am, Rachael?"

It wasn't the first time he'd said her name, but previously she'd been feverish, vague. Now, she reveled in the way his voice caressed the syllables.

"Assuming you're not a delusional fantasy of mine, all the facts so far seem to indicate you're a ghost," she said.

"And that doesn't frighten you?"

The question surprised her: It really hadn't occurred to her to be frightened. She was pragmatic about psychic phenomena, but she'd always been cautious about it, as well.

She considered his query. No, what she felt about Jordan was far from fear, she thought, as her body tingled with memory.

"No," she said quickly, to catch her thoughts. "You've startled me, but you haven't given me any reason to fear you. Should I be frightened?"

He didn't answer right away. He took a thoughtful sip of his drink, as if trying to mask the hesitation. "No," he said finally. "Not of me."

"Then of whom? Or what?"

He rolled the glass between his palms. Light struck the crystal, shattered into rainbow sparks. "I believe we were discussing my corporeality, or lack of it."

Rachael knew he was deliberately changing the subject, and, for now, let him.

"My natural state now seems to be of…of nonsolidity, for lack of a better word," he said. "However, with effort, I can become partly or wholly substantial. The more solid I become, and the longer I do so, the more effort I expend. It can become extremely tiring. There are limitations, of course." He held up the glass. "I can drink, but I won't get drunk." His grin was rueful. "Believe me, I've tried. I can eat, but I won't get full. I bleed, but if I become insubstantial, the wound vanishes without a trace."

"So you were the one who rescued Brett and me at the river," she guessed. "I thought I saw you there."

He nodded. "Aren't you at all curious as to why you were able to see the fire at the cottage when you were by the river?"

She stared at him. "How did you know I saw it?"

"I saw your expression." He reached up and stroked her cheek with the back of his fingers. "You have a very open face: It's easy to tell what you're thinking."

"What am I thinking about right now?" she challenged.

He grinned lazily. "Last night."

She hadn't been, but the slow smile and smoke-green of his eyes spun her back in memory to her fevered forwardness. To her chagrin, she felt the slow enkindling of a blush rise in her cheeks. She knew he saw, too. She took a quick sip, feeling the brandy burn.

"Yes, well, I thought I was dreaming then," she said by way of explanation.

"Are all your dreams so...vivid?"

She felt her pulse throbbing, the beat echoing throughout her body. "So far, only those with you in them," she said, her voice husky from the brandy and desire. Her skin tingled, as if he were caressing it again.

She watched him take a deep, not quite even breath, and felt wickedly glad that she wasn't the only one having this reaction.

"Good," he said. "Otherwise I might have to get jealous."

"Of my dreams?"

"Of the other men in them."

This time, Rachael was the one to suck in a shuddering breath, reluctantly willing her mind back to the discussion at hand. "You haven't told me why I was able to see the fire."

"Right." He shot back the rest of his brandy and set the glass on the floor near the leg of his chair. "I believe it was because I carried you out of the water. Your touching me gave you the memories to see the fire."

"I normally don't get psychometric visions from people," she said.

Jordan cocked his head. "But I'm not a person, exactly. I'm a much closer link to the past." He crossed his legs, causing the charcoal-grey wool of his pants to stretch tight over his smoothly muscled thigh.

Rachael swallowed, forcing her eyes back up to his face. "How did you know about my power, anyway?"

"I don't know," he admitted, watching her. "I just knew as soon as I saw you. Again, it's probably because of what I am—although I think this family has always had a low-level psychic tendency running through it. Perhaps I'm just sensitive to it. Or perhaps I'm just sensitive to you."

He traced her lower lip with his thumb, and she closed her eyes, reveling in the erotic sensation. She was so caught up in the feeling of his hand caressing her sensitive skin that she almost didn't hear his next words, spoken softly, as if to himself.

"I would hate to see anything happen to you."

"Why would anything happen to me?" Rachael asked, opening her eyes.

His own eyes suddenly hooded, he pulled his hand away. Rachael curled her fingers loosely, stubbornly, around his wrist. The sudden action made her robe slip off one shoulder, but she ignored it.

"Who were you warning me about before?" she demanded. "What did you mean when you said the railing in the library wasn't an accident?"

"Rachael…" Jordan sighed. He seemed to be struggling within himself. "I don't—I just *know* that the railing wasn't an accident. It's a feeling, like knowing about your power."

"But when I asked you if I should be afraid of you, you said 'No, not of me.' If not of you, then of whom?"

"I don't know."

"You're lying." She was standing before him now, still clutching his wrist.

He ran his free hand through his hair. "All right, then. I might know, but I could be wrong. In any case, I can't tell you."

"Can't tell me?"

"I'm prevented from telling you."

"Prevented how?"

"I can't tell you."

She made a frustrated noise in her throat. "What do you mean, you can't tell me? Is this some sort of curse on you? Like Cassandra always having to tell the truth, only more frustrating?"

Suddenly he looked tired, his eyes reflecting weariness.

Can ghosts get tired? Is it polite to ask?

He smiled unhappily. "Something like that. Rachael..." He twisted his arm, and suddenly *he* was holding *her* wrist. He slid his hand up her arm, mirroring the motion with his other hand. Through the thick terrycloth she imagined she could feel the heat of his skin, even though a part of her mind questioned whether he could even exude physical warmth. "Please believe me when I say I want you to be safe." His eyes searched hers. "But I can't tell you everything because of...promises I've made, and things that prevent me."

"This is crazy," she said hoarsely. "You're not telling me anything, and you expect me to trust you."

"Yes."

"Maybe."

He stood, his body an inch from hers, his hands still on her arms. "I should go," he said.

"I'm not through asking you questions yet," Rachael protested, not sounding as forceful as she meant. He was too close, his breath stirring her hair (and yet how could that be?), and she tried to cling to what was left of her mental faculties.

His right hand trailed up to where the robe had fallen from her shoulder, and with one finger he traced the skin just along the edge of the robe, down along the exposed curve of her breast.

"I have to go," he said. He leaned down and gently pressed his lips to the bare skin at her collarbone. Rachael shuddered in delicious response. She felt him start to fade away, and clutched at him. But she was left clutching air, the memory of his kiss emblazoned on her skin.

"Ooh!" Rachael said between clenched teeth. "You come back here!" She wasn't surprised when she got no response.

She went to the bathroom and splashed water over her face, flushed far more than by the brandy. Then she returned to the sitting room and sat in the chair he had vacated, tugging the robe back up to its proper position. "You're sure you're not coming back?" she asked.

No response. Satisfied, she reached into the deep pocket of the robe and pulled out her recorder. She clicked it off, and tapped the small black machine thoughtfully against her upper lip. Jordan had answered some questions, but raised others....

She pressed play.

"I know you're around here somewhere."

Her own voice. The phrase was repeated as the voice-activation sensor skipped the silence while she had been reading.

"...I can be quite stubborn.... Thank you. Would you like a drink?"

Rachael hit the pause button in an almost unconscious movement. Her own voice, still, with nothing in between. No answer from Jordan. Carefully, thoughtfully, she pressed play again.

On the entire recording, Jordan's voice failed to appear. She heard herself, carrying on a one-sided conversation. She heard the clink of glass on glass as she poured him a brandy.

Rachael picked up the glass where he'd left it on the floor. A driblet of brandy rolled around the bottom, the bouquet mellow-harsh. The tape continued to roll. She heard the slight thud as he set the glass on the floor. Heard her own voice, husky and passionate. She felt her cheeks mantle. Heard her feet walking across the room, the sound of running water, walking. Then a click, signaling the end of the tape.

Rachael sighed, turning the glass in her hand and making the drop of liquor chase round and round, like a dog at its own tail. She wasn't sure exactly what she'd accomplished by proving Jordan's voice didn't record, except to reinforce her own theories and what he admitted.

Ghost, spirit, specter, haunt—he certainly wasn't of this world.

And he certainly had something to hide.

*

Rachael sprinted the last quarter-mile down the driveway, feeling her calf muscles lengthen and stretch. Her breath came in easy, measured strokes—in, out, in, out. The sweat beading around her bandanna caught coolness on the breeze. She'd run the length of the driveway, then about half a mile down the road and back; she was back up to her daily routine. She was surprised it felt so good today, surprised her endorphins flowed so easily, surprised her muscles agreed not to tighten or cramp.

She hadn't slept well, of course. She had Jordan to thank for that. Jordan who invaded her dreams—and she knew they'd been dreams this time—invaded her mind, invaded and inflamed her senses. She'd spent half the night reading about the history of the MacPhersons, rather than toss about restlessly, sleep a fleeting promise.

The fact that he knew about her psychometric power had disturbed her as well. She'd never told anyone about it, and the fact that he had gleaned it without her knowledge was even more disconcerting. He'd seemed almost uncaring about her power, but her old fear-demons had threatened to rise up again.

Until, that is, she realized the absurdity of worrying about a ghost revealing *her* secret. Jordan had enough secrets of his own to keep; he wasn't at all concerned with hers.

At the end of the driveway she slowed to a brisk walk, cooling down before heading inside.

"Darlin', you are nuuuuts!" a voice called. Mildred Shay was hanging precariously out her window, waving. Rachael grinned and waved back before looping around the driveway one more time, then heading in.

As she crossed the front hall, she did a mental calculation of the windows along the front of the manor and realized the Shays were in the room next to hers. She wondered if they'd heard anything last night. She doubted it; her bedroom would have served as a buffer between her sitting room, where she'd talked to Jordan, and theirs. At least, she hoped so.

If they had heard anything, they didn't mention it at breakfast an hour later. Mildred looked covetously at Rachael's cream-cheese slathered bagel and eggs Benedict and remarked that she understood why Rachael got up so early and punished herself like that. Earl smiled and speared his wife's sausage on his fork while she wasn't looking.

When breakfast was over, Rachael stood on the sunroom porch. Brett and another boy were playing with Chewie on the lawn near the fountain. If not for the other child and the heather-grey clouds scudding low across the sky, the scene looked like the first morning she'd been here, when she'd jogged across the back expanse of grass.

She found herself wanting to ask Brett if *he'd* seen the ghost again, and wondered what his reaction would be if she told him she'd seen the ghost. Then she wondered what Karyn's reaction would be when the story got back to her, and had to laugh.

Brett saw her, and waved. She returned the gesture and headed across the lawn to him.

"This is the lady who rescued me," he solemnly told his friend, whom he'd introduced as Jeremy. "She's a gen—genie—genieogolist."

"Genealogist," Rachael corrected gently, relieved that he hadn't lingered on the subject of her supposed rescue of him. "That's a person who studies people's ancestors," she added for Jeremy's benefit.

"Why?" Jeremy asked.

"Well, to see where they came from. For example, Brett's last name is Cappricci, which sounds Italian to me. If we traced his ancestors 'way back, we might find out his great-great-great-great third cousin twice-removed was Michaelangelo, the painter."

"Really?" Jeremy's eyes rounded wide; Brett was similarly enraptured.

"Well, probably not," Rachael said good-naturedly. "But you never know. Even if you weren't related to someone famous, it's sometimes fun to learn about who your forebears were."

"Are you going down to the river?" Brett asked, already losing interest. At her nod, he gravely said, "Be careful."

She held up her hand in the Boy Scouts' salute. "I promise not to stray off the path or get too close to the water. See you later."

As she entered the confines of the trees, she glanced back. The boys were running off toward the front of the house. Good, she wouldn't be interrupted. She knew she wasn't going to enjoy what she planned to do.

A woodpecker rat-a-tatted against a tree, and somewhere overhead, so far away she almost couldn't hear it, a plane puttered on. Rachael didn't pause on the bridge, but marched over, single-minded. Only at the edge of the cottage foundation did she pause, flexing her hands thoughtfully.

This wasn't going to be easy, and she wasn't sure if she would like what she found.

She waded though the scrubby, calf-high grass and surveyed the scattering of foundation stones. Some were cracked, others half-buried by the effects of time. Finally she chose one in a line of three; the tallest, standing straight beside one that tilted drunkenly into another. She brushed a crackling of bright leaves from the flat, rough grey surface as she knelt before it.

Carefully, Rachael placed her hands flat on the old substructure. She blanked her mind, forcing out the images of the fire that she had witnessed; she didn't want to taint the images to come with her memory.

Then she closed her eyes, letting her consciousness sink down into the stone and asking it to reveal its memories, give up its secrets.

Chapter Seven

The stone felt rough beneath her fingertips, and cool, shaded from the morning sun. Somewhere, a partridge chittered. Then all the present sensations faded as Rachael concentrated on opening herself to the past.

She heard the sharp bright laughter of a child, a boy. Ian as a child? Or farther back—Jordan or Shane? *Then she saw it was Brett, poised on the stone, king surveying his land, Chewie dancing around him.* Too new, too recent.

Back, back... She tried, without knowing quite how she did it, to specify the time period she wished to see. Back...

But, only darkness, and silence. No visions, no sounds, no smells visited Rachael from the past. The cottage stones refused to reveal whatever knowledge they had. Slowly, Rachael brought herself back to the present. The sharp end of a stick dug uncomfortably into the knee of her jeans, and she stood, slightly cramped.

The stones were too far buried in the foundation to carry any recollection of the night of the fire, or any other events at the cottage while it stood. She'd thought that with whatever heightened power she had received from Jordan, she'd be able to coax out something more. But either that enhancement of her powers had faded, or there was simply nothing there to be seen.

Rachael sighed, shaking out her stiff ankle. A burnished leaf wafted down, suddenly loosed from a tree. She caught it as it drifted by. She closed her hand around it, but it was newly minted and only crumpled, didn't crush to leaf-dust. When she uncurled her fingers, it slowly spread back out on her palm like a hesitant starfish, brick-red and waxy-fresh. Absentmindedly twirling it on its stem, she headed back to the manor.

The carpenter hadn't been in yet, so the library was still off-limits. Unwilling to waste the morning, Rachael went to her room and sat down at the computer. She typed in notes from the book on the MacPhersons, then began sketching out the few details she already had about the manor and the family.

The shape of her research began to mold under her fingers, and she found herself engrossed until it was nearly time for lunch. Even then, only a soft rap at her door brought her back to the present. Liz, one of the day maids, handed her a note from Ian, which requested she have lunch with him in half an hour.

The request startled and confused her. Ian, though polite, had made it clear he wanted nothing to do with her research, and she'd assumed that also meant he wanted nothing to do with her. She hoped he wasn't going to try and dissuade her from her job, even though he'd said he wouldn't interfere.

In the end she agreed, and after shutting down her laptop and freshening up, she accompanied Liz downstairs, not to one of the dining rooms, but to one of Ian's private rooms.

"This is very impressive," she commented as she prowled the den. One wall was taken up by an enormous flat-screen TV, and shelves on a side wall contained the high-tech stereo equipment. "Surround sound?" she asked, admiring the array of speakers around the room.

"Yes," Ian said, looking up from a cabinet in the wall across from the TV. He sounded surprised.

"A college buddy of mine was a real techno-buff, and taught me all the ropes of quality stereo and video equipment," she explained. "I've been slowly acquiring a system—on my limited budget, that amounts to about one piece a year, though. It's certainly nowhere as impressive as this."

"It's lovely to talk to someone who thinks so," Ian said. "Most people can't seem to appreciate all this—Celeste, for one, refuses to understand why it's necessary to have a pre-amp *and* a power amp."

"Because in an integrated amp, where both of them are together, the power amp delivers head current magnetic fields that can adversely affect the sensitive circuitry in the pre-amp," she said promptly. "While separate ones aren't necessary, they're better for the equipment."

"I'm impressed, too," he said. "It's rare to find a woman who understands the technical concepts like that."

Rachael smiled. "That techno-buff buddy of mine? *She's* now a production engineer for Sony, and making a lot more money than I'll ever see."

"Rachael, I'm sorry." Ian moved around the couch to her. He seemed about to take her hands, but hesitated, clearly uncomfortable with the physical contact. She noticed that he was a tall man, but his childhood injuries kept him somewhat hunched over, so that he was only an inch or two taller than her. "I shouldn't fall into stereotypes like that." He laughed ruefully, the smile pulled lopsided by his scars. "It seems as though every time we're together, I offend you somehow. I'm sorry," he repeated.

"No offense meant, so none taken," Rachael said firmly, also smiling. "Now..." Lightly brushing against his left hand, she moved around him and led him to the cabinet. His leather glove felt buttery-soft beneath her fingertips before he eased away. "I believe you were trying to choose some music for us to dine by?"

She sensed him relaxing, and felt glad she had eased the tension. Though she knew Ian didn't want or need her sympathy, she could easily guess that he had little social contact outside of his family. It was one thing to conduct a professional business transaction over impersonal telephone lines and computer link-ups; it was quite another to carry on leisurely small-talk face to face.

If the entertainment set-up had been impressive, his collection of compact discs was nothing short of astonishing. Rachael estimated there were at least five hundred lined neatly along the shelves, and she was half-afraid to open the other cabinets, where she might find just as many DVDs.

"Any suggestions?" Ian asked, leaning over her shoulder. She smelled the expensive but discreetly pleasant, musky aftershave, remembering it from their first encounter in his office.

"May I?" She slid a slim jewel-case from the top shelf. "Bantock's Celtic Symphony, please. I've only heard *Sea Reivers Poem No. 2*, and I've been dying to hear the rest."

He laughed again, heartily this time. "A stereo aficionado with a discriminating taste in music," he said, taking the CD from her and walking to the stereo center. "Rachael de Young, you are a wonder indeed."

"Oh stop," Rachael said, waving her hands about to bat away the compliments. "You'll be horrified to know I usually listen to rock—it's more accessible, I guess. But I do love certain types of classical music, mostly the lighter stuff, like traditional ballads, Renaissance lute music, that sort of thing."

"Really?" The music began to waft from the speakers around the room. He settled into an armchair and motioned her towards the sofa. "You strike me more as the Romantic type—Wagnerian, perhaps."

"Pompous German," Rachael retorted, dropping onto the soft cushions. "Overblown."

"Are you saying *The Ring*—"

"Yes, I am. Four separate operas for one story? I mean, really…"

They were still deep in the friendly bickering when lunch arrived, and only then did the conversation dwindle in the face of broiled salmon and spinach-pasta salad. The symphony reached a crescendo during dessert, and they listened quietly. Rachael stole a glance at Ian over her glazed pear in cream sauce. His eyes were closed as he welcomed the music slipping into his soul. Though the stereo equipment in the room could bring the music to symphony-hall quality, it still couldn't take the place of a live orchestra, something Ian in his self-imposed seclusion had probably never experienced.

In many ways, she realized, he reminded her of Vincent from the old *Beauty & the Beast* TV show. Knowing the real world would never accept him, Vincent prowled the mazes of tunnels beneath New York City, where, accidentally acoustically perfect pipes gave him a seat at any concert. But that still wasn't the same as sitting in the balcony, and never could be.

The symphony ended.

"That was beautiful," Rachael said.

"It was," he agreed. His next words were so quiet that Rachael wasn't sure she was intended to hear them. "So much so that I sometimes feel guilty, as if someone such as I is unworthy to share such beauty." He paused, as if collecting himself, and then opened his eyes. He spooned up a mouthful of pears and cream. "Any time you'd like to listen to more music, feel free to use this room. I think I can trust you with the equipment," he added with sly humor, having obviously shaken off his brief melancholy.

"I think you can," she joked back. "And thank you."

"Let me know when you do," he said. "Perhaps I'll be able to join you."

"I'm not keeping you from your work now, am I?" She set her dessert plate on the coffee table.

He glanced at the gold Rolex fastened over the cuff of his black glove. "I do need to be getting back soon, but I reserved this time so we could lunch." He leaned forward, any traces of humor gone. "I hope what I'm about to say doesn't upset you, but Rachael, the more I think about it, the more appalled I am at what happened to you in the library yesterday."

"I'm fine," Rachael insisted. "Accidents can happen."

"I'm so glad you weren't hurt," Ian said seriously. "Tell me: Did you see anything unusual on the catwalk before the accident?"

Rachael opened her mouth, closed it. If she said she'd heard a noise, but no one was up there, she'd sound insane. Her mind skipped back to Kevin, but he hadn't been on the catwalk, just in an anteroom. "No," she said. "I went up there to look at the books. I shouldn't have leaned on the railing, is all." Why was Ian asking if she'd seen anything? Did he know Jordan had warned her? Did he— "Why do you ask?" she blurted.

"Oh, I just like to be aware of all the facts," he said hastily. "I wouldn't want to think vandalism was involved, though there's slim chance of that, of course. I really must be getting back to work now."

He stood, and something fell from his pants pocket onto the sofa. He snatched it up, but not before Rachael saw what it was: a gold lighter, similar to the one Celeste had. Odd, for she hadn't realized he also smoked, although she supposed he could be as solicitous about it as his aunt.

"Again, I can't tell you how glad I am that you weren't injured," he said, and she saw that his hand trembled slightly where it closed around the lighter. "Do be careful. Thank you for lunching with me—we'll do this again soon." He hurried out, smoothing his hand over his hair.

Rachael sank back into the sofa, shaking her head. What had all that been about? Why did the library incident disturb him so much? She remembered his startled reaction to her question about Jordan's scar the night before. Did that have anything to do with this?

She sat forward and thoughtfully toyed with the silver spoon lying in the puddle of cream in her dish. Why did both Jordan and Ian think the broken railing hadn't been an accident? And why was everyone suddenly so concerned with her welfare?

If it hadn't been an accident—if someone *was* inexplicably trying to harm her—then there would probably be another "accident." She'd have to be alert for that. Rachael stood and paced the room, wrapping her arms around herself. She noticed that Ian had forgotten to shut off the stereo system, and reached out to the CD player. She hesitated. An "accident" could be electrocution....

"Oh, now *that* is ridiculous," she said aloud. The sound of her own voice seemed to ground her somehow. She firmly pressed the off button, and repeated the motion on the pre-amp and the power amps for each of the two main speakers. Such thinking wasn't getting her anywhere, and she had research to continue.

She sought out Karyn and learned that the carpenter had indeed been and gone, so she returned to the library. She soon found a series of birth certificates and transcribed the information, also recording the dates on a hand-drawn family tree. The fact that this arm of the family clustered in Heather Mountain made this aspect of her research easier, as most were born in the manor or at local hospitals.

That line of study sent her in search of a family Bible. She found it in the anteroom of the library that contained books passed down through the family. Thumbing through the beginning pages, Rachael blessed whomever had taken the time to record important family events, especially baptisms. She made a note to herself to pay a visit to the local church and its records.

In fact...she made a mental assessment of the dwindling stack of papers that represented what she hadn't gone over. Yes, tomorrow would be a good day to head into town and drop in at a number of different places.

She sat back, chewing her lip in frustration. She was still finding gaps in the history—and they still surrounded Jordan, Marion Roark, and Emilie Shaw. Marion's absence wasn't surprising, because she had been a first wife. Husbands or second wives frequently rid their house of old, painful memories—a fact that Rachael understood as a person but abhorred as an historian.

Emilie and Shane's marriage was recorded in the family diary, and a dated entry about a year later heralded the birth of Ian. There was another entry about a year and a half after that, but the words had been scratched out, obliterated. She tried the old trick of shading another piece of paper with a pencil over the faint dents on the next page, but all that showed up was the hatch marks enshrouding the original writing.

Her mental comments brought her back to thoughts of Jordan, and she pulled the photo album toward her, flipping carefully through the yellowed pages. The faint, musty smell tickled her nostrils. She reached the pages that had previously been stuck together. She froze. Stared, disbelieving.

The pages were empty. Only the black tabs remained. One, nearly unglued, dangled tenuously skewed.

She flipped a few pages forward and back, making sure she was on the right page. She was, and the pictures hadn't somehow slipped out into another section of the album.

Rachael remembered propping one of the pictures at the back of the desk the day before, but she was sure she'd replaced it before packing up for the night. Just to be sure, she crawled down under the table and scrounged around. Not so much as a dust bunny.

She backed out and sat down on the chair, laying her hands on the desk on either side of the scrapbook. The temptation to touch it and learn who had been there was very, very strong. All she had to do was touch it, lay her palms flat on the thick pages, and ask. So many questions could be answered, so many truths told, so many secrets revealed....

But no. In one great, swift movement she slapped the book shut, sending up another rush of musty odor, and shoved it aside. She wouldn't succumb to the provocation. She shook her head. Since she'd arrived at Manor MacPherson, she'd either been wrestling with unwanted visions or fighting off the enticement to abuse her powers. Either way, she wasn't accomplishing much.

She made a methodical search of all the papers on the table, in case the photo album had somehow innocently been jostled or moved and the pictures had slipped out. She didn't have much hope in the quest, and so wasn't greatly surprised when the photos remained missing.

Between "accidents" and suddenly missing research materials, the library was no longer a safe place to work, she decided. Having spent enough time in manor houses to have a good idea where the kitchens might be, she found them here with little difficulty. She spotted Liz in a supply room off the massive main kitchen.

"Good afternoon, Miss," Liz said in answer to Rachael's greeting. "What can I do for you?"

"Well, I was wondering: Has anyone been in the library since the carpenter left?"

"I went in to see if there was any tidying up to be done after he left," Liz said, deftly wringing out a mop. "He'd left a bit of sawdust, which I cleaned up. As far as I know, no one else has been in."

"Did you do any straightening near where I was working?" Rachael asked.

"Why, no, Miss." Liz grinned. "You keep it so neat there, we were thinking we should hire you."

Rachael laughed. "I've got enough work to do, thanks. I'm glad I'm not causing you more work. I'm amazed at how clean you can keep a place this size." Liz nodded her thanks, and Rachael asked, "Who besides Karyn has a key to the library?"

"Let's see... Each of the family has one, I believe, and of course Mrs. Rabideau does. We normally don't keep it locked, except in cases such as last night, and during the All Hallows Eve Ball. We can't keep track of all the people then, you see, so we close off some of the rooms. I believe that's it for keys, though. There isn't a problem, is there, Miss?"

"No," Rachael said hastily. If someone *had* taken the photos, she didn't want him or her to know she was suspicious. And if it had simply been an honest mistake, or if she'd misplaced them, she didn't want to cause a ruckus. "I was just concerned about something happening to the family papers. Some of them are very old and delicate, and accidents can happen. At any rate, I think it's going to be more convenient if I do the research in my room, where all my supplies are. Do you have an empty box I could borrow to haul the stuff in?"

Liz found her a large cardboard box that had originally housed a case of Clorox bleach, and Rachael returned to the library to pack up the paperwork. She packed each item separately, rather than in stacks, just to triple-check. Nothing. Not unanticipated.

She lugged the box to the door of the cavernous room, set it down outside, turned, and firmly closed the doors. Lifting the box again, she headed down the hallway, considering her route. It would probably be best if she didn't meet up with anyone; she didn't want to upset Karyn or Celeste or Ian with her decision. Better to explain later, over dinner, that it would be easier for her to research in her room, where the computer was set up. So, back hallways it would be.

The west wing was easy, since Karyn had given her the grand tour; she had no trouble picking a private path. She hurried across the front hall, glad that the manager's office door was closed, and slipped into a corridor at the back of the east wing. She leaned against a wall, and grinned in spite of herself. She'd always liked skulking. If she hadn't become a genealogist, she might have gotten a job with the CIA, another option open to history majors.

Skulking was taking its toll on her physically, however. The papers and books felt innocuously light when they were separate, but their weight increased quickly when they were grouped together in a box. Her arms and lower back were beginning to feel the strain.

"Wimp," she chided herself. "When I get you back home, you're getting back into weight training."

She glanced around, looking for a place to set the box down and rest. The east wing was the guest wing, so no rooms were off-limits, at least as far as she knew. A partly open door lay to her left; the room, she guessed, would overlook the back lawn. She crossed the hall and nudged the door wider with her hip.

The music room.

Even if she hadn't seen Jordan's portrait, she would have been able to name the room because of the gleaming black grand piano that dominated the long chamber. Nudging the door a bit further, she entered, and dropped the box on a loveseat along the side wall before shutting the door. Rubbing her lower back, she drank in the room.

Just as in the portrait, a simple bronze candelabrum holding white spiral candles sat atop the closed piano, reflected in the polished ebony surface. The walls were unadorned, the windows covered with blinds rather than fabric curtains: both to facilitate better acoustics. A cabinet with low drawers probably held sheet music.

Rachael walked over to a stocky object in one corner of the room and lifted one end of its rich, brown velvet covering. As she had suspected, it was a full-sized harp. The instrument's reddish wood gleamed in the last light glinting through the windows. She touched the strings gently. They thrummed out of tune; someone had had the foresight to loosen them when the harp wasn't being played, so the wood wouldn't warp. Smiling, she let the cloth drop.

The piano drew her attention again, of course. She slid onto the padded bench and raised the cover. Her fingers danced over the keys, barely touching, making no sound. She rested her fingertips along the black wood just in front of the white keys. They weren't yellowed with age; the piano, like everything else in Manor MacPherson, was kept in immaculate condition. The only reason the place didn't feel like a museum was the accessibility of everything inside.

So, here we are again. She gazed down at the keys. She could imagine Jordan's long, artistic fingers urging music from the instrument. He wouldn't have played it, no, not exactly; he and the piano would have created, played each other in mutual consent.

All she had to do was rest her hands on the keys, and she'd know so much about him. Anything that ever happened while he was playing....

Well, here was an interesting conundrum. She'd sworn never to use her psychometry for personal gain, and never to use it to learn about a living person. But Jordan wasn't living: He was very definitely dead.

Amazing—she hadn't done so much moral soul-searching about this since she gained her power.... Well, what was the call? Was Jordan fair game, or what?

Her fingers caressed the keys, skidding along their smooth tops without enough pressure to coax out their individual notes. Memories surged beneath her fingers, fighting to break forth.

Unfortunately, Jordan destroyed every concept of *Death* that she'd ever held. Stomped right over every definition she knew. He was dead—shot, and probably killed right then, and fire had laid to rest any question of his survival as it burned his body almost beyond recognition. But she'd spoken with him, touched him.

How the hell do you classify a ghost?

She ran the tip of her forefinger along the coolly slick surface of a D-flat.

Well? What's your answer?

No. No, it's not right.

He's not "dead."

As long as I can ask him questions, it's not fair to inveigle, or pry, the answers out of inanimate objects. I won't do it. Case closed.

Pinggg.

The sound startled her, but it was only the sound of her finger suddenly resting heavily on the piano key. She pulled her hand back.

Then, out of the corner of her eye, she thought she saw something. There, beside the piano. She forced herself not to look directly at the spot. A misty shape of a man.

The form solidified, became Jordan. Now she could look at him fully, with an unwavering gaze. He casually leaned both elbows on the piano, head turned to look at her.

"I didn't want to startle you, so I came in slowly," he said. His eyes were darkly warm.

Rachael wanted to say something, but didn't know what.

"I figured you were tired of me only appearing at night," he said, as if answering a question she hadn't even consciously formed. He smiled. "Well, are you going to play something for me?"

"Ohhhh no." She snatched her hands away, rested them firmly in her lap. "I can't play."

"You were touching the keys as though you knew your way around a piano," he pointed out.

"I had the obligatory lessons as a child," she said, tapping at one of the keys not hard enough to elicit another ping. "I had no talent for it, though, and Mom understood not to push. I love music, but as a listener, not a performer."

"Well, then." He set the candelabrum on the floor and, in a practiced movement, raised the piano lid and propped it open. He slid onto the bench next to her. She began to scoot off the other side, to give him room, but he encircled her forearm with one hand.

"Stay," he said simply.

She complied. Two people on the bench meant close quarters, and his thigh pressed against hers. A closeness, a pressure that she tried to ignore, but couldn't.

He played an experimental run on the keys, and she watched his blurring fingers in fascination. He paused, his eyes closed as he decided what to play. Rachael snuck a glance at his face. She wanted to run her fingers down his smooth jaw line....

She kept her hands resolutely in her lap instead.

He began, idly playing snatches of different melodies rather than settling on one piece. Rachael recognized some of the songs, but others were unfamiliar to her. She leaned back so he could reach down the keys, and watched the muscles in his shoulders and back move beneath the fabric of his shirt.

"Feel free to interrupt with any requests," he said, glancing at her. She shook her head. "Let's see..." he murmured. "How about this." He switched to something a bit more up-tempo, and she murmured in surprise when she recognized a song by one of her favorite rock groups.

"How...?"

"The joys of modern radio," he said. "If I hear it enough, I can figure it out."

"You seem to know all my favorites."

"You were listening to it on your computer." He flashed a smile at her. "'Greensleeves,' on the other hand, was just a lucky guess." He finished the rock ballad, and switched to the traditional song, idly picking the melody with one hand.

"So, you can learn new things, even though you're..." Suddenly she wasn't sure if she should have asked.

"Even though I'm dead?" He stopped playing, turned to look at her. The warmth of his leg against hers seemed to contradict the word *dead*. "Apparently so, and thank God, because otherwise I would have gone insane long ago. I don't age, don't change physically, but I can learn, absorb new information, new ideas."

"You play beautifully," she said. "Why didn't you pursue music professionally?"

"Why don't you write best-selling historical romances instead of what you're doing now?" he countered.

"That's not the same thing," she protested. "I love what I'm doing, and if I wrote romances, I'd be compromising myself."

"Not exactly the same thing," he agreed. "But you're doing what you want to do, and loving it. I knew that if I turned my passion into a profession, music would change for me—I'd no longer be doing it for *me*. Besides..." he shrugged, "there was the family business to consider."

The family business, Rachael knew, was maple syrup. When Birney MacPherson built the manor, he took advantage of the acres of maple trees on his property, learning to tap them for sap. By the time Jordan's father took over, the business had grown to a national corporation.

"Did you have the option not to take over the business?" she asked curiously.

"I certainly couldn't have been forced to do it," he said. "But I wanted to, and I knew the alternative was terrible, even if Father didn't."

The alternative would have been someone else taking over the running of the company, and the next likely candidate would have been...

"Shane."

He nodded, not elaborating. She could tell from his expression that he probably wouldn't, even if she asked. Celeste had said Shane had racked up some minor gambling debts in his time; it didn't take a great leap of imagination to question his business sense. She rose, and leaned her elbows against the open side rim of the piano.

"Tell me about yourself, Jordan."

His eyebrows raised. "Is this for your book?" he asked.

Her shoulders tightened. Did he know that she'd taped him last night? she wondered guiltily. But no, how could he?

"No, not for that. For me."

He sat sideways on the bench, leaning back on his hands. His white shirt stretched tight across his chest. "What do you want to know?"

"Anything. Everything. All I *do* know is that you were musically inclined; you loved your Irish setter, Finn; you never married; you were close to your family, especially Celeste and Felicity...."

"You've learned an awful lot in just few days," he commented, vaguely approving.

"Well, some of it I figured out all by myself," she retorted good-humoredly. "How did you get along with your parents?"

"Now you sound like a psychiatrist." But he sobered. "My mother died shortly after I was born, and Father remarried quickly. Shane is—was—only two years younger than me, you know. I suppose I always harbored a bit of resentment against Anne because she replaced my real mother. Felicity and Letitia spent more time mothering me than Anne did, but then, she had a baby of her own to contend with. What do you want me to say, Rachael? That I resented Shane, too, and that festered in me until the night of the fire...?"

"No." Rachael didn't wince from his sarcasm; instead, she had the somewhat irrational urge to hold him, or perhaps hold the motherless boy he had been. She didn't know why Malcolm had remarried so quickly, although it explained in part the absence of information on his first wife, and she didn't know what kind of woman his second wife, Anne McKenzie, had been. Had she been loving to Jordan, or had she favored her own son?

And then there had been Jordan's comment about Malcolm not realizing how terrible the alternative of Shane taking over the family business would have been. How had Malcolm treated the two boys?

"No, I don't think you're that kind of person, Jordan MacPherson," she said. "I think you're smart enough to see beneath the surface of things, to understand that people are fallible and sometimes even stupid when it comes to people they love. But you don't strike me as the type to hold grudges."

He sat up, and leaned one elbow against the piano, his eyes searching, and very, very green. "You're pretty astute, too, Rachael de Young, especially for someone who spends her time dealing with long-dead people, not living ones."

"Putting together the pieces of a family history can show a lot about interpersonal relationships," she said. "Some things don't become obvious until a generation or two has passed."

"True," he said. He turned so that he faced the piano again, and played a line of music with one hand. "I've had a lot of time to think," he said finally, stating the obvious without a trace of irony. "Time changes things—makes you realize what's important, and what's trivial. Holding grudges is trivial. Oh, I was always quick to temper—that's the MacPherson curse, to go along with our motto—but I've learned not to stay angry."

"What's not trivial—what, have you learned, *is* important?" Rachael asked softly.

His eyes unfocused. "Promises," he said, even more softly.

She guessed what he was reliving. "Jordan, what happened...the night of the fire?"

For a moment, it looked as if he were going to answer automatically. Then he paused, and looked at her again. "I don't remember," he said.

She stared at him, trying to fathom from his tone of voice, from his expression, if he were telling the truth. Trying not to get distracted by his eyelashes, which were unfairly long, or the dark sprinkling of hair that she could see in the vee of his shirt.

She failed on both counts. She didn't know if he were lying, and she was fast becoming mesmerized with the top button of his shirt.

"You don't remember?" she repeated finally.

"No, I don't," he said. "I think it's a blessing, don't you? All things being equal, I'd rather not remember the moment of my death, particularly since it was a violent one."

There was an edge to his voice, but she didn't blame him. She could see his point. The discussion obviously upset him, but she had so many questions.... How much of the evening *did* he remember, for one? Who had brought the gun to the cottage? What had really been his relationship with Shane? With Emilie?

She didn't know what made her blurt out her next question.

"How well do you know Ian?" At the startled query in his eyes, she faltered, "I mean, what do you think of him?"

"You should have been an investigative reporter," he commented. "You like to throw people off guard by changing the subject." He stood, and reached to put the top of the piano down. "Why do you ask?"

She moved away to give him room, and shrugged. "I don't know. He's a hard man to get to know. I seem to be getting mixed signals from him, and I don't know what to think."

"Mixed signals? You sound as though he's your suitor."

She caught a hint of something in his voice, and her eyes widened when she realized what it was. "You sound as if you're jealous," she said, amazed.

He had the good grace to look abashed. "Well," he said, blustering, "you did kiss me. Several times, in fact."

"I told you, I thought I was hallucinating," she teased, leaning back against the piano.

"What about last night, lady?" He stood directly in front of her, very close, his voice a tangible caress.

"*You* kissed *me*."

"What about right now...?"

Chapter Eight

He was going to kiss her again. He dipped down toward her in apparent slow motion, his lips parted ever so slightly, his green eyes shadowed with passion....

"Oh, no you don't." She put up her hands just in time, her palms contacting with his strong chest just before his lips contacted with hers.

Surprise flickered in his eyes. "I don't?"

"No, you don't."

He still leaned close, very close. Too close. Instead of keeping him at bay, her splayed hands were trapped between them. Rachael could feel his thighs pressing against hers. She swallowed. "Every time I start asking you questions, you try to squirm out of the situation by distracting me."

By kissing the holy bejeezus out of her.

"Sheer coincidence," he protested, his breath warm on her lips.

"Is it?"

"Rachael." He almost groaned aher name. "Yes, there are things I can't tell you. But I would never, ever try to...seduce you in order to avoid answering your questions."

"Then answer them," she challenged, her voice huskier than she meant it to be.

"What was the question?"

"I..." She'd forgotten what she'd last asked him. Her mind backpedaled hastily. Why had she asked him about Ian? And what had she asked before that? Something about the night of the fire.... "The fire?"

"I told you I don't remember. Next question?"

She shook her head mutely. Although one part of her wanted to grill him on what had happened, her conscience wouldn't let her. If he didn't remember, then he didn't. And if it pained him to think about it...

"Well, then, I can seduce you with impunity, yes?"

Yes, Rachael's libido answered, nodding vigorously. *No*, her brain said, but her brain was fast being overruled. Her fingers flexed against the muscles of Jordan's chest...

"Hello?"

...sank right through.

"Oh. I'm sorry, Ms. deYoung, I thought I heard voices in here." Maria's dark head poked around the door.

"You probably heard me talking to myself," Rachael managed, flustered, and amazed at how quickly Jordan managed to vanish. At least, his form had vanished. For all she knew, he was still standing in front of her, ethereal, incorporeal, intangible. Great. Let the servants think you're a loon, carrying on conversations with yourself. "I often take notes on a recorder, you see."

Maria nodded. "Have a nice day." Smiling pleasantly, she ducked out.

Rachael made a frustrated noise, somehow knowing Jordan wasn't going to make a reappearance any time soon.

*

Rachael double-checked the address on the scrap of paper, and pulled into a driveway off Heather Mountain's Main Street. The town was so small, nearly everything of note was located on Main Street, including the town Historical Society, which just happened to be situated in the Town Historian's house.

A low sloping cement ramp led up to the front door, but a sign pointed her to the side of the old, traditional log cabin. Rachael followed the path of natural stones sunk into the lawn, careful to step only on the stones, not the grass. It was one of those holdover superstitions from childhood, that old step-on-the-crack-and-break-your-mother's-back mentality. She wondered why there wasn't a smooth sidewalk, as in front of the house leading to the road, and decided the stones must have some historical significance, were somehow connected to the log home she approached.

A sign by the side door stated that if she were visiting between Town Historian hours (10–12 & 2–4, weekdays), she should come in, and holler if no one was about. Rachael's watch said 9:59; she took the chance and swung open the screen door—no storm door was needed on this unseasonably balmy October day—and entered. Since someone was about, she had no need to holler.

"Can I help you?" The woman behind the desk looked up and smiled warmly. Rachael gauged her age to be about sixty-five, the same as Celeste, although this woman's hair had stayed stubbornly black except for some white strands sluicing through the front. She wore her hair long, parted in the middle, emphasizing her round face.

"You can if you're Vera Ducharme. I'm Rachael deYoung."

"Rachael!" Vera's voice held welcome and pleasure at meeting with a fellow historian. As Rachael stepped forward, hand extended, she maneuvered out from behind her desk, and returned a solid handshake.

"Rachael, I can't tell you how excited I am to be helping you with this project," Vera said. "I've known the MacPhersons for years—since I was born, really—and they've long deserved this kind of attention."

"Celeste said that you two were old friends."

"School chums from the beginning," Vera said with a laugh, "which isn't hard when your high school graduating class amounts to only eight people." She leaned back in the wheelchair, folding her hands on her lap, hands that Rachael suspected wouldn't be still for long. "Have a seat. Now, where do you want to start?"

Rachael had come armed with a series of questions, but the list fluttered to the wayside as one answer led them to another topic, another memory, another relevant fact, over the course of the next hour.

"The MacPhersons literally built Heather Mountain," Vera said, returning from the kitchen. She handed Rachael a chilled glass of lemonade. "The basic story is that Birney MacPherson came over on a visit and fell in love with the area because it reminded him of Scotland."

Rachael nodded, taking a sip of the sour-sweet drink. Ice cubes clattered as she set the glass down. "That much I've heard. What brought him up here in the first place?"

"That I can't tell you," Vera said, shrugging. "It was untamed land then. Hunting, or exploring, perhaps? Anyway, Birney tapped into the maple sugar business—pun intended—and the town grew up as the business grew." She moved to a bookcase and, barely having to look, plucked a book from the shelf.

While Vera had been out of the room, Rachael had taken the opportunity to browse, delighted, among the book-lined walls. The town historian had a very complete library of information about Heather Mountain and the North Country in general, including old town records and the like.

She had explained to Rachael that while she studied and stored the records and most of the photographs, the Historical Society was in charge of the artifacts, and had a rotating display at the Town Hall. The library housed old newspapers and census records. Between the shelves, the walls were the same unfinished pine logs as outside; the only difference was that these weren't weathered.

Vera handed the volume to Rachael. "This is an overview of the history of the sugaring industry in the area. I know you'll go to original sources for your book, but this will give you a place to start."

"Great—I don't know the first thing about sugaring."

"You'll have to visit an authentic Adirondack sugar-shack, then," Vera said eagerly. "I'm sure you'd enjoy that."

"The running of the MacPherson syrup business has passed down through the generations, I understand," Rachael said. She glanced at the dates scribbled in her notes. "Who took over after Jordan and Shane were killed?"

"Malcolm kept on to the day of his death—he didn't know the meaning of the word 'relax,'" Vera commented, tapping her fingers on the arm of her chair. "A real—what do you call 'em?—A-type personality? Anyway, after the tragedy, Celeste and Arden came back to the manor, and Arden helped some; it wasn't really what he was interested in, though. But Ian expressed an interest in the business fairly early on, and assisted Malcolm during the final few years. He has quite a business sense, that Ian."

"You said you grew up with Celeste—did you know Jordan and Shane well?"

"They were older than us, enough to be legends," Vera said, a grin spreading across her plain face. "Jordan had graduated high school before we hit junior high, and Shane graduated two years later. All I know about Jordan is that he was a bit of a ladies' man."

"What do you mean?" Rachael asked, frowning. She'd never liked that phrase, and now it left a particularly sour taste in her mouth. Her Jordan? Then she wondered what on earth had caused her to think that. He wasn't "hers," unless you counted the fact that so far as she knew, she was the only one to whom he appeared, except once or twice, perhaps, to Felicity.

She forced her attention back to Vera.

"Oh, I don't mean he was the 'love-them-and-leave-them' type," the historian said. "But he was a real heartbreaker, especially to my friends and me, since we were younger. He had—well, the best way to describe it is that he had bedroom eyes. He looked at you, and you felt like you were the only person in the room. The only person in the state."

Well, that was true. Rachael had been on the receiving end of that encompassing, consuming gaze.

"Every woman in town had a crush on him. And when he set his sights on someone—whoosh! she was doomed. He was always loyal to whomever he dated, although he never really seemed to get serious enough about anyone to get close to marriage. I think part of that was the family loyalty, knowing he had to give a lot of attention to the family business. Anyway, Shane was quieter, less charming, really. I suppose he felt shadowed by his brother, but I really don't know."

"What about Ian?" Rachael asked. "How well do you know him?"

Vera shook her head. "He didn't attend local school; he had tutors all the way through, and took correspondence courses. The few times I've met him, he's been quite gracious and polite." She pursed her lips, thinking back. "He turned out well, despite Celeste's worries...."

Rachael cocked her head. "What worries?"

Vera raised a cautioning hand. "I'm not normally one to gossip," she said firmly. "However, I understand your professional reasons for asking. I can't tell you much, though; Celeste never spoke much about what troubled her. I believe she worried about Ian's emotional health. The tragedy obviously scarred him more than physically. I got the impression that perhaps he had some violent spells while growing up, but again, I never heard anything specific."

"As you said, he's a gracious and polite man now," Rachael said, tucking away the information for later consideration. She spoke the words truthfully—he'd always acted that way around her—but she'd also seen evidence of extreme emotion. When she'd blundered into his study that first day, he'd reacted with untoward anger.

And what was that comment Karyn had made? *"Ian will be furious; we'll all just have to stay out of his way for a while,"* she'd said when she learned about the near-accident in the library.

Rachael realized Vera was waiting for another question.

"Jordan was going to take over the business after Malcolm—I assume," she added hastily, realizing she'd gotten the information from a source she could never explain to Vera. At the woman's nod, she asked, "How did Malcolm get along with his children? What kind of a parent was he?"

"You're venturing into murky territory with me again," Vera said. "Remember, I was Celeste's peer—Malcolm was an adult, of another generation. Anything I tell you is tempered by the memory of a child. Also, the MacPhersons were the Family on the Hill, so to speak."

She moved her hand in a forewarning motion again. "While they were in no way snobbish or pretentious, neither was Malcolm someone who dropped in for supper. That said..." Her eyes unfocused as she conjured up memories of the former MacPherson patriarch. "He was every inch a businessman: professional, cordial, yet stern. I gathered that he was the same way at home. Oh, I'm sure he loved his family, but as I said, he worked constantly. I never got the impression that he spent much time with the children. The only time I ever saw him loosen up was at the Halloween parties."

"Did you attend the balls every year?" Rachael asked.

Vera nodded, smiling with memory. "They always had a party for the younger children in another part of the manor, and it was a great Rite of Passage to be deemed old enough to attend the 'grown-ups' party." Her crisp blue eyes flashed mischievously as she added, "Of course, before that year, we always managed to peek in and see the festivities. I think the servants purposely turned their heads for half an hour so we could.

"The balls were elaborate affairs, even more so than now. The manor would be brimming with guests—they'd start arriving weeks before the event. The decorations were superb—a jack o'lantern in every window, that sort of thing. And the costumes…oh, they were magnificent, breathtaking. People certainly went overboard, each trying to be more ornate than the other. Back then, it was more of a masquerade party than a costume-type deal. Nowadays people try to outdo each other with uniqueness, not intricacy."

Rachael opened her mouth, but before she could ask anything, Vera reached over and playfully smacked her arm. "Oh, I know just what your next question is going to be. We historians do think alike, you know. The answer is no, I wasn't there the night of the fire. It was a few months after my accident—" she gestured unselfconsciously at the wheelchair "—and I was still in rehab at the Medical Center down in Albany. I didn't even hear what happened until a couple weeks afterwards. Do you know that after my accident, Jordan sent me flowers and a personal note? That's the sort of man he was, Rachael. He barely knew me—I was some young friend of Celeste's—but he took the time and was honestly concerned."

She paused to drink some lemonade. "But we're off the subject again—you asked about Malcolm. As I said, he loved the balls—I suppose they were his way of letting his hair down once a year. He would appear in the same costume every year: traditional Scottish highlander, in the MacPherson tartan, of course."

"What were his wives like?"

"Hm. I don't really remember Marion, although my mother said she was very friendly, very gregarious. She was tall and slender, with dark hair; Jordan took after her in many ways. Malcolm seemed devoted to her, so everyone was surprised when he married Anne so soon after Marion died. Shane took after his mother: the stockiness, the florid skin. Anne was prone to anger, and, looking back, I get the impression that she ignored Jordan while doting on her own son."

"What about Letitia and Felicity?" Rachael asked, hoping Vera, who seemed to have a limitless knowledge of the family, knew something about the two women.

"What? Felicity hasn't bombarded you with stories yet? Just you wait," Vera warned. "Ask her about the Roaring Twenties, and she won't quit. She and Letitia were flappers, and apparently they did more than their fair share of roaring through the decade. They were both quite independent, especially for that time. Felicity never married—she was devoted to her art and achieved a fame few women of that time did. Letitia never married, either, and refused to name Celeste's father. Even more defiantly, she refused to be ashamed or hide out during her pregnancy."

"Did that cause a family scandal?" Rachael asked. Celeste had already provided her with the information about her birth, which explained why her maiden name was MacPherson.

Vera considered. "Yes and no. Her actions—both their actions—were scandalous for the times, but the family rallied around them. There's an incredibly strong sense of family loyalty running through the MacPhersons."

"Like Clan loyalty," Rachael commented. "That's why they don't like to talk about the night of the fire, of course."

"If anything untoward was going on, it was family business, nobody else's," Vera agreed.

Rachael found that her list of questions had been momentarily exhausted, and she was surprised to discover it was nearly 2 p.m. "I've overstayed my welcome," she said, gathering up her notes and the book Vera had given her.

"Oh, not at all," Vera said. "Those hours posted outside are only so some high school student doesn't show up at 9 o'clock the night before his local history research project is due. Before you go, let me give you a few more things...."

A few deft moves by Vera, and Rachael found herself being weighted down by book after book—a history of Heather Mountain...a photographic survey of the great hotels of the Adirondacks...*Journal of a Small Village Doctor?*

"That doesn't really have anything to do with your research, but you might enjoy it," Vera said, fluttering her hands a trifle apologetically, as if to indicate she knew her enthusiasm was getting the better of her. "It was directly transcribed from the journal of James Pope, the town doctor who practiced here from 1921 to 1967. He probably delivered a few MacPhersons—maybe you'll find something helpful after all."

Rachael thanked her profusely, and somehow managed to wedge all of the books carefully into her attaché case. In answer to Vera's question, she said she'd be going to city clerk, church, and assessor's offices the next morning, and the library within the next few days. Vera promised to let the librarian know she was coming.

"And you let me know when you want to see the Historical Society's collection," Vera added. "I know we have a number of things from the MacPhersons that you'll find helpful."

*

Rachael stopped at a Stewart's Shop on the way back to the manor, topping off Celeste's car with gas as a courtesy and buying Diet Pepsi and several bags of Goldfish crackers for sustenance. Back at the manor, she returned the keys via Nancy Rabideau and snagged a locally grown Macintosh apple from the kitchen before retreating to her room.

The information Vera had given her was invaluable, even if some of it was hearsay and conjecture. Rachael paused in the process of typing up her notes to take a bite of the crisp apple, the tart juices electrifying her taste buds. If nothing else, the material gave her a springboard, a place to start asking more questions.

Unfortunately, a great deal of those questions led her right back to Jordan.

She whacked the save button with more vengeance than she intended, and leaned back in her chair, munching on a handful of Goldfish. She'd hoped that leaving the manor for a while would have given her some perspective, but instead, every time Vera had mentioned his name, Rachael had felt a pang deep in her soul. Each sudden, surprising shock of feeling had sent her blood surging, making her wonder if the heat showed on her face.

She wasn't sure if she was glad that Vera hadn't known Jordan well. On the one hand, the last thing she wanted to do right now was to meet someone who'd had a crush on Jordan, or, worse yet, had dated him. On the other hand, by not knowing him, Vera hadn't been able to provide much information about him except for the memories of an acquaintance and anecdotes about his honor.

Nibbling on more crackers, Rachael scrolled through her new notes. It was interesting, she thought idly, that the streak of temper running through the family didn't seem to come from the MacPherson side, from the people with the strict warning for a family motto. Anne, Malcolm's second wife, had been prone to anger, Vera had said, as Ian apparently was now. What about Shane, the link between Anne and Ian?

At this point, all she knew about Shane was that he wasn't particularly good with animals and that he wasn't a particularly good gambler. Wait. What else had Celeste said? Brushing crumbs off her hand, Rachael found her notes from that interview. "Shane had a temper, and was quick to judge...."

But that still didn't say much: It didn't point a finger at the guilty, nor absolve anyone of any crime. Jordan apparently had been beyond reproach; then again, he had been alone in the cottage with Emilie before the shootings. But that didn't prove anything either....

Vera's voice trailed back to her.

"Every woman in town had a crush on him. And when he set his sights on someone—whoosh! she was doomed."

Had Emilie Shaw MacPherson had a crush on her husband's brother? And had Jordan set his sights on her...and "doomed" her? But that didn't match with the descriptions of his family loyalty and honor.

She wanted Jordan to be innocent of everything, she discovered with a sharp smack of realization. She could hardly believe at this point that he could be capable of murderous, destructive violence anyway. Not the talented, devastating man with the passion-fire eyes and the mocking, seductive grin.

Then again, he had no explanation of what he'd been doing that fateful night. He said he couldn't—but she suspected he wouldn't—tell her.

She didn't like that very much at all.

Suddenly she heard her brother's voice. Richard, by virtue of being only one year older than she, had appointed himself to be the brother who teased her mercilessly. She could just imagine what he would say about this.

"Hey, did you hear about Rach's latest? He's dead, and a possible murderer to boot!"

"Jordan is *not* my boyfriend," Rachael muttered aloud, annoyed.

"Oh? Just like Andy Jacoby wasn't your boyfriend—how many weeks did you get grounded after Mom caught you kissing him behind the house?"

"It's nothing like that!" Rachael said loudly, forcefully. Great, if the maids heard her talking to herself again, they were *really* going to think she was looney.

But Richard would be wrong—it wasn't anything like that. She and Andy had barely been fourteen, and only kissed on a dare.

"Whatever you say, Rach."

Nothing like that. But if it wasn't, and he wasn't her boyfriend, what was he?

Dammit, I don't know. Rachael angrily stuck her hand in the goldfish bag, and looked at the stack of books and information Vera had given her. She just didn't want to face reading all that now. As much as she enjoyed research, she couldn't read intensively for long periods of time without going stir crazy. The best research, she felt, wasn't done by paperwork anyway.

Right now, she needed to clear her head.

And she knew just where to go to do just that.

*

Dry, brittle autumn leaves crackled beneath her sneakered feet, sending up a pungent, earthy smell. To her left lay the remains of a stone fence. The grey rocks, once piled carefully, now tumbled haphazardly, half-covered by dirt and mulch. In some places, the pile vanished completely, only to reappear a few yards later where a stone still perched stubbornly atop its neighbors.

Something white caught Rachael's eye, something disturbed by the passage of her foot scuffing through the leaves and dirt. A fragment of a china plate. She picked it up, rubbing away the clinging earth. A simple cobalt-blue pattern was visible along the outside edge, no more than two inches long. Rachael turned it over, knowing even as she did that there would be no identifying marks on the back; those would have been stamped in the center of the plate's back. She dug the toe of her white high-top in the dirt, but unearthed no other fragments. It would have been too much to hope for a garbage dump here, so close to the road. She sighed, continued walking, absentmindedly rubbing her thumb on the smooth surface of the china shard.

The cemetery Celeste had told her about—the one just past the property line—had hovered in the back of her mind since their conversation. Though Celeste had said that the family mausoleum in the town graveyard held the remains of her ancestors, Rachael hadn't discounted the importance of this tiny cemetery. Perhaps no MacPhersons lay here, but those people who did must have been, at the very least, passing acquaintances of the family.

The directions Celeste had given her were simple: go out to the end of the driveway and turn left, go about a mile along the curved road, and then turn in at the old stone fence that marked the end of the MacPherson's property.

Even if there hadn't been the barest connection between the MacPhersons and this graveyard, Rachael's interest would have been piqued. Cemeteries were a wellspring of information for an historian, not to mention that she found them serene places, somehow comforting. The militant, even rows of polished stone; the close-cut carpets of green lawns; the well-tended, carefully placed shade trees....

Old, small churchyards had their charm as well, the weathered, rough stones crowded together like families huddled against a storm; the remains of a wildflower bouquet, tied with a bright ribbon, laid before a tiny stone marking an achingly tiny grave.... And each stone represented a life, a person, someone who had lived and laughed and cried and in some way, small or large, made a mark in history.

Rachael skirted a dead tree, picking her way around the branch-tangle, and then there was the graveyard. She stopped, dismayed by the disarray. Celeste had said she tried to have their groundskeeper come out once a year, but it was obvious that the cemetery hadn't been tended in several years at least. Several of the rough-hewn wooden posts had fallen, dragging the rusty barbed wire down with them. Rachael stepped carefully over one of the low spots, balancing herself on one of the wobbly weathered grey posts in order to avoid tripping over a gravestone that listed drunkenly against the springy wire.

She sank onto one knee and brushed her hand across the chiseled surface, removing enough green-brown moss and dirt to read the words.

"She lives in memory/One so dear/Though lost to earth/Is cherished here," she read haltingly, sadly. "Not so very cherished anymore."

She stood again and surveyed the area, which didn't measure more than fifteen feet square. Only a few of the gravestones remained standing straight, still defying the cruel elements of wind and rain, wet heavy snow, crack-inducing ice, gravity. The rest of the markers leaned at various angles or had toppled over completely, the earth around them eaten away. Several of the stones, she noticed, had snapped in two, the base part still imbedded in the ground while the top lay beside.

Rachael wandered purposelessly around the area, fighting through the wild grass and clumps of knee-high ferns. She bent over and pulled upright one of the few marble markers, and traced a finger over the now-faint picture of a fountain, hundreds of delicate carved lines depicting the flowing water. She scuffed at the dirt behind the stone with her sneaker, trying to pack the earth down so the gravestone would stand proudly again. The dark loamy odor filled her senses. She succeeded, but knew it would take only one hard rain to sluice away the mud and ease the ponderous tombstone down again.

Many of the actual graves were apparent as long mounds of earth: the hard-packed dirt over the coffins remained while the surrounding ground had been worn away. Rachael noticed that, whether by vandals or the passage of time, some of the markers had been moved away from the heads of the graves, lying several feet away, marking nothing.

Most of the trees around the graveyard were thin and wiry, fighting for what meager sun they could touch. One large tree, an ancient wild-apple, grew next to the graveyard, its trunk substituted for one of the posts in the fence. The barbed wire bit into the trunk where the flaking bark had layered over it through the years.

One thick branch dipped low into the yard. Rachael pushed at it experimentally. It gave, bounced back, held firm. She hoisted herself onto it, leaning her back against the trunk and propping one foot ahead of her on the branch. Her other foot swung in a melancholy arc, occasionally brushing against a gravestone partly beneath the branch. The stone had snapped in two; the top piece leaned against the bottom section and the tree trunk.

She should have brought paper and crayon to do some rubbings of the stones, she thought idly. She'd done that in elementary school—what grade had that been? Third? No, fourth; she remembered Ms. Peavy taking them. Rachael had been enthralled, moving from headstone to headstone in a state of young awe. Some of the boys had tried to scare the girls by hiding and then leaping out, hollering about ghosts, but she'd ignored them. One of the girls had been terrified to even enter the cemetery, despite the bright afternoon sunlight and Ms. Peavy's gentle coaxing. What had her name been? Amy Somebody. Amy Sandusky? Sandrewski?...

"This upsets you."

Her foot abruptly ceased its lazy dangle, her stomach lurching at the unexpected voice and the unexpected speaker. Jordan sat at the end of the branch, apparently not all "there" because no weight tugged at the limb. He swung a hand to indicate the decay. "This hurts you," he clarified.

She willed her heart to stop pounding so ferociously. "Yes," she answered simply, frowning, in her eyes an angry storm. "How did you—I thought…I thought you couldn't follow me here."

"What do you mean?" he asked curiously.

"Well, I'm no expert on paranormal phenomena," she snapped, "but I didn't know ghosts could travel."

"Ah." Realization flooded his green gaze. "You thought perhaps I was bound to the house." She nodded. "Actually, if that theory were true, I'd be forced to haunt that burnt-out shell of a cottage. Thank goodness that's not the case."

"Then why do you stay?"

"I said I wasn't bound by the house, not that I wasn't bound," he said, a quiet note of resignation in his voice.

"What binds you?" she asked softly. The sky seemed suddenly darker; only a mournful bird call broke the hushed stillness of the tiny, final resting place of long-forgotten ancestors.

He looked at her. He hadn't moved, but somehow he seemed more distant than a moment before. "A promise," he said, and turned away.

Rachael didn't know what to say to that. Her anger began to subside, filtering away through the half-bare branches. She hadn't wanted him here, but now here he was, and though his presence made her emotions rock like a boat on a storm-tossed sea, it was also somehow succoring.

A late afternoon sunbeam pushed its way through the thicket of trees; dust swirled, patternless, blinded, in the bright path. Still frustrated, she sighed.

"It pains you that history is being destroyed here," Jordan commented, back to his first topic.

"Destroyed, ignored, forgotten, disrespected—the end result is the same," she said bitterly.

"Emilie loved this place, too," he said thoughtfully, as if not speaking to her. "She used to sit right where you're sitting, with her feet propped up on that tombstone. It wasn't broken then." He slid his hands into the pockets of his pants. "Like you, she came here to think...to get away."

Does he know what I was trying to get away from? "Did you come here with her?"

He glanced at her sharply, eyes piercing. "Sometimes," he said. His lips tightened; he knew what she thought. "If she wanted company," he said pointedly, "I would accompany her. But usually she wanted to be alone, and I respected that. She would sit there and write in her journal."

"Journal?" Rachael's interest piqued with a vengeance. A journal could be an historian's boon—properly taken, of course. All "facts" recorded couldn't be taken at face value, but impressions of events, surroundings, other people could speak reams. "Emilie kept a journal? Where is it now?"

He shrugged. "I don't know. I don't think anyone at the manor has it. She used to write in it out here, away from—so no one else would read it."

And who had Emilie been hiding her most private thoughts from? Rachael thought, somehow guessing Jordan wouldn't reveal that information. It made sense that Celeste and Ian didn't know of the journal's whereabouts; otherwise, they would have given it to her for her research. "Emilie must have trusted you, since she let you know of the journal's existence," she commented. When he didn't answer, she pressed on. "Did you care very deeply for her?"

His eyes had gone the color of that storm-tossed sea; fury barely kept in check.

"She was my sister-in-law," he said tightly. "Of course I cared for her."

And then he was gone.

"Of all the—" Rachael muttered, startled and annoyed. She huffed back against the tree trunk, folding her arms across her chest. At least his reaction had given her some information: His angry defensiveness told her that he had indeed cared for Emilie. But in what way? As a sister-in-law, as he said? And what had she felt for him?

But no. She had come here to clear her thoughts of him for a while, not fill her mind with his lean form and mellow-smooth voice. She leaned her head back and closed her eyes, breathing in the calm. A breeze shushed through the dry, papery leaves; soft murmurings, gentle rustle-sighs. Without intending to, and yet knowing all along that she would, she let herself drift backwards: backwards in thought, backwards in time, backwards to another's memories. Here, here Emilie had sat, journal propped on her knees.... Rachael dangled both feet down, reaching her toes toward the splintered crack of the tombstone, sitting as Emilie had.

Summer. She knew because the leaves clung green to the branches; because the sun felt hotter, hot enough to spring sweat along her brow, across her shoulders, beneath her breasts. No broken gravestones now, only uneven rows, uneven-sized stones, set in a small expanse of lawn bordered by bright, perfumed flowers. A blue jay lit on the headstone with the fountain carving—the design distinct, clear-etched—and seemed to bow its head to drink from the marble-frozen liquid.

Emilie smiled at the sight, then turned her eyes and thoughts back to the leather-bound book on her lap. The smile faded; she chewed uncomfortably on her lip as she gazed at the words there written, put pen to paper again.

Rachael leaned toward her, over her shoulder, straining to see the neatly inscribed words. But they seemed so indistinct, so hazy. She urged her mental self closer, closer than she had ever approached someone whose memory-imprint she chased. The words were there, but she couldn't read them.

"Emilie."

Jordan stood across at the entrance to the cemetery.

"Emilie, it's time to go. Shane's been asking for you."

A tear hung, caught crystal-bright by the sun, on Emilie's pale, high-boned cheek. She closed the book slowly and set it in a silver box.

Rachael, looking over Emilie's shoulder, tried to read the expression in Jordan's eyes, but the sun cascaded around him, casting his face in shadow.

Emilie slid slowly from her perch, and moved across the graveyard. Jordan held out his hand....

Chapter Nine

Rachael gasped, jerking back to the present, guilt streaking through her stomach. She hadn't meant to see so much, watch so long. She should have stopped when Jordan first appeared. The clue of Emilie's journal was no excuse.

But why hadn't she been able to read the words?

She swung her leg over the branch to dismount, leaning her weight on the broken, angled top half of the gravestone. It shifted beneath her weight; she heard and felt it scraping against a rock buried in the soil as it ponderously toppled to the ground. Again guilty—thoughtless, foolish action—she yanked her foot away.

The question of the illegible diary entries nagged at her as she hiked back to the house, and beyond, through dinner. Back in her room, she poured herself a brandy and settled down on the window seat with her large sketchpad on her knees. Perhaps drawing the scene would bring the words focus-clear.

Closing her eyes, she made her breathing deep and even, the gestures automatic after years of frequent meditation. Bit by bit, she relaxed her body—face, shoulders, arms, torso, legs—until her hands felt numb and heavy, distant. When she was completely tranquil, she counted backwards from ten, with each breath backing farther into the self-hypnotic state.

One...

Rachael opened her eyes, unseeing but for the empty white expanse of paper. She glanced ever briefly away as she fumbled for the colored pencils in their display case. Selecting several—sweet leaf-green, rough stone-grey, bright sun-yellow—she began to draw.

The movements of her fingers, her wrist, were not from any talent or art study. Instead, they came from somewhere deeper, somehow connected to her psychometric ability. Independent of conscious thought, her hand caused the pencils to fill the page with what she had scene and perhaps, she hoped, what she hadn't seen.

Her only plan for this picture was to draw a general sketch first, of Emilie in the cemetery, writing in her journal. Then, she planned to do a second drawing: a close-up of the diary.

But when she finished the first illustration of the past, Rachael forgot about the second one.

She had captured the twisting ballet of sunbeams through the applause of leaves, and in the foreground, the questioning head cock of the reviewing blue jay. And she had captured the instant after Jordan appeared, when she had looked at him over Emilie's slim shoulder.

At that moment, Emilie had turned and slipped the box into a hole in the tree, letting the fresh, covering branches spring back into place.

*

Events of the next day propelled Rachael almost helplessly through the hours: an early appointment at the county clerk's office for copies of various documents; a hastily arranged meeting with a former MacPherson Maple employee who was leaving for a winter home in Florida the next day; another stack of paperwork from Ian; an update for Celeste. Rachael wasn't able to head out to the graveyard until late afternoon, the dinner hour worrying at her mental heels.

When she reached the tiny worn cemetery, Rachael hiked herself onto the branch and twisted around. She ran her hand along the tree. There was the hole, now gaping, the young fresh branches long since died and snapped away.

Empty, of course.

Rachael lay her hand on the trunk, wishing she could see more, but knowing the visions from this place couldn't take her to where the journal now rested. She wouldn't be able to see beyond the graveyard, beyond Emilie's actions here.

The sunbeam that provided a stage for the mindless dust-dance now slashed lower through the trees. It was getting late: She had just enough time to wash up and dress for dinner. She slid off the branch and paused, looking guilt-filled at the broken gravestone that she had disturbed the afternoon before. The least she could do was prop the top piece back up against its other half. She crouched down and dug her fingers beneath it, heaved up, revealing an ugly fresh gouge in the earth. As she set the stone against its twin, she saw something glint in the moist black dirt. When it fell, the stone hadn't ground against another, but against something metal.

She brushed her fingers across. Sharp metallic edge. She hesitated, unwilling to unearth something best left buried. But metal? She slid her fingers along the edge of the object, sinking her nails into the loam, and determined that the squared edges sized a chest not nearly big enough to be a coffin. Finding a flat, palm-sized stone, she dug around the box until she could curl her fingers beneath it and lift it free, and balance it in her hands.

The box was tarnished except where the tombstone piece had scraped streaks in the side, revealing bright silvery metal. Rachael rose from her crouch, leaning a hip against the apple tree as she rubbed at the top of the small chest with trembling hands.

There. Gleaming dully in the fading sunlight, on the top of the box, the ornately inscribed initials *ESM*.

*

Rachael slipped on a pair of gold tassel earrings that echoed the gold braiding on the neckline of her slim, wine-colored dress and the gold tassels at the ends of her twice-wrapped belt. She'd pulled back the sides of her hair and secure them with a gold clip, but her hair still looked rather wild; then again, it usually did, and she didn't have time for further fixes now.

She glanced at the clock. The cocktail hour would be ending in about five minutes, and she didn't want the others to wait dinner for her. She bit her wine-colored lip, looked over her shoulder at the tarnished secret on her desk.

Succumbed to the temptation.

The tumblers within the tiny brass padlock crumbled away, and she carefully slipped the lock out through the hasp. Peremptorily dislodged, silver-rust flakes drifted down as Rachael worried at a clasp sealed shut by moisture, dirt and time. No lock had been necessary: the box stubbornly guarded its secrets with cementing corrosion.

Turning the box in her hands, she wondered if she should wait and take it to a jeweler—she didn't want to harm a potentially valuable piece. But she had some knowledge of antique care, and to her adequately trained eye the clasp already looked too far gone to be worth saving. She propped the box back on her knees and wiggled the clasp again.

A rap sounded at the door. Rachael jerked with irrational guilt. "Just a moment," she called, and glanced hastily around the room for a convenient hiding place. She didn't want to announce her discovery just yet. Desk drawer? Too low—the box wouldn't fit. Under the bed? Too far away, in the next room.

She swung around in the petit-point cushioned desk chair and pulled open the small door to the recess that housed the personal refrigerator.

The hot pot and accouterments took up all the space on top of the fridge, so she yanked the door open and tucked the box on the shelf beneath the remaining cans of Diet Pepsi. She hastily brushed slivers of rust from her skirt as she hurried to the door.

"Ian?" He was already self-consciously edging his way into the room, so she automatically stood aside, surprise and confusion momentarily blotting out basic politeness. She was astonished that he would take the chance of coming into the guest wing, even at a time when the guests should all be downstairs. He must have felt something was terribly important.

"Good evening, Rachael," he said, glancing at the door. She closed it. "Celeste said you didn't have cocktails with the other guests—is something wrong?"

"No. I was just about to come down to dinner, in fact." She eyed the clock. "I'm not late, am I?"

He shook his head, tugged at the end of his glove, agitated. "She also said you've decided not to work in the library any longer. Is it because of your accident on the catwalk? I can't tell you how upset I am about that."

"No, that's not it," Rachael interrupted soothingly. She picked up one of her pumps and braced herself on the back of the desk chair to slip it on. "That was an accident, nothing more." She repeated the action with the other pump. "It's just easier to do my work here, where my computer's set up."

"Is that the new Apple laptop?" he asked, stepping closer to the desk, sounding relieved at the subject change. Taking his lead, she told him about the specs and why she'd chosen this model, how at home she hooked it up to a larger monitor and extended keyboard.

"Shouldn't we get going?" she suggested finally, checking the clock again.

He nodded, half-hearing her, looking around the room as if he'd never seen it before.

"You have everything you need up here?" he asked.

"Well, a personal masseur would be nice, but other than that..." she joked. Again only half-hearing her, he barely laughed, just gave an uneven smile. But he slowly moved toward the door behind her, still looking around. Rachael took her room key from the pedestal table by the door and, at his gesture, preceded him out the door. She guessed that just politeness wasn't the only reason for his action, and checked each way down the hall before stepping out.

Quickly locking the door behind them, she fell into step with Ian. She noticed that it took him a moment to remember to arrange their pace so that she walked on his unscarred side. Was this because of his preoccupation since being in her room, or because he was getting used to her presence? It was difficult to reconcile the man whom everyone said had a temper with the one who seemed to be, in his own way, reaching out to her.

In some ways, he made her understand the cliché "tortured soul." Yet she still felt uncomfortable about something...the inevitable sense of tragedy about him, and the knowledge that what had happened to him had affected him in ways she could never comprehend.

"You're sure you don't need anything?" Ian asked again. "What about a printer? The ones in my office are wireless."

"Access to a printer might be helpful, now that you mention it," Rachael said. "But I don't understand—why are you trying to help me? You're opposed to my research."

"It's true, I didn't agree with the decision to hire you," he said, turning down a narrow corridor that led to one of the wing's back staircases. "I really don't see any benefit in what you're doing. But you're here, and I respect Celeste's wishes. As a family, we must stand in agreement. I certainly don't want to hinder your efforts."

He paused at the top of the narrow steps. Unlike the front staircase, this one was wall-lined, close and dark. Rachael stood next to him, wondering at his seeming change of heart. That, and the fact he'd come to her room. Was there another reason for his erratic behavior? She stared down the dim descent of wooden steps, for some reason remembering her near-tumble on the front stairs her first night here.

Ian's body suddenly tensed, and at the same time she thought she sensed another presence with them, standing a few steps down. Jordan? For a brief second she felt a flood of reassurance, like a silent message: *You're safe.* Then Ian touched her elbow, and she jumped, stepping backward automatically. But he cocked his head at her, and she realized he had been motioning her down the stairs.

She started down. Whatever presence she'd thought she'd felt was gone now. She'd probably imagined it, as well as Ian's momentary agitation. He was no doubt on edge because he didn't want to meet up with one of the other guests.

They reached the family dining room without incident; Celeste and Felicity were already there. As she accepted a drink from Ian, she noticed a wedge of black dirt beneath the nail on her right forefinger. She'd washed up after she returned from the graveyard, and thought she'd cleaned away all the dirt from digging up the box.

They sat down at the long table, and surreptitiously, Rachael tried to pry the stubborn dirt out from under the nail with another fingernail. The dirt remained imbedded, darkly obvious beneath the pale pink polish. She glanced down at her hands, then back up at Celeste, who was commenting about some economic reforms the President had suggested, which had been discussed on the evening news.

She started to reach for her drink with her right hand, paused, and took up the glass with her left. Ian made a spirited rejoinder to Celeste's last statement. She fidgeted, worrying at her nail again, wishing dinner would get on the table sooner. She'd barely had time to try to open Emilie's box, and all she wanted to do was bolt back up the stairs to her room. Now she understood how Pandora felt.

She had debated about whether to tell the family of her discovery, and decided to at least wait until she opened the box. Shaking the box had told her nothing; the journal could fit snugly in a padded interior. Or it could be empty. The journal could have been destroyed by the elements over the past forty years. There could be something else altogether in the box, something that wouldn't be helpful. She couldn't believe that would be true.

Of course she would give the box to Celeste afterwards, no matter what was in it. It was still a piece of the family's history, and an antique. Battered and timeworn as it was, the case might clean up nicely and make an interesting addition to the house's display.

But, just for a short while, she wanted to savor the treasure herself. While it was nothing like unearthing the treasures of a pharaoh's tomb or a sunken pirate ship, this find had personal significance and, therefore, satisfaction. It was A Clue, another step toward solving the genealogical mystery, another piece in the proverbial puzzle....

"Rachael?"

"I'm sorry, what?" She looked up, guilty, realizing she'd lost the thread of the conversation.

"You seem preoccupied—is something wrong?" Celeste asked.

Rachael denied any problems, begging off her distraction as thoughts on her work.

"Well, it's nice to know I'm getting my money's worth," the older woman said with a smile. "Really, though, you don't have to work twenty-four hours a day. But, since you brought it up...how did your meeting with Dan Wilson this morning go?"

They chatted about her work for a few minutes, while she continued unobtrusively to try to dislodge the dirt. As their attention was diverted by the arrival of the first course, shrimp cocktail, she felt a nudge on her arm. Smiling conspiratorially, Felicity, who was sitting next to her, passed her a metal nail file.

*

The night was going to be a cold one, Celeste had warned her as they parted ways after crème de menthe and coffee. In fact, it already was. A cool breeze spun itself around Rachael like invisible cotton candy as she headed down the hallway to her room. Her heels thudded against the carpet runner, sounding loud in the quiet hall; the other guests had apparently already retired for the night.

The moment she touched the doorknob to her room, she knew something was very wrong.

The metal knob burned her palm as if someone had taken a psychic blowtorch to it. She snatched her hand and the sensation immediately vanished.

Someone had been here.

And whoever it was had been up to no good, and recently, because she'd never felt such a red-hot psychic imprint before.

Cautiously, she put her hand out and grasped the knob again. Now that her mental defenses were up, all she felt was the slightly chilled metal beneath her fingers. Her hand shook slightly as she twisted the key in the lock. Then she flung the door inward, just in case, and jumped back.

Nothing. She peered carefully into the dark room, but couldn't sense anything wrong. Again very quickly, she flicked on the light, then snatched her hand back. Again, no one grabbed her wrist or leaped out at her. So far, so good. Still wary, she eased into the room and nudged the door shut with her hip.

The box. Rachael yanked open the closet that housed the small refrigerator, her heart an angry thud in her chest. Nobody knew about what she'd found, of course, but what if someone had found it? A thief might have broken in—dear lord, hadn't she read once that the freezer was the first obvious place a thief looked? Or could Ian have somehow seen her before he came in the room? Or Jordan...?

Please, not Jordan.

A dim light spread across the floor as she opened the small refrigerator and peered inside. Rachael let out a whoosh of air. The box sat where she'd placed it, beneath the cans of soda. She touched it carefully with one finger, and felt nothing untoward.

What, then? Methodically, Rachael checked the few belongings she had brought with her to the manor. Her purse still lay inside the closet, money and credit cards intact. Nothing missing from the jumble of jewelry on the dresser.

Standing in the archway between the bedroom and sitting room, Rachael turned in a slow circle, lower lip caught between her teeth and the towel dangling from the hand on her hip. Something *had* to be out of place—otherwise, why would someone have taken the trouble to break into her room? What could the intruder have been looking for? Even if the person hadn't found anything, wouldn't he or she have disturbed something? But what? What was different?

The bed, carefully made up earlier by a conscientious maid, looked unrumpled. The refilled brandy decanter sat on the small table near the window. She hadn't noticed anything out of the ordinary in the bathroom. Her clothes were untouched.

"Oh, my God," she murmured, a chill tickling her spine so forcefully that the hair on the back of her neck bristled against the onslaught. The computer's screen was flipped up. She *always* closed it after she finished working. She knew she had done so before she went out to the graveyard, and it had been down when she returned.

Slowly, Rachael crossed the room and sank into the chair before the desk. She almost didn't want to know, and that reaction made her hesitate for a moment before she reached out and flicked the ON switch.

The laptop took an excruciatingly long time to turn on, it seemed, but then the icon blazed bold on the screen. Rachael expelled the breath she hadn't realized she'd been holding. So, whoever it was hadn't destroyed the whole operating system. Tapping a few keys, she tried to open a folder of files.

Nothing.

Starting to curse under her breath, she tried opening the genealogical program.

Nothing again.

Swearing louder, she tried Word, and when that didn't work, she smacked her fist on the desk and let out a string of imprecations that her mother had no idea she knew.

*

"Whoever it was didn't have to know computers very well," she said to Celeste as the woman frowned in consternation at the desk. Her call downstairs had roused Nancy, who had in turn alerted Celeste. Now, both women were in her room, along with Ian and Felicity. "It's easier to delete files than to create them."

"I don't understand why someone would do this," Celeste said. She was already dressed for bed, wearing a green, quilted-satin dressing robe. Her feet had been hastily stuffed into polished loafers. Felicity also wore nightclothes, in the form of a high-necked, lace-edged Victoriana gown. Nancy still wore her apron; she'd been in the kitchen finishing the dishes. Ian was still fully clothed, save for his tie. "You said nothing else was missing?"

"Nope." Rachael rubbed the back of her neck. "If someone broke in to steal something, I'd imagine they'd take the whole damn computer."

"Why would anyone do such a thing?" Celeste said again. "I just don't understand."

"I don't know," Rachael said quietly. She shivered, but not from the cold. Someone was obviously trying to sabotage her research. As Celeste asked, why? And who? The family hadn't left her sight during dinner. She might have suspected Ian, with his computer knowledge, but for that fact. "Were all the guests accounted for during dinner?"

"They were all there," Nancy said. "I helped serve them, and no one left long enough to get all the way up here."

"How did whoever-it-was get in?" Ian asked.

"Through the door—I imagine," Rachael added hastily, realizing she couldn't explain why she was so sure the intruder had entered that way. "The windows weren't open. There's no secret passageway I'm not aware of, is there?"

"No," Celeste said with a short laugh. "Not unless we're not aware of it, either."

"Then it was someone with a key," Ian said. "Was the door locked?"

Rachael nodded. "You were with me when I left—you saw me lock it. And I had to unlock it to get in." She paused. "Who has keys to access all the rooms?"

Nancy answered firmly, "I do, and I only give them out to the maids during cleaning hours. All the other employees went home before dinner, except for George and myself, and Maria, who served the guests." She raised her chin, as if daring Rachael to accuse one of her staff. Rachael, unable to imagine why a maid or gardener would want to trash her computer files, nodded reassuringly.

"I have a skeleton key, and so do Ian and Felicity," Celeste put in. She looked at her relatives. "Have you lost yours recently?"

Felicity shook her head and drew her key out of the neckline of her frilly nightgown, where it hung on a long strand of thin silk rope. Ian reached into his pocket and produced a heavy key ring.

"Karyn has keys, too," he pointed out.

"She left before dinner," Celeste said. "We can ask her in the morning. There's no sense calling her now and waking the child as well."

"Since there's no emergency, we might as well wait until morning to call the police," Ian suggested.

"Oh, do you think that's really necessary?" Celeste protested, concern making her frown. "That might cause bad publicity for the manor, Ian, and we can't afford that right before All Hallows Eve. Since nothing's been taken..."

"They could at least dust for fingerprints," he pointed out.

"Damn," Rachael said, shutting the laptop, her gesture abrupt and frustrated. "I touched the doorknob, the computer—everything. I didn't even think about fingerprints."

"There, you see?" Celeste said to Ian.

He scowled. "At the very least, I'll inspect the grounds tomorrow morning to see if the intruder was from the outside."

"'...And knew the intruders on his ancient home'," Felicity said. "Matthew Arnold, 'The Scholar-Gipsy'," she added meekly when Celeste pressed a disapproving look on her.

"That's a very good idea, Ian," Celeste agreed, tugging her robe closed at the throat. "If someone did break in to the manor, then it might be wise to call the police. For now, though, I think we'd all be better off with some sleep." Rachael noticed the older woman looked pale without her careful makeup, and tired. The others filed out, but Celeste paused and turned back to her.

"You won't be frightened staying here tonight, will you?" she asked solicitously. "I could have Nancy make up another room...."

"I'll be fine," Rachael assured her. "I don't want to be any trouble, and I don't think the intruder will be back."

Celeste hesitated, as if unsure whether she should voice what she was thinking. Finally, she said, "I hope this doesn't seem callous, Rachael, but this will slow down your research, won't it? Please be assured I understand, and I'm willing to pay you for whatever time it takes for you to finish chronicling our history, but—"

"It won't put too much of a crimp in the research, actually," Rachael said. She was almost surprised that she could smile after the last half hour, but she did feel rather smug that she'd foiled the potential saboteur. "There's that old saying among computer users—and forgive me if I sound like Felicity for quoting—'There are two types of computer users: Those who have lost something, and those who will.' Being one of those who have, I make backups religiously. I keep them away from the computer, of course, and I had a chance to check them before you came upstairs—everything is intact. I'll have to load everything back in tomorrow, but that won't take me very long at all."

Celeste's smile of relief banished some of the haggard lines on her face. "I'm so glad to hear that," she said, taking one of Rachael's hands between hers. "And, more importantly, I'm glad you're unharmed. You just haven't had much luck since you've come here, have you?"

Rachael shook her head and said no, unwilling to upset the woman by pointing out that much of what had happened hadn't been bad luck, but the work of someone. Someone who, apparently, didn't want her to continue her work.

Someone who had sneaked into her room during dinner, when all of the manor residents, all of the servants and all of the guests were accounted for.

Someone who could get in a locked door without a key, and leave no traces.

Someone who could move like a ghost.

*

After Celeste had gone, Rachael locked the door, and stood in the center of the sitting room, hugging herself against the remaining feeling that she had been violated.

"Jordan, are you here?" she demanded aloud. Nothing. "I know you did this, Jordan. You keep away from me, dammit. If you're hiding something, I'm going to find out. You can't stop me. Unless you want to tell me what happened forty years ago, you just keep away."

"Rachael."

He appeared in front of her, swiftly, so swiftly that he startled her, even though she'd been watching for his presence. He looked solid, strong, substantial, and she wanted to fling herself into his arms and let him protect her from violation.

But she didn't have that option. Not only did her very psyche rebel from such weakness, but he was the prime suspect, and that frightened her even more.

He must have sensed her confusion, because he held his hands out to her, features anguished. "Lady, please."

She backed up a step. "Please what? You want to tell me what happened here tonight?"

"I don't know. Rachael, you've got to believe me, I don't know!"

She wanted to believe him, but she couldn't. Not with the damning evidence.

"No, I don't have to believe you," she snapped. "Here are the facts: Someone wiped out my computer files. Whoever it was broke in without a known copy of the key, which narrows it down to a very good lock pick—or someone who doesn't have a problem with locks. And all the manor residents and guests were accounted for. Except you."

He ran a hand over his hair, a brusque gesture. "I was with you all evening, as a matter of fact. I can tell you everything you ate, what you said."

"And you can move pretty quick, too. You could've appeared here, done the dirty work, and been back downstairs before the soup course became salad."

Again the imploring expression. The look in his green eyes smacked her in the gut, and she gritted her teeth. She wanted to hold him, or have him hold her. Rachael wrapped her arms around herself again instead.

"Why would I do something like this?" he asked.

"Because you don't want me to continue my research. You don't want me to find out what happened that night." Why else would someone destroy all the work she'd done?

"No, someone else doesn't want you to learn—"

"Then tell me who," she demanded. "I'm sick of your fudging and your excuses. You made a promise to somebody? It could just as easily be a promise not to let anyone find out what happened. So I don't want to hear your excuses."

Jordan sank into the armchair, shaking his head. He looked so tired, defeated. "First of all," he said finally, "you could be wrong about your door not being unlocked. Somebody else might have a key."

"Okay, that's true," she conceded. Anger began to abandon her, and suddenly she felt as weary as he looked. She sat on the very edge of the desk chair, still unable to relax; still scared. "But why would someone else screw up my files? You've got the best motive for that."

"So does—" He stopped. She pounced.

"Who?"

He shook his head, stubborn, mute. Rachael stared at him, at the way the side lamp sent his cheekbones into sharp relief and made the strands of dark hair shadow on his face to look like scars. Anger returned, and she gave it easy passage, jumping to her feet.

"Dammit! You can't keep hinting that someone else is responsible! If you keep refusing to tell me who, then I have to assume you're lying, and you're doing all this."

"Why would I warn you if I was responsible?" he asked, his voice even.

She had touched a nerve by questioning his honesty: She could see that in the set of mouth, the proud glint in his otherwise hooded eyes. For a brief moment, she could almost imagine him capable of fierce, wild rage. But murder? Suddenly uncertain, she nonetheless plunged on.

"Maybe you're warning me to throw me off balance," she said, the words tumbling out. "To make me trust you. I mean, you could've set the library railing to break, then come and warned me so I'd suspect anyone but you." As the sentence left her, she gasped, fear knotting in her stomach. She hadn't thought about what she was saying, but suddenly the full import of the words crashed over her, nearly drowning her in the wave's intensity.

"Is that what you think?" The expression in his eyes changed, but she didn't have time to register that before he was on his feet and in front of her. She tried to back away, but the chair tangled her step. Jordan caught her, pulling her against him.

"Rachael."

The name was torn from him. His lips pressed against her temple, and she imagined her pulse beat wildly beneath his mouth. How could his touch do that to her? Sweep away reason, logic…leave behind emotion and passion and a desperate, aching need. His breath whispered across her brow.

"You must believe me—I would never do anything to hurt you."

His words, softly and tenderly spoken as they were, served to shatter the spell. She stiffened, and when he reacted by trying to hold her tighter, she put her hands against the hard planes of his chest and pushed back. Reluctantly, he released her.

"I'm sorry, Jordan," Rachael said, and she was. Despite all her fears and suspicions, she was very, very sorry. She closed her eyes. "That's not enough. I can't trust you if you can't tell me what's going on." She was going to say something more, but before she could, she sensed him leaving. She opened her eyes in time to see his form, barely visible, his eyes a brighter glow of regret before he faded away altogether.

Rachael somehow made her way across the room to the armchair and allowed her shaking knees to drop her into the seat. The cushions contained no lingering warmth from Jordan's body, and they never would. She buried her face in her hands.

Finally she stirred herself into action again. Because she was convinced that Jordan was the culprit who'd broken into her room, she was even more determined to find out what was had happened in the past. If Jordan had sabotaged her computer, then he didn't want her to continue her research, which meant she might be close to learning something he didn't want anyone to know. In that case, Emilie's box—and, she hoped, the journal within—might hold a key to what he was trying so desperately to hide. There was no way on earth she was going to be able to fall asleep right away, so she opened the refrigerator and drew out the box.

She made sure her windows were tightly shut against the cold, then held a long, slender match to the arranged pile of logs in the fireplace in her bedroom. The kindling caught, the bark flickering with orange, a thin spiral of smoke curling specter-like from the dry wood. Satisfied that the fire would grow, she replaced the spark-screen and returned to the sitting room.

The box waited patiently, as it had patiently waited these forty years, on her desk, the metal slowly warming. Still cool though, she learned, setting her palm on it. As much as she wanted to explore it again, she decided to wait a few more minutes to let it return to room temperature. She carried it to the hearth, then slipped out of her dress and hung the garment in the closet.

As she did, something tugged gently at the pocket, and she reached in to discover she'd forgotten to return Felicity's nail clip. Juggling it in her hand, she snuggled into the peach robe. She dragged a comfortable chair to the fire and buried her feet in a pair of warm socks.

Firelight played over the box, bright fingers of flame recarving the detail of the initials on the top. Rachael cradled the box on her lap again, and lightly ran her finger around the rough edges of the clasp. She tried to pull up on the clasp, but the corroded metal bit into her fingertip. She needed something to wedge beneath it....

She glanced at the nail clip in her other hand, then flipped the instrument open so the slender file stuck out. Carefully, she inserted the strip of metal beneath the edge of the clasp, and attempted to slide it upward, beneath the sealed part. The fastener creaked its displeasure, spitting more rusty slivers onto Rachael's lap.

She pulled the file out, blew gently on the area. More bits of metal puffed away, and she slid the file beneath again, shimmying up and down. Suddenly, with a faint shriek of mortal protest, the clasp popped up, rebounding against the top of the box.

Heart thumping, Rachael dropped the nail clip on the hearth and gently raised the top of the box. Layers of soft red material lay inside. The seal must have been tight, for she could find no evidence of moisture damage, although she detected the musty smell of mildew. Carefully, she unfolded the velvet, and there, nestled in the bottom of the box, was a book. She knew before she even touched it that it had to be Emilie's journal.

Tenderly, Rachael lifted the book from its niche. The burgundy leather cover did have some spots of mildew on it, but otherwise, the volume seemed unharmed. With gentle fingers, she drew back the cover, wincing as the browned edges of the pages within crumbled. On the first page, in the flowing script she recognized from her vision, *Emilie Shaw MacPherson*. She drew the page over.

And discovered she still couldn't read the writing.

*

"Don't you threaten me," the first man said, warning in his voice. There was little warning in his stance, though; he slouched in a chair by the fireplace. The fire within was the only source of illumination in the room, and its light failed to reach the other man, who leaned against the bedpost.

"Then don't threaten *her*," the second man said, his voice tight.

The first man sat up straighter and leaned on one padded arm of the chair, looking across at the bed. "You know," he said, "at first I thought you were trying to protect her because of her work. But that's changed, hasn't it? You're falling in love with her." There was a faint, unpleasant sneer to his voice.

The other man didn't answer at first; instead, he restlessly began to prowl the space by the bed. "If I am or if I'm not, it doesn't matter," he murmured, ignoring or avoiding the challenge in the first man's tone. "She must be allowed to continue with her research, whatever it reveals."

The first man turned away, looking into the heat of the fire. "Sometimes I think you're right—maybe it would be better if the truth came out and everyone knew our secrets."

The second man seized on the words—but cautiously. "Perhaps."

Flames found a pocket of sap in a log, and hissed. The man watching the fire said, "Just keep in mind what that would do to the family…and to you."

"And to you."

"But I'm not the one falling in love with her." The first man's face twitched. "I don't have that luxury."

Chapter Ten

"Dammit," Rachael said out loud, but she sounded more amused than angry. "Well, this just bites it. The woman had to write her diary in damn *Gaelic*."

It made sense, in a way. Emilie had been Scotland born-and-bred, and had probably grown up bilingual. Either she was more comfortable writing in her native tongue, or she'd done it to keep prying eyes from knowing what she wrote.

The ploy, unfortunately, worked all too well. Forty years later, Emilie's secrets were still safe from everyone, including Rachael.

Rachael gently closed the book, trying not to flake off more ecru page corners. One hand splayed across the wine-colored cover, she looked down at the book on her lap. If she couldn't read the secrets within, maybe she could learn them another way.

She could, but not right now. Now, she felt tired; no, not just tired—bone-fatigued, mind-wearied. She closed her eyes, listened to the unintelligible whispers of the fire. She'd learned so much today—and so much of it raised more questions. Especially about Jordan. Particularly about Jordan. And between her overwrought emotions, the break-in and the crème de menthe, she was in no shape to psychically delve into the journal's past. That could wait until tomorrow.

Standing, Rachael ensured the screen in front of the fireplace was firmly set, so that no sparks could arc free from the fire. She held the diary in her hands again, considering. Without knowing why, she felt a strong need to store the volume in a safe place for the night. Perhaps it was because her research in the library had been tampered with; but the need was stronger than caution, bordering on urgency. She scanned the room, gauging. The most secure place would be close to her.

Pulling a scarf from her suitcase, Rachael gently wrapped the book, then slid it between the mattress and box spring of her bed. If someone tried to get at it, she'd know immediately.

If that someone were Jordan, would she know? The thought struck her after she'd slid, shivering contentedly, under the heavy soft covers.

What would Jordan want with the diary, anyway? Wouldn't he already know what was in it? another part of her mind argued, and before the two sides could finish battling out the problem, she slipped into sleep.

*

Celeste's prediction about the weather had proved correct: Come morning, Rachael's window was etched with frost, and the ground was similarly fairy-laced. As she reached the end of the driveway, she had already slowed her run; a proper cool-down was essential now. She took a deep breath, let it out. Through the mist of her breath, the manor seemed fog-enshrouded, looming from a misty highland moor.

As the cloud dissipated, she focused on the left-hand tower, the one across from Felicity's studio. Pale morning sunlight glinted off the windows, making it impossible to see inside. White-dusted grass crunched beneath her running shoes as she crossed the front lawn at a brisk walk.

She wondered if the tower was used as another workroom, or storage, or whether it was open to guests. Karyn hadn't mentioned it on the one brief tour they'd taken; but then, they'd gone through less than half of the manor. She made a mental note to ask someone about the other tower; and then, as she ascended the front steps, her mind returned to the thoughts that had been with her since she awoke: the journal.

*

Concern for the safety of Manor MacPherson and its guests had prodded Celeste into calling the police, despite Ian's objections. The two state troopers from Ray Brook arrived in an unmarked car in deference to her wish for discretion. Rachael, forewarned, met them in her room.

"Do you know of anyone who isn't happy with your research?" Trooper Parker enquired. Although his tone was even, he seemed to be upset, probably because his forehead bore a perpetual crease, a double set of vertical lines furrowing down to his brows. In contrast to their bushiness, his hair was thinning and swept ineffectually across the top of his head.

A dead guy, Rachael answered mentally. Aloud, she said, "I can't think of anyone. It's not like I'm doing investigative reporting or writing for the *National Enquirer*—I'm just chronicling the family history."

"Skeletons in the closet?"

More like ghosts in the music room. "You'd have to ask Celeste about that," Rachael said diplomatically. "The family history includes the tragedy forty years ago, but most people already know about that. The point is, this is a history for the family, not for mass publication."

"So you're saying the perpetrator isn't someone outside the family?"

She fought back a smile at his officious use of jargon. "I'm saying I don't know of anyone outside the family who would care so much about this, or even know about it."

He nodded, a noise of assent rising from his throat, and made a notation in a small notebook. Across the room, Trooper Stefanick dusted for prints, even though Rachael had said it was probably a futile task. His lank hair, so blond it was nearly white, bore the indentation from his hat. He didn't look up during their conversation, but Rachael suspected he heard and mentally noted every word.

"Is your computer able to get Internet through the—what's it called?" Parker said.

"Wireless," Stefanick said without pausing in his work.

"Wireless," Parker repeated. "Maybe this could be the work of a random hacker."

"I'm running a system-level firewall," Rachael said. "I checked, and there's nothing unusual in the system logs."

"Virus?" Stefanick suggested, flicking at the white powder with a small brush.

"I've got a good anti-virus program—plus, hey, it's a Mac," she said.

Parker grunted again, apparently realized he was being rude, and mustered a half-smile before moving to test the door lock. Rachael, feeling dismissed, sat on the window seat to stay out of the way and watched the troopers complete their investigation. Stefanick's efforts had produced only one complete, usable print, and chances were high that is was her own.

"If anything else strange happens to your computer, or if you discover anything missing from the room, have Mrs. Jenner give us a call," Parker said. Stefanick shook her hand, and then they were gone.

*

Celeste turned the tarnished box over in her carefully manicured hands. She glanced up at Rachael. "You found this in the cemetery?"

Rachael refrained from repeating her diatribe about the gardener who obviously wasn't doing his job. In fact, she knew that Celeste's question was rhetorical—she'd thoroughly described the situation and answered Celeste's numerous questions.

"It was a fluke," she said. "I'd never have found it if I hadn't accidentally pushed over the broken gravestone." What she purposefully failed to mention was her vision and sketch, and her discussion with Jordan. Would she have noticed the box otherwise?

She didn't know. As it was, she was achingly aware of the fact that her power had done nothing other than confirm what Jordan had said: that Emilie sat on the convenient branch and wrote in her diary. Rachael's vision hadn't done anything to help her find the book.

A knock; the door opened before Celeste could say anything. Ian stood in the office doorway, his slightly hunched shoulders tensed, his face flushed. He looked at Rachael.

"You have something of my mother's, the message said."

Wordlessly, Celeste held out the box. He shut the door and sank into a chair next to Rachael. Reverently, he accepted the coffer from his cousin's outstretched hands.

For a moment, he simply held it, gazing at the inscription. Then he set it on Celeste's slate-topped desk and opened the top.

"It's in Gaelic," Rachael supplied at his questioning look, after he opened the journal and attempted to read the lettering within. "I can't read it, but I know someone who could translate it. With your permission, of course," she added, looking at Celeste. Despite Ian's overtures of help, she felt safer dealing with Celeste.

Celeste, she somehow guessed, wasn't hiding her motives; she simply wanted the mystery solved. Ian, on the other hand...Rachael wasn't sure what Ian wanted. Or, she realized with a spiked prick of guilt, what Jordan wanted.

Except that he wanted her. Something fluttered, deep inside her, at that thought. She forced herself back to what Celeste was saying.

"...you know someone who can translate this?"

Rachael explained that she had a colleague—and friend—in England who spoke Gaelic fluently and often did translation work. It would take some time, of course, to mail him the diary and for him to do the work, but she certainly thought it was worth the effort. Celeste agreed. Ian was more hesitant.

"I don't think it's safe to send the book off like that," he said. "What about copying somehow?"

"Photocopying might damage it, and hand-copying would take an awfully long time," Rachael said. "And a great deal could be mis-copied and lost that way. Colin—Dr. Pryke—is an expert in preserving antique books, too," she added meaningfully. "Top of his field."

Ian still frowned. "You trust this man?"

Rachael nodded.

His gloved hand clenched, almost possessively, around the leather-bound book.

"Rachael's suggestion sounds more than reasonable to me, Ian," Celeste said. Rachael wondered if the older woman would also bring up the fact that she had chartered this family research, so she should have the final say in the matter. Celeste didn't strike Rachael as the type to use such an argument, but, on the other hand, Celeste felt very strongly about Rachael's work going smoothly.

Ian stared at the book, then abruptly looked up at Rachael.

"How long have you had this?" he demanded.

Suddenly, concealing her discovery overnight no longer seemed like the good idea it had the night before, and she felt guilty.

"I found the box in the cemetery yesterday, just before dinner, and didn't have a chance to open it until afterwards," she explained.

"Rachael says the cemetery hasn't been tended to properly in years," Celeste told Ian. "We'll have to have a talk with George."

He wasn't listening to her.

"I wasn't even sure if the box contained anything, so I saw no need to raise a fuss until I'd looked at it carefully," Rachael continued. "And then I forgot all about it in the confusion when my computer files were trashed. I finally remembered it after everyone had left my room, and told Celeste first thing this morning, after the police left."

He humphed, looking at her oddly, almost suspiciously.

"I understand it's important to you, being something of your mother's," Rachael said in a rush. "It must have been hard for you to lose her so young, not have much to remember her by."

A dark red flush crept up from the carefully knotted tie at his collar, making his scars stand out, white and vulnerable.

"My mother," he began, and then stopped, obviously fighting for control. "My mother was a weak, ineffectual woman who hid herself away and had no idea what it meant to make a mark in this world." While more subdued, his voice still held the hint of a snarl. "My father was the one who taught me what I needed to know to survive."

Stunned at his outburst, Rachael could do nothing more than stare at him. But he was through with her. To Celeste, he said, "I'm not pleased with the idea, but if you think it's for the best, I'll go along with your wishes." Then he rose and left the office, closing the door not very gently behind him.

"Oh, dear," Celeste murmured, gazing at the door, her green eyes troubled.

"I'm sorry I upset him," Rachael said, more guilty, but also confused. Not only was she taken aback by his carefully restrained hostility, but the look he had given her before his diatribe bothered her, and she didn't know quite why, didn't know how to interpret the stare. "I did what I thought was best."

"No, no, you did the right thing," Celeste said firmly, smiling quickly at her. "It's the journal's very existence that bothers him, I think. He doesn't remember much of his mother. Please make sure the book comes back in one piece—I know that is very, very important to him."

*

Karyn waved when Rachael entered the office, the phone receiver wedged between her ear and shoulder. She scribbled something in the margin of an already full sheet of paper, and hung up.

"How are you doing?" she asked, clipping her earring back on. The gold dolphin matched the tiny blue ones frolicking on her white turtleneck. "Celeste told me about what happened last night—it's horrifying. I can't believe someone broke into your room." She shuddered. "Someone smashed my car window in college and stole my stereo, and I felt violated. It took me forever to feel safe again."

"I'm more confused than anything else," Rachael assured her. "I don't understand why someone would do it. But I do daily backups, so no permanent damage was done."

"Well, if you need to talk about it, just let me know," Karyn said. "Now, to what do I owe this visit?"

"I have a package to mail overseas," Rachael said, and explained what had happened. Karyn's pale-lashed hazel eyes widened at her tale of finding the diary in the graveyard.

"I always thought there might be treasure hidden in these walls," she said, grinning.

"The diary's not worth much, except to the family," Rachael said. "It could be a great help to my research, though—once Colin gets through it."

"I'll be going to the Post Office around four or so today. Just drop it off—there's usually a stack of packages and letters to go out sitting there." Karyn pointed a pencil at the chair by the door on which Rachael sat. "Now, I have a request for you: Will you come to dinner tonight? As a little thank-you for saving Brett."

Rachael started to demur, but Karyn cut her off. "No, I insist—*Brett* insists. He's been bugging me to have you over. It won't be anything fancy like you get here, mind you. I was planning on spaghetti, if that tells you anything."

"Sometimes we need a break from 'fancy,'" Rachael said, cheerfully relenting.

"Great! Brett will be thrilled—and to be honest, so am I. I'm in serious need of some 'girl talk.' I should be back from town by five; we can leave after that, if that's okay. I'll let Celeste know you won't be at dinner tonight."

*

Rachael tucked her legs beneath her and considered the leather-bound volume cradled in her lap. She felt somehow hesitant to learn its past. Would she get any information she could use? Or would it be like yesterday afternoon at the cemetery: nothing helpful, nothing new?

No. She had to be positive, or she'd find nothing. She'd learned long ago that her power wouldn't work well if it were forced, or if she were emotionally overwrought. Worrying would only make things worse.

Closing her eyes, she breathed in deeply. The odor of moldy leather and age-browned pages filled her senses. The book hadn't always smelled like that. When Emilie had first obtained it, it had probably been new, with a fresh, pungent leather tang and crisp white pages that snapped back and forth instead of crumbling....

Again, the image in the graveyard: a tear hanging bright on Emilie's cheek as she replaced the diary in the tree trunk. No, Rachael urged: deeper, more....

Clutching the journal against her breast, as if protecting it from a rainstorm, Emilie crossed the main hall, her feet moving swiftly over the polished wooden floor. She reluctantly moved one hand from the book to the handle of the western tower. Rachael could almost feel the woman's relief at reaching her place of sanctuary.

Then a large hand clamped around her wrist.

Emilie gasped and turned, pain evident on her face from the tight grip the man had on her delicate, small-boned arm. The man towered over Emilie, his eyes dark and angry.

"Where have you been?" he demanded, harsh-voiced.

Emilie shrank back—as far as she could in his grasp—unable to hide the book any more than with her other hand. Rachael smelled her fear, wished she could help, knew she couldn't.

"Well?" The man shook her arm, and Emilie's whole body shuddered from the action. Her fingers loosened, but she managed to catch the diary before it fell.

"What's this?" The man's pale brows rose. He reached toward the book. Emilie tried to twist away from him, but her pained cry told of his cruelly tightened fingers on her wrist.

"Shane."

Everyone turned. In the doorway of the parlor, Jordan leaned easily against the wall, arms folded over his chest. But despite his casual pose, his carriage was tense, and his green eyes spoke volumes.

"Could I speak with you, please?" Jordan asked levelly. His eyes flicked briefly, meaningfully, to where Shane's hand dug into Emilie's arm.

Shane's face twisted with rage, but he let go of Emilie. Or, rather, he flung her arm away, and she stumbled backwards. Shane turned toward Jordan, but Emilie ignored them, yanking open the tower door. Thankfully free, the woman didn't dare look backward; she plunged into the stairwell, pulling the door behind her. And then—

Darkness. Not the darkness that would have enveloped the unlit spiral staircase, but a darkness that barred Rachael's vision. Something, something in the tower prevented her from seeing anything, prevented her power from working....

With a gasp, Rachael pulled herself from the trancelike state. The warmth of the room—the heat in the manor had finally kicked in, it seemed—caused sweat to trickle down her back, but over and above that she shuddered with a chill no thermostat could dispel. She pulled her hands from the book, clasped them together.

What was it about the tower that prevented her from seeing? She'd felt nothing untoward in the eastern tower, when she visited Felicity. But something in the western tower blocked her power—and she had never encountered anything like it before.

So...that was Shane. She shivered again. That he was nothing like Jordan was her first thought. "Shane had a temper," Celeste had said, but that seemed to be an understatement. Emilie had been terrified of him, and although Jordan had stopped him from harming her or snatching the journal, Rachael couldn't know what then took place between the two men.

At least her vision had given her new information; relief coursed through her. But what did it all mean? In essence, all she had was more questions. What was Shane and Emilie's marriage really like? Why was Jordan so quick to champion Emilie—was that all that Shane was angry about? And why couldn't Rachael see anything in the tower?

She wanted to try again, but her first effort had tired her, especially because of the exertion of trying to mentally see in the tower. She could try again after Colin returned the book; his translation would probably provide even more important, concrete information. Reluctantly, she put the diary down, and dialed England.

Colin, fascinated by her current project, enthusiastically agreed to translate the journal. Because of his eagerness, she also asked him if he could find any information on Birney MacPherson previous to his move to America—perhaps a reason for his decision to relocate—and anything on Emilie's early life.

"And what do I get in return?" Colin asked, the warm humor in his voice cutting through the transcontinental line.

"A case of M&Ms?" Rachael suggested, remembering how much he preferred them to Smarties, the British version of the candy.

"Splendid! You are such a dear. And I shall send you a case of Cadbury Crunchies."

"Wait," Rachael protested, laughing. "Now I'm owing you again. I'm running out of things to give you."

"How about your undying passion?" Colin suggested cheerily.

"You already have that, crazy man."

"Then I have everything I ever wanted," he said, his voice pitched dramatically. "Very well then, love, I shall keep watch for your package, and see if I can't dig up something on your MacPhersons. Ta."

Still smiling, Rachael packed the journal securely in a well-padded box, sealed it up, printed the address clearly on the top, and took it downstairs. Karyn wasn't at her desk, but Rachael spotted the promised pile of letters and small packages on the wooden chair inside her door. She set the wrapped diary on the chair, along with a note asking her to send the package registered with the maximum amount of insurance, and headed back to her room to start on her work for the day.

*

"I thought you lived pretty close to the manor," Rachael commented, slipping into the passenger seat of Karyn's grey four-wheel-drive Subaru.

"I do. I brought the car to run those errands today," Karyn explained as she let off the emergency brake and started around the oval part of the driveway. "Usually I walk. It's only about a half mile, and I like the exercise."

They arrived at Karyn's cottage a few minutes later. Brett, already home from the friend's house where he stayed after school, ran out to greet them, a wilted bouquet for Rachael gripped in his fist. Since most of the native flowers didn't grow in the fall, the arrangement mostly consisted of tall brown grass and a few hearty weeds. Rachael thanked him profusely anyway, and Karyn found a jar for her to set them in.

Karyn changed into a comfortable pair of jeans, and while she defrosted a container of spaghetti sauce left over from the last batch she'd cooked, Rachael shredded lettuce and chopped vegetables for a salad.

The small cottage reminded Rachael in many ways of her childhood home, with the sort of organized chaos only a household with children could create. Karyn's decorating taste ran toward country, with accents of delft blue and white. She'd chosen practical furniture, and seemed uncaring that the blond-wood dining table was scratched and scarred and bore faint crayon illustrations. The artist's later work, now created with paint and paper, adorned the refrigerator, and the *Star Wars* theme was carried on in the stack of DVDs beneath the television.

After dinner, Brett cleared the table and then, tiring of the "grown-up's" conversation, asked to be excused.

"He's a good kid," Rachael commented, cradling a mug of coffee in her hands and watching as he raced out of the room.

Karyn smiled fondly, freckled nose crinkling. "Yeah, I think I did a pretty good job with him, considering," she said, her voice betraying her pride.

"Being a single mother must be rough," Rachael said, and then, realizing how that must have sounded, "I didn't mean—"

"You're not prying," Karyn assured her. "It's not something I keep secret." She propped her dock-shoe clad feet on the coffee table. "Brett's father and I dated when we both were at Cornell. I was getting my Master's in Hotel Management when I found out I was pregnant. He couldn't deal with it, and left. I graduated, had Brett, and took a job at a big hotel in New York City. I hated it. It was a high-pressure job, and with a new baby…it was too much. This job was a godsend. Celeste is wonderful about giving me time off when I need to be with Brett—and, in turn, she knows I'm happy here, and not going to run off to some better-paying, more exciting job. Plus, I have some cousins who'd moved to Lake Placid, so I didn't feel totally alone moving here."

"This does seem like an ideal situation for you," Rachael agreed, assuming Karyn didn't expect or need her to comment on the unplanned pregnancy. She had been wondering why Karyn had invited her, but now she realized that the other woman really did need female companionship. "You must get to meet some interesting people, too—like Mildred and Earl."

Karyn hooted, rolling her eyes. "Mildred! What a loon! They're staying for the All Hallows Eve Ball, did I tell you?"

"What have the ad guys been up to? I haven't seen them around lately."

"Goodness, they left days ago."

"They did?" Rachael paused in the act of setting her mug, which said "World's Best Mom" in rainbow colors, on the table. "I thought they were staying another week."

Karyn shook her head, the ends of her blunt-cut hair swinging back and forth. "They didn't get the authorization they were hoping for. Just between you and me," she said in a mock-conspiratorial whisper, "I think it was because they weren't getting a whole lot done while they were here! But anyway, they left…Sunday morning, I think. Yep, that's when it was."

Rachael accepted Karyn's offer of another cup of coffee and some homemade banana bread, and they settled down to chat some more.

"Ten thirty!" she exclaimed a while later, looking at her watch. "I'd better be getting back."

"I'll drive you," Karyn said, getting up.

"That's okay—I don't mind walking," Rachael said hastily, seeing her glance at Brett's bedroom door. The boy had gone to bed over an hour earlier. "You shouldn't leave Brett alone. Besides, it's a lovely night out."

Karyn loaned her a heavy-duty flashlight and pointed her on the path that led through the manor grounds. "If you go up to the chapel and cut through, you shouldn't get lost, since you've been there before," she said. "See you tomorrow."

Rachael waved goodnight and headed into the dark night, zipping up her leather jacket against the chill. The moon curved only quarter-full, but the stars glittered brightly, crystal on a jet sky. Her feet crunched across the brittle grass; otherwise, only silence. The flashlight's beam pooled pale golden on the ground before her. Darkness milled restlessly at the edges of the light, waiting for any chance to slip past the barrier.

A beautiful night. Romantic. The kind of night that two people should take advantage of, hands clasped together for warmth as they walked....

With a start, Rachael realized she hadn't thought about Jordan in hours. Oddly, the awareness made her feel suddenly lonely. She felt as though she hadn't seen him in weeks, and yet, they had last spoken the night before, in her room, and the day before that, at the cemetery. She remembered with surprising clarity the way his dark hair curled over the collar of his white shirt as he'd sat on the branch, commenting about Emilie and the diary. She'd been angry at his intrusion. Now, she almost wished for it, for his company. Despite...

Despite the fact that he may have been a murderer, and might be trying to harm her.

Rachael shook her head. She couldn't believe he had been responsible for any wrongdoing, past or present. She knew this belief wasn't anchored in fact or in intellect, but in emotion. A gut feeling, an instinct—nothing more.

The last thing she needed was instinct. Instinct had always helped her in the past—but in her work. This had gone beyond a job, beyond being hired to chronicle the MacPherson genealogy. Even if Celeste hadn't asked her to try to find the answer to what had happened on Halloween Night, 1953, she would have sought the answer herself. She wanted to know. She wanted to prove that Jordan was innocent.

And instinct only clouded her judgment now, because of her feelings for him.

Something caught suddenly in the flashlight's beacon, large and Cimmerian and yet somehow glimmering. The pond, she realized with a shaky release of breath. She stepped forward and peered at the inky liquid where it met the shore, unmoving and silent. The waterfowl had gone to wherever they rested at night.

Rachael thought that was an excellent idea. She wanted to be back in her room, fire flickering low, quilts piled high. The chill seeped beneath her jacket; she held the flashlight in benumbed fingers. With that thought, she turned and headed down the path through the trees.

And then she heard it. A soft rustle, just like the rustle of her own feet as she walked. She turned, swept the flashlight in an arc across the area behind her. Nothing. But she knew, with a prickle of angry fear, that someone was back there. No one spoke. If it had been Karyn, she would have said something, called out. This person didn't want to be heard.

Rachael resolutely began walking again, her stride confident and purposeful. Then, abruptly, she stopped. As she suspected, the steps behind her stopped, too.

The beam played over a low building; she recognized the dog run. She wasn't too far from the house now. As she started walking again, her stride still swift, she snapped off the flashlight so her pursuer couldn't see her. In response, the steps behind her quickened. She broke into a trot. Her toe caught against an exposed root, and she stumbled, almost falling. She didn't dare run any faster, unable to see the rough trail.

Sensing something near, she flicked the flashlight on for a hairsbreadth second, and saw that she had veered and nearly crashed into a tree. In the instant the light was on, she picked out the path ahead, then flicked the light back off, continuing as swiftly as she dared. Shouldn't she be able to see the lights of the manor soon? Should she turn and confront her pursuer? The element of surprise would be in her favor, and the heavy flashlight was a decent weapon....

No noise, but then someone grabbed her, not from behind, but from the side. The flashlight flew from her unfeeling fingers as someone dragged her into a copse of trees, one hand clamped over her mouth.

Chapter Eleven

Rachael twisted frantically in her attacker's embrace, trying to open her mouth enough to bite the hand pinned across it.

"Ssssh." Warm hiss in her ear. "Be still. Wait for him to pass."

She knew that voice, surprised to recognize it so quickly because she hadn't known it long. And she knew the feel of that long-fingered hand from an intimate caress....

She stopped struggling, and leaned back against his chest, trying not to gasp aloud. Heavy breath scraped her lungs. Quick footsteps sounded by them, slowed; then a soft curse. A point of light appeared as her pursuer finally relented and turned on his flashlight. The light swept around, but didn't penetrate the thick web of pine needles. After a moment, and another curse, the steps continued away, toward the manor. Jordan had removed his hand from her mouth, and now his fingers lay against her neck, not cold and not warm, almost dipping beneath the collar of her jacket.

Her eyes began to adjust to the dark; her heart, to a normal rhythm instead of pounding painfully in her chest. The pines grew in a neat circle, and a bench ringed just inside of them, breaking only at the entrance where he'd pulled her in.

"Who...?" she asked, her voice no louder than a breath.

He shook his head. She could see his eyes, darkened with concern. "I don't know. Are you all right?"

"I...yes, I think so." A faint, bruised ache in her upper arms where he'd grabbed her; otherwise, her breathing had steadied. The cold air bit her dry lips, and she swiped a tongue across them. "Just frightened."

"You're safe now," Jordan said, and she believed him. "I could go, try to find out who—"

"No." Her voice was sharper than she expected, the pitch higher. "Please stay," she added quietly. She needed him there, needed his comforting presence, his reassuring proximity.

"Are you sure?" His hands flexed on her arms, as if ready to release her if she made a move to bolt. "Last night, you said you didn't want to see me unless I was ready to tell you the truth. You made it extremely clear that you don't trust me."

"Yes...that's true," she admitted slowly. "But you couldn't be out there with a flashlight and in here holding me at the same time."

"I could be in cahoots with the person who was following you," he pointed out reasonably.

"I doubt it." She looked up at him. The moonlight hollowed his proud cheekbones. "You don't strike me as the type."

"Where does that leave us?"

Rachael shook her head, uncertain. "I know you weren't chasing me just now, so someone else is involved. In which case, he's probably the one who broke into my room." She paused. "Do you know who he is?'

"No, I don't." Jordan stared unseeing into the trees. "It's not...who I initially suspected, anyway. I don't know who was following you."

"Well." She leaned closer to him again. "I'm still not happy with what you're holding back, but right now, I just need you to stay with me."

He stepped backward, leading her down onto the smooth wooden bench, his arms still around her. With kiss-light fingers, he brushed the hair at her temple. The silent still of night descended around them again, bringing with it a sense of timelessness. Through the whispery-needled branches, she could see the slender pale moon pricking at the sky, leaving a trail of stars.

Her alarmed trembling ceased, and in its place, surprisingly, she didn't shiver with cold. Though Jordan didn't seem to radiate body heat, his solid form pressed her own warmth back against her. Without thinking, she slid her numb hands beneath his arms, up his sides.

His fingers stilled their movement, and he pulled away from her slightly, looking down at her. She murmured a protest at his leaving, and when she tugged him back and rested her head against his shoulder, he bent to kiss her.

The kiss was gentle at first, as though he still tried to comfort her. But they both needed more, and their lips quickly grew more urgent, more desperate. The hand at her brow slipped behind her head, urging her closer; the arm around her crushed her against his lean body. Her own hands snaked around to his back, molding to his shoulder blades.

His teeth rasped against her lower lip, his tongue following to instantly soothe the sensitive flesh. Pleasure pulsed through her at the savage-soft intrusion. Then his lips left hers, to trail along her cheekbone, down her jaw. She arched her neck in invitation. His tongue slipped into the tender hollow behind her ear, and then his teeth nipped at the tendon on her neck. She moaned softly, his name, then inarticulate, surprised that the desperate sound came from her own throat. Surprised at the intensity of her response.

Turning her head, Rachael sought out Jordan's mouth again, and brought her hands around between them. She plucked at the top buttons of his shirt, then skimmed her hands inside, brushing against the dusting of hair on his chest. Her fingernail grazed the sensitive nub of his nipple, and he gasped. The sound sent a thrill of desire through her. She pressed her lips to the pulsing spot on his throat, flicking against it with her tongue.

Somehow her jacket had gotten unzipped. The skin on her belly prickled with gooseflesh as he slid his hands up beneath her sweater. His fingers splayed out, teasing the bare skin just below her bra. Rachael shivered, not from cold but from the erotic sensations his touch evoked. At his urging—or just from her own?—she leaned back, back until she lay on the narrow bench, pulling him down with her. His thighs pressed against hers, muscles flexing as they both squirmed slightly to shape against each other. She felt the hardness of his arousal pressing against her hip, too, and she moved her hands restlessly up and down his back until they dipped low enough to cup his buttocks.

Then, above the soft moans and gasps of desire they both made, she heard a voice calling her name. Not Jordan; no, this came from farther away. Rachael tried to ignore the sound at first, concentrating on the feel of Jordan: his lips and tongue, his hands, his body. But then his head raised from hers, and he stared into the darkness, tense, like a wolf casting for the source of an unfamiliar, possibly threatening scent.

Rachael started to question, but even as he shook his head to warn her to silence, she recognized the voice.

"They've come looking for me," she whispered. He sat up, helping her to her feet, tugging her sweater down. She shivered with regret, her hands shaking from passion as she tried once, twice, again finally to zip her jacket.

Jordan caressed her shoulders, then pulled her hard against him. He kissed her softly, as when they'd begun, and she felt the restraint in his hands and mouth. Then she held nothing, as he faded away.

The bobbing glow of flashlights approached as she stepped from the copse.

"I'm okay! I'm right here!" she called. A light glanced up, blinding her, and she raised a hand to shield her eyes. George Rabideau lowered his flashlight to point at the ground again.

"Rachael, thank goodness," Celeste said, tucking her own flashlight under her arm as she came forward. "Karyn called to tell you that you'd dropped your wallet out of your purse at her house, and she was worried when I said you hadn't arrived back yet."

"I dropped my flashlight, and it went out," Rachael lied quickly. George's beam swiftly picked out the glint of metal where it lay in a tangle of exposed roots, and she picked it up. "I was feeling around for it; I'm glad you showed up."

"I'm just thankful you're all right," Celeste said. "My goodness. First you nearly drowned, then you nearly fell off the library walk, and now—"

"Now, nothing happened," Rachael said firmly. "Except that I'm terribly cold."

"Of course. Let's get you back to the house."

She was glad when the flashlights' glow illuminated the way to the manor, no longer pointing at her. Her lips felt swollen and bruised; no doubt her eyes looked passion-drugged as well.

Rachael wondered why she had made the hasty, split-second decision not to tell Celeste about the person who had chased her. If someone were prowling about, trespassing on manor grounds, Celeste and Ian should be informed. But somehow, Rachael felt hesitant to say anything. Like Celeste had said, it seemed as though she was going from one mishap to the next. The near-drowning hadn't been anyone's fault, but the broken catwalk...that was another story, and another thing she hadn't been willing to fully tell Celeste about.

Then again, how could she? The carpenter had apparently found no sign of tampering, and all Rachael had as proof was the warning of a man who had been dead for forty years. And how could she explain how she'd outwitted her shadowy pursuer?

She declined the offer of a hot drink and went straight to her room after they returned to the manor.

"Jordan?" she asked softly. No reply. Dropping her leather jacket on a chair, she held a match to the fresh pile of wood in the fireplace and watched as the flames flickered hesitantly to life.

A hot shower restored her body temperature to normal, although every time her mind wandered back to her pursuer, she shivered again. Though she spoke Jordan's name aloud several more times, he never answered, never appeared. Had he remained solid too long, and tired himself? She hoped he hadn't harmed himself, trying to protect her. Although "protection" wasn't the word for what he had done once they were alone. She smiled, lightly touching her fingers to her tender lips.

Thoughts like that weren't going to help her get to sleep, although she felt comforted by the fact that Jordan seemed to be watching over her. Still, she double-checked to make sure her door was locked, before she crawled into bed.

But thanks to the night's emotions, sleep eluded her. With a sigh, she turned the light back on and padded across the room for a splash of brandy. On her way back to bed, she picked up Journal of a Small Village Doctor, and snuggled back under the quilt-soft covers with book and glass.

Instead of inducing sleep with dry medical comments, the journal proved fascinating. The doctor had kept his diary mostly separate from his medical reports, instead using his cases as a springboard for musings on life and death, human interaction and psychology.

Today I set Teddy Bouchard's broken leg. This time he had been trying to move the hay bales in the barn and fell from the loft. Will the boy never learn what he's old enough to do and not? I suppose this is his way of spreading his wings and cutting from his mother's apron strings, but I do wish he would find less dangerous and painful ways of doing so.

Rachael chuckled, thinking that in this day and age, Teddy Bouchard would probably have ended up in therapy. She paged through more entries, but didn't find his name again. She learned of the drunken exploits of a past mayor, shared the loss of a beloved townswoman who died on her ninety-ninth birthday, and silently cheered the healing of various patients.

Finally feeling relaxed enough to attempt sleep again, she was about to put the book down when an entry caught her eye. What it said made her sit upright, shocked.

Although it is not my place to speak this aloud, I must say here that I fear Emilie MacPherson will not live out her natural years, yet I am helpless to intervene. I was called to the manor tonight to oversee the birth of her child—a child that, unfortunately, never took its first breath. I warned her that she may be too frail to bear more children, but I could tell she discounted my words. Still, perhaps her stubbornness will see her through the coming years. I would have asked her husband about the bruises on her, but he was not to be found. Imagine, a man not even in the house as his wife labors.

Rachael sought back in her memory. Unless she had confused her dates, the birth of the nameless child coincided with the marked-out entry in the family diary. How sad that someone had had the foresight to write it in, probably moments before the child died. Who had taken that task with Shane missing, uncaring? And who had so violently scratched it out?

With a frustrated sigh, Rachael shut off the light, and watched the fire's orange glow pulse on the walls until she finally fell asleep.

*

Rachael paused at the top of the stairs, looking over the railing at the silent hall. The heavy chandelier hung dark, and above her, stars glinted through the skylights above. Hearing nothing, she began down the steps, the filmy white nightdress swirling like heavy mist around her ankles.

Again? What was this with putting me in a damn fluffy nightgown? But the image persisted, the dream stubbornly keeping to its course.

She carried the many-tiered candelabrum again, as she had in her first dream.

Her bare feet made no sound on the smooth wood as she crossed the main hall. As if to echo the mist-like quality of her gown, she felt a faint, cool breath of air curling around her legs. The breeze seemed to be coming from her apparent destination: the western tower.

As she neared the door, she experienced the distinct, back-of-the-neck prickling sensation that someone stood behind her, watching her. She got a mental picture of her earlier vision, of Jordan casually slouched in the parlor doorway. She spun around. No one there. No one lurking anywhere, she determined after a visual sweep of the room, including the cross-balcony that connected the two staircases.

Still, the feeling persisted as she approached the tower door. She expected the door to open easily, but it resisted. Frowning, she wiggled the latch. It didn't feel locked; no, the knob turned easily, and she couldn't feel the tug of a bolt. Perhaps the wood was swollen with moisture? There was space between the door and the frame, no warping. She tugged again, bracing her feet on the cold floor. It felt as though someone—or something—pulled at the door from the other side. Placing her right hand on the door jamb, she grasped the handle again and jerked, hard. The door seemed to give, very slightly. She fortified her position again, yanked again. This time, the door did move. Bolstered by her success, she pulled again. Suddenly the door flew free, and she stumbled backwards from the unexpected movement.

Darkness billowed from the opening, thick and sooty, like the smoke from the cottage fire. Indeed, she found herself struggling to breathe beneath the surge of heavy blackness, coughing as she had when she inhaled the visionary smoke, lungs afire. With streaming eyes, she tried to peer through the cloying dark, and thought she made out the outline of the stairs spiraling up.

Blinking in a feeble attempt to ease her stinging eyes, Rachael tried to walk through the doorway, step inside the lower part of the mysterious tower.

And hit what felt like another, invisible, door.

Something, somehow, blocked her from entering. She felt the same sensation as when she had her vision, and tried to see inside the tower. The dark-smoke surged around her, pushing at her, around her, pressing down. Again, she tried to enter, and failed, flailing against the unseen barrier.

Then, someone grabbed her arm, tight fingers wrapping around her wrist.

Rachael turned, expecting the dream to follow the vision, expecting to see Shane.

But through the haze, she saw Jordan, and before she could read the tight expression in his eyes, she woke up.

Gasping, the sound loud in the silence of her room, she sat up, fumbling for the lamp switch.

With the light flooded reality, sweeping away the last tendrils of sleep and dream. She half-sat up, clasping a pillow as she tried to make rational sense of the dream.

She couldn't help but compare it to her earlier vision—she often dreamed like this after using her psychometry—and still felt the aftershocks of surprise at finding Jordan behind her. But, she reasoned, that could have been culled from their encounter this evening. And the phantasm darkness could simply be another image of the fire's smoke.

Why she had been blocked from entering the tower? The force, or barrier, that kept her out echoed the fact that she couldn't "see" inside when she held Emilie's diary.

Rachael sat up for a few more minutes, replaying the dream in her mind to see if there were any details she might have missed, anything that might answer questions or reveal clues to some of the mysteries she faced. Satisfied that there was nothing else, she turned off the light and buried herself back under the covers.

But sleep didn't come easily this time. Her mind relentlessly circled back around to the obstacle that kept her out of the tower, both mentally, and, in her dream, physically.

Punching the pillow into a more pleasingly fluffy state, she huffed down on it again, and closed her eyes. An image of Jordan flickered beneath her eyelids. The last time she'd dreamed so intensely, she'd woken to find him there. This time, he didn't appear. That fact made her feel lonely again, and yet unnerved by the look she'd glimpsed in his eyes. She tried to turn her thoughts to something else, but Jordan linked her back to the dream, and again she found herself wondering about the obstacle and his presence by the door.

Finally, decisively, she threw the covers back and got up. She wasn't going to be able to sleep until she satisfied her curiosity. She pulled a sweater and jeans over her pajamas, and slipped on a pair of heavy socks. Taking up Karyn's flashlight, she headed downstairs, ensuring the door to her room was securely locked behind her.

She reached the main hall, and instead of heading straight down the stairs, she paused by the railing, feeling a sense of déjà vu from her dream as she looked down on the darkened, silent space. When she began down the stairs, she could feel the cold whispering up her legs, although the house, shut tight, afforded entrance to no breezes. The spacious hall simply didn't respond to central heating the way smaller, enclosed rooms did.

The sensation of being watched also carried over from her dream, but a quick, sweeping glance told her that her imagination was on overdrive. She purposefully crossed the floor to the closed, almost forbidding tower door.

Locked. She could hear the bolt catch in the lock as she pulled. Nothing otherworldly held the door closed to her curiosity.

A curiosity that wasn't yet satisfied. There might be a bolt on the door now, but her psychic vision had apparently been blocked by something within the tower—something more than a conventional lock.

Her hand resting on the latch, Rachael considered what to do next. Going back upstairs to bed was a strong temptation. But still, curiosity nagged, tugged, demanded answers. She'd already used her power once today, and the day before as well. Her visions became less clear if she tired herself, forced herself to overuse the gift. Her lack of sleep tonight, plus her overwrought emotional state due to being followed, would further serve to dim her vision.

She was here. She might as well try.

Rachael set the flashlight on the floor, the beam creating a glow at her feet against the doorsill. Bowing her head and closing her eyes, she placed her hands, fingers splayed, on the polished wooden door, and waited for the visions to come.

Come they did, almost immediately, startling her with their powerfulness.

First, a recent image—she could tell by the fresh imprint in her mind. *A black-gloved hand, reaching for the door handle.*

She pulled back, brushed that vision away. Obviously Ian; too early. Back…back…

Then, what she had seen earlier: *Emilie, hand on latch, whirling to face an angry Shane, saved only by Jordan's timely (deliberate?) intervention.*

Then, suddenly—

Emilie stood before the door. Behind her, the hall froze in dark, empty secrecy. The warm glow from a lantern near her feet provided the only illumination. Next to the lantern lay a silver flask and a book, its black leather binding old and worn, white patches in evidence. But she did not need to consult the tome. This ritual she knew by heart, passed down to her by her mother and her mother's mother before her, and back through the ages to when this was practiced openly, not smothered in secrecy, not feared and hated and punished.

Murmuring the ancient words in a reverent voice deeper than her normal voice tone, Emilie raised her hand and sketched a design in the air a hairsbreadth from the wood of the door. Somehow, the movement left a blue trail, sudden, bright, and then gone, like the path of a shooting star. Energy thrummed and crackled, too low to be heard and yet still felt, deep inside. The current vibrated through Emilie as she drew the wards on the door. Protecting the tower from unwanted visitors, from prying eyes, from evil forces.

Rachael recognized the symbol Emilie etched, invisible, on the door.

*

Rachael rolled onto her stomach and pressed the pillow over her head, a vain attempt to stem the relentless throbbing in her temples. Through the pain, she tried to remember what she had drunk the night before that would give her such a hideous hangover.

No, she'd been at Karyn's; hadn't had any alcohol. The evening fast-forwarded through her mind: the walk home, the pursuer, Jordan, home, dream, door...

There. Her midnight excursion to the tower. A wave of agony crashed across her head. She had overused—no, abused—her power. Psychic hangover. Like a regular hangover, it was somehow unfairly easy to forget the pain when indulging. The next morning, however, was agonizingly similar.

Mentally backing up, she tried to retrace her steps back from the tower. Nothing. She had no memory of returning to her room, of shedding the outer layers of clothes, of crawling back into bed. She'd never experienced that before, that blacking out, like a psychic drunkenness. Or had she, and just didn't remember?

The fact that she couldn't remember drove her from the bed, moving relentlessly through the pain-haze to the door. Locked. At least she'd had the presence of mind to do that. She shuffled to the bathroom for a glass of water and some aspirin, then retreated to the bed again.

In her mind the boundaries blurred between the memory of the dream and the memory of going downstairs. Had that trip been a dream, too? No, it couldn't have been, or else she wouldn't be battling these buffeting waves of pain.

That left only one conclusion. She'd seen Emilie sketching a pentagram on the tower door.

Which meant Emilie was a witch.

*

Rachael rubbed the back of her neck and tried again to concentrate on the book in her lap. The incessant pounding had subsided to a dull throb, a band of pain squeezing around her forehead and temples, still making it hard to concentrate. She'd known there was no way to face the monotonously blinking cursor on the computer, but she was trying to be somewhat productive by doing basic research, reading the book on the history of maple-syrup production.

A thump at the door. Not a knock—no, this sound was heavier, and seemed closer to the floor. Rachael frowned, and set the book on the table next to the decanter of brandy, which had been refilled by a conscientious maid the day after Rachael and Jordan had drunk and talked.

Thump. She opened the door to find Felicity, cane tucked underneath one arm, holding a silver tea tray loaded with pot, cups, and an assortment of other containers.

"I brought something to make you better," she said sprightly, relinquishing the tray to Rachael. "Cook said you weren't feeling well and hadn't been down to eat."

"Cook?" Rachael set the tray on the desk.

Felicity pursed her lips. "Whoops, I mean…Nancy. One year Father kept firing the cooks, and I could never remember the name of each new one, so I took to calling them all Cook. Celeste calls it one of my quirks. She thinks I have many amusing quirks." As she spoke, she lifted up the lid of the teapot and began sprinkling in a variety of herbs from the containers.

"What exactly is that?" Rachael asked warily.

"Irish Breakfast tea, with a bit of help from me," Felicity said. "And, for medicinal purposes, lemon, honey and whiskey." After pouring the tea, she squeezed in juice from two lemon slices, splashed in some whiskey, and stirred with a spoon dolloped with honey.

"Pardon me for saying, but it sounds hideous," Rachael said.

Felicity tsked and handed her a cup. "It's good for you. Drink."

She sniffed, and found the mixture of scents pleasing. Still, she sipped cautiously; then her eyes widened in surprise as the flavors burst brightly on her tongue. Felicity hummed contentedly, smiling an "I told you so" smile.

Rachael felt her headache slowly receding, ebbing away like a painful tide. Felicity took a drink from her own cup and tilted her head to read the title of the book on the table.

"Ah yes, MacPherson Syrup Industries," she said. "I suppose I should put syrup instead of honey into the tea, but I always forget. Father never taught me much about the business—that was saved for Jordan, the ubiquitous male heir—but I do have some lovely sketches of the older sugaring buildings."

"I'd love to see those," Rachael said, feeling strength seeping back into her limbs and professional curiosity into her mind. "I have some more questions I'd like to ask you, too, when you're free."

"Well, dear, what about this?" Felicity set her cup on the tray with a dangerous jangle of silverware. "I'll be working in the greenhouse this afternoon. You drink up, and call Cook for some food. Then, trot on down to the greenhouse, and we'll chat. The air there will do you good."

*

Rachael somehow doubted the cloying, humid air would do her or her headache any good, so she was surprised when she stepped inside the bright, glass-roofed area and shut the door carefully behind her.

Her headache had almost completely subsided, thanks to Felicity's mystery tea concoction. By then it was nearly lunchtime, and she'd managed to swipe a few cucumber sandwiches from the buffet on the sideboard before the other guests came down to lunch.

Now, she breathed deeply, inhaling the sweet, warm flower scents. The fragrances brought back memories of visiting botanical gardens with her parents, of fascinated exploration of the exotic plants. She trailed a finger along the edges of a leaf, feeling the sparse fuzziness tickle her skin, and felt herself relaxing.

It took her several moments to find Felicity amongst the well-tended jungle, but she was loath to call out and break the tranquility. Instead, she wandered through the maze of terra cotta pots and wooden boxes, past rubber hoses and metal sprinklers, around the white storage bin of trowels and hoes. Felicity knelt on a small padded pillow, packing the dirt around a fresh seedling with gentle finger-pats. The row of already-planted seedlings attested to the work she'd done, and a flat wicker basket beside her held the rest of the frail tiny plants.

"Rachael, dear," she greeted, reaching for the next plant. "Feeling better?"

"You'd be surprised if I weren't," Rachael said with a smile. "Thank you for whatever it was you gave me."

"Family secret, but maybe I can be persuaded to divulge it someday." Felicity winked and set the last seedling in place. She rose slowly from her crouch, gestured for Rachael to follow.

Around another corner, to a table covered with an astonishing variety of greenery. Felicity said something that sounded like incomprehensible garble, but then Rachael realized she was giving the Latin names of the plants.

"In other words, herbs," the older woman said. She pinched off a small leaf and crushed it between her fingers. She sniffed, then held her hand out to Rachael.

"Spearmint!" Rachael said as the pungent odor filled her senses.

Felicity smiled contentedly. "Cook uses whatever fresh herbs we have, of course," she said, and then she was leading Rachael through the labyrinth to another part of the room. Here, they were surrounded by low shrubs bearing tiny urn-shaped buds of purple-pink, some shading to grey, some almost to blue, some nearly white.

"*Callurna vulgaris*," Felicity announced. "Heather Mountain's namesake.

> 'Thro' the rare red heather we dance together,
> (O love my Willie!) and smelt for flowers:
> I must mention again it was gorgeous weather,
> Rhymes are so scarce in this world of ours.'"

She smiled again. "C.S. Calverley," she said, settling down onto a scarred wooden stool by the shrubbery. Rachael had just enough time to pull out her recorder as Felicity launched into a definitive history of heather and its introduction to the Adirondacks by Birney MacPherson.

Rachael propped one hip up onto the low stone wall surrounding the heather patch, and listened in silent fascination to Felicity speak, watched as she brushed a patch of heather or lifted the evergreen leaves to illustrate a point.

"When he had time, Jordan would help me out here," she commented at one point. "He loved the flowers, the mountains—like a true MacPherson, he had loyalty to the land, just as he had loyalty to the family. He was quite a man of honor."

Those words again, Rachael thought: loyalty, honor. She was beginning to sense that herself, in his protection of her. And, yet, he was still protecting someone else—what would happen if those two things came into conflict?

Felicity deftly snapped a sprig free and handed it to her. Rachael caressed the soft buds, which seemed to glow from within, a bluish-pink hue. On a whim, she brushed it across her cheek, feeling the kiss of the velvety petals.

"Just there," Felicity said suddenly. Rachael jerked, her hand dropping. "No, no, hold it up like that. Don't move."

Rachael acquiesced in startled confusion, and watched as Felicity flipped open a large, flat canvas case that she'd earlier leaned against the wall. From it she pulled a portable easel and a large pad of drawing paper.

"Felicity, I—"

A brief, determined glance up from Felicity, and Rachael's protest trickled back down her throat. The artist deftly set up the easel and scraped the stool across the dirt floor. "Now," she said, a pencil poised in her long fingers, "without moving too much, tell me what it was you wanted to ask me."

Rachael had nearly forgotten that she was the one who'd arranged this meeting so she could ask Felicity some questions. For a moment, she couldn't even remember what they were.

"What did Emilie use the other tower for?" she blurted.

Felicity's hand stilled, and she peered around the canvas with curious green eyes. "Now, how did you know about that?" she asked.

Damn. There was no way she could know: She'd learned that through her visions. Between them and everything Jordan had told her, she had a lot of information…little of which could actually be used when she sat down to write the family history.

"I saw it mentioned in the diary," she improvised quickly, hating to lie. "'Tower' is one of the few Gaelic words I can recognize. I assumed she meant the left tower, because you're in the right one."

Felicity nodded, apparently mollified by the explanation, and went back to sketching. "When Letitia and I were girls, we each claimed one of the towers as our own," she said fondly. "Two princesses in twin towers. I eventually turned mine into my studio, my garret-away-from-Paris. Letitia used hers as a studio, too—she was an actress and singer, you know. Oh, she was a wonderful singer…such a lovely voice. She used to just hop up on any stage in New York and start singing. There was one time…"

Felicity's voice took on a dreamy quality as she revisited the tale "…we snuck out of here one night, after the All Hallows Eve Ball. We still had our costumes on. Felicity wore a blue beaded gown; I remember she sewed those beads on for months before the ball. We caught the night train to the city, and the next night we found some party that was going on, some club that was open. She didn't even ask the band for permission; she just sashayed herself up on stage and started singing. The whole room fell silent…."

She softly hummed a slow jazz tune, swaying slightly as her pencil dipped and darted across the paper like a seabird over a calm ocean. Barely moving, Rachael glanced down to make sure the recorder was still on. They'd gotten off the subject of Emilie, but tales of Letitia were integral to the book, even if they didn't bring answers to the specific quest Celeste had sent Rachael on.

However, Felicity somehow apparently sensed what Rachael was thinking, for she seemed to awake from the past.

"But I'm not answering your questions about Emilie," she said. "Letitia turned the tower over to her after she arrived, since she really hadn't used it much after Celeste was born. Too much running up and down the stairs, she said. So she and Jordan would fight over the music room. Truth to tell, I don't know what Emilie did up in that tower. She was a very private person; didn't talk much, very quiet."

"That's pretty much what everyone has said," Rachael commented.

"She came from a small town in the highlands, and most people in small towns kept to themselves, and to their traditions. Emilie was a very traditional girl, still faithful to the old traditions, beliefs, religion. I don't think she was very happy to be away from her family. Anyway, she fiercely guarded her privacy in that tower—never let anyone else up there."

Rachael envisioned the two towers. "Could you see across into it from your studio?"

"There are windows that face each other, but Emilie kept the windows curtained—she liked the room dark. Tilt your head a little to the left, dear. That's it." Felicity regarded her for a moment with an artist's detailed stare. An odd smile flickered across her lips, then she turned her attention back to the sketch pad.

Just then, Rachael felt something on her shoulder. Not a hand resting there, not exactly. No more pressure than the delicate breath-caress of heather against her cheek. She looked up, then glanced quickly back at Felicity. But the woman was intent on her work, humming softly again.

She hadn't seen Jordan, one hand resting protectively, possessively, on Rachael's shoulder, smiling down on her.

Chapter Twelve

The talk at dinner that night centered on the upcoming All Hallows Eve Ball. Rachael was surprised that the event was approaching so swiftly. She hadn't expected to spend so much time doing research at Manor MacPherson—then again, she hadn't expected to be asked to solve a decades-old mystery, nor had she expected to meet a decades-dead murder victim, and fall in love with him.

"Not to worry," Celeste said when Rachael expressed dismay at her own lack of planning. "I asked Karyn to make an appointment for you with Angie Jones. She's a local seamstress who makes costumes for nearly everybody in town. She always saves a few slots for our guests who don't come prepared."

"I haven't even thought about what kind of costume I'd want," Rachael said, setting down her salad fork. "I don't have any ideas. What are you all going to be?"

"Tut tut," Felicity said, shaking her finger. "That's secret."

Celeste smiled. "Part of the tradition is that everyone's costumes are a secret until that night. That's one of the reasons Angie's the only seamstress: She loves to talk, but she's never let slip about what anyone's wearing."

"Another part of the tradition is the masks," Ian said. "Although it's not required, most people wear masks, which are removed at midnight, if the wearer wishes."

Ian must like that part of the tradition, Rachael mused as she watched him dab at his lips with a white linen napkin, his face carefully turned away. From his contribution to the conversation, she assumed he would be attending the ball. He probably wouldn't do that if not for the masks. She found it sad that his only physical contact with people outside his family came on the anniversary of his greatest tragedy, and that contact was limited by a barrier of disguise.

Later that night, too restless to attempt sleep, she changed into jeans and a sweater and went for a walk in the arboretum outside the greenhouse. Pale moonlight trembled between the latticework of white trellis and green vines, bringing with it a mournful chill that her jacket couldn't completely keep at bay.

When she felt Jordan appearing—slowly, so as not to alarm her—she wasn't startled; in fact, she was gratified.

"You're appearing a lot more frequently, it seems," she commented as he stood before her, dark hair tumbled over his forehead. She longed to brush the strands back, then slide her hand down to cup his cheek. She wasn't sure why she held back, instead relying on conversation.

"I've noticed this happens every year. My strength, you could call it, increases the nearer it gets to Halloween," he said.

"Because that's the night...?" She couldn't bring herself to voice the words describing the terrible event.

He shrugged. "Either that or because of what Halloween represents—ghosts and goblins and all that."

"All Hallows Eve," Rachael said thoughtfully. "The Celts called it Samhain, and believed that on that night, the boundary between the worlds of the living and the dead grew thin enough for spirits to pass through."

"So they say."

"So they say," she agreed faintly.

A sudden gust rattled through the trellis, bringing with it the smell of frost. She shivered. Jordan held out his arm, and she moved into its comforting crook.

"Ghosts and goblins," she repeated as they began walking. "Witches are associated with Halloween, too. Jordan, did you know Emilie practiced Wicca?"

Before it had been bastardized into the clichés of ugly, wart-nosed evil hags, Wicca—or at least an early form of it—had been a bona fide religion, Rachael knew. Pagan, Goddess-worshipping, it had been one of the beliefs nearly trampled out when Christianity invaded Europe, and despite that, it was still practiced today.

There was the slightest hesitation in his step, and then he said, "I won't even ask how you learned about that. I'm impressed that you found out." Before she could accuse him of avoiding the question, he added, "Yes, I did. She swore me to secrecy, though."

"Who else knew?"

"Felicity knew, I'm fairly sure, but not Letitia. Not father or Anne. I seriously doubt Ian did; he was too young."

"What about Shane?" she asked gently.

"Shane may have guessed, but I don't think he knew for sure," he said. "She took great pains to hide it from him. Then again, he often didn't care much about what she did, so long as it didn't interfere with what he wanted."

"What did he want?"

"Power. Money. A devoted, quiet wife—someone to possess and control."

And an heir, to prove his virility and to carry on what he had started, Rachael added silently, basing her assumption on the type of man she guessed Shane to have been. He'd had his heir, Ian, and she wondered if Shane had wanted more children. Or if Emilie had, for that matter.

From what Rachael had seen in her vision, Emilie hadn't just subscribed to Wiccan beliefs. She'd also had some psychic power as well. When Rachael had discovered her own talent, she'd researched what little was known about paranormal psychology. Some believed psychic power was inherited and inheritable. As far as she knew, she didn't have any relatives with similar abilities, and it would be difficult to determine if Emilie had.

But what about passing it on? Did it take two people with psychic ability to produce a child with power? Or could Ian have received any powers from his mother? Rachael hadn't sensed anything in him, but then again, that wasn't where her talent lay.

She shivered again, this time in fear of the unknown pieces in the puzzle, a puzzle in which she herself had become a piece, instead of merely being the arranger. In response, Jordan's arm tightened around her. The gesture, as well as his presence and strength, reassured her somewhat. She wished she could simply give in and enjoy the feelings, but Jordan held some pieces to the puzzle that he wasn't yet willing to give up.

"Jordan..."

"Yes?" His voice stroked a musical caress out of the single word.

"Why were you the only one to return as a ghost?"

He answered her with another question. "Why does anyone become a ghost? All the stories I've heard say ghosts have unfinished business that keeps them on this plane."

"Do you have unfinished business?"

He swung her around to face him. "I certainly have some with you," he said as he descended for a kiss.

The kiss knocked the breath out of her with its intensity. He claimed her mouth as if trying to reaffirm his current place in the living world, and she clung to that reality, answering him with equal passion. Her tongue slipped between his lips, and somewhere in the back of her mind she idly noted that he had no taste. But he had a faint smell, undeniably masculine, and she breathed it in, inhaling it like a desperately needed drug.

The cold night air and the arboretum faded away, leaving only Jordan and the feelings he evoked in her. His hands splayed across her back, pressing her against him. He kissed her cheeks, forehead, eyelids, before trailing down to nip at where her jacket collar exposed her throat. She moaned at the sensation of almost-pain, the sound dwindling to a whimper as his tongue and lips soothed the spot.

Rachael moved her hands to his waist, tugged at his shirt. It pulled free, allowing her to slide her hands under and up along his back, caressing the hard muscles that flexed at her touch. He released her then, long enough to mirror her action by slipping his hands beneath her sweater. A flash of chill air accompanied his hands, and when his fingers brushed against her nipple, it was already hard. But the sensation he evoked made her gasp with pleasure.

"Oh, Rachael," he groaned into the curve of her neck. "Lady, you drive me wild."

She pressed her hips against him, felt the hardness pulsing there, confirming his words and eliciting another groan from him.

A hot fire kindled within her as he continued to stroke the aching nub that yearned for escape from its satiny prison. The smoldering heat engulfed her, consumed her, until she felt only a fiery yearning desire that enflamed her senses. So she was confused at first when Jordan reluctantly pulled his hand away and cradled her gently in his arms again, murmuring, "You're shaking like a leaf. I'm sorry, Rachael. This is neither the time nor place...I've forgotten how the air can chill...."

She *was* shivering, she realized, from a combination of the cold and the passion that continued to resonate through her like the last note through the strings of a piano.

"You don't look so good, either." Of course the cold air didn't affect him, but even in the dim moon-luster, she could tell he was fading ever so slightly. He seemed less tangible, one step away from opacity. Though Rachael realized she should have come to expect this by now, she felt a pang of concern for him.

But his grin was decidedly wicked. "I've been expending an awful lot of energy."

"Oh!" Hoping she wasn't blushing, she socked him lightly in the arm. Jordan caught her wrist and pulled her against him again for a gentle kiss, which spread a touch of warmth through her again.

"The least I can do is see you back to the house," he said. He entwined his fingers with hers, and together they walked back through the arboretum.

Just out of range of the path of light from the sunroom door, he paused, squeezing her hand. He was definitely blurred at the edges now, and his expression bespoke seriousness.

"You're getting close—that much I can tell you," he said. "But the closer you get to the truth, the more dangerous it will be for you. Be careful, Rachael. Please be careful. I'm trying, but I can't always be there to help you."

He leaned down once again to kiss her, and then he faded away, leaving her with the memory of the imprint burned onto her lips, and the vague concern that for all his care and concern, he had once again deliberately avoided her question.

*

The next day, Rachael had an appointment with the seamstress, then made her way to the public library to do some much-needed research there. After being in Angie's talkative presence, it was almost a relief to enter the quiet building. Rachael was amazed that this was the woman who kept everyone's costume a secret. Within ten minutes of entering her house, Rachael had learned all the events leading up to Angie's career, had her measurements taken, been offered milk and cookies, and met Marzipan, a tiny but thankfully non-yappy dog who put his paws up on Rachael's shins the moment she sat down. A pair of limpid brown eyes, peering between mop strings of fur, begged for a lift.

"I've met cats twice your size," Rachael muttered, giving in anyway and hauling Marzipan up. Angie hadn't heard her, because she was in the process of telling a story about the time she made four bridesmaid's dresses in less than twenty-four hours, because all the women flew in from different parts of the country the weekend of the event.

"Oh, what a wonderful idea!" Angie exclaimed when Rachael explained her idea for a costume. "And with your figure, you'll look stunning, absolutely stunning. No one else has done anything similar to that."

"Are you allowed to tell me that?" Rachael asked curiously. "I thought you were sworn to deadly secrecy."

"Oh, well I am, of course," the middle-aged woman said, only looking hurt for a brief moment. "I'd never tell you what someone else was planning. But if I knew someone else were going to wear a similar costume, I'd try to steer you away from that. Sometimes that doesn't work, though. I worry so much that someone will be angry when they see someone else in the same costume. But he insisted."

"He who?" Rachael had lost track of the conversation while attempting to keep Marzipan from eyeing the butterscotch-oatmeal cookies.

"Well, I can't tell you that, of course," Angie said, helping herself to a cookie. She was one of those soft-bodied people who was never outright overweight, but who never engaged in formal exercise. "But all I can say is, it's amazing how similar the two costumes are. It's almost as if the two got together and planned this. Which they might have done, come to think of it."

The police scanner sitting on the microwave in the corner crackled loudly, and she jumped up. "Joe—that's my husband—is a volunteer firefighter," she explained, turning down the volume. "Now, what kind of fabric would be best for your costume…"

Yes, the library was a welcome change. But soon the walls throbbed with silence, as Rachael settled in with a pile of microfilm rolls. The small room where the old-fashioned library had shoved the once-newfangled machinery felt tomblike, with the only illumination the glow of the microfilm reader's screen.

Shaking her head, Rachael fed in the first roll with practiced ease. Unlike most historians, she actually enjoyed this part of the research. She felt like a detective searching for clues, searching for that one spark of important information shining out in the middle of red herrings and useless facts. That rarely happened so neatly, but the image stuck with her.

The library's microfilm index was sketchy, but Rachael knew the date of the fire, and intended to read the papers both approaching and after that day. The articles she had found and copied before coming to Heather Mountain had been the only ones available through the research service she'd used. That made sense, because only the fire, not the annual ball, would be of anything more than local interest. And the fire was news mostly because of the multiple deaths, not the destruction of a minor outbuilding.

The first article, titled "MacPhersons Begin Preparations for Annual Ball," appeared about a month before the event, and mentioned not only the newsworthy information regarding the preparations, but also a brief history of the balls. No one was interviewed, and the passages had a pedantic feel to them, as if they had been copied from something else. Probably from the yearly article the paper ran about the ball, Rachael guessed, nonetheless dropping a quarter into the microfilm machine and making a copy of the article. It might make an interesting addition to the book of MacPherson history. She'd eventually go through and check every year's newspapers, but for now she wanted to concentrate on the special project to which Celeste had bound her.

Successive articles contained little information of note, although a few listed prospective guests, including a short item announcing that Celeste MacPherson Jensen and her husband Arden would be arriving from New York City a week before the party. Rachael listed the date and page of each article along with a brief note of its contents.

The work was slow and tedious; she had to skim every article in every newspaper because there was no helpful index. She rose and paced the three steps back and forth in the renovated closet as she had done several times before, stretching out and resting her eyes from the unrelenting glare of the machine and the cramped, blurred letters of the old newspapers.

Reseating herself, she glanced at the date of the newspapers and felt a rush of relief when she discovered it read October 29. Two days to go until All Hallows Eve. The last few articles had merely given more details of preparations, with the numbers of servants and amounts of food scrupulously listed. Interesting to her historian sensibilities, but not helpful in terms of the mystery. None of the servants' names were mentioned, so she made a note in her digital recorder to ask Celeste if any rolls still existed somewhere in the house. If any of the people still lived in the area, they might remember something that had slipped through the cracks earlier.

She had an appointment to tour a sugar house in an hour, so Rachael decided to end her research after the first fire article and continue in a few days. The next articles focused on the guest lists, and she copied those, again with the idea of possible interviews in mind.

"Tragedy struck last night at Manor MacPherson when fire ravaged an outbuilding, killing three family members and seriously injuring another...."

She barely noticed the words that began the first article she had read about the MacPhersons. It was the photograph next to it, which the research service hadn't copied when they found the article for her. There was one photo of the fire, the horror of it not dimmed by the black and white reproduction. The editor had also chosen to run a photo taken earlier in the evening, at the start of the party.

Patriarch Malcolm dominated the picture, his heavy brows lifted in a moment of rare gaiety. Beside him stood Anne, his second wife, coyly holding a peacock-feathered mask to her eyes. Around them crowded various members of the family; Rachael picked out a young Celeste dressed as some sort of fairy princess, Felicity and Letitia in what were no doubt their favorite beaded flapper dresses. Rachael felt a flutter of desire in the pit of her stomach at the image of Jordan. Arms crossed over his chest, body language betraying his discomfort, he wore the high boots, tight black pants and ruffled shirt of a dashing pirate, his plain black mask dangling from a string around his wrist.

His discomfort no doubt stemmed from his proximity to Shane, she surmised. Jordan's half-brother, standing beside him, was garbed as an incongruously tall Napoleon, the hat perched carefully atop his head. Emilie looked as uncomfortable as Jordan, and probably for the same reason. She seemed to be trying to hide behind Shane, but couldn't find the space; instead, she half-turned from the camera. She had, unsurprisingly, chosen (or been required, Rachael thought) to dress as Josephine, and her arms looked painfully thin in the puff-sleeved, empire-waisted gown as she rested her hands on her stomach.

Rachael stared. Granted, the dress' style wasn't flattering on anyone, even women with the most boyish of figures—falling from just beneath the breasts, it hid the natural inward curve of the waistline. In effect, the style could make nearly anyone look pregnant.

But unless she was hallucinating, Emilie was standing in that pose to hide what the dress only made more obvious: She *had* been pregnant.

*

The Range Rover bumped along the road, lurching as the wheels slipped into frozen mud-ruts, nearly snatching the steering wheel from Rachael's hands. She toyed with the 4-wheel-drive lever, pulled her hand away. Living in the flatlands, she'd never had to deal with such things, and she was half-convinced the transmission would crash to the ground if she popped the truck into 4-wheel-drive at the wrong time. Despite growing up with brothers, she was most definitely car-impaired. She made a mental note to take a community college course when she got home, gritted her teeth, and struggled to keep the steering wheel in line.

The Range Rover stumbled its way to an open area that was more like a field than a parking lot. But Rachael knew she'd arrived at the right place. She'd seen enough pictures in the books on maple sugaring to recognize an authentic Adirondack sugar house when she found one.

Of course, it wasn't sugaring season now. The sap flowed in the spring, when the woods were still shrouded in thick layers of snow; though the temperatures plummeted at night, the sun warmed the air to above freezing during the day. But the MacPhersons saw the monetary potential in keeping a house running throughout the year, for tourists. Few tourists took advantage of it during foliage season, however, so Rachael knew she wasn't displacing any visitors even though Celeste had called ahead to request that she be the only one given the tour that afternoon. "So you'll have a chance to ask questions, really get a feel for the place," she'd said, and Rachael had to admit it was a good idea.

Ned, the caretaker, also proved to fit her mental picture of an Adirondack sugarer, with his red flannel shirt, stained overalls, and chewing tobacco, which he decorously spit out upon her arrival.

The soaked heat inside slapped her in the face like a wet towel, and she quickly eased out of her jacket. The moist air was even hotter than that of the greenhouse, with a heavier, darker smell; an odor like woodsy, earth-tinged syrup.

Ahead of her mawed an open "arch" or firebox, angrily digesting thick chunks of wood with a burning roar. Ned tossed a few more logs in, getting dangerously close to the sizzling coals as he poked around with the last tree remnant. The pans that fit in above the arch sizzled as he added more water, which he used for display when there was no sap.

"So you're writing a book about the MacPhersons, eh?" he asked.

Pushing up the sleeves of her purple sweater, Rachael explained her job and her work for the MacPhersons. "Maple sugar production is such a huge part of their history, and I know almost nothing about it," she concluded. "That's where you come in."

Ned led her through all facets of production, showing her the vats where the thin sap boiled down to thick syrup, and further down to maple sugar. She sipped cautiously at a tiny paper cup of seal-brown, brackish-looking thin liquid, and was surprised to find it palatable, though dull. Like a diluted dollop of Mrs. Butterworth, it had a watery, smoke-pale flavor that lingered on her tongue.

Outside, he showed her a set-up of a series of tapped trees. In the past, he explained, a wooden or metal spout had been pounded into each tree, and a bucket had been hung beneath each to catch the sap. When the sap was running well, he said, the buckets had to be emptied by hand at least once a day. Now, spouts were connected by what looked like rubber surgical tubing, and all fed through a filter into the evaporator pans in the sugar house. Of course, he added, for major production, a sugar "house" was a much larger, modern building.

"The old houses were open at both ends; we had doors put on this one so I don't freeze my a—tush," Ned explained.

They were barely back inside, the heat another physical blast, when the phone rang. Ned kicked his work-boot-clad feet through the toss of wood chips on the hard-packed dirt floor. Through the office door, Rachael caught glimpses of a grimy phone, a rickety metal desk covered with papers, and a girlie calendar tacked up on one wall. The noise from the fire and boiling vats made it impossible to hear what he was saying, and his back was to her, but she saw his body tense just before he slammed down the phone.

"Dammit," he said upon returning. "Someone's been messin' with the lines near the main building. You can stay and read some of these brochures. I shouldn't be gone too long."

Grabbing a grimy, navy blue ski vest from a peg by the door, he left. Rachael heard the faint bark of his ancient pickup as he drove away, and hoped for the MacPhersons' sake that the damage wasn't too severe.

She picked up one of the brochures, which featured a picture of a maple tree in full autumn splendor, but instead of reading it, twisted the glossy paper in her hand.

Was this latest incident somehow connected to the damage to her computer? Everyone had assumed that mishap had been directed at her, but had it been nothing more than part of a series of negative events? Rachael thought back. First the library railing had failed—or been tampered with. Then the computer incident. Then she'd been chased. And now this.

The song from *Sesame Street* about things not being like one another danced in her head. The first three events were similar—she'd been somehow involved in each one. She rolled the brochure into a tighter tube. No, this couldn't possibly be related.

That thought was firmly in her head when, over the furnace's clamor, she thought she heard the door open. She started to turn, started to ask Ned if the damage had been severe. But all she got was the glimpse of a backlit, obscure figure and a descending arm, a sudden bright flash of pain, and then the world went black.

*

Her own coughing jerked her back into consciousness. How much later? She tried to take a deep breath to clear her lungs, but instead inhaled viscous air that choked her more. She opened her eyes, and they stung, tears obscuring her vision.

Blinking rapidly, she cleared her sight enough to realize that the room was filled with smoke. Her head ached, and the muscles in her shoulders pulled, stinging.

That knowledge immediately led her to the discovery that her arms were bound behind her, behind the back of the desk chair. She peered through the smoke. Yes, she was in the office, bound to the cracked leather of the old chair. A tug proved that her wrists had not only been tied together, but somehow to the chair as well. The hemp rasped painfully against her skin.

"Ned?" she called, her smoke-roughened voice breaking. No answer. And why would there be? He had gone to investigate some vandalism. He hadn't been the one who'd hit her, she knew that for a fact. The dark figure in the doorway had been of moderate size. Ned, on the other hand, was well over six feet and at least 250 pounds, judging from his straining belt.

Tugging uselessly at her arms again, Rachael tried to calm her racing heart, tried to take stock of the situation. It didn't seem to be all that much hotter in the house, just smokier. That meant, hopefully, no fire.

No matter—she had to get out of there—get untied, and get outside before she collapsed from smoke inhalation. She tried to crane her neck and look over her shoulder, and the action made the chair seat dip stomach-lurchingly backward, its spring stretched from years of abuse.

She briefly considered tipping the chair over so she could squirm out of it, then abandoned that plan. With her hands still bound behind her back and to the chair, she'd be just as bad off on the floor. Perhaps as a last resort, if the smoke got too thick, she could do that to breathe the clearer air near the ground.

Wait. The chair had wheels, and her feet weren't tied. She could push it to the front door. Without hesitation, she began kicking her feet against the ground. The old wheels groaned, but obligingly rolled her backwards. A few more pushes, and she was in the doorway to the main room. The door had been conveniently left open—or maybe not, Rachael thought, horrified: The smoke had easier access to her this way.

The sound was louder here, as the fire roared unchecked in the furnace. The flames didn't seem to have escaped, however; what was causing the increase in smoke? No time to wonder. A roil of sooty air sent her into paroxysms of coughing again, her eyes watering.

She struggled to roll the chair towards the front door, the wheels turning painfully slowly in their rusty coasters along the pocked floor. One wheel caught on an uneven board, and she nearly pitched over onto her back.

Extricating the wheel from the rut, Rachael redoubled her efforts. Sweat streaked down her face, pooled in the small of her back.

Come on, just a little farther.

Instead of craning around to see where she was headed, she positioned the back of the chair in direct line with the door. She bent her head, trying to take in a full breath of air without choking again. Then, with a flurry of kicks, she put the chair in motion.

With a sudden smack, she hit the door. Her arms, caught against the back of the chair, screamed a protest at being slammed and pinched. The pain made her swear, then cough, adding to the ache of her raw throat.

Her fingers scrabbled blindly, uselessly against the door. Where was the latch? Rachael twisted around to see. From her seated position, the knob was shoulder-height. There was no way she could reach it with her bound hands.

Her breathing was more labored now, each inhalation a thick effort. Frustrated, she hit the knob with the corner of the chair's back, jerking her body with each thwack. Nothing.

Pulling forward, she swung the chair around, trying to peer at the door through the constant haze of grey tears. Maybe she could turn the knob with her shoulder and chin, or her teeth? She brought the chair close to the door, pressing her knees against it, but she when she tried to lean forward, her bound arms yanked her back. It wasn't going to work.

With a sob of frustration, she slumped forward, ignoring the pain in her shoulders. She was trapped.

Chapter Thirteen

"Rachael..."

Her head jerked up, and she squinted frantically through the billowing gloom of smoke. "Jordan?" she whispered, a blossom of hope unfurling.

"Rachael, lady, don't give up."

She couldn't see him anywhere, her eyes so clouded with tears. His faint voice hovered, intangible, in the air by her head. "Jordan, help me."

"Burn the ropes."

Suddenly, she could no longer sense him, no longer feel the urgent brush of his voice at her ears. Biting her lip, she choked back a whimper of abandonment. Why hadn't he helped her? Why hadn't he stayed? His words echoed, mocking, in her mind....

"Burn the ropes."

She certainly couldn't untie them, and there was no one to do that for her. It made sense that the only other way to get free was to destroy the ropes that bound her to the chair. But how to do that when her hands were useless?

Amassing her strength, Rachael pushed away from the door, back toward the long low arch in the center of the room. Because it was the source of the smoke, she felt as though she swam into thick ocean fog, blind, without the steady comforting blink of a lighthouse to guide her. She moved slowly, unwilling to suddenly slam into the red-hot metal, inching herself forward instead of pushing backwards. After what seemed like an eternity, she spied the glow of the fire in the arch's opening.

The heat was much greater here, so strong that it took away what little breath she had. Her skin burned from the sheer proximity, and she again gave mental thanks that the fire hadn't spread from the stove.

Ignoring the pain, she carefully turned the chair around, little pushes of her feet slowly twisting her position, until again she faced away from the huge firebox. Then she deliberately pushed back.

Cautiously, Rachael moved her wrists the inch or so they could move, and pressed them against the searing metal. She hissed in pain and jerked away as her left pinkie caught against the stove. Fighting the urge, and unable anyway to put the finger in her mouth, she gritted her teeth and cautiously pressed back again. The stench of burning hemp sliced into her nostrils.

She was barely breathing now, barely able to choke the thick, smoke-filled air into her lungs. She closed her eyes, concentrating on pulling the air slowly in through her nose, and on the gentle pressure of her wrists against the firebox, tense for the moment when the fibers would give way.

Suddenly, the ropes parted, and the same finger glanced against the metal. Pulling the chair away from the heat, Rachael scrabbled to extricate her wrists from the smoldering strands that bound her to the chair. As soon as her hands were free, she flung herself out of the chair, landing with a thud on the sawdust-strewn dirt floor.

For a moment she could do nothing more than gulp at the relatively clear air, shaking with relief. Then she began dragging herself towards the door by her elbows and toes, keeping her head down. When she reached the door, she raised up on her knees and fumbled for the knob. For a brief, panicked second, she thought the door had been locked from the outside, but then the latch gave and the door swung out.

Rachael tumbled forward, scraping her palms on the cracked cement doorstep, her face inches from a pair of scarred work boots.

*

The paramedics pronounced her fine, though suffering from mild smoke inhalation and a tender bump on the head. Rachael smiled and thanked them hoarsely, sipping at hot tea and thinking that she could have made the diagnosis herself.

The ambulance left, bouncing along the rutted road; before it was out of sight, the BCI detectives arrived, swarming into the sugar house after a brief greeting to Trooper Parker. The trooper stood at her blanket-wrapped perch on the tailgate of Ned's truck, where he'd been waiting for the paramedics to leave.

"We've been seeing a bit of you lately, Ms. deYoung," he commented, propping one foot up on the tail and opening his notepad.

"Nothing personal, but it's really not something I'm happy about," she said, a stab at levity.

"No offense taken. Gotta ask you the same questions again, though: Any idea who might have wanted to do this to you?"

"It wasn't Ned," she said quickly. "Whoever hit me on the head was shorter, smaller. But I didn't see any features."

The trooper nodded. "We know Ned wasn't involved. No motive, and there were more than enough witnesses at the main building who saw him come to inspect the lines. The vandalism was minor, by the way. No footprints there, like here, what with the ground being so hard."

"Makes it sound as though the vandalism was just an excuse to get him away from the sugar shack," Rachael mused. "You know, maybe this had nothing to do with me, personally. Maybe the person didn't know I was here, and whapped me on the head in a moment of panic."

Trooper Parker's expression clearly said what he thought of civilians trying to doing his work. Rachael gave him a guileless smile, which he didn't seem to fall for.

Trooper Stefanick emerged from the sugar house and gestured to his partner. When Parker returned, he said, "The chimney was plugged, presumably so the shack would fill with smoke," he said. "The ladder outside was one Ned leaves there, ironically, so he can periodically do a safety check on the roof and chimney. If someone really wanted to do damage to the building, he'd've set the place on fire, not fill it with smoke."

"So what you're saying is, someone tried to kill me." The words tumbled from her mouth almost before she realized what she was saying. When she did, a fresh chill of horror covered her in clammy breath. Although she'd known that inside, she hadn't had time to consider it until now, and now she shivered despite the blanket and tea. She found herself craving Felicity's secret recipe tea and its miracle effects.

The BCI pair joined Stefanick outside the sugar house, and the three came over to gather around the tailgate as well.

"Well, now, I suppose I am." Trooper Parker leaned forward, his pale blue eyes serious, his words making cloudy puffs in the chill air. "Why would someone do that?"

What could she say? If she told them about her research...no, she'd only be able to give them half-truths. Much of what she'd learned came from sources she couldn't name, or even explain. Her research affected no one but the MacPhersons, and the only MacPhersons who would be directly affected by her research into the tragedy were dead.

She settled for an outright lie.

"I don't know," she said.

*

"I warned you not to hurt her!" he roared, raising a hand to strike.

The other man took a limping step backwards. He stumbled, banging his hip against the sharp corner of the desk. But his face held no fear, only twisted triumph, as he faced his attacker.

"Have you forgotten your vow so quickly?" he taunted. "Forgotten that you were charged with protecting me, and who charged you?"

"But *she* didn't know what you'd done—she didn't know how evil you were." The man lowered his arm, but the dangerous glint in his green eyes bespoke the unquenched anger within him. "And have you forgotten that she also charged me with exacting revenge?"

The other man paled, but held his ground. "After all these years, I don't think you could go through with it," he said, his lip twisting into a sneer.

"Don't push me," the first man said. "If you try to hurt Rachael again, I won't continue being an impartial witness. I've been covering for you for far too long."

"She's getting too close. Besides..." The second man narrowed his eyes in triumph. "I wasn't the one who tried to kill her."

The first man's hands clenched again, this time in frustration. "I know you're behind it, though. And I'll hold you responsible if she's harmed."

*

It took three shampooings before her hair stopped smelling of smoke. Rachael spent a good half-hour in the shower, fighting off bouts of shivering panic.

With effort, she tried to turn her thoughts to her work. If someone were truly trying to kill her—a part of her mind continued to opt for the safer theory of coincidence—then it must have something to do with her research. Apparently she was getting too close to learning something that someone didn't want her to know.

The possibility still remained that an outsider had shot Jordan or Emilie, or both, and set the fire in the cottage. But how would an outsider know the details and extent of her research? The question left the same conclusion she kept trying to avoid: that one of the MacPhersons was responsible.

Celeste certainly didn't seem the type for violence, and besides, she had no motive that Rachael could ascertain. Ian had been but a small child when the tragedy occurred. Felicity was harmless. That left Jordan...no. Rachael was convinced he hadn't been the one attacking her. He couldn't have been the one chasing her in the woods—in fact, none of them could.

Karyn knew about her research, being involved in the day-to-day activities of the hotel. Motive? She'd mentioned that she'd had relatives in the North Country. Maybe one of them had been involved, and gotten Karyn involved....

Rachael laughed aloud at that as she stepped from the shower and wrapped a thick peach-colored towel around herself. She was grasping at ridiculous straws now. Karyn might be physically able to clamber up a ladder and stuff the chimney, but she certainly wasn't the one who knocked her out or tied her up. And again: Motive was vague enough to be nonexistent.

Thoughts of Karyn reminded Rachael that she had a question for the hotel manager, so as soon as she'd dressed and dried her hair, she headed downstairs. She found Karyn in her office, contemplating an open bottle of antacids on her desk and harriedly tucking her blond hair behind her ears.

"Bad day?" Rachael asked sympathetically.

"Not when compared to yours. How're you feeling?" Karyn asked, getting up to give her a quick hug.

"Better, now. Just some smoke inhalation and a good scare. What about you—why're you eating those things like candy?"

Karyn ran a hand across her face. "Work. Life. Everything. The assistant cook quit—can you believe it? Right before the ball—because she says she found a burned mouse. It must have gotten into the oven or something; I don't know, she wasn't too coherent. Then I got an irate letter from the owner of that ad company those execs were from—I couldn't even understand it, something about us being somehow responsible for his employees not working. I gave that to Celeste; I'll let her handle it."

"I thought those guys left weeks ago."

"Two weeks ago, Sunday," Karyn said, not needing to check the calendar.

Rachael remembered the men joking that they didn't want to go back to work, but she couldn't imagine any of them failing to do their jobs. Kevin, for example, had spent extra time making a list of names for her, and even sought her out to deliver it.

She frowned. That had been on a Monday, hadn't it? She shook her head. It must have been Sunday, before they left.

Karyn peeked out from behind splayed fingers. "Please tell me you didn't come down to see me with a problem."

"Nope, just a request. I wanted to get the receipt for the package you mailed for me, so I don't forget to put it on my itemization of expenses for Celeste."

Karyn dropped her hand. "What are you talking about? I've been meaning to ask *you* when you were going to give me the thing to mail."

It was Rachael's turn to look confused. "I gave it to you the same day I told you about it. I put it right here, on top of the rest of the mail on this chair."

Karyn slowly shook her head, her usually bright blue eyes troubled. "It wasn't here when I gathered the mail to take into town, Rachael. I swear it wasn't."

"I believe you," Rachael said; Karyn did sound honestly confused. She leaned forward in the chair. "This is really strange."

"I'll ask the servants if they've seen it, and get back to you," Karyn suggested, reaching for a pen to write herself a note—and for the antacids. "I don't know what to tell you. This place is getting stranger by the minute."

Thinking of the resident ghost, Rachael added silently, *You'd be surprised.*

*

When she got back to her room, Jordan was waiting for her.

Before she had time to react, he had swept her into his arms, with a kiss that left her breathless. He paused long enough to say, "Rachael, praise God you're all right," his tone aching, and then he kissed her again.

"I'm sorry I couldn't help you," he said when he released her from the kiss' spell. "But I can't abide fire, can't deal with it—can't become solid so near to it."

"I wouldn't have escaped if you hadn't told me what to do," Rachael said gently, desperately wanting to erase the deep pain and concern in his eyes. She laid a hand on his cheek, feeling the cool, smooth skin beneath her palm. Her thumb brushed over the scar on his chin.

"I don't know...I don't want to lose you," he said in a sudden rush of passion, looking as surprised as she felt by his words. "I couldn't bear it if something happened to you," he added, his voice softer.

Rachael stared at him, at the way his dark hair curled around the taut lines of his face. Conflicting emotions surged and writhed within her: the morning's revelations, the afternoon's panic and fear, and now, her feelings for him.

"I don't want to lose you, either," she admitted finally, to herself as much as to him. "But what choice do I have? You're a ghost. Whatever time we have together *is* limited by the very fact of what you are."

She was very conscious of the way he held her against him, the way his hips pressed against hers, his chest against hers. She imagined she could hear his heartbeat, throbbing with her own rhythm, and knew it was a fantasy.

Jordan pulled away from her, and ran his hands down her arms until he clasped her hands in his.

"Well, then," he said, carefully, eyes searching her face, "I should think we should make the best of our time together." To his words he added a slight tug on her hands. He'd made it a question, and left the final decision up to her.

"I should think so," she answered, and smiled.

She wasn't sure who pulled whom to the bed, only that suddenly they were upon it, Jordan's satisfying weight pressing her down into the soft pillows. She'd kissed him before, so his kisses were familiar. They didn't have to experiment, didn't have to explore; instead, the familiarity was combined with the urgency and knowledge that their time together was limited and thus precious, to be savored. His tongue thrust into her mouth, and she welcomed his entrance, jolting with passion as they touched.

He parted the top of her button-down shirt and nipped at her neck, first here, then there, throwing her off-balance. She moaned as his teeth found her earlobe, then as his tongue licked the sensitive skin behind her ear. He drew back slightly, but only to roll her to one side and hold her hair gently aside so his mouth could find the back of her neck. Her hands dug into the pillows as the sensations at her nape seemed to writhe their way through the rest of her body.

He let her hair drop, and she moved onto her back. He knelt between her thighs and took her wrists, tugging her arms up.

"Hold on," he said, his voice husky, and she complied, lacing her hands behind his neck. "With everything." Realizing what he wanted, she wrapped her legs around his waist, hooking her ankles together.

For a long moment he paused, and she stared at him, gazing into his passion-glazed eyes, tense with her need for him. Then he leaned back, carrying her with him so that when he knelt upright, she sat on his thighs, his arousal separated from her own by a few layers of clothes. She wriggled her hips, fitting tighter against him, and he closed his eyes. She chuckled, and kissed him lightly. The next thing she knew, he crushed her face against his, kissing her desperately, and she answered him in kind, with an intensity she barely recognized as her own. Such an intensity that when he pulled back, she gasped for air.

"Oh lady," he said finally. "Sometimes when I'm with you, I forget to breathe."

He voiced her own reaction, and Rachael couldn't help but laugh. The laugh turned into a groan as he cupped her rear and pulled her hard against him, reminding her—as if she could be unaware—of his reaction to her.

Jordan lowered her back onto the bed, and tugged off her shoes and socks. He pressed his lips to the arch of her foot before sliding his hands up her legs to her waist. She reached up and fumbled with his shirt, trying to pull it free from his pants, and he helped, finally slipping it over his head. He released a hiss of breath as she ran her hands across his chest, shadowed from the single lamp on the night table.

Not to be distracted, he deftly undid her belt, then her jeans. The zipper rasped as he slid it down. Rachael obligingly lifted her hips so he could pull off her jeans.

"Very pretty," he approved, caressing the silky, emerald green panties. "Very nice," he added, this time looking at her face, watching her reaction as his fingers glided between her thighs.

Suddenly shy under his scrutiny, Rachael caught her lip between her teeth. The action didn't help quell the whimper that escaped as he caressed the fabric, and she knew he felt the heat beneath them.

"So wet," he murmured, pulling the panties away. His eyes never leaving her face, he dipped his fingers into her, stroking.

Rachael forgot to be shy, forgot everything except the feel of his hand against her. She cried out at the suddenness of the sensations that rocked through her, that pulled her hips from the bed and then sent her grinding back against the mattress.

When she had enough sense to be aware of things again, she saw him reaching for his own belt. The motion reminded her of something, of a practicality she'd never been able to forget, even in the throes of passion.

And, yet, it wasn't necessary here. The implications hit her, and she grabbed Jordan's wrist.

"Rachael?"

The concern in his voice sent her over the edge, and to her horror, she began to cry. He gathered her into his arms, his thumb catching a teardrop. "Rachael, what is it?"

She took a deep breath, fought for control.

"I'm sorry," she whispered. "It's stupid, really."

"Tell me."

She took another breath. "It's just, well, I thought about—about protection, and then I realized you wouldn't need it, and then I realized just how insane this is. Our time together is limited—everything is limited for us. There's no future. No relationship, no kids—nothing. I thought I'd thought of that, but I was just thinking about now. I'm sorry," she ended, another sob catching her words.

She'd never removed her oversized shirt, and now Jordan adjusted the white cotton across the tops of her thighs. The complete understanding in that simple gesture made her heart catch painfully.

"Lady, don't ever apologize," he whispered, his breath stirring a spiral of hair. "I should be the one to apologize—I'm the one who can't offer you all the usual things in a relationship."

"But—"

"Sssh. Just accept this moment in time, when I can hold you."

The emotions had exhausted her, and she wasn't aware of slipping into sleep, only waking again, in Jordan's arms. The afternoon shadows had been consumed by dusk. Rachael sighed, unable to stop her mind from reviewing the insane day in reverse. Jordan, and before that, the police, and the sugar house…

"Jordan?"

He moved his head from where it nestled in her shoulder. "Yes?"

"Why is someone trying to kill me? Am I getting too close to something?"

With a small sound of pain, he dropped his head. Finally he raised it again and gazed at her with eyes verdant with worry. "I won't let anyone harm you."

Rachael pressed her lips together. "You can't always be there to help me, love," she pointed out gently. "But I wanted to tell you something I found—no, I wanted to ask you."

He sat up, pulling her with him into his arms. "Go ahead."

"Did you know Emilie was pregnant on the night of the fire?"

His lips quirked. "Now there's a leading question. But I'll answer it in all aspects: Yes, she was pregnant, and yes, I knew it."

Rachael took a deep breath, trying to decide what to say next. "I'm already sure of the answer to this, but I need to hear you say it. Was it your baby?"

"Ah, lady, after all we've been through, after this trust, you still need to ask?" He wrapped a long strand of her sable hair around his fingers and tugged gently. "No. Emilie was like a sister to me."

"I know. I'm sorry." She kissed the sharp line of his jaw. "Did anyone else know about the baby?"

"Surprisingly, no. She did a good job of hiding it. As you've seen, or guessed, she kept to herself a great deal—she didn't have enough contact with the others for them to notice anything was wrong. I only found out later that night, when she came to me for help."

"That's why you went to the cottage with her?"

He nodded slowly.

"What did she need help with?"

"I can't tell you."

With a frustrated noise, Rachael pulled away from him, wincing as her hair untangled from his fingers with a jerk, and got out of the bed. "Dammit," she said, shrugging into her bathrobe and savagely jerking the belt into a knot, "why can you answer some of my questions and not others?"

"Because of the promises I've made." He stood and found his clothes, tugging on his pants. "Rachael..." She was standing at the window, gazing out, her back rigid beneath the terrycloth. She heard him come up behind her, and he put his arms around her waist.

She stiffened, but didn't try to pull away, her anger warring with the need to be in his arms.

"Forty years is too long," Jordan said softly. "Perhaps it *is* time for the truth to come out. Because I'm bound by things I can't even explain, I can't just tell you everything. But I'm not going to keep you from the truth. If you ask me to confirm something you've already learned, I'll be honest with you; I'll answer your questions."

"That's really stupid," she said finally. "But I don't understand everything that you've gone through, and I guess I'll just have to accept what you can give me."

"I'll give you this." He turned her around, cupped her face in his hands. "You are getting close, and you are in danger. I don't know why, but I think this is all going to come to a head on Halloween. Maybe it's because of my own strength then, I don't know. But you'd best find out all you can before then, and please, lady, be careful."

*

The next day, Ian invited her to lunch with him again.

"Thank you for agreeing to join me again, Rachael," he said, stepping aside to let her enter his sitting room.

"I appreciate the invitation," she replied. "Aren't you terribly busy, between the ball preparations and your other work?"

"Well, yes, I am." He was considering the CD rack, his back to her, and she couldn't see his expression. "But I suppose one must take a short break now and then. Would Tchaikovsky be all right?"

"That's fine." A spinach salad, topped with crumbled bacon and hard-boiled egg slices, already sat on the coffee table, along with two tall glasses of mahogany iced tea. Rachael eased down onto the sofa. The invitation couldn't have come at a worse time, and she was dreading what she had to tell him.

"I must admit, I have an ulterior motive for asking you here," Ian said, now occupied at the stereo.

Oh, no. Celeste must have told him already. "Oh?" she asked, picking up her drink. The cool-sweated glass nearly slid from her hand; she tightened her grasp.

"I'm curious to hear how your research is going." He joined her on the sofa, as usual at her left, holding on to the arm as he carefully sat, wincing slightly at some old, not-yet-vanished pain.

Rachael let out a rush of air, and sipped her iced tea, delicately moving a mint leaf away from her mouth. But she still had to tell him.

"It's going very well," she said. "I found some letters that Birney MacPherson wrote to his wife, Elisa, before she moved over here to be with him. He was a very eloquent man, and passionate about this area. I think the theme of the history is coming clear—the attachment of your family to the mountains—both the land and what grows upon it."

"The maple trees certainly made our fortune," he agreed. "I only wish Birney had chosen a warmer place to settle." He set down his salad and went to the fireplace to poke at the logs within. One of them collapsed, sending up a burst of starry sparks.

Rachael wondered at his ease with the flames. She would have supposed he would be uncomfortable with fire, considering what had happened to him. But he claimed to remember nothing from that night, and so might not have retained an unconscious fear of fire. In fact, he spent more time than necessary rearranging the logs with the iron poker. She felt as though he prolonged the inevitable, even though she was the one who had to speak. She waited until he was seated again before she did.

"There has been one minor setback," she said carefully. "Your mother's journal seems to have been...misplaced."

He forked a spinach leaf into his mouth and glanced at her, eyebrow raised questioningly.

"I packaged it to mail it to Colin in England, but it wasn't with the mail when Karyn went to town. I'm sure we'll find it soon—it's just been misplaced," she repeated in a rush.

"Of course," he said unconcernedly, spearing a piece of egg. "In a house as big as this one, things are always getting misplaced. I hope this doesn't hinder your work."

Rachael tried not to stare at him, tried not to blurt out anything in her astonishment. He had been so possessive about Emilie's diary a few days ago, and now he barely seemed to care. She supposed she should be glad that he wasn't angry, but she couldn't help being curious about his reaction.

"I've done some thinking," he said abruptly. "While I in no way intend to hinder your research—and, in fact, I find some of it quite interesting—I retain my initial objection that the past is gone and has no bearing on the present."

Including his mother's own written words? If she'd been a psychiatrist, Rachael thought, she might conclude that Ian was in denial. The symphony swelled, reproduced to near perfection through his speakers, its powerful melody a counterpoint to her own inner discordance.

"Well, I'm glad to hear you're not opposed to my work," she said brightly, all too willing to change the subject before he changed his mind. "I was hoping to ask if I could use your printer this afternoon. I'd like to print out some preliminary pages for Celeste to look over."

"What? Oh, yes, that would be fine. Anytime this afternoon," he said, as if he'd barely heard her. A knock at the door got both their attentions. "Ah, Mrs. Rabideau, you've brought the cheese soufflé—excellent timing."

She told him a little more of his family's history while they ate, but the conversation studiously danced around and away from the generation before his. Rachael wondered if it was her imagination, or if he remained distant, asking only polite questions to keep the discussion going. He was probably distracted because of the upcoming ball, and the memories attached to it, she decided.

When she left Ian's study after lunch, she heard a voice calling her from down the hall. Breathless, Karyn hurried up to her.

"Any luck?" Rachael asked her. They had scoured the house that morning looking for the diary, to no avail, as Rachael had reported to Celeste.

"None. The servants are clueless. I've asked a few of the guests, and I'll get to the rest of them this afternoon. How did he—" she inclined her head back at the door "—take it?"

Rachael shrugged helplessly. "Fine. He didn't seem to care all that much."

"Weird," Karyn said. "Then again, this whole place is weird sometimes. Especially now."

"Having another bad day?" Rachael asked, sympathetic. She had guessed that even before Karyn spoke. Though still her casual, well-groomed self, the hotel manager was obviously out of sorts. She still kept fitfully tucking her hair behind her ears, and her cardigan was slightly askew. Rachael gently tugged it into place for her as they walked toward the main hall.

"You betcha. Would you believe George found a dead squirrel today? Looked like someone tried to barbecue it. It's a good thing he's not freaked by these things as the assistant cook was."

"Another burned animal?" Rachael was aghast.

Karyn pursed her lips, considering. "I'll let you in on something: This happens every year around Halloween. It stops right after. No one's been hurt, other than a few small, furry woodland creatures. Celeste figures it's some local prankster. It's creepy, though. I'm terrified that Brett might find one."

"What do the police say?"

"Celeste doesn't want to tell them. She's usually very cooperative about such things—it's Ian who avoids outsiders. But she says it's just a prankster who'll eventually stop once he realizes he can't get a rise out of us. But it's been going on as long as I've been here." Karyn shuddered. "I'm just glad to have Chewie around to protect me."

They parted ways outside the office, with Karyn promising to contact her immediately if the journal turned up. Rachael went up to her room and finalized some of her notes.

She couldn't shake the uneasy feeling she'd gotten during lunch. She wished Jordan were there to talk to, but he didn't make an appearance. He'd come to her that morning, and, she thought with a lecherous grin, between then and last night, he'd probably worn out his corporeality for a while.

A few hours later, she'd finished what she wanted to show Celeste, and headed back downstairs to Ian's office. His door was closed, and she hesitated a moment before knocking, remembering her first and only visit to the room. His possessiveness about the sanctity of his office equaled his initial reaction to the diary, and she doubted that his abrupt change carried to all fronts.

His call of "Who is it?" seemed abrupt, but he smiled when she opened the door and greeted her pleasantly enough. Still, it wasn't enough to make her relax completely. Once her laptop found the printer via the wireless connection, he went back to his own desk.

As Rachael watched the pages emerge from the machine, she found herself thinking about some of the things that she and Ian had in common—music and the technology surrounding it, computers—and how easily they could discuss those subjects.

Suddenly, she wondered if Ian's abrupt changes in behavior had anything to do with his feelings for her. She stole a glance at him. He sat at his wide desk, scowling over some papers spread in front of him. He probably hadn't had much experience dealing with single women, she mused. Perhaps he was just unsure how to deal with her?

Making a face, she turned back to the printer. *Talk about ego*, she chided herself. But that left her back where she started, with the niggling feeling of unease at Ian's recent conduct.

She heard Ian pick up the telephone receiver and punch a button. "Celeste?" he said after a moment. "Have you read this latest report from the APA? No? I'll bring it to you." He stood and moved carefully around the desk, pausing at Rachael's side. "Everything going all right? Good. I won't be gone long, if you need anything."

Unfortunately, he was gone long enough for her to need something. Five minutes after he left, the printer ran out of paper. Rachael checked in the cabinet beneath the printer, but only found extra toner cartridges. Hands on her hips, she surveyed the room, trying to logic out where the paper would be. A low cabinet of polished walnut and brass at the other side of the main desk looked like a good place for office supplies, so she went to it.

At first the doors seemed locked, but then she felt a click, and the latch gave way.

"Damn," she muttered, finding only bound files and corporate reports. She was about to close the door when a dark object in the back caught her eye. "No," she said, reaching for it, but it was what she first suspected.

In her hand, she held the still-wrapped, carefully addressed journal of Emilie MacPherson.

Chapter Fourteen

Rachael stared, dumbfounded, at the package in her hands. Ian had had the diary all along? That might explain his lack of concern when she'd told him it was missing, but she couldn't understand why he'd taken it in the first place. She turned it over, noticing it hadn't been opened. If he really hadn't wanted her to mail it to England, he could have asked her not to, but he'd acquiesced to her and Celeste's wishes. Had he taken it because he didn't want Celeste to know how important it was to him? Rachael shook her head. She had no answers, only questions, and the damning evidence in her hand.

Just then the door opened. She turned. Ian froze in the doorway, his eyes fixed on the package. Slowly she dropped her eyes to it, then raised them back to him, questioning, unable to speak.

An almost visible shake, and suddenly he was walking towards her. She resisted the impulse to back away, feeling cornered, vulnerable. Trapped.

"I was looking for paper. For the printer," she explained lamely. His explanation was more important than hers, so she stood her ground, eyes fixed on him.

He stopped, and cleared his throat. "I meant to tell you," he said. "It completely slipped my mind, between setting you up at the printer and that damned APA report." He made as if to reach for the package, but hesitated when she instinctively hugged it closer. "After you told me it was missing earlier, I got to thinking. I knew I'd seen a package somewhere, under a table. I found that under the table in the foyer. Karyn must have set the mail down on the table when she was getting her coat on, and the package fell beneath the table and got kicked back."

The explanation was good—too good, too well-rehearsed. Rachael didn't say anything. She didn't mention that she and Karyn had searched all around the foyer—including under that table—before she'd even told Ian the journal was missing.

"I put it there for safekeeping, and I meant to give it to you when you came down to use the printer," Ian added.

Rachael hoped her voice would remain even when she spoke. "Thank you for keeping it safe," she said. "I'll be sure to let Karyn and Celeste know so they stop worrying."

He had begun to turn away, but stopped at her words. "Celeste knew it was missing?" he asked.

"We told her this morning." Rachael wondered at his sudden concern.

"Yes, please be sure to let her know it's been recovered," he said, and moved around his desk to slowly sit down. His chair squeaked faintly, reminding her of the chair at the sugar shack, and she shivered.

"Ian?" Rachael held the package close. He looked up, keeping the scarred side of his face turned away from her. His expression was questioning, but otherwise blank. "The printer paper?"

He opened a closet behind his desk and gave her a ream. Luckily she only had a few more pages to print, because she felt on the verge of screaming if she didn't leave the room soon.

The tension building up inside the back of her head pulled her neck muscles taut. She wanted to lay her hands on the printer, on the package, on something, and get the answers with her power, but she knew she shouldn't, and couldn't.

And wouldn't.

Ian must have taken the diary from Karyn's office. But it didn't make sense, didn't fit with the rest of the puzzle. Ian couldn't have chased her in the woods, or tried to kill her in the sugar shack. Was this incident even related to the others? She could feel Ian watching her as she faced the printer, willing the last pages to feed out quicker. She didn't know why he'd taken the diary, other than perhaps a sudden possessiveness.

But there was something else: something that didn't connect, something that wasn't quite right. It spun around inside of her head, darting this way and that, and she couldn't catch it, couldn't pin it down.

The printer reluctantly released the last page from its clutches. Rachael grabbed the stack of paper and thrust it into her attaché case, fumbled with her laptop. Ian was on the phone, so she merely waved a farewell as she backed out of the office.

She began to pull the door shut, but juggling her case and the bulky package proved to difficult, and she lost her grasp on the package. As she knelt down to pick it up, she glanced through the nearly closed door.

And could have sworn she saw Jordan standing next to his nephew.

*

The next days passed in a frustrating blur of work and flurry of preparation for the ball. Rachael had several more fittings for her costume, and through Angie and her volunteer firefighter husband, met the fire chief, who was more than happy to let her sift through the records at the station.

The old papers proved to be of little help, other than adding an interesting note that the night had been so cold that one firefighter slipped and broke his leg on the frozen water from the pumps. There had been an investigation into the spilled lamp oil, but it had been written off as an unfortunate accident that had caused the fire to ignite the cottage with a devastating swiftness.

The coroner's report from that night confirmed that Emilie had been roughly six months pregnant on the night of the murders. Celeste agreed with Rachael's hesitant suggestion that Ian not be made privy to that fact. Rachael had already told her about Ian's disturbing behavior concerning the diary, and Celeste confided that he always became agitated at this time of year.

"This has always been a hard time for him, dealing with the memories. I appreciate your discretion, Rachael."

"I'm not sure I like the idea of suppressing information, though," Rachael told Jordan one night when he appeared while she was reading in bed. She twisted the bed sheet between her fingers, forming a haphazard skein.

He gently rescued the sheet from her grasp, pulled her to him, stroked her hair. She forced herself not to tense at the action, or her own physical reaction. She wanted him badly, and sometimes found it difficult to accept his comforting actions without aching for more. That he understood her feelings—and suffered the same problem—made her care for him even more.

"You've said yourself that family histories can't be too in-depth—that families don't want every last detail, but a fitting memorial for their ancestors," he pointed out. "If you were writing just about the night of the fire and the people involved, or a book for the public, then I would agree with you. But a small fact like this, taken in the context of over 250 years of MacPherson history...it doesn't matter."

Rachael took the journal to town and mailed it herself.

Celeste had approved Rachael's preliminary notes, and Rachael was immersed in finalizing the text and deciding which of the piles of photos and documents should be reproduced in the book itself.

She'd almost had to admit defeat in complying with Celeste's request that she solve the forty-year-old murder. The facts she'd gathered had confirmed conjectures and pointed out motives and suspects—the distrust between Jordan and Shane, the unhappy marriage of Shane and Emilie, at least from Emilie's point of view—but while she could form possible theories about the shootings, she was still in the dark about who started the fire, and why.

Unfortunately, she wasn't sure which was more dangerous: the knowledge she had, or the knowledge she lacked.

*

Halloween morning dawned cold and overcast, the sky heavily padded with thick sluggish clouds that reminded Rachael too much of sooty smoke. When she went outside for her morning run, swathed in sweats, knit hat, and gloves, wind raked through the trees, the nearly barren, black branches clattering together. By late afternoon, a light dusting of snow was falling, covering the dead grass of the lawn with a fairy-white mantilla of frosty lace.

The phone pealed as she fumbled the key in her chilled fingers. She burst into her room and lunged for the receiver.

"Rachael, love! I was hoping I wouldn't miss you."

"Colin!" Rachael dropped into the wing chair and began to pick at the laces of her running shoes, trapping the receiver between her shoulder and chin. "Did you get the package?"

"I did, and I've had a bit of a look at it." Colin's accent smoothed across the transcontinental line. "You are in the midst of a weird one, aren't you?"

Thinking of her spectral companion, Rachael smiled. Aloud, she said, "It's certainly proving to be...interesting."

"If that's what you want to call it." Colin sounded bemused at her fudging. "I'd call it a bloody soap. Anyway, I started work on this diary right on, because I knew you were waiting. First off, did you know this woman was staunch Pagan?"

"I'd found other evidence to that fact, yes," Rachael said, wincing at the memory of the headache that evidence had caused. "What do you mean about this being a soap opera?"

"Let me read some of this." Colin paused, presumably to find the passage he sought. "'S. struck me today, again. It seems I have not yet learned the signs of what angers him and what does not. I fear for the life of our unborn child, who moves so sluggishly within me.'"

Rachael wondered to which child Emilie referred: Ian, the stillborn baby, or the one that had died with her on the night of the fire. But instead of asking for the date of the entry, she let Colin continue.

"And here's another: 'Sweet Goddess, the sickness that drives my husband has begun to infect my Ian as well. He adores his father so, and try as I may, I cannot halt the spread of the disease.'"

"Yikes," Rachael said. What disease? Was Ian showing signs of brutality at such a young age? Celeste's comment—a lifetime ago, it seemed—about Shane's inability to keep a pet suddenly took on new meaning. She felt close to retching.

"Quite so," Colin agreed. His familiar, positive voice grounded her. "Who are these people, anyway?"

"'S' is Shane, her husband, and Ian's her child," she supplied.

"Well then, who's this 'J' fellow? Listen: 'Would that I had met J. before S. came into my life—and would that I had not made the mistakes I have. But the past cannot be changed now, and I must deal with my fate as best I can.'"

Rachael struggled with irrational jealousy at Emilie's admission of caring for Jordan. But Colin's next quote helped assuage her possessiveness.

"'J. has been a savior to me, and though I know he will always treat me like a beloved sister, that is far enough for me. Nothing can ever happen between us but the confidences I am able to share with him. I have begged him to protect Ian, if he possibly can.... Only he seems strong enough to stand up to S.'"

"Jordan." She found it difficult to speak his name, but she managed to tell Colin. "That's who 'J' is. He was her brother-in-law. Colin, how soon do you think you'll have the whole translation done?"

"A few more days at most, I think," he answered. "I'll send it right out when it's done. And Rachael, love? Be careful, will you? I've not got a good feeling about all this."

Rachael hung up, thoughtfully jiggling the phone in her hand. The journal absolved Jordan of any improper doings with Emilie—something she'd believed in her heart.

But instead of relief, she felt unsettled. Frightened, even. The journal also indicated that Emilie had asked him to protect Ian—was he still doing that? She wondered if Shane's negative energy might be at the root of all the problems here. She wasn't sure how to find out. All she knew was that she agreed with Colin: She was in the midst of a weird one.

A troubled sigh released from her chest. Stripping off her running clothes as she entered the bedroom, she prepared for a much-needed hot shower.

*

Unable to concentrate on her work, Rachael went down to the ballroom, where Karyn was supervising the decorators. In her element now because she was fully in charge of the proceedings, Karyn no longer looked harried or worried. Instead, Rachael found her efficiently instructing a rail-thin man on how the ornate jack o'lanterns should be placed in the windows. Nodding, he carried one carved like a snarling cat's face to the nearest window, and glanced over his shoulder as he set it down. She gestured, and he turned it slightly to the left. Karyn gave him a thumb's-up.

"You're in good spirits today," Rachael commented. Karyn looked imperturbable in brown slacks and a pumpkin-colored turtleneck, a single strand of pearls around her neck.

"You bet." She lowered her voice. "Those problems I told you about? They always clear up by tonight. Haven't had a problem in a day or two, even. I still don't have an explanation for that ad agency, but Celeste is dealing with them." She spread her arms. "Party plans are on track. I am in control."

"Are we still on for tonight?"

Karyn adjusted the tan leather strap of her watch. "The guests are due to being arriving at seven. These guys should be done by five, and Nancy's in charge of the caterers and the musicians, who've been here every year and know what they're doing, anyway. Brett is going home after school with a friend and coming to the ball with them. I'll run home, grab a quick snack, and meet you in your room at six. Sound good?"

"Works for me," Rachael said. She looked around the massive, high-ceilinged room, impressed how the festive decorations enhanced, rather than overshadowed, the rich blue-and-gold decor. She hadn't been in this room since the day Karyn had shown her the portrait gallery. It seemed like a lifetime ago.

The sudden urge gripped her to see Jordan's portrait again, to see all the portraits, to visit with the people whose lives she now knew so intimately.

"Is the emergency exit unlocked yet?" she asked Karyn, who was calling something up to a woman on a high ladder dusting one of the chandeliers.

"Not yet, but it's on my list." Karyn pointed at the clipboard on a folding stepstool.

"I'd like to take a look at the portraits again, so I'll open everything up for you," Rachael offered.

"Would you? That'd be fantastic. You can give me back the keys tonight." Karyn gave her the ring of keys, and waved as she headed across the room to the side of the orchestra balcony.

The room seemed so changed, not so much from the decorations, but from the people scurrying around, cleaning and decorating, she mused as she pulled aside the heavy velvet curtain. She looped a gold-tassled tie-back around it so the door remained visible. People gave new life to empty rooms.

She remembered the last time she had been in the room; just herself and Karyn...and Jordan. Her mouth curved at the memory, but it was a smile tempered with melancholy. He'd danced with her then, but he wouldn't dance with her tonight.

They'd savored their time together these past days, but Rachael was constantly aware of the limitations. He hadn't needed to remind her that he couldn't offer her all the "usual things" in a relationship, as he'd phrased it. She knew he couldn't dance with her at the ball, couldn't stay with her the night through. Her work here was almost done, and though she tried not to let the thought come forward, she knew, deep down, that he wouldn't be able to come with her. Vows she didn't understand bound him to this house. And if those vows were fulfilled, then nothing kept him in the mortal realm. In a few days—perhaps tonight, if his powers waxed full on Halloween and then waned too suddenly afterwards—they would have to say good-bye.

Rachael fitted the key into the antique lock and opened the door, then turned back to the ballroom. Squinting, she tried to imagine what the scene had been like forty years before.

Amidst the glittering finery moved three dark souls whose lives would end that night. Emilie, pale and thin except for the disguised swell of her belly, shying away from the overbearing intensity of her husband; Shane, sullen and arrogant; Jordan, silent in his piratical finery, soon to be an unwilling participant in some mysterious drama that would link him to the earth in an unholy bind, perhaps forever.

The door to the portrait hall opened easily, setting free a rush of stale air that Rachael in her life and work had somehow become accustomed to, almost fond of. The pale light from the sconced bulbs illuminated the portraits. She walked slowly around the room, memorizing the faces of this branch of the proud MacPherson clan. *Touch Not the Cat Bot a Glove.* The cat lurked near, and if she made a false move, he would lash out, ripping her skin with razored claws.

Hands slid around her waist, frightening her, but then a soft voice melted in her ear.

"Lady, when are you going to learn to be more careful? Don't you know this sneaking off alone could get you into trouble?"

"Oh, Jordan," she said, laughing, turning in his embrace to face him. "Don't you know that it's only when I'm alone that I find you?"

He kissed the tip of her nose. "I just wish you'd take more care."

The worry in his voice sobered her, and she nodded, her hair tumbling in her face. "I know. I'm sorry."

Smiling, he brushed the curls away from her cheek, and released her from his embrace, leaving one arm snugly around her waist. He surveyed the portrait she had been studying, the one of him at the piano.

"This was always my favorite," he commented.

"This was the portrait that truly captured my interest in you," Rachael said. "I recognized you from the river, and this just seemed to give you life. I can see the love of your music in your eyes."

"Do you know that one year I came to the ball as Mozart?" Jordan said, his eyes still on the picture of the man he had been. "Full wig, ruffled shirt—everything. I spent most of the night at the piano taking requests from the guests."

Rachael chuckled. "I wish I could have been there to see that."

He buried his face in her hair. She felt his lips move as he said, "So do I, lady. So do I."

But that was an impossibility, just as having him forever was. So many things an impossibility. She couldn't go back in time, couldn't have him with her when she left. She only had him now. He'd asked her to accept this moment in time, all he could give her.

And if that was all he could give her, that was what she would take.

"Jordan," she said, pulling away slightly, "remember when you said we should make the best of our time together?"

He cocked his head, acknowledging and waiting for her to continue. She took a deep breath, staring for a moment at the top button of his shirt.

"I know there's no future for us. That I'll leave here and maybe someday find someone with whom I can have a future. But this moment in time—our moment—it's all we've got, and I want to make the most of that."

He cradled her face in his hands, those artistic hands she would never forget. "Lady, do you know what you're saying? Are you sure?"

"I'm sure," Rachael said, and the conviction in her voice was conviction she truly felt.

She didn't remember getting from that wing of the house to her room. She was barely aware of fumbling with the key in the door to her room. None of that mattered. What mattered was now.

Now, as Jordan deposited kisses on her cheeks, her eyelids, her forehead, before blazing a trail to her ear. There, he nipped, drawing from her a startled gasp of arousal. Rachael wove her fingers into his silken hair as he dragged his teeth down the cords of her neck. Pulling him hard against her, she heard him breathe in her scented flesh as a drowning man gulps air.

His hands roamed beneath the hem of her sweater, and she knew he felt the way her stomach muscles fluttered and tightened as his hands passed over her sensitive skin. Aching to feel more of him, feel him the way he felt her, she pushed him back so that he rolled over. She rolled with him, straddling him, feeling his arousal press against her, as if no clothes were barrier between them. She nibbled at his neck, sweeping a slow path with her tongue, and chuckled seductively as he groaned in response.

Her hands worked to undo the buttons of his shirt, and when she was done, she pulled the two halves aside, exposing him. Fine dark hair dusted his chest, and she ran her hands across it, feeling it tickle the pads of her fingers. A white scar puckered the skin above his left nipple. Over his heart. Rachael didn't have to ask about the cause. For a moment she stared at it, unable to speak, unable to move. She sensed Jordan watching her, waiting for her response. Then, slowly, she bent forward and pressed her lips against the scar. She felt Jordan's hands come up to gently stroke her hair.

Finally she moved down his chest to lap at his flat nipple, which sprang to attention under her ministrations. His hands tightened in her hair as her teeth skimmed the sensitive nub. She trailed her lips across his broad hard chest to the other nipple.

Jordan went back to her waist, insinuating his hands up under her sweater, reaching higher to caress the soft skin beneath her bra. She sat up again, this time to facilitate the passage of his hands, and crossed her arms down to grasp the edge of her shirt. She pulled it over her head, momentarily blinded, and allowed no other sensation but the tantalizing feel of his hands on her; then she pulled it free and tossed it aside, smiling down at him through a haze of hair.

"Ah, lady," he breathed, "you're so beautiful."

Rachael guided his hands up to the front of her powder-blue flowered bra. Jordan's hands fumbled with the clasp at first, but he murmured something about the wonders of modern clothing, and the fastening gave way. Her breasts spilled out, heavy in his hands.

"So beautiful," he said again, shaking his head, his hair dark and curled against the white pillowcase.

Rachael moved her hips against him in a seductive slow circle, luxuriating in his pulsed response. His hands flexed around her breasts. Now it was his turn to pull her down, hard against him, and pull her beneath him, capturing her mouth again before moving lower to bury his face between her pliant mounds. His moist breath warmed her cleavage. When his teeth captured one tender nipple, she cried his name aloud. The action sent a shock of arousal through her, striking lightening-quick to the center of her need. She writhed against him as he caught her other nipple and flicked his tongue against it, and she felt him throb in answer to her movement.

"Jordan, please...." She wasn't sure what she begged him for, and she was almost beyond caring. She cried out wordlessly when he left her, but he was only moving to kneel at her feet and unzip her jeans. He tugged them off, and lifted one of her feet to press a kiss against the inside curve of her ankle. A husky laugh was his only answer when she moaned again in delicious frustration.

He flicked his tongue against her calf, the back of her knee, her tender inner thigh. He skimmed his mouth along the edge of her panties, holding her down with firm hands when she tried to wriggle closer to him. One palm pressed between her legs, feeling the moist fabric. His smile was wicked. Then he slipped his fingers under the elastic, and pulled away the last barrier to her.

"Jordan—" She began to moan his name, but choked off with a cry of pleasure when his mouth found her most intimate spot. The smoky curls of pleasure that had begun suddenly burst into full flame, flames that grew hotter and higher until they ignited an explosion that rocked her to the core.

For a moment they lay still, Jordan's head resting on her stomach, listening to her gasps as she spiraled down from her climax. She felt a low vibration as he whispered, "So beautiful." Then he stood, and stripped off the rest of his clothes.

She reached for him, but he gently captured her wrists and held her hands away, telling her it would be too much for him, that it had been too long. Rachael rose up to her knees to meet him in another driving kiss, their mouths and bodies crushed together.

They used no words, only movement and motion and an inherent sense of what to do. The urgency, the need was upon them, and there was no desire for tenderness now. Rachael gripped the headboard, looked over her shoulder at Jordan as he entered her. She felt the hard length of him slide into her, and shuddered in responsive need, a rush of desire roiling through her as they connected, joined. He bent down to brush away her hair, kiss the back of her neck as he began to move within her.

"Oh lady, oh Rachael…my love…."

The curls of flame kindled within her again, a promise of another fiery eruption. She knew Jordan felt it, too. His hands were tense upon her waist, and as the sensations heightened for her, they did for him, too. His pace quickened, his mouth moving to her shoulder. His words abruptly smothered as his passion overcame him, and his teeth grazed her shoulder. His reaction triggered hers, and Rachael spiraled into blazing hot ecstasy with him.

*

"Okay, I give up. Who exactly are you supposed to be?" Rachael asked after helping Karyn into her somewhat shapeless, long white robes.

"You wound me," Karyn said, picking up a brown wig. "I'm clearly Princess Leia. You should see Brett—he makes the most adorable little Han Solo. I was afraid he'd want me to be Jabba the Hutt—or Slave Girl Leia. As it was, he made some mumblings about *Pirates of the Caribbean*, but I quelled those as fast as I could. Thank goodness I haven't let him watch *Jurassic Park*, or I'd be standing here explaining that I'm a velociraptor."

"Movies seem to be a big theme this year, then," Rachael commented after she finished laughing at the mental picture of short, curvy Karen as a sinewy, vicious dinosaur. She pulled her own costume from the closet. "Although I was also thinking of the TV show."

Karyn had to stretch out the long, slinky black dress before she figured out what it represented. "You're not—" Then she looked at Rachael's hair, which had been painstakingly blown out in a straight fall of black. "That's wonderful!"

"I've always wanted to be Morticia Addams," Rachael admitted, slipping out of her clothes.

"I bet you just liked her house," Karyn teased, holding up the dress so Rachael could slide into it.

"Yeah, until I saw Raul Julia in the movie. What passion!" Rachael dramatically held the back of her hand to her forehead. A long sleeve trailed down from her wrist, ending in a flowing point.

The dress was crushed velvet, a black so dark that it seemed to suck in the light around it. Long and skin-tight, it had a square neckline that hinted at cleavage but wisely showed little. The unrevealing upper half of the dress balanced the slit in the front that traveled from the floor to mid-thigh, allowing Rachael to walk. In the back pooled a short train, night captured in the fabric.

"Too perfect," Karyn pronounced, stepping back to admire. "I would never have the guts to wear something like that."

"I'm surprised I do," Rachael admitted. "This night just brings out the fantasy in us all, I guess."

She'd already glued on blood-red fake nails, and now she applied simple but stark make-up, taking care not to skewer her eye. Her skin, snowy white; her lips, scarlet to match the nails; her eyes, kohl-rimmed.

"All set?" Karyn asked, toying with her peacock-featured mask while she glanced at the clock.

"I think I need a few minutes to practice walking in this dress," Rachael said. "You go on down and start greeting the guests. I'll be down soon."

It was only a half-lie; she did take some turns around the room, getting used to not striding too widely. But she also whispered Jordan's name, inviting him in, welcoming him to view her in her All Hallows Eve costume.

But he didn't come.

*

Rachael paused on the landing, just out of sight of those in the entrance hall below. The MacPhersons had really outdone themselves, she thought, surveying the scene. In the center of the front hall stood a full-sized pumpkin carriage. Doormen dressed as footmen in red uniforms with tassled gold epaulets greeted guests, took their coats and directed them to the ballroom.

Celeste, Felicity and Karyn welcomed the guests after they entered. Though costumed and masked, they were easy to identify. Rachael wondered where Ian was. She supposed he didn't like the attention, being in the spotlight as people came through the front door. On the other hand, she couldn't imagine him making a grand entrance in the ballroom after the guests had arrived. Shrugging, she fiddled with her black satin half-mask, hoping the red-lace edge was straight. Then she minced carefully down the stairs to join the others.

"You look fabulous!" Celeste said, taking her hands and holding her out at arms' length to see her costume. The hotel owner was garbed as an astronaut. Felicity seemed to be dressed as some artist; she turned and presented the side of her head, and Rachael, seeing the makeup obscuring her ear, laughed.

"So do both of you," she said warmly. More guests were coming through the front door, shaking powdery snow from their coats, so she told the family she'd see them again at the ball, and made her way down to the ballroom.

Accepting a dance card from a footman at the door, she entered, and gasped at the change in the room even in the few hours since she'd been there. Fairy dust seemed to hang in the air, shimmering from the chandelier's muted glow. The impression was echoed by the fine snow falling again outside the windows, twinkling against the dark night. The decorations transformed the ballroom, sent it back in time, and somehow magnified the pagan element of the holiday without offense.

Rachael was surprised at how many people she actually knew. As the room filled, she recognized town historian Vera Ducharme dressed as a mermaid, her wheelchair cleverly disguised with crepe paper seaweed; and Trooper Parker, unsurprisingly in the guise of a Keystone Kop. And there were Mildred and Earl in all white, over which they wore clear plastic garbage bags stuffed with colored balloons and labeled "Jelly Belly." Angie's costume, as expected, was the most detailed of all, some sort of many-layered, be-pearled gown with a matching headdress that glinted in the lights. Rachael thought she recognized some of the newer hotel guests, but she couldn't be sure. Concealing masks, ornate costumes and elaborate wigs shrouded everyone else from her recognition.

The effect was more than a little unsettling, Rachael realized. While she could see people's eyes, it was hard to fully judge expression from just that, with other facial features obscured. That, she supposed, was part of the mystery and excitement of such a ball. Masks allowed people to be someone else, if only for a short while.

Before she had time to ruminate on the history and psychology of masks, she felt a tap on her elbow and turned to find Trooper Parker. Wordlessly, he tugged gently at the dance card where it dangled from her wrist on a silken gold cord. Bemused, she released it to him, and he signed his name within.

Over the next minutes, several other men came and added their names to the list, including Brett, who signed his name with earnest concentration, the tip of his tongue peeking from one corner of his mouth. Karyn had been right: He *did* make a most adorable Han, his tousled blond hair poking up behind a carbonite mask.

A lull gave her the chance to get a cup of punch, and she retreated to a non-jostling corner while she sipped, observing the crowd. The room was almost filled, with guests either standing or sitting in the chairs that ringed the dance floor, and she saw Celeste ascending the low steps to the musicians' balcony. As the woman began to welcome everyone to the party, Rachael felt a tap on her shoulder. Expecting it to be Trooper Parker come to claim his dance, she turned.

The Phantom of the Opera stood silently before her, white mask obscuring half his face, and she knew it must be Ian. She smiled a welcome, knowing that an acknowledgment of his identity would only discomfit him. He nodded in greeting and understanding.

"May I be so bold as to request a dance from you?" he asked, his voice pitched low to avoid interrupting those who listened to Celeste.

"That you may," she replied, offering him the card. The black leather gloves, she noted as he signed his name, complemented his costume. In fact, the persona was achingly right for him, with an irony that she guessed was only too obvious to him as well.

Celeste finished her welcome, and the orchestra swelled into the first song. Trooper Parker finally did come to claim his dance, and Ian melted into the crowd.

"I trust nothing strange has happened to you since our last meeting?" he asked as he moved her onto the dance floor.

"If by 'strange' you mean sabotage or attempted murder, then no, it's been very quiet," Rachael said pleasantly, deftly slipping a foot away before he stepped on it. The man danced like his costume-character. But she appreciated his concern.

"Good," he grunted. He glanced around the room. "Well, nothing's going to happen tonight, in a room full of people." They danced for a moment in silence. Then he asked, "And how is your research going?"

"Book's almost done, as a matter of fact." His nightstick banged against her hip, and she winced.

Rachael was glad when the dance ended and Angie's husband Joe came to take his turn. He, too, inquired after her research, and so did most of her next partners, until she seriously wished she could forget her work and enjoy her evening. She danced with Brett, who performed his duties solemnly and then scampered off to the separate party for children in another room.

Her dance with Ian was strained, stiff. He danced gracefully, despite his limp; knowing the music, but without feeling. He spoke little, answering her comments with monosyllables. She guessed that he was uncomfortable, felt him tense anytime they came too close to another couple. But there was something more, something she couldn't quite grasp or define. Resting on his back, her fingertips tingled, as if wanting to eke an answer from the jacket of his tuxedo. She resisted, forcing her mind to remain in the present, all the while wondering why the urge persisted, and what was wrong.

Just as the music ended, she felt something. But it wasn't something wrong.

It was the tingling sensation, the knowing, the expectation she always felt when Jordan was about to appear.

A ripple went through the crowd, and suddenly Ian made a harsh noise. His face had turned as white as his mask.

Because a man was moving through the room, a tall, beautiful, dark-haired man wearing the ruffled white shirt, short jacket and tight leather pants of a buccaneer. His hair curled rakishly along the back of his neck, and his plain black mask couldn't disguise the strong nose or sensuous mouth.

Rachael felt a melting warmth, weakening her limbs, swelling her throat. Tears welled in her eyes even as a gasp of joy threatened to escape her mouth. Jordan easily found her in the crowd, and he smiled lazily, but his steps took him to the orchestra balcony. All eyes seemed to follow him. Of course: This was a small community, and the man was a delicious mystery to them all. Who was this enigmatic stranger? A hotel guest?

Or a ghost, risen from the grave?

Rachael glanced around, picking the MacPhersons out of the crowd. Ian was already slipping away, slinking painfully through an assemblage that paid him no heed, his face a harsh, pale visage. Celeste stood with her head cocked, one hand at the throat of her costume; even at this distance Rachael could see her puzzled frown. It had been forty years since she had seen her uncle; the memory had dimmed, with only a few faded photographs stuffed in an album and portraits in a dark back room to remind her. Something about this unknown man piqued her recollection, but she couldn't quite say how. Rachael caught a brief glimpse of Felicity, who had stood when the man appeared. Before she returned to her seat, Rachael saw her smile slightly, but it was a cryptic look that she couldn't define.

Jordan spoke briefly to the orchestra leader, who nodded. Then he turned and walked to Rachael, the guests parting like waves around the prow of a schooner. His gaze never left hers as he approached, and she lifted her chin, answering his look. When he reached her, he bowed low, a sweeping gesture. Humor glinted behind the verdant of his eyes, but his voice held seriousness as he said,

"My lady, may I request your company for this dance?"

Rachael held up her wrist, presenting her dance card. He eased it from her, but instead of signing his name within, he folded it and put it in his breast pocket, claiming her for the rest of the evening. And as she folded into his arms, the band began to play "Greensleeves."

They didn't speak during that song. Jordan sang the words softly to her, too low for anyone else to hear. Rachael pressed her face against his jacket, blocking out everything but the sound of the music and the feel of him against her, moving with her in a dance she had never thought possible. She remembered the first time she had been in the ballroom, when she'd imagined she'd danced with him. Or maybe she had. She raised her head and looked up at the ceiling, watching it move in slow circles above them, and it seemed they were the only people in the room.

The song ended, but he didn't release her, and when the next began, they continued to dance. The first blush of excitement for the guests had worn off, and they moved away as they danced, no longer hovering near to catch a snippet of information that would tell them more about the stranger.

"Jordan... How can you be doing this?"

"Ssh, lady." He put a finger against her lips, then moved it away to kiss her. "Did you think I wouldn't squire you to the ball? What kind of lover would I be then?"

"But Ian, Celeste, Felicity—they might recognize you."

"Masked and costumed, in a room full of masked and costumed people?" He glanced around, slight worry at the corner of his eyes, but then he shook his head. "They might think I look like a former relative, but do you honestly think they'd believe in ghosts?"

"Felicity probably does," she answered, remembering the woman's cryptic statement about Jordan asking her not to tell anyone what she'd seen. "Ian might. He nearly died of shock when he saw you. I told you I saw you in his office last week."

"Just because you saw me doesn't mean he did," he pointed out again.

She opened her mouth to reply, but then she noticed that the children had been allowed back in the ballroom for a short while. Brett was watching them. When he saw her looking, he gave her a thumbs-up.

"I think more people know about you than you realize," she commented. Brett, in fact, had told her he'd seen a ghost the first day she'd met the boy.

Jordan followed her look. Brett wasn't paying attention any longer; instead, he was nudging the child beside him and pointing at the buffet table.

"Adults don't realize how observant children can be—children see and hear things adults never intend," he commented. He smiled. "Besides, children have always been able to see things that adults, by the very nature of their age, no longer can."

Rachael laughed. "I don't know whether to kiss you or smack you upside the head."

"I vote for the kiss," he said, and gently branded one on her forehead. The action sobered her suddenly, and a sense of loss swept through her, causing her to cling to him.

"I know, lady. I know," he said, lips warm and soft against her skin. "The time's so short. Don't think about it. Just feel."

The song had ended and another had begun, and she hadn't noticed. It was the same with the next song, and the next. They danced together as if they'd been destined to, not thinking of the past, or the future, but just the way it felt to hold one another and float on the gentle music of their love.

Eventually, though, she felt him tremble with the exertion of being there. She squeezed his hand in understanding.

"Walk with me," he said. They made their way through the crowd to the door and down a private hallway, dim and small compared to the light and space in the ballroom. "I just need to rest for a while; I'll come back," Jordan promised, kissing her. The imprint of the kiss lingered on her lips even as he faded away. Rachael blinked back tears, holding her hand out where he had been, as if she would be able to feel traces of him on her skin. Slowly, she turned and made her way back to the party.

Craving a glass of punch, she tried to make her way to the buffet, but she was barely into the room before Karyn appeared out of the crowd.

"Rachael! Who *was* that? Where have you been hiding him?" she demanded excitedly, her blue eyes alight.

"Who was that masked man?" Rachael quipped. "Would you believe me if I said I didn't know?"

Karyn reared her head back, squinting her eyes in bemused suspicion. "Somehow, no, but I get the feeling that's your story and you're going to stick to it."

Rachael spread her hands in supplication. "He was wearing a mask and a costume. How should I know?"

"Some people have all the luck," Karyn grumbled good-naturedly. Then she looked at the doorway and added, "Then again, maybe not. Looks like Ian wants to see you."

Rachael turned. Ian gestured at her. He seemed less upset now, his skin a healthier tone, but his movement suggested urgency. "Grab a glass of punch for me, would you, please?" she asked Karyn. "Hopefully this won't take too long."

She found him waiting outside the wide set of double doors. Without preamble he said, "I've found something of my mother's."

Chapter Fifteen

He spoke barely above a whisper, his voice low and mumbled; she hardly made out his words. Still, they sent a flare of excitement sparking through her.

"What is it? Where did you find it?" Rachael demanded.

Ian ignored her question, instead turning and walking away. She was vaguely annoyed at his assumption that she would follow, but she did anyway. His silent abruptness disturbed her, but she supposed his own shock was to blame.

They were nearly to the front hall, Rachael hurrying to keep pace with him in her heels, when she realized that he no longer limped. Could shock induce that, too? She'd heard of people gaining great physical strength in moments of adversity, to the point of lifting cars and saving companions, but his limp was caused by a physical deformity. She slowed, to view him from the back, but he sensed that, and turned.

"What's wrong?" he asked, his shoulders tensed, one hand jammed into the pocket of his tuxedo jacket. "Hurry."

No longer muttered, his voice still sounded wrong. She hesitated.

His hand vacated his pocket, and she saw the dull metallic gleam of a gun barrel.

"I said, come on," he commanded, his voice hard. Rachael complied. Grabbing her upper arm, his grip painfully tight, he pushed her along next to him. She walked quickly, taking small steps to avoid stumbling. He held the gun close to his body, almost hidden in the folds of the black swirling cape.

Certainly one of the footmen would see them.... But all the guests had arrived, so the front hall was empty, the pumpkin coach mockingly silent, empty windows dark and unseeing.

He pulled her to a stop in front of the door to the western tower, shifting her to the right so that the gun poked painfully into the small of her back, and opening the door with his left hand. No lock deterred him; the door swung outward, and he shoved her inside.

Surprised that she could even enter, after what she had seen in her visions, she tripped forward, catching herself on the banister that curved upwards in graceful parallel with the spiral stairs. The wooden rail wobbled in her grasp, the end no longer attached to the wall. She heard the door shut behind her, the lock sliding home, and for a moment blackness engulfed her. Then a bare bulb on the wall flared to life, its unshaded light glaring, harsh.

Rachael turned. Ian was pulling off the mask that obscured his face. But it wasn't Ian who was revealed by the action. She gasped.

Kevin. A reddened line slashed across his face where the edge of the Phantom mask had cut into his skin. The mask had also matted his hair, and he absently scratched his head. He still wore the black gloves, and she remembered "seeing" a black-gloved hand on the door handle. She'd assumed it had been Ian. How long had Kevin been using the tower?

"Get upstairs," he said, indicating the way with a wave of the gun. "Be careful—some of the steps are rotted through."

"Why are you doing this?" she asked, nonetheless putting a foot on the first step, not wanting to antagonize him. The steps were wooden, and open behind; not solid, and obviously old. The tower was unsafe, someone had said, and that was obviously true. "What do you want from me?"

"I don't want anything," he said from behind her, following her up, letting her know he and the gun were right behind her. "He asked me to bring you here, that's all."

"Who, Ian?" A stair bowed beneath her weight, and she hastily moved to the next one. Knowing the banister was relatively useless, she placed her other hand against the stone wall, putting some of her weight on it as she carefully moved up to the next step.

"Of course. He's the one who hired me."

"Hired you for what?" *That's why his boss was angry: He'd never come back to work*, she realized.

"Never mind," Kevin said sharply, as if realizing he had overstepped his bounds. The gun prodded her in the back again, and she ascended another step. In the next one gaped an angry, ragged hole, and she shivered, glad she wasn't the one who had broken through. Gingerly, she stepped higher, over it.

Things were falling into place now, almost faster that she could catch the pieces and arrange them to fill in the puzzle. Ian hadn't been directly responsible for any of the "accidents"—he'd had a middleman. The person who chased her in the woods…the person who sabotaged her computer…the person who tried to kill her in the sugar shack…. They had all been Kevin, whom she had seen a day after he was supposed to have left the manor. A minor slip on his part, but one she hadn't caught until too late. He'd probably been responsible for the broken railing in the library, too. His sneakers' squeak echoed in her memory.

But why? Why had Ian gone to such lengths to prevent her from doing her research?

They were about halfway up when a step shattered beneath her.

Rachael flung herself forward, straightening her body so she didn't land with all her weight on another rotting step. Splinters dug into her palms, and she hissed in pain. For a moment she could do nothing but lie there, trying to calm her frantic gasps, her cheek pressed against the uneven wood. She watched pieces of wood tumble into the blackness, and it was a long time before she heard them hit the stone floor far below.

"Are you okay?" She felt Kevin's hand on her back.

"What the hell do you care?" she raged, getting on her knees. "You've tried to kill me!"

His expression changed, almost startled, then went blank: another mask. Rachael doubted he held any personal ill-will toward her. He worked for Ian, for whatever reason. Maybe he was reconsidering his actions? Carefully, she eased over, sitting on a step that didn't sag when she pushed at it.

"You don't really want me to get hurt," she said softly. "You just tried to help me—you were worried about me, weren't you? Kevin, you know this is nuts, and it's wrong. What say we just go back downstairs and pretend none of this ever happened?"

His eyes narrowed. "That's a bunch of bull," he snapped. "You'd go straight to the police. Now, get up." When she didn't move immediately, he leaned over her and pointed the gun at her, barrel inches from her face. "I said, get up."

Biting her lip, she complied, forcing herself not to panic and move too fast, and fall again. Her knee ached where it had smacked against a jutting piece of broken wood, and she saw that her pantyhose had torn. The velvet of her dress was matted and dusty, and for a sudden, irrational moment, that bothered her.

"Why, Kevin?" she asked softly. "At least have the courtesy to tell me why you're doing this."

A pause, and then he answered, his voice shooting bitterly over her shoulder. "Help U Sell Advertising has never realized my talent. With the money Ian's giving me, I'll be able to set up my own agency—and then I'll get the big bucks I deserve."

"Is the money really worth being an accessory to murder?"

"Who said anything about murder? All I've been trying to do is scare you, so you'll stop your research."

"Oh, come on, Kevin, do you really believe that?" Rachael took the chance of stopping and turning to look at him again. "What do you think he's going to do with me? Have a nice little chat over a spot of tea?"

"Shut up, and *move*," he said. The edge in his voice frightened her, and she complied. "Yeah, that's all I know, that he's going to talk you out of finishing the book. What the hell can I do now, anyway? It's too late for me to back out."

"It's not—"

"If you talk one more time," he shouted, "you'll be happy if he does kill you."

She sensed from the hysteria in his voice that whether he'd ever thought this would lead to her death before, he knew it now, and he was scared enough to shoot her if she provoked him any further. They made it the rest of the way without incident, Rachael always aware of the gun at her back and the treacherous spiral stairs. The door at the top was half-open, and Kevin reached around her to push it the rest of the way, nudging her through.

The room was a mirror image of Felicity's studio, but after the basic building design, the resemblance ended. Heavy drapes in sun-faded burgundy and green covered most of the windows, shunning light. The single bare bulb illuminated the fact that the place was, for the most part, filthy. Grime coated the once-polished wooden floor, making her shoes stick. Threadbare blankets crumpled atop a single cot, and the corners were stuffed with tattered newspapers and magazines, old clothes, and something that looked and smelled suspiciously like moldy food. The room also smelled of stale urine, and it occurred to her that if Kevin had been living up here since his ex-coworkers had left, he would have had to make do with a chamber pot. The only other furniture, besides the cot, were a card table scarred with burns no doubt made by the ancient oil-burning lamp upon it, and a single grey metal folding chair.

Kevin tossed a rumpled pinstriped Brooks Brothers shirt off the chair onto the bed, and motioned for her to sit. She complied, unwilling to antagonize him further, hoping he wouldn't tie her up as he had at the sugar house.

"Well," he said, to her relief, "I'd better get back to the party before they notice the Phantom is gone too long." He paused in the doorway. "Oh, and don't bother screaming," he said. "This old place was built so well, sound's protected from escaping."

It's protected in more ways that you'd understand, she thought, listening to the bolt clunk into place on the other side of the door. She waited, giving him time to start down the stairs, before she stood to make an inspection of her tower prison.

More than half the windows overlooked the front of the house, a sheer drop down to the ground. No one was outside. A fresh layer of snow had fallen on the tracks leading in, and glittered on the cars parked along the sweeping curve of the drive. Even if some guests left the manor, there was no guarantee they would look up, or understand her frantic gestures if they did.

Several windows faced across to the other tower, which was silent and lifeless with its usual occupant off at the ball. Star-shards were trapped on the sharp ridge of the ice-painted roof. Windows along the back of the tower showed another sharp drop down onto the peaked center of the roof.

She supposed she could always tie blankets together to form a rope and shimmy down that way. A quick check of the bed revealed only two shabby blankets; even adding a pair or two of Kevin's pants wouldn't make a long-enough rope. Besides, she had annually failed rope-climbing in gym class, and seriously questioned her ability to make the descent unscathed.

Hoping Kevin would be away from the tower by now, Rachael crossed the room to the door. She wasn't surprised when she tugged and the bolt showed no signs of giving way. The stairs might have begun rotting through, but the door proved to be of much sturdier ilk. Even pounding on it produced only a faint thudding noise that probably didn't even reverberate to the other side, much less down the stairs to where someone would hear. Kevin had been right about the sound-proofing quality of her cell.

Defeated, she returned to the chair and sat down heavily to wait. Wait for what? Kevin had gone back to the party, dressed identically to Ian, so no one would notice if the real Ian wasn't present. She hoped someone would notice the lack of limp, or the different voice, but it wasn't likely. No one would question Ian lurking silently, uncomfortably, attending the party but not enjoying it. Kevin and Ian, she realized, must have been the people Angie had mentioned when Rachael had had her first costume fitting: the two who requested almost matching disguises.

How long would it be before someone noticed that she was absent from the ball? Karyn had seen her leave with "Ian," so he'd be questioned. He'd probably use the same excuse—that he'd found something of Emilie's, and that she was examining it. He'd tell Celeste that she really couldn't go off and leave her guests, and turn her attentions back to the party. It would be a while, probably all night, before anyone thought to worry or search for her.

So now Kevin had gotten her out of the way and gone to play interference, but for what? What was Ian planning to do, and to whom? She shivered.

As Rachael scanned the room, trying to conjure another possible method of escape, her eyes picked out the faint remains of a large pentagram on the floor. This had been Emilie's room, her haven, her escape from an abusive husband and her place of worship. She would have had a small altar, possibly beneath one of the windows, with her candles and athame and cup. The symbols on the door and up here kept her safe, kept Shane out.

Had she allowed her young son entrance to her sanctuary? Ian had spoken passionately about his father, and she'd extrapolated that as a child, he worshipped the man. Even if he considered his mother weak and ineffectual, at some point he'd obviously discovered her tower room and its contents. She sensed the faint impression that he'd spent much time here, even before he'd hidden Kevin here to do his dirty work; his presence overpowered Kevin's, even though Kevin's clothes and dirt and smells permeated the room.

Rachael shivered again. Ian had obliterated much of what Emilie had had here. The pentagram on the floor was blurred to near obscurity, and she knew from experience that floor, so constantly walked on by so many, was useless for picking out a specific memory. The altar was long-destroyed, and the current furniture was too new to have been used by Emilie. The only item that looked old enough to have survived forty years was the oil lamp on the table. Rachael turned, reached out for it.

A brief touch, and she snatched her hand back, surprised the lightning bolt hadn't been visible as well as felt. She pressed her fingers against her lips, trembling. Not Emilie, but Ian, and memories so strong, they burned her before she saw anything.

Rachael debated what to do. She'd sworn never to use her powers to learn about another living person.

After what he's done to you, all bets are off.

But...

And before he's done more to you, maybe you'd better find out what's going on. Before it's too late.

Personal gain...

This is a matter of life or death. Yours, specifically.

Conscience tried to gnaw at her, but the facts lashed back like a lion-tamer's whip. Yes, she'd made a vow to herself, but she'd never considered this possibility. Ian had tried to have her killed. She didn't know where he was now, or what he intended to do. If she didn't find out before something happened....

Turning the chair around, she faced the table, and the lamp. In the harsh light of the uncovered bulb on the ceiling, the green-tarnished brass refused to glow, refused to shine, and smoke stains begrimed the glass panels. The oil inside looked sludgelike, unhealthy, tainted like the memories it hid.

With a deep breath, Rachael closed her eyes and reached out to touch the lamp, steeling herself against the sudden rush of recollection. She laid only her fingertips upon it, in an effort to filter the visions and emotions slowly, carefully.

The lamp swung crazily in the child's—Ian's—hands, casting distorted shadows along the path down the lawn. Ahead, a black-on-black line indicated where the tree line began, almost unseeable. Behind, not enough light spilled from the wide heavy house to help illuminate the way. A shriek-burst of laughter darted out, only to be swallowed by the night.

He was following his father, Rachael remembered from Felicity's recount of the events. He'd seen Shane go down to the cottage—or, at least, to the woods—and wanted to be with him. Or maybe it was simply curiosity that had led young Ian into the fray of that horrible night.

The trees closed in, the shadows now menacing, creeping from behind the bushes, ducking back out of sight when he turned to look. Ahead, a faint light shone through the trees: the cottage. Resolutely, the boy continued on, and as he approached, he heard the door bang open against the wall, and a loud, angry voice. Shane. Ian crept to the front door and tiptoed inside to the hallway. Setting down the lamp, he peered around the corner into the room.

Emilie lay on a cot in the simply furnished room, her party finery rumpled and torn. Jordan had been kneeling next to her; now, as Ian watched, he slowly rose to his feet to face the man who had just entered. Face the man, and the gun in his hand, pointed at them.

"So, here you are," Shane spat. "I finally have proof of what I knew was happening all along."

Jordan made an angry gesture, but checked himself as the gun raised, the threat acknowledged. "Dammit, Shane, are you blind? We're not here having some illicit tryst. Your wife is ill."

As if to add credence to his statement, Emilie moaned, clutching her belly, her gaunt face drained of color. Jordan dropped back down on one knee, and turned over the moist cloth on her forehead.

Shane snorted, his face twisting, ugly. "Then why is she lying there with her legs spread like some common whore?"

Jordan swore, raking a hand through his now unruly hair. His mask lay crumpled, forgotten, beneath his booted foot. "You are blind—or insane. She's losing her child."

"Child?" Shane's eyes narrowed, flicked to his wife. "You're pregnant again?"

Unable to speak, she nodded, gasping as pain wracked her thin body again.

"She never told me," he said, almost defensively, and without compassion.

"She didn't tell anyone," Jordan answered, no longer looking at him. He cradled Emilie's head in one hand and held a cup to her lips, urging her to drink. The smell of Felicity's secret tea-concoction wafted up with the steam. "She was afraid to, after what happened last time. Of course, your beating her didn't help matters any."

"I've told her I don't like her running off to that graveyard. I can't help it if she doesn't learn easily." Shane spoke as if she wasn't even in the room, making his words all the more chilling. She was a possession to him, and a willful one at that.

Emilie moaned again, a low sound of agony that lingered in the air. A wet crimson rose was blooming between her thighs.

"She won't be running off anywhere if she doesn't get help," Jordan said. "Go to the house and call for Dr. Pope."

But Shane approached the cot. Languidly, he used the end of the gun barrel to lift up the edge of Emilie's skirt. "And how," he asked, feigning unconcern, "do I know this child isn't yours?"

His reserve snapped, and with a snarl Jordan launched himself at his half-brother. Shane brought the gun up, but Jordan was too close, and he knocked it aside.

Ian dove away, his ears shrieking in pain from the echoing report of the gun. An agonized scream followed the bang, an ululating wail that finally, finally trailed away.

"Holy Jesus," he heard his uncle whisper hoarsely in the sudden loud silence that followed. Cautiously, he crawled back to the doorway, peeked around.

Another rose blossomed in his mother's chest. Jordan clutched her hands. Shane stood at the foot of the bed, staring at them, his expression unreadable. But the gun shook in his hand.

"Jordan." Emilie's voice was barely audible. Pink frothed at the corner of her mouth. She somehow found the strength to disengage one of her hands from his, and she pressed two fingers against his forehead. "Jordan, I charge you. Avenge my death. Exact revenge from my murderer. Swear it."

"Emilie—"

"Swear you will not rest until I am avenged. Swear it!" Her voice suddenly gained force. Even though it wasn't much louder, it resonated with power, rippling through the room on the wave of her demand.

Shane blinked, as though coming out of a trance. "I don't think anyone's going to be avenging anything, my dear," he said, and raised the gun again.

Ian clapped his hands to his ears, but the gunshot still sent a shock of pain through him. Jordan slumped forward, his head near Emilie's on the pillow. It was *possible that he whispered something; then his body gave a jerk, and he toppled to the floor, the thud heavy and solid.*

His hands now over his mouth, Ian scuttled backwards, away from the door, nearly knocking over the lamp. He snatched out to right it, then paused, considering it, chubby cheeks hollowed as he pursed his lips, an oddly adult expression.

Papa always told him that if you did something bad, you should cover it up so no one else found out. Papa had showed him how he made sure no one found out when he did something bad in his work papers.

Rachael gasped, but the sound was very far away, through an aural fog. She'd never been able to feel emotions so strongly, certainly never heard their thoughts as though they were her own. She tried to pull away from the vision, but inexorably she was drawn back, helpless, into the scene....

Papa was still busy in the room. But Ian could help him, make sure no one found out the bad things Papa had done.

He went out to the kitchen and, one by one, opened the cabinets until he found the big heavy jug of lamp oil. He dragged it to the front door, then tipped it, allowing some oil to spill out. He tugged the jug outside, and spilled more. Walk, drag, tip, spill. Walk, drag, tip, spill. At the bedroom window, he stood on tiptoes and peeked in. Papa was doing something to Mama and Uncle Jordan, but his back was to the window, and Ian couldn't stretch up long enough to watch. Instead, he went back to the jug. Walk, drag, spill, until he was back at the front door. By now the jug was just light enough to carry, and he gripped the oily handle with both hands, hauling it inside. It dripped a trail of oil behind as he made his way to the bedroom. Shane was standing at the foot of the bed, where the two bodies lay heaped together.

"Papa?"

Shane whirled, surprise and then fury in his eyes. Startled, Ian took a step backwards. His heel caught against the doorjamb, and he fell backwards, landing with an oof. The jug slipped from his grasp, oil spurting out from the force with which the container hit the ground.

Shane took a step towards him, but his foot landed in the spattered oil, and he, too, fell, his knees making a sharp sound on the wood. On his hands and knees, he shook his head, slightly stunned.

"Papa," Ian said, pulling himself up, "I wanted to help you. You can cover it up so no one will know." He took a step forward.

And kicked over the lamp.

A sudden whoosh, and flames exploded in the pool of oil, exploded up to surround Shane. Screaming, he heaved to his feet, slapping his arms against his body to blot out the fire, but the movement only fueled the flames.

And behind his father, his mother's arm weakly waved through the air, a gross parody of Shane's motion.

Ian opened his mouth to scream, but his throat moved soundlessly. He turned and bolted for the front door. But the fire raced him, eating along the track inadvertently provided for it, and it had a head start. By the time Ian got there, the blaze had leapt outside to eagerly consume the dry grass around the front step. The old wood of the door frame lovingly coaxed the flames along its length.

His voice returned.

The scream reverberated in Rachael's ears, first deafening, then muted. As it gained intensity again, spiraling louder, she realized it was no longer Ian, but herself who howled in fear. With all the strength she had, physical and mental, she tore her hands away from the lamp and leaped to her feet. The chair clattered as it toppled over.

Rachael hugged herself in a vain attempt to stop her trembling, her mind tumbling over with what she had seen.

And then she realized she was no longer alone.

She turned. Ian stood, watching her, his face expressionless. He'd removed his mask, and his cloak.

"It was you," she blurted.

He moved toward her, and she backed away, but he walked to the card table instead. From a deep pocket, he produced his gold-plated lighter, and with a practiced flick, held it to the lamp's wick. He picked up the flickering light and gazed at it a moment before speaking.

"Yes, it was me." The small flame sent light and dark dancing over the burn patterns on his face. "I started the fire—though not in quite the way I intended. As a result, I killed my father."

"Emilie..." Rachael managed.

His green eyes, now flecked with red-gold, flicked up at her. "Oh, yes, I killed my mother as well."

Rachael remembered the arm weakly moving as the fire began to rage. "Dear Lord, Ian, I—"

"Don't pity me," he snapped, and she took another involuntary step backwards. "I don't want any pity. She was weak, anyway."

"Avenge my death. Exact revenge from my murderer. Swear it."

They hadn't been the words of a weak woman. Everything was falling into place now: Jordan, the reason he couldn't tell her what happened. He'd been asked to exact revenge, but when Emilie bound him to the promise—not weak, that binding—she thought her murderer had been Shane. She never suspected her death would actually come at the hands of her six-year-old son.

And Jordan had never exacted that revenge.

"Now, Rachael, the problem is you," Ian said, pacing with his familiar halting step through the room, heedlessly swinging the lamp, occasionally bump-bumping it against his leg. "What am I going to do with you, now that you know?"

She was beginning to recover from the terror of her vision and the shock of finding him behind her, and she leaned a hip against the rickety card table, feigning nonchalance.

"What makes you think that I know anything dangerous?" she asked.

"I know about your power."

The sharp cat's claw of fear slashed through her again. "How——?"

He lifted one shoulder in a shrug. "I inherited a bit of the Sight from her. I knew something was different about you the moment I met you."

"But no one else knows, so why do you have to do anything with me?" she asked. "I have no real proof, so who would believe me? And why would I even tell? You were a child, Ian, and it was all a mistake—"

"You and your damned lover!" He turned on her suddenly, and she straightened, feeling the table wobble with the sudden motion. "You both want to forgive me. You won't understand that it wasn't an accident."

But it *had* been an accident: He'd never intended for his father to die. Over the years, the horror of what he'd done had obviously festered in his psyche, twisting the reality into his own personal fantasy-nightmare. The tragedy had claimed one more victim than anyone had realized, that of Ian's tortured soul.

"I did it on purpose."

Ian punctuated his last words with steps toward Rachael, but she held her ground, casting about for an avenue of escape, or perhaps, a weapon. If she could dart around him, she might make it to the door.... She could see over his shoulder that he'd left it unlocked, and she was surprised he'd overlook a detail like that. She could probably reach the chair before he did, maybe hit him with it and slow him down, but she'd still be trapped unless she managed to knock him out and find the key to the lower door. Doubtful he would have neglected to lock both.

Best if she kept him talking, kept his mind on other things.

"So, you know about Jordan," she said, recalling his words: *You and your damned lover*. "Damned" was such an ironic word. That he even knew about her and Jordan was unnerving, but she didn't let him know.

"Of course he knows," responded another voice, just as she felt the familiar tingle of his approach.

Chapter Sixteen

Ian sensed him immediately, too, and he whirled at the words. Jordan stood in his usual pose, arms folded across chest, leaning in seeming casualness against the wall. Incongruously, he still wore his buccaneer costume, although the hat lay at his feet.

"Of course he knows," he repeated. "I've made it my afterlife's work to try and keep him on the straight and narrow, as it were." In one fluid, graceful motion, he pushed himself away from the wall and began moving toward them. "I've kept his secrets, and I haven't done what his mother charged me to do on her deathbed forty years ago."

"I never asked for your pity," Ian snarled.

"It wasn't pity that stayed my hand, believe me," Jordan said, stopping at a point between them. Rachael could hear the tension in his musical voice, the fury that counterpointed his words. "I searched for signs of compassion in you because I knew your mother wanted me to find it. She never could, in Shane or in you." He shook his head. "I can't go on protecting you any longer, Ian." He looked at Rachael, his green eyes expressionless except for the love she knew was there, and back at Ian. "I think

Emilie would understand why I have to break that vow. She understood what love was. I told you I wouldn't abide you threatening Rachael, and now you've taken it too far."

"Another thing you can't abide is fire," Ian said, and swung the lantern at Jordan.

Jordan threw up a hand to ward off the blow, and their arms collided. The lantern flew from Ian's hand, skittered across the table, and bounced once on the floor, landing beneath one of the long burgundy curtains. Flames greedily leapt onto their prey, hungry scarlet teeth tearing at the fabric.

Rachael swore, pushing the table aside in her haste to get to the fire. Kicking the lantern away, she grabbed the curtain in both hands and yanked, pulling it from the rod. It tumbled down in dusty swaths, choking her. She beat at the flames, and managed to put them out. But the rolling lantern had ignited a trail along the floor, and the blaze leapt to another curtain, chewing up the hem, devouring the heavy emerald cloth.

A crash demanded her attention, and she looked up to see Jordan and Ian grappling. Despite Ian's bulk, with his old injuries he was no match for Jordan. Still, his desperation gave him might, and he struggled to push Jordan closer to the growing fire.

Rachael threw the first curtain onto the next, trying to smother the flames. When the thick curtain landed, however, it sent up a fire-spray of sparks and burning threads, which in turn ignited another drape.

Jordan spun, putting Ian between himself and the blaze. And Ian's former nemesis proved his downfall again, as he slipped in spilled oil. He fell to his knees, thumping hard against the wooden floor. Fighting to regain his footing, he grabbed at the curtain next to him. But it tore free from the valance and tumbled down in fiery folds, wrapping about him like the devil's cloak.

With an inhuman cry, Ian lurched to his feet. But instead of trying to beat out the flames, he instead launched himself at Jordan, arms spread wide to embrace him in the conflagration.

Jordan backed up, trying to get away, but Ian was too quick. He fell against Jordan, and the two slammed back against the door. It swung outward. Rachael screamed as the two men toppled into the blackness beyond. Her voice was lost in the hideous wave of crashes that followed, as the rotted wood splintered under the weight of the falling men.

Then—suddenly—silence, except for the crackling of flames that munched through the drapery and along the floor.

Rachael rushed to the gaping doorway. The single bulb at the top of the stairs provided little illumination, just enough to see that most of the steps were gone, only jagged edges remaining. Dust swirled up in the light's glow. Below, darkness.

"Jordan?" Rachael called. "Jordan!" Her voice echoed in the now-empty space. No answer. Just the mocking reverberation, reminding her that the only exit to the burning tower had been destroyed.

Choking back a sob of fear, Rachael stumbled back into the room. The cot was alight now, Kevin's Brooks Brother's shirt writhing in the flames. She ran across the room to a window and tore down the burning curtain, throwing it aside as it scorched her hands. The window was painted shut, probably years before. She stared across at the other tower, and the narrow, ice-covered ledge that separated her from it. Then she picked up the metal folding chair and smashed it against the window.

The old, thick glass repelled the attack, her wrists twisting painfully as the chair rebounded. Gritting her teeth, she hit again, and this time, she felt a pop as a ligament snapped out of line, the sprain agonizing. Rachael cried out, almost dropping the chair. Gripping it as best she could, she raised it again.

This time, the glass shattered, sparkling pieces flying outward like falling stars to scatter in the glittering snow on the roof, raising little puffs of white as they landed. Wrapping her hand in a piece of curtain that hadn't burned yet, Rachael punched out the rest of the glass.

Chill air silently breathed into the room. There was no breeze, but it felt as though a wall of air inexorably pushed at her. The fresh air fueled the fire, which roared its delight. Swirls of smoke made her cough, and her stomach twisted. She'd barely survived something like this not so long ago, and the lingering memory intensified her fear.

Rachael began to unwrap her hand, then thought the better of it and tied the cloth on with another strip, tugging the knot tight with her teeth. She repeated the action on her other hand. This way, her palms would be protected, while her fingers were free to grip the roof.

She glanced back into the room. Most of Kevin's clothing had been littered on or around the bed, and had gone up in flames. But another pair of slacks had been tossed into a corner away from the windows, and had so far escaped the conflagration. Rachael tore at the front slit of her dress, ripping it up to her waist, and grabbed the slacks, pulling them on. She and Kevin were about the same height, and luckily he was stocky. She tugged the belt to the last notch. There was nothing she could do about shoes; her pumps would be no help outside. Poking her head outside to take a deep breath of clean air, she swung one leg over the sill.

It wasn't a long drop; in fact, she was able to keep hold of the sill and lower herself onto the narrow ledge, no wider than a balance beam, instead of dropping down onto it. The weight of her body made her injured left wrist twinge, and she sucked in between her teeth. The cold air nearly snatched her breath away. Already she was shivering, and she hadn't even begun to cross to the other tower.

Slowly, so she didn't slip, Rachael turned around, straddling the slender, precarious perch. To her right, the front of the manor fell away, the ground a good three stories away. To her left, the wall also dropped, but only to the main part of the roof. She considered sliding down there, but decided against that course of action. It was at least five feet down, maybe more, and she wasn't sure she could pull herself back up when she got to the other tower. Even if she had the strength to pull up, swinging herself back onto the narrow wall was more acrobatic than she cared to attempt.

"Onward ho," she muttered. She brushed away the snow ahead of her, to ensure no glass shards lurked beneath. Then she stretched forward, rested her hands on the wall, and shimmied herself ahead. She repeated the sequence, and again, keeping the movements small and careful.

A flaming spark, perhaps of cloth, floated down, landing just in front of her to fizzle out on the snow. Rachael brushed it away, trembling, and turned to look back at the tower. But the movement caused her to slip, and she began to topple right, off the wall. Snow billowed off the side like a white waterfall leading the way.

Her stomach lurching, a burst of adrenaline sending everything into hyper-sense, she grabbed at the wall, flinging herself forward and flat against the narrow abutment. That stopped her downward slide, but she was still leaning dangerously. Rachael prodded about with her left foot, found a narrow crack in the wall. Hooking her toes into it, she cautiously pulled herself in that direction. Her left hand slipped on the icy stone, and she nearly fell to the right again, just catching herself. Her movements still slow and deliberate, she tried again, and finally succeeded in pulling herself upright.

Her limbs weakened as the adrenaline trickled away, and Rachael sobbed from fear and stress. She pressed her cheek against the snowy stone, willing herself to calm.

Finally, she sat up, still keeping her center of gravity low, and fixed her eyes on her target, the other tower. Visualize, that's what she had to do—visualize herself there, and no sudden movements. And don't look down.

Rachael inched along, trying not to listen to the crackles of the fire behind her as the inside of the western tower succumbed to the fiery attack. What would happen when the wood paneling and floor had burned? The outer part of the tower was stone, so perhaps the fire would burn itself out. She shuddered inwardly at the thought of any other part of the manor being damaged. The western tower had officially been closed off, but smoke detectors should have been installed. But if Ian had spent much time up there toying with the smoky lantern, he might have dismantled them. With any luck, someone would smell the smoke, or an alarm in the main part of the house would go off before the fire caused further injury.

Orange antishadows flickered and twisted on the snow around her. The sharp smell of smoke pierced the crisp wintered air, still pungent though it seemed a normal part of her world now.

She reached the halfway point, and paused to rest. Her wrist barely throbbed, but only because her hands were almost completely numb; the feeling had fled from the tips of her fingers. She flexed her hands, breathing on them, willing them to life, just long enough to get her across. Her toes had also gone lifeless, though she wiggled them and tried to find sensation. She gripped the roof with her knees, trying not to rely on her benumbed feet for purchase and movement.

Almost there. Her breath rasped, searing her lungs with glacial air. She tried to breathe slowly, through her nose, to reduce the icy slice of pain. Thankfully no wind blew; the air hovered, silent but for the fire's angry sounds. Rachael clenched her jaw, trying to keep her teeth from chattering uncontrollably. Shivering was a part of her now, and she prayed the spasms wouldn't make her lose her balance.

She inched the rest of the way to the eastern tower, and rested her forehead on the outer sill for a moment, thankful. Inside, a small lamp glowed, keeping silent watch over Felicity's paints and pastels and canvasses.

Rachael stretched to push the window up. The movement made her slip again, and she tried to grab the sides of the window. Though her hands retained no feeling, she must have succeeded, her downward slither halted. Leaning against the window, she pushed with one hand, but to no avail. Either it, too, was painted shut, or firmly latched.

Then, above the fire's roar came another noise: a shout? A door slammed open, and another shout, louder—there, below. Cautiously, she leaned forward, hugging against the slick window, and looked down. A guest pointed at the tower; another guest, in answer, ran back inside. Rachael tried to call out, but the sudden frigid air closed her throat. The first guest, full flowing skirts swirling around her ankles, stared up, but at the fire, her shocked face flickered with red and orange and gold. Then she scurried inside as well.

"Damn," Rachael muttered, the word a pale cloud puffing from her lips. She waited, but no one else came outside to view the conflagration in the tower. No doubt the guests who had seen it had called the fire department and alerted everyone else. Even when others did appear, there was no guarantee they'd see Rachael's dark-clad form near the other tower, or hear her call over the sounds of the fire, the shouting, the fire engines.

Fear grew in her, bubbling like acid, eating through her defenses with a vicious burn. Rachael tried to swallow it back, dilute it, but desperation lent strength to her movements as she balled her hands into deadened fists and pounded at the window. But desperation proved her downfall, because her sudden action sent her tumbling, with no chance of catching herself, toward the roof below.

Stomach-wrenching terror as she fell, and Rachael felt herself tense, anticipating her body slamming against the slate-topped roof. She knew relaxing would prevent more serious injuries, but she couldn't help herself. The stars, she noticed, were very, very bright. And then—impact.

Her landing actually proved less hard than she expected; the snow, apparently, helped cushion her fall. Her breath whooshed out of her chest, and for a moment she could only gasp feebly, ineffectually, before her lungs allowed air in again.

After a moment, she struggled to a sitting position. Her left wrist refused to hold any weight, so she made do with her right. She attempted to stand, but the shreds of her dress tangled sodden around her ankles. Rachael plucked it away, her movements slow and clumsy from the numbing cold. Another try, and she pulled herself to her feet.

The snow had fallen thicker up here, up to her shins. The trees and wind had kept too much from accumulating on the ground, but on the unobstructed roof the flakes had had free access, and were sheltered by the surrounding walls.

Rachael slogged the few steps to the stone wall that rose up to the tower, the wall off which she'd tumbled. In her journey across, she had swept away most of the snow upon it, and now it loomed black but for the flickers of orange and red, like flaming autumn leaves. She stretched her arms up. The wall was low enough for her to easily curl her hands over the top.

Gathering her strength, Rachael tried to pull herself up. A second later, she fell back, crying out as pain lanced through her left arm. Her sprained wrist wouldn't allow her any purchase at all. She tried again, pulling with her right arm and trying to find a foothold in the stones of the wall. Again she fell back, the stones too smooth and her own body too weakened by the cold, the stress, and the pummelings she had taken so far this night.

Sobbing in frustration, she raked her hands through the snow at her feet and threw some at the window. But the snow was too dry to pack properly, and the flakes filtered apart before they reached the glass.

Rachael heard herself calling for help, rasping and hoarse, a sound no on else could hear but which made her feel more hopeful. She cried out for Jordan, even though she knew he couldn't answer, couldn't help her. "I can't abide fire," he'd said, and he'd been engulfed in it when he and Ian plunged down through the tower stairs. And anyway, with Ian dead, the curse upon him was lifted. He was free. And she'd never see him again.

So she thought she hallucinated, an ice-fever dream, a moment later when his face appeared in the window. She saw his lips move as he shouted, and then next to him were Celeste and Karyn. *But that's impossible*, she thought clearly, as they all worked together to heave the window open. *They can't be able to hear him or see him.*

Then the window clattered upward. Rachael watched in amazement as Jordan shimmied out onto the ledge, then jumped down beside her. He laced his fingers together and she placed her frozen foot into the makeshift step, one hand on his back for balance.

"Jordan," she said, her voice a faint rasp from the smoke and cold. "How...?"

"Ssh, lady, let's get you inside first," he soothed. "On three—ready? One, two..."

He lifted her up and she did her best to aid the momentum. Hands reached out for her: Troopers Parker and Stefanick. The rush of warm air made her cheeks sting with pain, and they pulled her inside to safety.

*

The next hour passed in a blur. She was in her room, in her bed. Ironically, a fire spat and popped on the hearth, Celeste and Karyn hovering concernedly by. Sgt. Parker, taking what she was certain was a garbled statement, telling her that Kevin had been picked up and confessed his involvement. Paramedics, treating her for smoke inhalation—again—taping her sprained wrist, pronouncing her free of frostbite. In the distance, fire sirens wailing, shouted commands, the hiss of sprayed water, and the rattle of that water against the manor. The rhythmic pulse of red lights. And through it all, Jordan, in the background, always there, holding her hand, watching, murmuring encouragement.

No, it couldn't be. He was gone; nothing held him to this plane. And yet she felt his touch, heard his voice, saw him there—and so did everyone else.

"She needs rest, eh," a paramedic said, urging everyone out. Jordan lingered, uncertain. She knew he couldn't be there, and yet she reached out for him. "Five minutes," the paramedic said firmly, and shut the door.

"Jordan," she said clearly, though the words rasped painfully in her throat. "You can't be here."

"But I am, lady. I am." His smile was tender as he cupped the side of her face. His skin felt warm, alive. *No.*

Rachael struggled to a sitting position, despite his protests, despite her body's protests. Her hands and feet had feeling again, but tingling with pain, and she was so very tired.

"You can't be," she protested.

"But I am. Feel." He grabbed her uninjured wrist, pressed her hand against his chest. Beneath her palm pulsed a heartbeat. She tried to pull away, but he held her fast.

She shook her head. "It can't be. How...?"

He shook his head, hair spilling about his face. The odor of smoke, caught in the strands, wafted through the air. There was still a smudge of charcoal-grey high on one cheek. "I don't know, exactly. But I'm here. I'm with *you*."

"But you're a ghost. Emilie charged you with seeking revenge on her killer." Rachael coughed, pain a band around her chest. She gripped his hand. "My God, Ian killed her. The wound from the gun didn't—the fire did. Her own child set the fire that killed her."

"And that's what he had to live with, all these years," Jordan said softly. "His father had already poisoned his mind against his mother, against everything, but it still ate at him. All these years, he lived with the knowledge that he killed his parents, and scarred himself, both physically and emotionally."

"But why didn't you—?"

"Why didn't I exact revenge like Emilie made me swear?" Jordan's green eyes darkened as he stared into another vision, the past. "In a way, he was innocent; he didn't mean to kill her or Shane. And she didn't know Ian would be the ultimate cause. In fact, before that night, she had begged me to keep him safe, to stop Shane from twisting his mind. So somehow, I couldn't destroy him. All these years, I've been trying to save him. I've tried to stay his hand, keep him from causing harm." He shook his head again. "I've been his conscience, though it did little good."

"But you tried." She tugged him down for a kiss; his mouth felt warm and soft and sensuous against her lips. She sensed his reluctance as he pulled back. "But that doesn't explain why you can be here, with everybody else."

He swung his legs up onto the bed, cuddling into the pillow beside her. Though he lay above the covers, she sensed his heat, his presence, more real than he had ever been. He wriggled an arm behind the pillow, beneath her neck.

"Ian is dead," he said. "I didn't mean for it to happen."

"I know," she said gently, stroking along his fingers. "No one could have survived that fall. And perhaps—perhaps it was meant to be." She knew her words were weak, but she didn't know what else to say. He had done what was right, though it had seemed wrong.

"All these years I've protected him, and now I've seen him killed...." Jordan buried his face in her hair; she felt his lips move, shuddering the tangled locks.

"None of that," she said, "explains why you're here now. You've done what Emilie charged you to do. But you've been here with Celeste and Karyn and everyone—they can see you."

"I'm not sure I entirely understand it," he said slowly. "But it seems I've been given a reprieve. Perhaps because I chose not to take revenge on an innocent child. Perhaps because I chose, in the end, not to let Ian harm you, despite everything I'd vowed. I don't know. But what you see now is me, whole and real and alive. I've been given another chance at life."

"But how can you explain that to everyone who knows you died forty years ago?"

Again he shook his head. "Apparently time has...changed. They don't know anything is different, or wrong."

"But if you hadn't died, you'd be over sixty years old," Rachael protested. She couldn't resist a coy laugh that turned to a half-cough as she ran a hand along his hard thigh. "You're the finest looking sixty-year-old I've ever seen."

He laughed, covered her hand with his. "Just to make things that much stranger, I'm not me. I'm my own son."

"What?!"

"In this...timeline, the first Jordan had a son before he died in the fire. That son is me."

"What happened to your mother—his wife?"

"She died shortly after I was born, of pneumonia."

It was Rachael's turn to shake her head. "And no one else knows about this?"

"Just you and I." He paused for a long moment, his fingers stroking her hand. "It seems like only yesterday we agreed that we should make the best of our time together."

"And now we have all the time in the world. Oh, Jordan..."

He covered her lips with his, gently, warmly, aware of her injuries. When he drew back, he eased her head into the hollow of his shoulder. Dimly she felt him stroking her hair, but her thoughts were elsewhere.

"You're your own son," she murmured. "Damn. Now I have to rewrite half the book."

*

Her wedding dress was a white satin-and-lace copy of her All Hallows Eve gown, only slightly less high-slit in the skirt. She wore no veil, only heather and ivy in a circlet on her head, white ribbons streaming down.

"It's not quite the style I would have expected you to choose," her mother murmured, leaning back to study her as she twitched a fold into place. "But you do look wonderful; so beautiful," Elizabeth added, her eyes sparkling with unshed tears.

Karyn, Rachael knew, understood the significance of the dress. The hotel manager—and her maid of honor, looking comfortably elegant in pale pink linen and pearls—merely smiled when she saw Rachael's dress.

And when Rachael paused on the balcony, surveying the gathered people in the front hall, she saw the look in Jordan's eyes, and it made her want to cry and laugh at the same time.

The reception was held in the ballroom. The All Hallows Eve decorations were gone, of course; the pumpkins a warm pie-memory in everyone's stomachs. Now simple flowers tied with white bows graced the room, and the delicate patterned frost on the windows seemed to mimic the lace on Rachael's dress.

In honor of the family history being completed, Celeste had decided to move all the portraits from the near-hidden portrait hall to the ballroom. Newly reframed, they hung in measured cadence on two of the walls, ancestors watching the progression of time and family as Rachael was accepted into the MacPherson clan.

Even Ian's portrait had been kept with the series. The true story of what happened the night of the first tragedy remained only with Rachael and Jordan, and Rachael truthfully reported that the fire in the tower had begun by accident. Because no one could know of Jordan's involvement that night in the tower, Ian's death had been ruled a tragic accident.

The fact remained, however, that he had tried to kill Rachael more than once, and when she was considering what to do with the portrait, Celeste had asked Rachael her opinion.

"How would you feel to see it hanging there?" she'd asked. "Would that bother you terribly to face it every day?" Celeste's concerns, Rachael knew, ran deeper than the portrait. The older woman had confessed that she'd known Ian wasn't well, but had protected him just as Jordan had.

She'd never suspected he would ever threaten anyone, she said, begging Rachael to believe her. Rachael had assured her she understood, but only time could fully heal Celeste's guilt.

"It's not my decision to make," Rachael had protested. "This is a family matter."

Celeste, with a small smile, had lifted Rachael's hand. The antique engagement ring, a MacPherson tradition, sent a spark of light though the office, glancing off the slate-topped desk. "But you are family, now," she'd said.

In the end, they'd agreed to include the portrait. Rachael and Jordan had echoed Celeste's sentiment at the hanging: "He was a tortured soul, but sometimes I think he had a guardian angel watching over him."

Now, Ian's face seemed less intense, softer, without the tight edges of pain. Rachael wondered if the subtle shifts in time had perhaps brought him some peace.

Then she noticed a new picture at the end of the row, covered with a pale green cloth.

"This," Felicity said dramatically, "is my wedding present to you both. I painted it because it was meant to be painted. I think I knew something about you two long before you knew about it." She grasped a corner of the cloth. "I knew you were in love," she said, and pulled the covering away.

Rachael gasped. It was the portrait of her in the greenhouse, brushing the sprig of heather against her cheek. Felicity had captured, with light and color and passion, the moment she had looked up and seen Jordan resting a hand on her shoulder. The woman's sight had been uncanny, for it was obvious from the looks in their eyes that they were in love, even then.

"That wasn't the only thing she knew about," Rachael whispered to Jordan as he led her out to the center of the dance floor. "Maybe the time change meant you were in the greenhouse that day, but if not, she shouldn't have been able to see you then."

"I always thought Aunt Felicity was a bit fey," he admitted fondly.

"I think it runs in the family," she said lightly, toying with the heather in his boutonnière.

He caught her hand in his. "I think so, too, lady."

And the band began to play "Greensleeves."

For a free electronic copy of *What Beck'ning Ghost*,
go to www.smashwords.com/books/view/322626
choose your favorite format,
and when you check out,
use the code DR24P

About the Author

Dayle Ivy eloped properly in Gretna Green, Scotland, rode off on the back of a motorcycle, and hasn't looked back since except to smile and sigh happily. Unsurprisingly, she writes romances that are sometimes sweet, sometimes spicy, sometimes spooky, and sometimes funny, but will always make you smile and sigh happily.

An unabashed romantic, she lives in an historic house near the ocean, and whenever she can, she travels the world for inspiration and loses herself in music.

Under a variety of names and sometimes with coauthors, she has published several novels and more than a hundred short stories in various genres, most notably erotic romance, erotica, and speculative fiction.

She'd love to have you over for a virtual cup of tea or glass of wine at www.cyvarwydd.com.

Also by Dayle Ivy

Novels
Blackwood House (forthcoming)
Waking the Witch

Short Stories
The Best Catch
Flowers for Marjory

For more information, visit Soul's Road Press (soulsroadpress.com).

Made in the USA
Charleston, SC
09 July 2013